ARCHITECTI

DEALS OF DARK DESIRE
BOOK ONE

RUBY ROE

Architecti - A Dark Gothic Romantasy

Copyright © 2025 Ruby Roe

The right of Ruby Roe to be identified as the author of this work has been asserted in accordance with the Copyright, Designs and Patents Act 1988.

All rights reserved. No part of this publication may be reproduced, stored in any retrieval system, copied in any form or by any means, electronic, mechanical, photocopying, recording or otherwise transmitted, without permission of the copyright owner. Except for a reviewer who may quote brief passages in a review.

This is a work of fiction. Names, characters, places and incidents within the stories are a product of each author's imagination. Any resemblance to actual people, living or dead, or to businesses, companies, events, institutions or locales is either completely coincidental or is used in an entirely fictional manner.

First Published September 2025, by Ruby Roe, Atlas Black Publishing.

Cover design: Andrew Brown, Design for Writers

www.rubyroe.co.uk

All rights Reserved

Also by Ruby Roe

Girl Games Series

A Game of Hearts and Heists

A Game of Romance and Ruin

A Game of Deceit and Desire

A Game of Love and Hate

A Game of Parties and Proposals

A Game of Vows and Vendettas

Kingdom of Immortal Lovers Series

House of Crimson Hearts

House of Crimson Kisses

House of Crimson Curses

House of Crimson Nights

House of Crimson Spice

Deals of Dark Desire

Architecti

CONTENT WARNINGS

This book is intended for adult (18+) audiences. It contains explicit lesbian sex scenes, considerable profanity, scenes and themes that may impact your mental health as well as some violence.

Your mental health is everything.

I have done my best to give comprehensive content warnings because sometimes we want to read the bad stuff, and that's okay, too.

Please see my website: rubyroe.co.uk and visit the book's individual page for information.

Don't come at me over the S and Z, this book is written in British English.

PLAYLIST

Scan the QR code below for the full Architecti playlist.

FINIS ACADEMY
SOCIETAS MORTIS ARCHITECTI
Bar
Specialism Building
House Inferos
Cemetery & Catacombs
Cloisters
Pub
Theatre
Restricted Records
House Mortis
Meeting Rooms
Chimera Hall
House Vitalis
Church Vitalis
Church Mortis
Refectory
Maze
Main Entrance
Cloisters
Garden of Death
The Great Library
Theoretical Student Lecture Hall
Eytomancer Lecture Hall
Memoria Lecture Hall
Hall of Unfinished Business
Negotiations Lecture Hall
Resurrection Lecture Hall
Weaver Lecture Hall
Veil Walker Lecture Hall
Visiting Staff Accommodations
Clock Tower
Admin Offices
Faculty Wings
Medical Wing

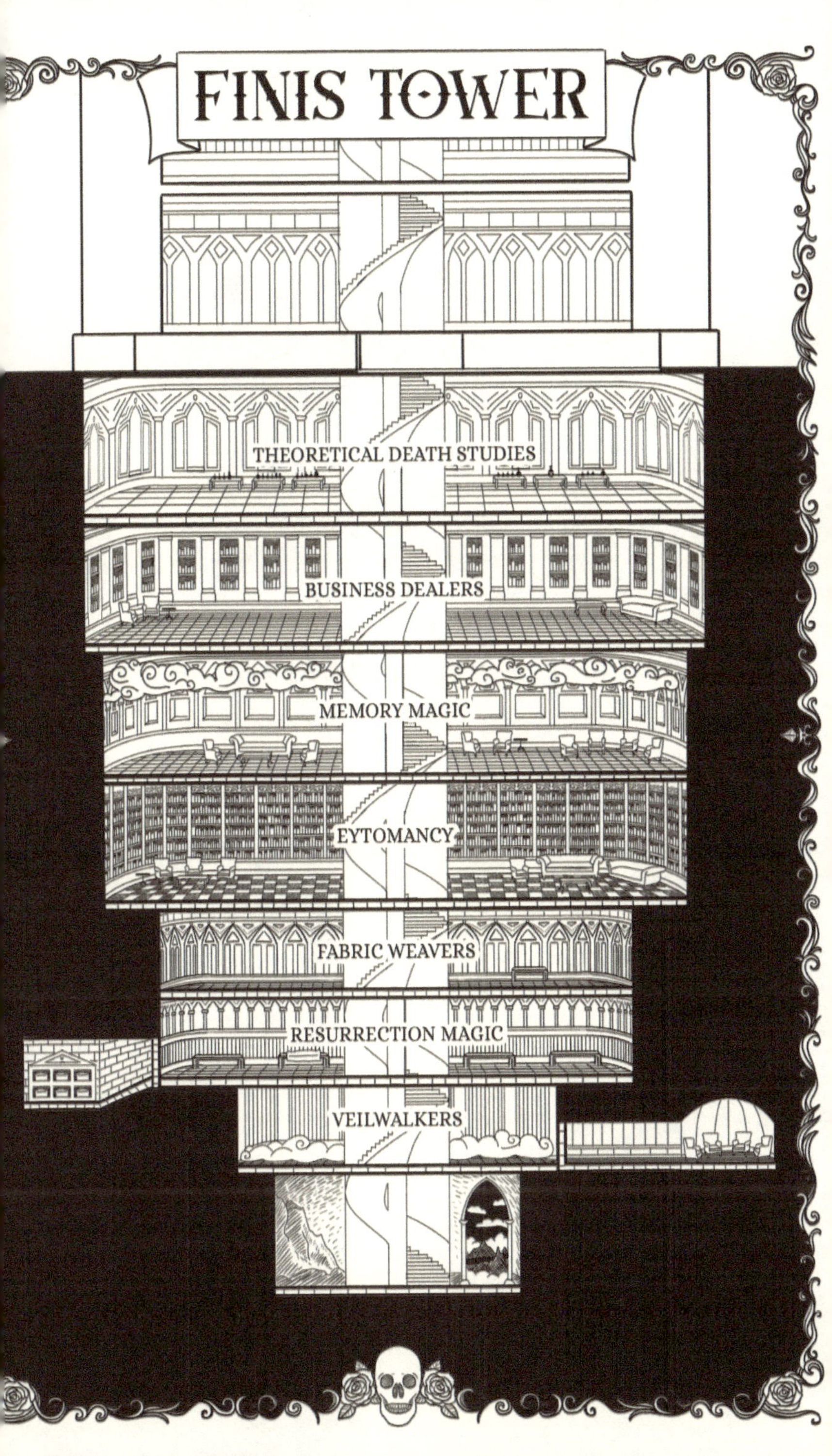

FINIS TOWER
THEORETICAL DEATH STUDIES
BUSINESS DEALERS
MEMORY MAGIC
EYTOMANCY
FABRIC WEAVERS
RESURRECTION MAGIC
VEILWALKERS

For all the people who hate the word pussy...

I have devastating news for you.

PROLOGUE

A sensible demon will spin you a line that goes something like: *I need you to know, I started out as a good person.* It's how they lure you in, you see. How they manipulate frail hearts and sweet minds.

I did, though... start out as a good person, I mean...

It's what happened next that ruined me.

I

ARCHITECTI

Aeons ago, or maybe right now?

Angels are supposed to be divine.

That's what the mortals think, and there are certain connotations, implications and presumptions that come with that.

Unfortunately, it is also what the demons assumed.

We have disappointed everyone.

Yet, angels are not gods, and as much as we are born with celestial blood flowing in our veins, we hold mortal hearts—metaphorically speaking, of course.

I rather think it unfair that these assumptions have been placed on us. We're all spinning on this universal plane trying to do our best. I certainly was.

Am?

It's confusing.

Everything is jumbled now, but I want to explain. I need to, so that you understand that what happens next is for the best.

Some angels are born good—innately birthed to bestow

light and love and creativity, and some are born of destruction.

And once in a celestial blue moon, you'll find twins.

Such a fascinating phenomenon, twins. Theoretically identical, but so often they manifest in such tragically different ways.

I was a twin.

I was supposed to be the good one and truly, I thought I was. Either the gods have forsaken me, or my twin is far, far more dangerous than I realised.

I know what they say about me—that I wanted to rule the underworld, that I caused massacres and killed thousands.

It's not true.

It wasn't.

Maybe it still isn't.

Or, at least, I don't think it is. It's all bewildering now. Jumbled and messy.

If I tell you my story, maybe you'll understand. Maybe you'll see the truth.

Someone's lying to you.

Someone is lying to all of us.

2
MIDNIGHT

Three Hundred and Sixty-Five Days Left

Last birthdays are meant to be filled with equal parts wrinkled people weathered by decades of friendship, and disinterested youths three generations down from your tired-ass genetics.

They are not meant to be in your twenty-ninth year, with a libido raging hard enough to euthanise an entire necromantic nunnery.

But here I am.

And here it is: *My last* birthday.

I scrunch the rejection letter up and get up from my kitchen table—I don't have time to sulk. I guess that's me fucked, then. This intake was my last opportunity to get into Finis Academy for a chance of saving my soul.

So that's it.

One year left.

I fling the parchment in the bin and kick the canister for good measure. I don't get why I was rejected—again. I mean, my role as a reaper isn't exactly seen as the pinnacle of respectable. But I'm fucking good at my job, plus there are enough reapers at the academy. The only thing I can come up with is that Ignatius is blocking me—like stealing my soul wasn't enough.

I'm not giving up, though; I'll find another way to break my contract. If for no other reason than to spite my bitch of an ex who put me in this position.

I grab my keys, shrug my leather jacket on and pick up my motorbike helmet. If I don't leave now, I'll be late for the rave. Some of the other reapers are dragging me to this pop-up club to celebrate even though that's the last thing I feel like doing.

I lock the house. It's crisp tonight and the night air slides off my skin like silk on glass. My street, like many Ora streets, split in opposites. One side is bright stone, gilded frames and turrets framing the skies, the other degrading buildings, chipped charcoal brick, greying windows and festering plants—like the city still can't decide if it belongs to angels or devils.

Nights like this are deceptive. They pretend, like summer wants to surrender to the first caress of autumn. The weight of reddening leaves makes the winds shiver and tremble. But I know better. All nights like this are filled with is trouble.

I sling a leg over my bike. It's sleek and black, the cog-addled engine roaring like mid-winter storms. The wheels are thick and grip the road when I take the bends a little too hard. It's built for racing, not cruising. Just the way I like it.

It's my first and last love, especially now I've written off women. Once you've been betrayed the way I have, you don't go back. I run my fingers down my equally sleek black helmet as a moth catches my eye. It wafts in the lamplight, fluttering like secrets in the breeze.

I squint at it, checking to see if it is actually a moth, or something I'd rather avoid. Its wings dance around my head: a soft caress of pink and hint of yellow.

"Shit," I groan. Definitely something I want to avoid. "Not tonight, arsehole," I shout at the moth like Ignatius can hear me. "Come on, Ignatius. It's my birthday, for fuck's sake."

Why is it always the fucking entropy moths and never the Architect's? I wish just once I'd get a moth that could create possibility instead of taking it away.

I swipe at the air, batting the entropy moth away, only to recoil— idiot. I replace my hand with my keys and lash out. I should know better than to touch them unless I want to wreck my evening. I slap it, and the moth plummets towards the ground, a wing crumpling against the keys. I press my lips together, smirking. I should feel bad. It's not the insect's fault.

But also, I am not working on my birthday. *My last birthday*, let us not forget.

I pick my helmet up off my tank as the moth surges up, fluttering like its miraculous little life depends on it. I chuck the helmet through the air, hoping it squashes the moth in its tracks. But the devious little cunt swerves out of the way.

"Motherfucker." I swing my head, ducking its attack, and shove my helmet on, twist the ignition and flick the kickstand up. I rev the throttle as a swarm of the bastards appear at the end of my drive.

"Oh, hell no." I click my visor down and push off, the bike engine growling like the simmering rage of a starved wraith. I surge through the swarm, smug as fuck that I've managed to avoid picking up any work—until I realise my mistake.

I covered my head, but in my haste, I forgot to put my

gloves on. My heart thuds hard, one loud beat as I spot one of the ashkissing dustfuckers landing on my knuckle.

I swear its antennae bristle—laughing at me. My teeth grit, I keep one hand on the brake, the bike balanced between my thighs and lift my other off the throttle, carefully balancing so I can slam it down and kill the moth before it can contract me.

I yank my hand up, but the bastard sinks its proboscis into my skin.

Fuck.

I squeeze the brakes hard, the back wheel swerves, kicking out. The sting of the bite pulses through my hand as I skid off the road into a rickety as fuck street. The pavement is worse for wear, another victim of the angels leaving no doubt. My feet slide across the ground, I dig my heels in and pin the bike between my thighs right as my vision whites out and the scents of day-old coffee, broiling flesh and stale tobacco hit me.

"Gods dammit, Ignatius," I groan.

When my sight clears, it's the entropy moth's mind I'm in. Ignatius's face shimmers into focus. By all accounts, he's handsome. His bones are chiselled in a way that screams model. He has eyes dark enough to haunt a serial killer's dreams. I think it's the lightly speckled salt-and-pepper hair shorn short on the sides and longer on top that softens him. Gives him the kind of 'fuck-me-daddy' vibes I'd sell an organ to own.

Though I swear I saw my first grey the other day. Makes sense with how dark my hair is, I'm bound to be fully grey by thirty-five—or I would be if I wasn't going to be reaped before then.

Ignatius must be at Finis Academy because he's wearing a dark suit with their crest emblazoned on it. He's the dean there, which is probably why I've been rejected so many times. Too selfish to let his reaper do anything other than work her ass off.

"Trying to avoid work, Midnight?" he drawls. His voice is deep and husky, like molten charcoal. If I had a lick of interest in men, he might be appealing.

"What do you want? I think I deserve a night off, all things considered."

I'm bolshy with him—actually, I'm bolshy with everyone. But it's dangerous with Ignatius. If I cross the line and piss him off rather than amuse him, it won't end well for me. As long as I stick on the side of funny, he'll tolerate it, which is saying something given I've never seen him tolerate diddly-squat from anyone else.

He smiles, his jet black eyes glittering with the kind of mischief reserved for demons and heroes. Of which he is both.

Forty years ago, he killed the biggest threat this city has ever seen: Architecti. Meaning, I'm not the only one in his debt. Ora City is, too.

I can't lie; he did a good thing.

Architecti was a bad bitch. A fallen angel. There are a million rumours about why she fell. Some say she was kicked out of the celestial realm for trying to usurp the hierarchy. Some think it was her desire to take over the underworld. Others say it was a sibling fight. No one knows the truth because the angels all up and fucked off out of our realm when Ignatius killed her.

Most—though not all—of Ora City hate Architecti. As for me, I have a quiet respect for a woman who sees what she wants and goes after it.

Those who want her back tend to be the loudest—protesting and rioting and using far-fetched necromantic resurrection techniques, none of which have worked, thankfully. Much as I respect a bitch, I don't think I want a homicidal angel running around Ora City.

But back to the demons. They objected to an angel—fallen or otherwise—taking over their realm.

I mean, fair, right?

Unfortunately for us mere mortals, Ora City was caught in the middle. We're a gateway, so when they went to war, we were royally fucked. Massacre upon massacre of humans, demons and anyone else stupid enough to have gotten in the way.

Ignatius saved Ora by killing Architecti, and thirty years later, the same heroic motherfucker doomed me.

"Don't be dramatic. It's just another birthday," Ignatius says, his figure drifting in and out of focus as the entropy moth struggles to hold both of us in its mind.

"It's not though, is it? It's my last one, unless you're opting out of our deal?"

He huffs out an indignant laugh.

It was worth a shot. I'm shit out of ideas now I've been rejected from Finis.

His grin widens, all white teeth and gums. His teeth are the only imperfect thing about him. A slight crook in his front teeth that only seems to make him more charming. I have to suppress an eye-roll. To me, he's about as charming as a healthy dose of necrotising fasciitis.

He pouts his lips in one smug jerk. "Oh, that's right. Almost time. How is Aurelia getting on?"

My mouth pinches. The prick knows damn well Aurelia and I broke up six weeks after I made the deal with him—almost a decade ago—and frankly, I'd rather reap my own soul than ever have to see her again. Ironic really, considering I'll probably have to do just that in three hundred and sixty-four days.

I take a deep breath, praying to the seven devils that he either reaps me now or hurries the fuck up with whatever it is he needs me to do. "Seeing as we're both agreed that my time is limited, are you going to tell me what you want, or do I need to pillage the moth's mind instead?"

He picks something off his jacket. "Just a small job. Be a good girl and reap someone for me before you attend your celebration. He'll be at the rave."

My nostrils flare, *be a good girl?*

I'm about to shove my mental scythe up his actual arse when he vanishes and the entropy moth's mind trembles and settles back into its normal mode of communication. It shows me a series of possibilities—all of them closed off. Paths and fates that are no more thanks to the deal the human made with Ignatius. Scene after scene ripples and swirls, curving through my mind like smoke and shadow.

Reason ten million not to make a deal with a demon. You might think you're getting what you want, but all a contract does is rewrite your fate. Seal off a lot of possible futures and paths that were once open to you.

Awful really.

A sick sort of twist.

In order to give you what you want, the devil takes everything else.

That's how the moths are created. They're the manifestations of closed-off futures. Meaning I can see the soul that Ignatius needs collecting and all the lives they could have lived. And Ignatius, having contracted the poor fool, can communicate with me through those dead futures.

A vision of a young man washes through my mind. He's

skinny and short and holds a wistful gaze that screams yearning.

I bet it was love.

A slide show of possibilities rapid fires through my consciousness. Dancing, kissing, fucking.

Yeah.

He definitely sold his soul for love. Rookie error. Ask me how I know.

As the vision fades, I let out a deep sigh.

The moth's proboscis pings out of my knuckle. It twitches, fluttering its wings, staring at me. I hold its gaze. That same smug twitch of its antennae shivers through its beady black eyes.

I slam my fist down. It crumbles, bursting into a puff of dust.

Cruel?

Maybe.

But I hate those things.

I flick the entropy residue off my hand and start the bike.

Do you know what I hate more than entropy moths? Puny ashkissers that beg.

Fighting? That I can respect. I'll go down fighting when my time comes too. I think that's why Ignatius likes me; I don't pander to him like everyone else.

But begging? Pathetic—unless it's in the bedroom, of course. A pretty bit of meat begging Daddy to stop making her come? Mmm. That I can get down with.

The rave is tucked in an abandoned graveyard behind a derelict building. Even though it's hidden from sight, there's no mistaking it's there. The air is filled with the constant beat of music, the faint hint of sweat and alcohol.

Alas, before I can join the fun, I have to deal with this grinner.

A dribble of piss leaks down the guy's trousers, and all I can do is wrinkle my nose.

"Please, I just need more time," he whines.

I scruff his shirt tighter, shove him against the building wall. "You know who loves begging?"

He trembles, his head shaking from side to side.

"The wraiths. You should try begging in hell. I'm sure that will help."

He lets out a sob. "I just wanted to be loved."

"We all *just* want something. How do you think I got in this position?"

His eyes harden, he spits on the ground. "Gravetether."

I tilt my head at him. "If you think insulting me is going to win you any favours, it won't. It's only going to get you sent to the underworld faster."

"Okay, okay, I'm sorry. Please, give me more time. I'll do anything." He grips my shoulders, giving them a pleading squeeze. Grinning at me, no doubt the same way he did to Ignatius.

"I'll pay," he squeaks.

"Sorry, mate. We're all pawns in this city. Are you Thaddeus Crowhurst, contractee to Ignatius Corvine?"

His bottom lip trembles as he nods confirmation. Tears spill over his lids. He gives me the most puppy-dog expression you've ever seen. Demons, give me strength. Why do they always have to make it hard? Like any of this is on me?

He made the fucking deal, and the guilt trip makes me feel like shit. It's not like I *want* to do this.

I figure I can give him another minute. "Out of interest, what was the d—" I ask.

"The love of my life. I wanted her to notice me."

I knew it. I shake my head. "Did she?"

He shrugs, a few tears spilling out. "For a while."

"Yeah, it's never long enough. Never works out the way you want. It's why we shouldn't fuck with fate."

"Hindsight," he sniffs.

Couldn't agree more.

"Do you have any last words?" I ask.

He sobs again. Falls to his knees, almost taking me down with him. I'm growing tired of this. He kisses my boots, screaming and pleading. Honestly, if a hot woman kissed my boots, I'd be wet right now, but this is vile.

I shuck him off. "Stop it. You're embarrassing yourself. Death comes for us all, eventually."

"But not like this. Please, not like this."

I unclasp my scythe. Some of the reapers I know choose enormous weapons, I prefer the handheld blade. This one is special, too. I stole it from Ignatius. The bone-white edge catches the moonlight in whorls like stardust. It's always been beautiful; it's why I took it.

It's more intimate and personal to stare into the eyes of a lost one before you rip their soul from their body, so I force myself to lock onto his.

May I never forget.

May I never judge.

For one day, it will be my eyes, and Ignatius looking into them as he reaps my soul.

What's odd is that reaping this many souls should resign me to my fate—and trust me, I've reaped enough of them to believe in fate. And still, I won't give up. If anything, having taken so many souls is pushing me to fight harder. I don't want to share these mortals' fates. I refuse to accept that a year from now I'll have to stare down eternal darkness at the hands of Ignatius.

I pick Thaddeus up by the collar and read him his final rites. "Whisper your last truth and I'll carry it to the dark with me."

His mouth quivers, like his lips are trying to find the words buried in the evening air. I bring the scythe to his neck.

"It wasn't worth it. Love. Not this way. It never felt real. I think a part of her always knew. Our love entropied, and I sold my damn soul for nothing."

I nod, understanding in that bone-deep way only someone who made the same mistake as you can.

Selling my soul wasn't worth it either.

"Thaddeus Crowhurst, all debts must be paid, in silence or soul. May the weight of your choices carry you gently down. The gods forgot you, the demons won't. Rest now. Omnia mors aequat. *Death renders all equal.*"

I slide the scythe through his neck, tensing and pushing hard when I hit his soul spine. It has to sever the cord, or I won't remove his whole soul, and that is not a fate I'd wish on anyone.

I shove hard. His mouth opens, a silent scream whispering into the air. His eyes widen and dull, his body growing heavy in my arms.

The scythe slips out the other side of his neck and I drop him to the ground. I wipe the blade on my trousers. Not that there's anything there. The blade doesn't cut skin, it only cuts soul. But habits are hard to break, and all blades need cleaning, whether it's from blood, brains or a beautiful soul. I glance down at him, all crumpled and piss covered. He seems small.

Poor bastard.

Death isn't kind to anyone, least of all the grinners.

A white cat appears, all fluffy and orange eyed. It's cute, though the scornful sneer it's giving me is not. I kneel down to stroke it. It purrs and rubs around my legs, its head butting my hands for harder chin tickles. It's pure white, like a ghost, save for a single black blemish over one paw, like a sock.

"You're a sweet thing," I say.

And then it bites me.

I yelp, but it just headbutts me again, demanding more strokes.

Strange creatures, cats. I get up and walk away, I don't have time for strays. When tonight is over, I'll have three hundred and sixty-four days to avoid the same fate as Thaddeus.

3

LUCY

I've been summoned like a common contractee. I might be bound to my father, but that does not behove him to summon me like the rest of his grinners.

It's insulting.

Before I push open the door to his office, I steady the clenching in my gut. There is nothing I dread more than alone time with my father.

The door opens and I find him perched on a desk talking to Professor Thessaly Grimwood who is, in a word, gentle. Her blue eyes are round and smiley, even when she's cross with a student. Her curves are soft and full, even her hair falls in loose waves around her face. And yet, get her in a classroom and she's vicious. A professor who demands excellence at all times. But what do you expect? She's the most respected Eytomancer in a couple of centuries, so the faculty claim.

As I step into the room, she hardens. Those bright blue eyes shift to frigid. Her jaw ticks as she lowers her voice.

"We cannot afford anymore budget cuts, Ignatius. See reason, for demon's sake." She lowers her voice.

Father reaches forward, clasping his hands over hers. "Professor Grimwood. I understand your reservations, but it's imperative that we bolster the Veil. Chancellor Arcadius will make an announcement tomorrow. But I'm approaching the subject leaders I have good relationships with to give them a heads-up."

She flushes. "I appreciate that, but how do you expect me to continue teaching without a resources budget? Let alone a budget to provide complex linguistic defence? Students need necromantic spells. I can teach the necro languages, but I am no expert in spell defence."

Father's face radiates enough warmth that my teeth clench, and my chest burns. It's rare he displays that kind of warmth towards me.

I crave it.

What girl doesn't want her father's love? I don't have a mother. I was always going to be a daddy's girl.

He chuckles, a summery rumble that billows from his chest like a bouquet of blossoms. "Why Professor Grimwood? Because you're the best. It's rare I've seen such creativity in the classroom. Your last fifteen cohorts of students have all received outstanding grades. You constantly innovate in order to push the standards. I hardly think a little snip cut of ten percent on the budget lines is going to do anything more than cause a bothersome afternoon for a professor of your standing."

Grimwood's hard stare liquifies, settling into an abashed smile. Once again, Father's charm penetrates right where he wants it.

Grimwood stands straighter. "I'll make it work. But I implore you not to make any further cuts."

Father squeezes her hand and gives it a gentle tap. "I hear you, and thank you, Professor Grimwood. It's appreciated, especially under these difficult circumstances."

She withdraws from his grasp and makes her way out, giving me a polite nod, her smile turning stiff as she does.

Father's office is old. Brown leather books fill the shelved walls. The glow of library-dim orange warms the space. Two Chesterfield armchairs, cracked and worn from the weight of study, nestle in the corners. If it weren't for the wall filled with plaques and honours my father has received over the years, it would be as unassuming as any other academy reading room.

Father's rigid, his skin pulling taut across his cheeks. All the affection he showed for Thessaly a moment ago has vanished. He wears the strain in his shoulders like a freshly commissioned soldier. He's all charm and confidence for Grimwood, but I know the truth.

"Good evening, Professor Corvine," he says.

"So formal, Father." I mock curtsey, which makes his lip flicker.

"Indeed. Congratulations are in order. I'm giving you what you wanted."

"You're freeing me from my birth contract?"

He rolls his eyes.

As well as saving the city from that wretched fallen angel, Architecti, he saved me from, well, being dead, I guess. Unfortunately for me, I've been paying for that graciousness ever since.

His mouth pinches. "As my daughter, how could you possibly think you'll ever be free of me? That's not how parenting works. I gave you everything. I raised you single-handedly—"

Demons above. How is it I'm forty years of age, and still

made to feel like a nine-year-old burden? I won't be pandering to him today.

"I'm aware. I owe you my life, etc, etc." I waft a disinterested hand in his direction.

He stands and looms over me. He's trying to intimidate me. But I stand my ground. My father hates disobedience, free thought, and independence. He's a controlling man. It's how he got to where he is. You can't blame him, really. He's done a lot of good. Saved the damn city. He's just not the most affectionate or loving of fathers if he's not getting his way.

His neck vein pulses. When will I learn? Poking him only leads to loss—for me.

"Do I detect insolence?" he snarls, peering down at me. His hot breath trickles down on me. That's close enough.

I shove him back.

A searing heat floods through the palm of my hand. I grit my teeth against the pain and curse the day he saved me. I hate that he has this power over me.

I can't hurt him or threaten him. Apparently, it's part and parcel of the magic in the contract he created to save me.

Which was highly illegal, I should point out. No under eighteens are allowed to be contracted, and yet, here we are. A vile abuse of power that saved my damn life, so I'm stuck with it. What's the alternative?

Death?

"No, Father. You detect a tired, middled-aged woman with several contracts lessons to prepare for the new term, an investigation into a fraudulent agreement, apparently impending wraith attacks, if I read the subtext of your conversation with Grimwood, and above all, a need for a large glass of wine and a good dance."

He perches on the edge of the table, folds his arms and beams. "You're being appointed Head of House Inferos."

My mouth falls open. "I did not ask for that."

"Of course you did."

"No," I say firmly. "I most definitely did not. That is a considerable amount more responsibility. I have several research projects I'm heading up. I don't have time to babysit new students. Let alone move across campus into House Inferos."

"It is not babysitting, and it's an honoured position. Professor Dregan retired rather suddenly. His wife was taken ill. They decided to leave the city and spend her last months together in peace. We're maxed out on staffing in other areas and we're in a state of constant vigilance with the Veil thinning, so I volunteered you. Besides, you're always saying you would like more seniority at the Academy. Therefore, you're welcome."

You're welcome? How dare he. My contracts research is vital to gaining funding for the Academy.

"No," I say, pouring as much authority into my voice as I can and standing a little straighter. Sticking up for myself against him has never been my strong suit. Not when it usually leads to weeks of cold shoulder and silence.

A single crease forms between his brows. He laughs once, short and sharp and runs his hand through his greying hair. "Would you like to try that again?"

I shrug. "I said no. I'm not going to roll over and take on more responsibility that will detract from my research."

His expression darkens, pupils pooling to hollow wells. "You will do as I say. I won't have you embarrass me."

I step towards the door, done with this conversation. I have one ace up my sleeve, a secret of his I unearthed. He flashes to anger every time I use it, but it is ruthlessly effective at getting him to back off. Not least because if I were to spill the truth, it would bring down everything he's built.

"You're not listening t—" I start.

He leaves his perch on the table and draws near. I shuffle away until I hit the door frame. He grips my chin and pulls my face up to his.

It hurts.

He holds me tight enough to show he's in control. But not so hard he'll leave bruises. Because, of course, that wouldn't look good to Chancellor Arcadius, academic faculty, or any of the other devils.

"I have already told the Chancellor you'd be happy to take the appointment. You will do this because it is good for both our reputations. Can you imagine? A dean and Head of House Inferos in our family?"

"You're already the city hero, *remember*," I say, dragging out my last word, making sure he understands the implication—that he remembers the secret I carry. "What more do you need, Father?" I hold his gaze, the threat clear.

He hesitates, huffs and drops my chin. "It's easy to win a city. Staying on top is much harder. Don't you see how good this would be for us? Just think—my daughter, Head of House Inferos."

He's lost, his eyes glazing as he thinks of a future I want no part of. He doesn't give a fuck what I want. I could plead all day, and he wouldn't hear me. Either he's ignoring my thinly veiled threat, or he's intentionally pretending not to understand.

My stomach heats, chest simmering with the kind of rage that could ignite a revolution. I swallow it down.

If I lash out, I'm the one that will end up injured. But occasionally, I can subvert the contract.

My hands plunge for his wrists. My nails dig into his flesh, deeper and deeper.

"I said, no. Or would you prefer me to remind the city just how much of a hero you are?" I snarl the words, savouring the way his skin swells; resisting, fighting, slicing. The delicious sensation of my nails sinking into his pulpy flesh throbs in my fingertips.

It is one glorious millisecond of triumph.

Then it crashes around me. The sting of tears wells in my lids, the sensation in my fingers turns hot and searing, as though I'm having my nails ripped from their beds.

I endure the agony knowing he is also suffering. How dare he take my choice away, again.

I dig harder.

Harder.

My nose heats, a blunt burn high in my cavities. Something runs down my nostril, splattering on the floor.

Blood.

Father's eyes glimmer. "Who is the city going to believe? A bitter young demon or a devil and hero to the city? The only person getting hurt here is you." His voice is caramel and coal. Smarmy, sleek and full of the smug knowledge that he's won.

There are days when I hate him more than life itself. When I'd rather carve my chest open and tear my crystalline heart from between my ribs and shatter it just to be free of him.

Hell, there would be no better vengeance than falling for a mortal and losing all my demonic power to them and ruining our family's reputation.

And then there are days like today where reality settles and I cave to him, again.

He softens, that charm and charisma brightening his

expression. He draws a gentle thumb under my nose and wipes the blood away.

"My bright, beautiful daughter, you are magnificent. This might be an inconvenience, but you are so capable. I just want to see you soar." He beams, genuine pride moulding his features into the same father I remember as a young girl.

The one who would clap and cheer every time I'd bring him a scroll with gobbledygook words written on it, proclaiming I'd made another deal. Who still, to this day, has the first one I scrawled as a toddler framed above his desk.

The room shudders, the plaques on the walls tremble so violently that one of the lower ones drops to the floor and shatters.

I release him.

His eyes dart this way and that as if he's expecting someone to be there.

"Tremors?" I whisper.

He nods, his eyes wide.

"How bad is it?"

He rubs at his thumb, his shoulders sagging. "I am concerned. Tomorrow, Arcadius is going to announce some changes, and the fact that we're anticipating Veil tears throughout this academic year... It is... not good."

I press my lips together. If he's worried, then things must be much worse than the faculty are saying. Father shakes himself off and brushes down his shirt.

"Fine, I'll do it," I say.

"There, was that so hard?" he says. "You'll make a fantastic Head of House Inferos. I expect you to show your gratitude by doing the role justice."

He bends to plant a kiss on my forehead. "I love you,

Lucy, I hope you recognise that. Everything I do is for your benefit. I want you to understand that I make a lot of sacrifices for us. Even now, when you're a fully grown demon. I do it to keep us safe and prospering."

He leaves me in his office.

I have never felt more alone. More disconnected. He's been there my entire life, and yet, *not.*

He's a façade.

A mask of a parent.

When it pleases him, he'll show others how good he is as a father. But there's more to parenting than ensuring I'm fed, watered, and educated. I hate that I want his love. I hate that I crave being told I've done well or made him proud. I want to gouge this yearning need for validation from my ribs because all the while I need it, I am not free.

I will never be free.

I know this, and yet I can't break away. It's a strange thing to love a parent who behaves like they hate you. There's a part of him—deep down—that loves me. Or at least a part of him thinks he does. But he can't see past his own selfish needs.

It's fucked up. But what else can I do? I have no other parent, no other family.

My chin aches from the press of his fingers. I rub my jaw and pick up the fallen frame.

My fingers skim over the words; it's signed by Professor Dregan. I wonder if his wife is okay. I can't imagine having spent aeons with the same person only to have them die.

Omnia mors aequat, death renders all equal.

Death is an oddity. We're here studying every facet of it, a few are even able to control some elements of it, and still, there comes a point where none of us can avoid it, not even the archdevil himself. Not forever. And yet, if we are all honest, that is exactly what we are here to do.

Avoid it.

Control it.

Tame it.

Make it our own.

Irrespective of whether you're mortal, demonic or somewhere in between, we all obsess over death here.

It makes me wonder whether it's really the mortals or us demons who are most afraid of death. We evade it for so long, live these luxuriously long lives that no one can take away, and yet, like every mortal I've encountered, it's never enough.

We crave more.

I make a mental note to seek out the professor when he's back from his trip and hope that I get a chance to say goodbye to Mrs Dregan. She was a real sweetie. She always interrupted his classes to bring him sandwiches and cookies from home. It was adorable.

I pop the frame back on the wall and make my way out of the tower. I need that wine and dance, and rumour has it there's a pop-up rave in an old graveyard in the city.

I rush across the campus, its grey, gloomy mist lingering around every corner. Even at the height of midday, fog often crawls along the campus's cobbled streets and clings to the buildings like a cloak. But tonight, it's a pale, globulous shroud. Even the ivy seems to tremble at what lurks in the dingy white cloud.

I find a carriage at the campus entrance. "Take me to Lendon's Cemetery across town," I say and lean against the seat, grateful that despite this afternoon's horrendous events, the night is not lost. I intend to drink myself into oblivion, and if I'm lucky, perhaps I'll find a woman, or better yet, a masc dom who wants to play.

4

MIDNIGHT

I make my way through the building and enter the graveyard. It's brighter than I expected. Enormous flood lights showering the cemetery with strobing colours and patterns.

The DJ booth is at one end with a bar to the left. I head there, grab a drink and scan the dance area, looking for anyone I recognise. My drink is bitter and cool, the ice clinking against the glass.

I spot Darwin, another reaper I hang out with, and make my way over to him.

He raises his beer to me. "Cheers, birthday girl."

"Thanks, Darwin," I say, tipping my glass at him and taking another sip. He has a hideous cut on his cheekbone. I wonder how he got it.

Unlike me, he has two years left. Which means he stands straighter and surer than me. The weight of *his end* isn't as heavy as mine. We all carry it, though. Wear the reality of our ticking clock like a cloak. Strange that most mortals are able to live in blissful ignorance despite the inevitability of their impending end.

I've always wondered how they do it. Is it because they have no certainty? Perhaps, rather than let the doubt eat away at their sanity, they stay in denial about death. What else can they do when none of them know whether the end is today, tonight or thirty years from now?

But reapers know.

Our clock is an incessant beat. A reverberation too quiet for humans. It hums through our veins like a second heart. A persistent threat, a constant reminder of the choice we made.

Ten years.

Five.

One.

A few more of the reapers I hang with appear, but each one of them has more years than me. And now I can't think of anything worse than celebrating. Who wants to be reminded that there's one day less remaining?

Robin, another reaper, flings an arm around my shoulder. "Happy birthday, chump," she says, squeezing my shoulder and plonking a kiss on my cheek.

We fucked once.

Or tried. We rapidly realised we weren't compatible in the bedroom, each as dominant as the other, and way better off as friends.

I smile and hug her back, and then she's prancing off with a group of girls. She has six years left. I'd bet she barely feels the weight of her clock.

Reapers need each other. No one else understands the relentlessness of the job and the fact we appreciate every day in a way that normal humans don't.

There's something about that collective limitation that glues a group together.

"Nasty gash on your cheek," I say to Darwin.

He nods, "The grinner's wife wasn't too pleased to see me. But what was I going to do?"

Ah. I get it. That's the other thing that unites us—the hate from fellow humans.

It makes sense. We're reaping the very souls of our people. What humanity forgets is that we will have ours taken one day, too. After all, *Omnia mors aequat—death renders all equal.*

He drags me towards the dance floor, and I go reluctantly. We hop over long-since abandoned graves and avoid those dug for the dead that were never used. Hardly the safest not to have filled them in before the rave.

The music cranks up a notch, and as is the way with raves—or at least the raves I attend—the clothes lessen. Bodies grind up against each other too close and too rhythmically to be *just* dancing.

The hours drift by. As we pass 1 a.m., the bar is drunk half dry, people fuck openly over gravestones, on the grass, in seats, leaning against fences, and I thoroughly enjoy the view.

I soon forget that it's my birthday until the gods drop a gift on my lap in the form of a stunning black-haired woman striding towards the bar. Her long, dark locks flow down past her shoulders. It's straight, with the slight hint of a wave. She turns and I catch flame-red streaks framing her face.

Fuck me.

She is both the most angelic and sinful being I've ever laid eyes upon.

My mind heads straight for the filth, envisioning her on all fours beneath me. Those red locks wrapped around my fist.

My pussy tightens.

I throw the thought away. I should wait until I know her name before I objectify her, it's only polite...

And yet, *it is* my birthday, and I won't get another one to treat myself.

She catches me looking at her. I smile to myself as her eyes roll down my body, very definitely checking me out.

Minx.

Her tongue glides along her lip.

Yeah, she thinks I'm hot.

Game on.

I slide my gaze away—on purpose. Women are playthings to me. Aurelia saw to that. Broke me hard enough I won't commit to more than a night. What's the point when I only have a year of them left?

I shift position and join a group of reapers, making sure I can see my dark-haired seductress over the shoulder of one of the lads. She's a little older than me, maybe a decade? Possibly more. Her skin has that indulgent look of a woman whose youth refused to leave. But her golden eyes carry something else—weight, I think.

It surprises me that she maintains such a serene exterior when it's clear she's carrying a heavy burden of secrets.

She is fucking radiant even against the beaming floodlights. A tailored jacket clings to her curves, it's black with faint filigree patterns embroidered in matching black threads. It screams elite, wealth and academia. I'll bet she's from Finis. She sports tight black trousers that hug her arse cheeks in a way that makes me ravenous.

I adjust my stance, my boxers soaked now at the sight of her, or more at the spiralling need of what I'd like to do to her.

She doesn't seem to give a fuck if anyone stares at her.

Hell, half the men and women dancing are throwing her glances, and she knows it.

I want to talk to her. But as I'm about to head over, another conversation seeps into my consciousness.

"Sorry?" I say, unable to comprehend what I'm hearing. I blink at Darwin, my face suddenly hot and stinging.

He grins at me. "Yeah. I got in. I can't believe it. I'm thrilled."

Inside, I'm kicking myself for not being able to paste on my best poker face. My expression falls, hard. On the one hand, I'm pleased for him, obviously. Who wouldn't be? It's a great achievement. But I am also deeply, deeply, fucking pissed. How is it he gets into Finis, and I don't? What is it about Darwin that makes him better suited?

I've reaped more souls, I'm a better reaper and the demon—nay, devil now—I made my deal with is the fucking dean. You don't get a lot more senior than that.

I swear I do my best to put as much happiness into the words as I can. "That's brilliant, mate, really chuffed for you. You all packed, then?"

I fear my smile didn't reach my eyes, though, because he falters. My failure to get in isn't on him. But let's be real, there's only so much happiness you can shit out when you have to watch your friends achieve the thing you've been striving for... for nine years. Shoot me for being a pathetic, bitter mortal.

I need a distraction. Where's the hot woman in the jacket? Still by the bar. Mmm. She is a way better option. I can shag my pain away rather than doing something reckless.

I hold my hand out to shake Darwin's, trying to push warmth into my grip. I clasp a second over the top of our shake and squeeze gently. "Good for you, man."

His eyes soften. Oh gods, don't do it, do not fucking pity me.

"I'm so so—" he starts.

I pull my hand out of his grasp.

He rubs his jaw, concentrating on where his toe kicks fresh grave soil.

"Tonight isn't about me. We should be celebrating your birthday."

I take a step towards the bar. "I think you've got something bigger to celebrate. Besides, there's always another birthday."

That hangs in the air between us, because of course, there isn't another.

Not for me, anyway.

His mouth opens and closes, but just like my future, there's nothing but silence and air.

"Goodnight, Darwin. And good luck, my friend. May you become the greatest Veilwalker that ever lived."

I give him a soft smile, and head for the bar. He must watch me leave because my spine is hot the entire way.

I park myself right next to the hot woman.

She cocks her head to look at me, her lips twitching.

"If you're going to spend the night checking a lady out, you could at least buy her a drink," she says.

She has sass. I wonder if she's a brat, too. Nothing like taming one. She puts her hand on her hip like she's expecting me to buy her a drink.

I run a hand through my short hair. "And what if it's my birthday? Shouldn't you be buying *me* a drink? Don't pretend you weren't checking me out."

She flags the barman down and orders. "A Palimpsest, please."

"A Palimpsest? What's that, bitter maturity and historical trauma...?" I wink at her just to see how she'll react.

Her lips purse. I've got to her already, and that knowledge does things to me. My insides light up, the first swirl of heat settling between my thighs. Those golden irises fire up, sass, fight and a little rage fuelling her.

She is magnificent.

"It's refined, *actually.* The orange bitters and bourbon mixed with the walnut liquor evoke the depth of the Great Library, and the kind of warmth age-old family recipes bring."

"Age-old is right—it's the same drink my grandad used to drink. Helped him on his way to the grave, too." I raise an eyebrow at her.

"Oh, and let me guess, a young thing like yourself is ordering what?"

The barman returns and slides the Palimpsest to her.

"Moonless Black, please," I say.

She outright rolls her eyes at me. "I might be middle-aged, but at least I'm not a cliché. And there I was thinking you were the refined kind of masc. A dom even..."

There's the opening. Oh, I am going to break her. Looks like this evening is perking right up.

"Bold of you to assume," I say and snatch her tumbler out of her grasp and take a sip. Her lips part, surprise coursing through her refined features.

Good, she strikes me as the type of woman that needs to be kept on her toes.

The bourbon hits first. A heated burn slips down my throat, but it's a nutty orange lingering on my tongue that makes it sumptuous.

She was right. It tastes like old books and aeons of knowledge. Warm fires and family dinners. Gods damn.

"Not so cocky now, are you?" She grins.

Oh, that's it.

I step into her personal space. She doesn't move, another hint of brat? Or perhaps she's a switch. What's clear is that she's sussing me out as much as I am her. I position us with her back to the bar, resting against it.

I press my body to hers, leaning against the bar for balance and knock my thigh between hers. I push up until I hit her warm centre and hold with just enough pressure on her pussy that she inhales.

"You have no idea how cocky I can be. Now, why don't you be a good girl and tell me your name."

This close, I inhale her scent. It's deep and exotic, like oud and amber and a little hint of rose.

Behind her, the barman places my drink down, so I take the opportunity to lean forward, my lips millimetres from hers, brushing against her jaw.

She sucks in a breath, her body trembling with want. It takes a monumental amount of self-control not to lose it and fuck her against the bar.

Her chest heaves up and down, heat radiating off her. "L-Lucy."

Fuck, I love getting under the skin of a woman. I jerk back, pulling my thigh away and giving her some breathing room. Her cheeks are tinged pink, her lips flushed. She secures a streak of red behind her ear as she sips her drink. She's not trembling anymore, but her knuckles are white as she grips the glass.

I bring my Moonless Black up, but to my surprise, she snatches it out of my hand and takes a drink herself, mimicking my earlier move.

I gawp at her. It's not often a woman surprises me. She

swirls the liquid in the glass before taking a sniff, followed by a gulp.

She lingers for a moment, contemplating the rich flavours. Black rum, a dash of cold brew coffee and a squirt of lime mixed with activated charcoal. Oh, and a sprinkle of anise to garnish. Perfection.

She swallows and hands it back. "Stale, slightly bitter and tastes childish. A bit like your moves."

My eyes bug wide. She uses two fingers to slide my mouth closed, places a kiss on my lips and fucks off to the dance floor.

What.

The.

Fuck.

I stare after her, watching her arse swing from side to side as she disappears into the crowd.

Oh no, oh hell no. I would genuinely reap a newborn for a night with that woman.

Just so I could break her, mind.

"This is hers," the barman says, handing me a glass of wine.

I grin. "What a shame. Guess I'll have to go find her."

5

LUCY

I left my wine at the bar hoping she'd take the bait. She does. Her energy beelines for me as I move to a secluded corner of the graveyard. Less people here, but no quieter. The rave music still blares bass and rhythm at visceral levels.

I duck under some overgrown trees. There are a couple of graves and one hole that was never filled to dodge, but it's hidden enough that several couples and groups of people are fucking here. Alongside an array of others quite obviously sniffing a cocktail of drugs.

Not the most refined of raves I've been to, but what did I expect? The woman slips under the overhanging branches and makes her way over to me.

"Smooth, getting me to carry your drink over here for you," she says, holding out my glass.

I reach for it, but she snatches it away and guzzles the lot before handing me the empty glass.

"The name is Midnight, in case you were interested."

"I wasn't. Unless you're here to help me drink or fuck my way into oblivion."

She tilts her head, not even trying to hide the fact she's mentally undressing me. She hands me her original drink, which I take out of spite and swallow in one go. It sears down my throat, and I have to suppress the urge to vomit it back up.

"Well, *Lucy*, I guess it's your lucky night. Those happened to be my exact plans."

"Convenient," I say, as disinterested as I can make it. Though I am far from it. Midnight wears tight leather trousers; I'd put money on her being a biker.

Gods, I bet she can do all sorts of things with leather. The thought makes me cross my legs as my clit decides to misbehave, pulsing in erratic beats between my thighs.

A hand scythe hangs from her hip. Interesting. A reaper, perhaps? Her bright blue eyes pop against tanned brown skin. And the more I look, the more I settle on the fact she has to be a reaper. A weight lurks beneath her expression. It lives in the quiet curve of her smile and the tension in her shoulders. She's going to die, and she recognises it in a way most humans don't.

Her hair is dark, shorn on the sides, long and floppy on top. What I would give to sit on those full lips and grind an orgasm out.

The thought makes me swallow.

"Where did you go, baby girl?" she says, her fingers guiding my chin back to her.

"Somewhere sordid, you wouldn't like it," I say, unable to hide the smirk. I'm not a brat, though I have my moments. I much prefer the release of letting go, letting someone control me. I spend every day in charge, making decisions, lecturing my classes. Sometimes, I just need to let go. Especially on a day like today. That's why I came here: a drink, a dance, and hopefully an orgasm.

Midnight leans into my ear, warmth radiates off her and trickles down my neck, straight to my nipples, which harden instantly. The scent of vetiver and grapefruit drift on the air. It's fresh, intoxicating and makes me want to sink my teeth into her flesh.

"I think you should tell Daddy every single sordid thought that ran through that beautiful head of yours," she says.

Daddy?

A bolt of excitement shoots straight to my clit.

A gasp escapes. I've never called anyone Daddy, never thought that was a kink I'd have or want.

"Well, Daddy…" I say, testing the word in my mouth, and gods, does it hit the spot. A part of me screams that it's wrong, that if I lift the lid on why I like it, I'll have to unpack a load of shit I don't want to deal with.

But this is just sex. What does it matter when I won't see her again? So I lean in and go full tilt.

"I was thinking about how much of a filthy little slut I was going to be tonight."

She stiffens against me, the faint rush of her breath escaping in rapid huffs. Her fingers grip my arm and waist. We're hidden beneath the trees, but not from the other couples.

"I only do one-night stands," she says, suddenly serious.

"Good, because I don't do anything more with humans."

"Demon?"

I nod. Something flickers in her gaze, but it vanishes as fast as it arrived. The fact she's an awful lot younger than me might have something to do with my fleeting hesitation. Though the way she holds me, assured, confident, safe, tells me she'd have no problem being anyone's daddy. And that makes my insides and any remaining fucks I had dissolve.

She runs her hand through my locks and then grips the back of my head and pulls me to her, plunging her lips over mine.

Her mouth is exquisite. Hard kiss against the soft curve of her lips. I think my heart leaves my body. She pulls off and growls.

"Get on your knees, Lucy. I'm going to take what I need from you, and then I'm going to make you scream louder than the music."

Oh, my gods.

I've never dropped to my knees faster. My mouth waters at the thought of tasting her, my underwear soaked at the image of her taking whatever the hell she wants from me, using me however she sees fit. My pussy throbs as she unbuckles her trousers and lowers her boxers just enough to give me access.

She loops her fist around my hair and yanks me to her pussy. As much as it makes my scalp sting with the force, my heart rate skyrockets, and my thighs squeeze together to muzzle the pulsing in my core.

I slide my tongue over her clit, sucking and licking and probing my way to her entrance. It's hard, the angle isn't right but maybe she doesn't want that. She doesn't spread her legs to give me access, so I take the message and focus on her clit.

"Oh gods, right there, suck Daddy's pussy like the dirty slut you are."

Fuck, I can't.

I've never had anyone this vocal in bed, and it's doing things to me. The filth coming out of this woman's mouth, her grip on my hair and the taste of her on my tongue has me levitating out of my body.

Her words curl around my clit, making me climb my way to an orgasm before she's even touched me. I undo my jeans button and slip my hand down to my centre.

But she tugs my hair hard enough to halt me. "Did I say you could touch yourself?"

I bite down a whine.

"Fingers. Now."

I display them, coated in a sheen that shows her just how needy I am.

She smirks, pleased with the affect she's having on me.

"Give them to me," she demands.

I hitch up onto my knees and reach up to her mouth. She sucks my fingers, her tongue swirling over the pads to clean up every drop of my excitement. My nipples harden to painful buds beneath my bra. I don't think I've ever needed an orgasm more in my life.

She guides me back to her pussy. Her clit is swollen against my tongue. She rocks her hips into me over and over as I lick and swipe and flick my tongue against her apex.

Her hips buck faster and faster until she's jerking and erratic, and then she stills, a gasp drifting on the air around us.

She releases my hair, using her thumb to pull my lower lip down and stroke the tip of my tongue.

"Such a good little slut."

I practically vibrate out of my skin.

She fastens her trousers back up and offers me her hand to help me stand. Then her lips are on me. They're soft and full and so very fucking hungry.

Her kiss is bruising and exquisite. She grips me with the

perfect amount of pressure that tells me she owns me in this moment. I haven't had sex like this in so long it makes me ache for the loss of when it's over.

She runs her palms under my thighs and taps, indicating for me to jump up. I do, and cross my legs around her waist. My hair falls, covering our desperate kisses.

She tastes like booze and mint and longing. I can't get enough of her. I devour everything she gives me, wrapping my hand around her neck and whimpering as she breaks off to nibble my skin.

She steps forward, carrying us towards the fence. I remember too late.

"Wa—" I start.

But we lurch forward and then tumble and roll, crashing to a muddy stop. I thunk down on top of her.

There's a beat. Two.

Did I kill her? That would be awkward.

She groans, wriggles and then flicks my hair off her face, takes one look at me sat on her chest and bursts out laughing.

I follow. Tears leak down my cheeks when I can't control the hysterics. "I guess this is an omen," I pant through the laughter.

She nods. "Well, we did say this was one night only. Landing in a grave while fucking kind of foreshadows it all."

I laugh. "That's dark, who hurt you?"

A flicker washes through her expression. Oh, she was hurt? I open my mouth to ask more sensitively, but she grabs me by the hips and flips me onto my back, attacking my trousers and yanking them and my underwear off.

"We're doing this in a grave?" I ask.

"Do you want an orgasm or not?"

I shut my mouth.

The pit isn't long enough for me to be on my back with her between my legs, so she swings underneath me and shuffles me up her body until she can lower me onto her mouth.

Her tongue slips between my folds, parting me as she laps up my excitement.

She moans into my cunt, rocking and tilting my hips as I slowly grind onto her face.

A sick thought washes through my head that I could sink lower, suffocate her and she's in a ready-made forever bed. But then I'd lose out on what is building to be an intense orgasm.

Her tongue flicks faster and faster. She uses her lips and flattens her tongue then makes it soft and light and it all drives me fucking wild.

My head tips back. She releases her hold on one hip and lands a smack on my arse as I rock harder and harder on her mouth.

My pussy tightens, my clit swollen and throbbing. Everything clenches and then releases. Electric pulses surge through my body as I twitch and rock, seeking out those final aftershocks of pleasure.

After my day, I needed this. And she has the perfect tongue. Perfect enough that I am gutted it's a one-off.

She frowns. "What's—" she points at my neck. "Never mind, I'm seeing shit."

"Seeing?"

She shakes her head. "I thought there was something on your neck, but it must have been the light."

That's not weird, maybe I take back my previous comments. We dress, she hauls herself out of the pit and lends a palm to pull me up.

I squint through the trees to see the dance floor thinning, the rave dying.

That eau du awkward found after a one-night stand orgasm fills the air around us.

"Well, this was great," I start.

"Don't be like that, let me take you home."

She leads me through the graveyard in silence, throwing scant glances back at me. But neither of us find any words to share until we reach the parking lot and she stops at a motorbike.

Oh, hell no.

"I don't think so," I say, edging away from the sleek black machine.

She glances around, looking for a carriage or some other method for me to get home, I assume.

There are none.

At this point, I'll be walking into town to catch a carriage.

"It's late. All the carriages are gone..."

She hands me her helmet, and I hold it by the chin straps like the heinous contraption it is.

"Put it on," she demands.

"I, umm. I don't..."

"Demon's sake." She plucks the helmet from my hand and examines me. I find myself lost in her expression, the careful attention she pays to pushing my hair away from my face and adjusting the straps just so.

Her fingers caress my skin. It's weirdly comforting, and I find myself leaning into her palm.

She catches herself and pulls away, bringing the helmet to the top of my head and sliding it on.

It's snug and muffles my hearing. My lungs tighten so much I have to force myself to breathe slower.

"I don't like it. It's suffocating," I say.

"You'll get used to it. It's like a hug for your head. Do you have a tie? You'll want to put your hair up, otherwise it will be a tangled mess."

I plait the end of my hair and tuck it down the back of my jacket.

"I'll help you on," she says and places her hands on my hips. Those firm, assured fingers press into me. Gods, I feel them all the way through my jeans down to my bones.

"Slide your leg over this," she says.

I glare at her through the visor, but do as I'm told.

"Good girl." She winks at me, so I slap her on the arm. "Where to?"

"Finis Academy."

Her eyes widen, her brow furrows, but she stays silent as she climbs onto the bike.

She flicks the kickstand up and cranks the engine, then revs the bike hard, making me squeal.

She laughs and shouts over the noise. "You'll want to hold on."

"To what?" I shriek.

"That depends if you want another orgasm or not..."

Even as she turns to push the bike off, I can sense her grin all the way through the tension in her muscles as I slide my hands around her waist.

I grip hold of Midnight like my life depends on it as she swings around the city streets. Our bodies move in sync after a few minutes, bending this way and then that. She gets so low to the road that I scream multiple times. I don't know if it's the bike rumbling between my thighs, the hard plains of Midnight's body, or the orgasm from earlier, but when we finally pull up to the mist-shrouded campus, I am hot, my heart pounding like galloping hooves and, I can't lie, I am soaking wet—again.

Midnight pulls off my helmet and grins. "Wasn't that bad was it..." she says.

My traitorous lips twitch.

She brushes her mouth against my ear. My stomach somersaults—yet another traitorous part of me.

"I think you want me to kiss you," she says, and her words are drugs. Like the silk tension of an infernal contract. It's enough to make me wonder if *she's* the demon and I'm the mortal.

Is it her words?

Her tone?

Or just the wanton need coursing through my body, and the fact I wouldn't mind calling her Daddy again.

I never do this.

Never take risks or throw caution to the wind. I'm sensible, deliberate.

I pay attention.

Her hot mouth brushes over my throat and short circuits every thought I had.

Fuck.

"We shouldn't—"

But she cuts me off, plunging her lips over mine. I moan into her kiss. Into the soft caress of her tongue kneading mine. My body melts so fast, she grabs me by the waist and hoiks me back up onto the bike seat. I briefly worry that it will fall over, but she kisses my neck, my collarbone, and my mind is lost to the sensation. My head lolls, baring my throat to her as her tongue slides over my pulse.

There's a beat, the whip of wind against my cheeks and a sweep of clarity—I can use this situation. Make an arrangement, use each other for relief.

But we can't. This was a one-off. I have a life, I'm stuck on campus most of the time, and she is young. Way too young for this to be anything. And that's without the fact she's a danger to me. Demons are forbidden from becoming emotionally involved with mortals because of the damage it does to our power. It's not like humans mean to. But their souls attract our magic, suck it out of our crystalline hearts and leave us vulnerable.

So, no. This must be a one-off.

I lean down, finding her lips and crushing mine to hers. My hands are all over her, waist, hips, breasts, arse...

Midnight curls her hand around my braid and uses it to tug me where she wants me. I wrap my legs around her waist.

She licks and bites her way over every inch of exposed skin. I grip her chin and crush my mouth to hers.

I kiss her hard.

I kiss her thank you.

I kiss her goodbye.

This could have been something wonderful, but it wasn't meant to be.

It's not our fate.

I pull myself away and walk towards Obidiah, our gate gargoyle. He scowls at me, but I wink at him, and the gates swing open.

I won't lie—it hurt not to look back, but what's the point? We were doomed the minute I said I was a demon.

Lucy vanishes through the gates which creak as they swing shut. My lips still tingle from her touch. What is it about the way a woman kisses you? It's heady, intoxicating, moreish.

I could have spent all night drinking her in, caressing her flesh, inhaling the scent of her.

She kissed me like this night had been everything... and nothing. My fingers drift to my lips, tracing the spectre of her goodbye.

I lean against the thick, leering iron railings. I wish I could get in for her... and if I'm honest, for me, too.

I reel back and punch the gate with nine years of frustration coiled in my fist.

It hurts, obviously. I'm made of bone and blood, and it is made of iron.

The gates are imposing in the same way the sandstone walls of the campus are. Towering threats that glare down at the mere mortals who deem themselves worthy enough to look upon the campus. The goyle watches me with narrowed eyes and a hint of a curl on its lips. But it doesn't talk to me.

I stare through the night at Lucy's receding form, mist curling around her body like the choking hold of ageing ivy.

I slide to my knees, leaning my forehead against the gate, and grip hold of the iron, pleading silently.

Please let me in. Give me one more chance. Let me attempt the Severance Rite and earn my way in.

When nothing happens, my stomach fizzes with a cocktail of emotions.

"What the fuck do you want from me?" I snarl. Like the gate is going to respond.

But just like the last nine years, my prayers go unanswered. A chill ruffles the trees, the crack and rustle of ancient oaks stretching and yawning in the night. A prickle skitters over my arms and down my neck.

I shiver.

This place is haunted, so the rumours go. No idea whether it's true. Only students, professors, or those with invitations can enter. Probably why the mist shrouds the campus— nothing in, nothing out, not even the faintest glimpse.

Not even the ghosts leave.

I pull my scythe out and rest it against the gates, wondering if it's strong enough to cut my way in.

The goyle now glares down at me, squinting, ogling but never speaking.

The gates hum beneath my fingers, the cool wrought iron heating under the press of my flesh to the metal.

I pull my hand away. But it's stuck.

"Oww, fuck," I hiss. The metal bites into my palm. "The actual fuck?" I kick the gate, my stomach clenching as I struggle to yank my hand off the iron bars.

Something sharp spears my palm, warm liquid puddles in the crook of my hand and then I'm released.

I stumble back, cradling my injury. In the centre of my palm are two circular wounds and on the wrought bar is a thin river of my blood.

"It bit me?" I glare at the goyle. "Did you bite me?"

He doesn't respond.

My blood dribbles down the iron rail. I'm not an idiot; I take heed of the warning and edge away. Maybe I don't want to attend Finis after all.

This place is cooked.

The world tilts.

My head swims. I stumble towards the bike. There's a flash of white fur. I swear I saw that white cat earlier. Am I hallucinating? Was my drink spiked at the rave?

Grey smatters my vision. Bile climbs up my throat.

I gag.

Wretch.

Fall to my knees and spew up the contents of my stomach. I crawl to my bike, my fingers outstretched.

Then there's nothing.

I come round on my bike with the streets of Ora City speeding past.

"What the fuck?"

I'm so startled I swerve, nearly knocking over a couple about to cross the road. I grip the handlebars, tension coursing through my body. My heart hammering against my ribs. I have no fucking clue how I got here.

Houses race past—neat, orderly rows of bricks.

Mansions dotted between. The further I get into the city, the denser the housing and the sparser the greenery.

I pull into my street, park the bike on the drive and scramble off, staring at it like an alien.

I don't even remember getting back on it, let alone how I started it and made it halfway across the city practically unconscious. My skin is feverish with the need to wash the evening off.

Key.

Door.

Quick glance over my shoulder.

Inside.

I enter the kitchen and sling my helmet on the counter. The evening's events gnaw at my insides, a malignant tumour that bloats with every step I take.

If I thought I was freaked out before, it's nothing compared to the way my veins turn to ice as I approach the kitchen table.

A Finis Academy envelope rests on the wood. But I threw my rejection letter in the bin. Didn't I?

Didn't I?

I swear I did.

No. I *did*. I'm certain I threw it in the bin.

My fingers inch towards the lid and lift it, convinced I'll see the crumpled parchment. There's nothing but food and wrappers. That tumour swollen with unease in my belly bulges. Am I losing it? My throat is thick and my skin aches where goosebumps rise.

I reach the table, my fingers tremble as I lift the envelope. It's sealed with the Finis Academy's logo stamped in red wax.

I can scarcely bring myself to crack it. Déjà vu is

messing with my head. I thought I'd opened this letter already.

The wax snaps, an awful sound that cuts through my teeth. I flinch as a tree branch clips the window. I need to get a grip.

The black card peels open. Wait, wasn't my rejection letter white? The dark colour almost shines; it reminds me of the imposing iron gates.

My eyes flit to the bin again but the original letter doesn't appear. I flip open the card, and my mouth falls open.

It's at times like this that I question every rational thought that has passed through my mind.

I should see the fact that the words are scrawled in a red ink the same colour as my blood as a warning.

I should also consider the fact some deep part of my mind is certain I was rejected, and this can't be happening, thus it's a warning sign.

And above all, I should heed the warning bells screaming in my mind: I lost an entire chunk of the evening. Something is very wrong tonight.

But I don't do any of that.

I don't care how I got the letter. Nor why.

I don't care that my gut is screaming. Nor that I feel like I'm losing my sanity.

I ignore the crawling sensation slithering through my veins, settling in my throat and curling around my lungs.

None of that matters.

Because what lays before me, is the glimmering promise of a future.

And that is worth everything.

7

MIDNIGHT

The thing about lesbians is that we fall hard and fast. The fact we u-haul right into lesbian bed death should be an alarm bell to warn us off moving so fast.

But lesbians will be lesbians.

We love different.

Harder, hotter, brighter. Our love burns like the light of a thousand stars. Lesbians love intensely enough they'd peel their skin off and climb inside the body of their loved one, just to get a little bit closer.

Our love is the definition of obsessive, addictive, consuming.

When our eyes lock on a girl, there is only her. It's what makes a woman's love so intoxicating.

And so. Fucking. Dangerous.

Aurelia and I u-hauled. *Hard.*

We met at eighteen. She became my world. And in that young, naive way I thought it would last forever. I thought I was grown up and understood the world, that I knew better. What I know now is that I didn't know shit back then.

I willingly gave her my heart.

I openly gave her my body.

And stupidly, I gave her my soul.

For two long years we lived in each other's pockets, breathed the same air, drank from the same young love Kool-Aid.

Until one night that changed everything.

8
MIDNIGHT

Ten Years Ago

Aurelia's skin is grey. It sets my teeth on edge. We're only twenty—we should look youthful, vibrant. Isn't that the greatest joy of being in your twenties? You get to drink yourself into oblivion, snort whatever concoction of drugs you want and fuck yourself silly, and there are no consequences.

Aurelia is growing steadily weaker, and greyer. The last month she's barely had any energy.

It's a sinuous truth I've been trying to avoid. I can't anymore, though. It sucks at my skin like the ravenous jaws of a parasite. Gnawing repetitive thoughts burrow under my flesh. My brain itches and skitters. I need to get it out. Find out what is wrong.

I've rehearsed the conversation a million times. Played it this way and that. But I can't seem to get the words out. It's as if my subconscious has worked out the answer and my conscious doesn't want to hear it.

I have to do something because Aurelia is shutting down.

Shutting me out.

We're supposed to be each other's everything. She is my everything. I don't have anyone else. My parents are dead. I have no siblings, no aunts.

Aurelia is it.

She was with me when they died. We'd only been together a year, and she'd held me tight, cradling me through the long nights of tears and heartache. She cooked for me and made me eat when I didn't want to get out of bed. She told me that even though they were gone, I'd never be alone because I'd always have her.

It felt like the truest thing I'd ever heard. The way those words curled around my heart, it was sacred—an unbreakable promise.

So why does it feel like a lie tonight?

Aurelia has seen me through my lowest moments, but tonight I realise I was naive for thinking it had bonded us. When you go through that kind of trauma, it either makes you or breaks you as a couple, right?

I thought it made us. Maybe it only made me.

"Aurelia," I plead as I perch on the edge of the bed. "Please talk to me."

I'm pathetic, needy. She's the sick one and here I am, desperate for communication.

I'm met with the kind of pregnant pause that sends stony chills through a person. My lungs are heavy enough I struggle to breathe. She rolls over, turning away from me.

This is what hurts the most. There is something wrong and instead of leaning on me, she's pushing me away. I don't want to say the words out loud, but they cling to the air. It's putrid, like the cloying rot of week-old rodents and festering tumours.

I reach over the bed to open the window and let some air in. But Aurelia slaps my hand out of the way.

"I'm cold," she snaps.

I bite the inside of my lip, rehearsing the conversation again: *Aurelia, please, I'm worried, we need to talk. There's something wrong. Let me help you. Let me help us.*

She pulls the cover over her shoulder, tugging her body further away from mine. I'm losing her. Our relationship is fading away. Why won't she confront this?

That's when I realise.

"Oh," I breathe.

One syllable.

One word that cuts through the thick swell of unspoken words.

Through the bullshit.

Through our entire fucking relationship.

Funny how even as mortals, our lives seem long, and yet it's not the decades that change everything, but the brief moments. The short words and shorter sentences that slip from our mouths like waves and sand. Smooth shores one second, waves obliterating us the next.

She flinches against my touch.

"You already know...?" I ask.

The silence that hangs between us is a dark, hungry maw devouring our relationship.

"It's over," she says.

Two short words.

One broken heart.

"What?" It's all I have left. I'm gripping the bed sheets so hard my knuckles are stretched white over bone.

"Either I do it now, or my body does it for us in a couple of months."

There it is.

The ugly truth.

"You're sick?" It comes out like a question, but it's a statement, an acknowledgement of what was held secret between us. Now it's a bloated fact hanging as pungent in the air as her illness is in her body.

She flips over, her eyes colder than I've ever seen them.

"Not just sick. Dying, Midnight. So no matter what, it's over. We. Are. Over. Today. Next week. In a couple of months' time. Does it even matter? It's done. You might as well get used to it."

"Gods, Aurelia. You think I'd just fucking leave you? You think that I'd let you deal with this on your own? After everything we've been through?"

She rolls back over. "You need to leave."

"Babe, please don't shut me out. Not like this. What doctors have you seen? There has to be someone else. A second opinion."

"Second. Third. And fourth. It's terminal, Midnight. I won't see next year. I wasted my life for nothing."

I recoil. "We're... We're not a waste. What does that even mean?"

"I could have gone places. Done things. Instead, I tethered myself to you and spent what little time I had here dealing with you and your fucking emotions."

My stomach hardens. My eyes grow cold with the press of wet tears. "You don't mean that."

"GET OUT," she screams.

My chest cracks. Tears splash into the dimples my fingers make on the duvet.

Nothing can ever hurt like this.

Nothing.

She doesn't mean those things. She's hurting, and I understand that.

Aurelia *will* see next year.

I'll make sure of it.

9

LUCY

It's Severance Rite morning—my favourite day of the year. The campus is alive even before the students arrive.

My day is only dampened by two things:

First, the fact that it will be my last in this apartment. Like the new students, I have to move into different accommodations as Head of House Inferos. I've pre-packed my underwear and unmentionables. But left everything else for campus maintenance to handle.

And second, the protests in the city outside the academy walls. They're loud enough that even buried this far in the campus, the echoes of their rage spill between the buildings like thunder.

Apparently, there are thousands of people at the gates. Both for and against Architecti's resurrection.

I just hope the new students can get in. Half the campus staff have been sent out to deal with crowd control.

I take a sip of coffee, savouring the rich, nutty aroma of the cup I poured earlier. It reminds me of Midnight's drink last night at the rave.

It's six thirty, I need to hurry up. I sip the rest of my coffee and review the contracts I prepped as examples for my third-year class this afternoon.

I wish finding a way to break the contract my father made for me at birth was as easy as third-year class prep. There's a ripple of movement in the air. I check the window wondering if I left it open, but it's closed.

I rub my face and wonder if I have time for another coffee. Exhaustion is making me hallucinate.

A bang on the door startles me, and I yelp, but jump up and pull it open. "Father." I beam. "Morning, are you ready for the new cohort?"

He leans down and kisses both my cheeks. "We need to talk."

He barges past me and paces up and down my open-plan living room.

"What's wrong?"

He rounds on me, his dark eyes full of winter and snow. I edge towards the door. This is not a good expression for my father to hold.

"Did you have anything to do with the invitations?" he says, blunt and authoritative.

"For the new cohort?"

He nods.

"No? I'm not on the invitation board..."

He storms up to me, grips my chin hard enough it will bruise. "Don't lie to me, Lucy."

I push his hand off me, hating when he behaves like this. I was hoping he got the bad mood out yesterday.

"Don't fucking touch me. If you can't come in here and be nice, then don't bother visiting at all."

My throat tightens, a warning from my body—from the contract—not to threaten my father. I rub my chin and neck trying to shrug off the throbbing shadow of his touch.

"Did you let her in?"

I fling my hands up. "Who? Seriously, I don't have time for this. I still need to put my prep materials in my first classroom and get some contracts back to Professor Morrow before attending the Severance Rite."

"Security saw you with a woman late last night." He unbuttons his blazer, relaxing as if my flat is actually his.

I don't like it.

Not one bit.

I don't want him to make himself comfortable.

I shift position, my eyes landing on the floor. "Saw me doing what, exactly?"

If he thinks I'm dating a human there would be severe consequences. That is one thing he has always been clear about. We Corvines do not sully ourselves with humankind, at least not relationship-wise.

His glare burrows into my ribs, infesting me. My cheeks flame under his penetrating glare.

"Her name is Midnight," he growls.

"How... how do you know her name?"

"I asked you a question, Lucy." My name spills from his lips all gnarled like a winter twig.

I breathe slow, trying to calm my thoughts, to work this through. Realisation dawns on me. "You know her..."

His adjusts his jacket, refusing to look at me. Oh, shit, he doesn't *just* know her. My mind flits back to last night, to the scythe on her hip.

"She's one of your reapers?"

His mouth turns into a nasty sneer. He rounds on me, gripping me by the shoulders, squeezing.

"You stay the fuck away from her."

I frown and slap at his hand, only to receive a blinding pain behind my eye.

"Father, wh—" But the last words are strangled as he grabs my throat.

"I don't know what you did or how you did it. But Midnight is *my* reaper. Do you understand?"

I nod, my cheeks heating and swelling under the pressure of his grip.

"I know her type. All charm and ego. I've no doubt she'll have eyes for you. Do not go there, Lucy. Do you understand?"

"Go wh—" I stutter, but his grip tightens.

What the fuck is going on?

"I do not need more controversy in my department. I had enough to deal with Professor Jorsin. Not only is it forbidden to fuck your students, you are a demon. And. She. Is. A. Mortal."

I shouldn't fight back, not when the consequences are so severe.

But my survival instincts kick in, and I claw at his wrist, my nails splitting and bleeding the harder I scratch and pull at him. I pull my knee back and shove it hard into his groin.

He yelps and stumbles back as my kneecap shatters. I scream and buckle as searing pain radiates through my leg. My nose joins in the fun and pisses blood, spraying the floor and splattering my white shirt with red polka dots.

"I don't know why you insist on fighting back, you know it doesn't end well for you," my father says.

"And I don't understand why you insist on treating me the way you do. I won't be single forever."

He hauls himself up off the floor and bends to offer me a hand, helping me upright.

"I am sorry. I didn't mean to use my anger against you.

That was awful of me. And you're right, you deserve a demoness worthy of you, someone to take care of you."

He pulls a handkerchief out of his breast pocket and dabs under my nose, then holds it there, squeezing the bridge of my nose until the bleeding stops. This is what I hate about him. The constant flip-flop. The emotional whiplash is exhausting. Sometimes I feel like he hates me and others, the remorse trickles through his tender touch.

"What aren't you telling me about her?" I ask, sounding extra nasally from all the blood lodged in my nose.

He sighs, examines the hanky and resumes the pressure when my nose decides it's not done haemorrhaging. My knee has stopped screaming at least. It tingles where the bones are matting back together beneath my skin. Though I suspect I'll be walking with a limp for the rest of the day.

"The student invitation list was complete. Then late last night, shortly after you returned to campus, another name appeared. A Mercedes Midnight."

"It wasn't me," I say.

He nods. "I realise that now."

"Why is it such a big deal if she attends. She's just a reaper. It's not like you don't have others."

He nods, though his posture is as stiff as his demeanour.

"Just promise me you won't go there. I can't afford for you to lose your power to a mortal."

I fold my arms. "Just because she likes women and I like women doesn't mean we're going to get hitched."

Though... if she wasn't a student, I wouldn't be making the same promise about fucking.

He huffs, checks the hanky and finally pulls it away.

"Yes, I'm not an idiot. I understand the principles of attraction." He takes a deep breath, rolls his shoulders and relaxes. "But with your new role as Head of Inferos, our reputation is key right now. With the Veil flailing, and…" He stops himself. Then continues. "I simply can't afford you to fall in love with a mortal and give up all your power. I won't have it. Do you understand me?"

"No falling for mortals. Got it," I drawl.

His eyes flash. "I mean it, Lucy. If the Veil actually fails, we are all in grave danger. If Architecti were to…"

"To what? Hmm?"

The truth hangs between us.

"Say it," I edge closer, my knee searing in agony, but I refuse to be weak, refuse to let him strip me of power. "Confess and this all goes away, Daddy," I say in a sing-song voice.

His nose wrinkles in disgust. "Just keep away from her. She's my best reaper. But she's still a fucking mortal. Do not sully your reputation with a grinner, of all things. If you want a husband, or a wife, I'll arrange for one for you."

"You'll do no such thing."

His lips pull into a sneer as he walks to the door, dropping his bloodied hanky in the kitchen bin on the way. "Then see to it that you keep your hands, and your power, to yourself. I swear, if you fall for a mortal and lose our family power…"

He opens my apartment door.

"You'll what?" I shove my hand on my hip, hold myself strong despite the throbbing pain in my leg. "It's my power, Father. Mine to keep, mine to give away."

His expression darkens. "I made you, Lucy. I can unmake you. Don't you forget it."

"Good morning, Dean Corvine," a sing-song voice chimes in the hallway.

"Morning," Father says, his expression morphing into

that charming warmth mixed with serious professional academia.

Bile claws at my throat. He turns to me, some of the sunshine melting away. He clenches and unclenches his fists, not quite able to meet my eye.

"I'll see you at the Severance Rite. I... I'm sorry. I do love you," he says, his voice soft.

I nod.

"I know," I say, and I do. He's a demon, and they're all flighty, angry types. And yet the churning in my gut tells me that it's not an excuse. That I deserve better. That I shouldn't tolerate it. But he's my father.

The only one I have.

The only family I have, and I'm afraid if I push him away, I'll be all alone.

The flat door closes, and I sag against my dining room table, weakness settling into my muscles, tears stinging my eyes.

IO

LUCY

I make my way across campus, from the faculty wing over the cobbled sandstone paths. There's a shortcut through the Veilwalker lecture hall and down the main path to the Great Library. The campus is stunning. Even to me, and I've lived here my entire life.

There's a secretive beauty to Finis Academy. At first glance, it's all archways and cloisters, creeping ivy crawling over sandy-coloured bricks. But if you keep looking, the truth lies in your periphery. An aged wisdom of sorts, buried in crumbling shadows that lurk and move in unnatural ways, a clock that never tells the truth, doors that move and shiver away when they don't want to be opened. A cemetery that doesn't want to let you out and a church that won't let you in.

The campus is alive in ways it shouldn't be. Perhaps then, Father is right, and Finis Tower is haunted. Or maybe my students wish the stories were true.

The Great Library is circular, an endless spiral building that houses our oldest tomes and grimoires and doubles as a kind of fortress protecting Finis Tower itself—the magnum opus of the campus.

Maldrip, the library's goyle, sits on an oak-studded door, the dark stone of his skin matching the black metal studs. He mumbles "Good afternoon," followed by a line of gravelly spittle sprinkling out of his mouth. It lands in a stone dust pile by my feet.

Delightful.

"It's very much the morning," I say.

"Professor Corvine, glad I caught you," Thalia Morrow calls from behind me.

She's a professor of Veilwalking, but has a specialism in contracts. She's brilliant and was my mentor through my own studies. She must be in her late sixties now, though her bronzed skin doesn't seem to have aged enough. Grey streaks her hair, except for the ends, which are dipped in black. It's graceful the way the faintest of lines kiss her eyes, all of them etching in smiles instead of grimaces. Don't be fooled though, we all carry an edge, and hers is terrifying. I never crossed her as her mentee, but the lashings she'll give the students that do are enough to give even the senior faculty members nightmares.

"Looking forward to term starting?" I ask.

"About that. There's an urgent staff meeting in Finis Tower. Everyone has been called."

I follow after her, and we pass through a huge stone archway and onto the bridge perched above the moat that lays between the circular library and the tower.

She tugs my arm and pulls it over hers. "Now tell me, how is the love life, hmm?"

"Demon's above, Thalia, do we have to talk about this?"

Thalia has known me twenty-five years at least. Since I was a teenager. She saw me grow up with Ignatius and often took, not a motherly role as such, but more of the naughty aunt always encouraging me to rebel-type role.

"Absolutely, you're not getting any younger, when are you going to meet a nice young woman to keep you warm at night?" She winks her golden eye while her blue one glitters at me in the early light.

"Thalia," I hiss. "Stop it."

"If I'm still getting it, why can't you?"

I open my mouth about to say something and stop. I guess she's right. But also, I don't feel like spilling the fact I fucked a total stranger in a grave last night, not least because if Midnight survives the Severance Rite, she'll be a student, and there are only two rules here. One of which is students are forbidden from fraternising with professors and vice versa.

"I don't have time for frivolities like sex," I lie.

She tuts at me and leads me to the tower entrance as the autumn breeze whips under my blazer.

It's not compulsory to wear Finis attire as a professor here. Thalia isn't. But I find there's something deeply satisfying about looking the part. It makes me feel more professional, like I belong here, more than rocking up in gym sweats or whatever.

Besides, the neat lines and pinched waist does wonders for my curves. Maybe I should take more leaves out of Thalia's book. I'm forty, not dead. The way the uniform flatters me, I'm convinced whoever designed it must have been a woman. If nothing else, the black and red fabric matches my hair.

When I reach the tower door, Mordax, our most grumpy of gargoyles, is chewing on his knocking handle. His wing-like ears ruffle as I incline my head at him.

"Good morning, may we gain entry to Finis Tower?" I say.

His stony eyes glide up to meet mine, all the while he chews on his iron ring.

"Don finkth soh," he mumbles around the handle.

"Much as we'd love to exchange pleasantries, we've been summoned for a staff meeting, so open up or I'll tweak your ring," Thalia growls.

He chews on the iron a little more aggressively, scowling at the pair of us, but the door swings open. I tickle him under his wing-tip ears, trying to appease the situation. He shivers in delight but continues to chunter insults under his breath at Thalia.

"Thank you," I say and can't help but smile in spite of the glare he's giving us.

The tower is regal as ever. It houses fifteen floors total: seven above and seven below and the ground floor smack in the middle. Each floor down is more demonic than the last, and each floor up more celestial than the previous.

Beneath them all lies a forbidden basement with a door to the underworld, and above them sits an ancient records room holding a door to the celestial realm. That's the other rule of the Academy: no one goes to the basement without training and permission. My father's permission.

Connecting each level is a single spiral staircase that carves a coil through the centre of the tower.

Seven floors for seven devils.

Seven floors for seven angels. And one ground level for Ora City, the gateway to everywhere else.

"Bloody goyles thinking they own the place," Thalia grumbles as she leads me into the largest of the lecture theatres on the ground floor.

We make our way through the foyer, our feet dancing over the chequered tiles. The building hums, thick and sticky with magic. Candles flicker in sconces, dim streaks of light paint the floor. Every wall is covered in shelves and books, jars, specimens and scrolls. The sweet musty smell of decaying paper fills the air. I inhale, wishing I could breathe in new magic, maybe a clause that would supersede my father's contract. I've tried; gods, have I tried. I've spent months searching the demonic library for my contract, to no avail. I must have glimpsed every other agreement we have stored but mine. Years I've spent studying and hunting for anything I can find about underage contracts. Contracts that save lives.

The air ruffles, and I glance over my shoulder but no one's there.

Thalia tugs at me, urging me towards the theatre. "You know it's not really haunted."

I squint into the gloom, but we're definitely alone. "So they say."

"Oh, come on, you're really superstitious?"

I give her a stern glance. "Is it really so hard to imagine the tower is haunted? It's literally our job to work with the dead."

She nods. "Then if it were haunted, don't you think a campus full of professors who all work with the dead would have heard about it?"

Once again, she has a point. Though it doesn't stop my skin from itching like the bite of nettles on flesh.

Thalia opens the lecture hall door, and we take seats near the front. I spot Father lurking in the stage alcoves. He nods at me, his face severe.

"Do you know what's going on?" I whisper to Thalia as she waves and greets various faculty members.

"No. But were you here last week when we had that tremor?" she whispers out the side of her mouth.

I shake my head.

"It was awful."

"I think—" she starts, but Chancellor Lucan Arcadius strides on stage, my father, the dean and second-in-command, two steps behind.

He'll hate that. Arcadius has an ego the size of the underworld. I mean, why wouldn't you as the archdevil. He is the highest ranking of all devils and has been around for longer than anyone can remember. He's completely unbeatable. Which is exactly why my father hates him. He'd cut off a limb if it meant he could rule the underworld, or be Chancellor, for that matter.

Thalia licks her lips as Lucan strides up to the lectern. I cock my head at her.

"What? A girl can appreciate a strapping man."

Strapping is right, his thigh muscles bulge through his trousers.

"I thought your ex was a woman," I say.

She shrugs. "I like who I like."

I glance back at Arcadius. His shoulders are as wide as a carriage. Two silvery-white horns slice through his hair, curving in a sinister twist above his head. Not all demons are horned, but some, especially the most powerful, tend to be. My father isn't, and he takes this as some emasculation of his demonhood.

Arcadius's eyes harbour the same swirls of black as Father's, with one difference. Where Father's hold darkness, Lucan's hold a cold kind of cruelty that screams sadistic bastard. Not in the spank-me-harder-daddy kind of sadism, either. His teeth are sharp, his nose patrician and regal and his dark brown skin curves and bulges with ounces and ounces of muscle.

He taps the mic on the lectern. "Finis Academy."

There's a rumbling in the audience as the professors who are less inclined to perform the arbitrary student response of *Good morning, Professor Arcadius* mumble responses.

"Those of you who have been here for more than the last academic year will have experienced the infrequent tremors and quakes that have been happening for the last couple of decades. However..."

Arcadius glances at my father, who produces a thin sheet of parchment and hands it over.

Arcadius reads it, nods and addresses the audience. "For those of you that stayed on campus last week, you'll be aware of the major tremor we experienced. Significant damage was done. Several cracks in Finis Tower have since been repaired. However..." He pauses, takes a deep breath and glances at the parchment again. When he looks back at us, his jaw ticks. "What you may not be aware of are the consequences of those tremors. Security forces had to dispatch more than two dozen wraiths, ashspawn and a handful of shades."

I join in the ripple of gasps erupting in the auditorium. Thalia raises her eyebrows and glances at me. "Did Ignatius not tell you?"

I shake my head. He said it was bad, but I didn't realise how bad.

Arcadius roars for silence. "All of the wraiths and ashspawn were dealt with quickly and effectively. I appreciate the concern, these are dangerous underworld creatures. But—"

"What about the Veil?" a male professor shouts. I crane my head to locate them in the room but there's too many people for me to trace their voice.

Arcadius's face turns incandescent, darkening at the interruption. "As I was saying. The Veil was stitched and repaired on both sides. A great debt of gratitude is owed to Professor Alistair Ironheart for walking the Veil and ensuring it was sealed on their side too."

The hall erupts into applause, whooping and hollering so much we sound like the students we teach. Alistair stands up in the middle of the lecture seating and flicks a dreadlock off his shoulder. His stark yellow demon eyes beam at the audience as he waves dramatically, fending off the praise. The way he grins tells me he loves it. A bubble of warmth fills me; I'm pleased for him. I'm sure this will be points towards another academic tenure or promotion. He deserves it.

When he sits, Arcadius continues.

"The Veil has been sealed. However, it does not take a genius to recognise that these tremors are occurring at a more frequent rate. It is the senior faculty's feeling that we are going to experience a complete rupture."

This time, instead of the explosion of gasps and chattering, a silence descends on the faculty.

It is so acute that Arcadius glances at Father, his shoulders visibly tensing.

"This will be shocking to many of you who have found Finis to be a sanctuary and place of safety. However, we have been monitoring these tremors and after significant analysis, it is our belief that we will experience a major rupture at some point this academic year."

"FUCK THE SOCIETAS," a female voice screams from the back of the tiered seating.

Chaos erupts. Bellows and shouts and disagreements are thrown across the room like warfare.

This is not good. We're supposed to be a professional faculty of staff that can debate these things. If you can't in an academy setting, where can you? And while the general consensus on campus is that Architecti should not be resurrected, given she wanted to merge celestial and demonic kind, there are professors who are on her side. Be it academically, theoretically or philosophically. Especially the Footnote professors—they love a good theoretical studies debate. Those against her seem to forget these professors are just debating, they're not actually trying to resurrect her.

The Societas, though, is an organisation hellbent on resurrecting her, and often the source of protests, riots and sacrificial slaughterings in the city.

Finis seems to have forgotten that we're allowed to disagree with each other and stay civil. The room erupts with voices, the atmosphere sharpening like a blade. I glance at Thalia, both of our hands are on our seat arms, ready to fight.

This is going to get nasty unless Arcadius gets control.

He slams his hand down on the lectern so hard it splinters down the centre and shatters into pieces. The mic drops to the stage floor. The thuds echo as they roll around the stage, each one like a gun shot.

That shuts everyone up.

"Thank you," Arcadius growls. "Now, we do not have concrete evidence that the Societas Mortis Architecti are behind these tremors, but early investigations indicate that it is likely. It seems they believe the source for resurrecting Architecti is on campus. Therefore, we need to assume that the campus will be under increasing fire.

Security will be increased. It also means a change for students."

The room chills, the collective drawing and exhaling of breath like a sluggish heartbeat. Thalia's rigid where she grips her seat. I slide my hand over hers. "It's going to be okay," I say.

"It won't be if the Veil rips and the underworld spills into Ora City." Funny how one sentence can age a person. Something passes across her expression that I can't place. I pull her hand off the arm rest and pop it in my lap.

"Arcadius won't let that happen."

He clears his throat. "I am going to need you as a faculty to push the students harder and faster than ever this year. We need them to be prepared for what will happen if the Veil does tear. You'll have files delivered to your quarters with my teaching expectations. This year will be gruelling. For us and the students alike."

That hovers in the air, every professor in here bearing a grim expression.

"However, we have two new professors here from Sangui City, both of whom have extensive experience in war strategy. Professor St Clair and Professor Randall."

Two women walk on stage, hand in hand, and wave at the audience. A couple then. They beam at each other, the softest gaze hanging between them as though they've been together millennia already, when I imagine they can't be much older than me.

Arcadius continues. "They will be teaching every student defensive strategies along with Professor Malrec, who will teach the necromancy elements of defence. Welcome, and thank you both."

They smile and make their way off the other side.

"That's it for this afternoon. I'll need you all to report any tears or cracks in the Veil. And of course, be on your highest guard. Dismissed."

This year has already not started well.

I just hope it isn't an omen.

II

MIDNIGHT

Morning light dribbles through the curtains as I stare at the dark paper in my hands. Thick ink is scrawled across the page in whorls of red—red that I am convinced is my own blood.

I don't understand it and I can't explain it, but I know it to be true. The little sleep I managed, the invitation crept into my dreams and gnawed at me as if it were alive. Sloping and crawling through my nightmares.

Taunting me.

Threatening me.

Whispers of hope. Of possible futures. New beginnings.

The promise of a chance to save myself.

I flip the card over, but it's blank save for the cracked red wax bearing Finis Academy's crest. I run my finger over the crumbling seal, the tower of twisted magic that rises as high in the sky as it sinks beneath the earth. So many secrets, so much magic.

My eyes skim the words again, scarcely believing they're real:

Mercedes Midnight,

You are cordially invited to attend the Sever-ance Rite. Should you successfully complete the entrance trial, you will be given a place at Finis Academy.

Please make your way to the entrance gates at 8 a.m. sharp tomorrow.

The last words are so faint against the dark paper. It looks like whoever sent it attempted to sign their name but the ink—my blood—ran out.

I take a deep breath. Finally.

Nine years. Nine attempts. Nine failures.

This morning everything changes.

I spent half the night packing and repacking. Pulling clothes and books out and putting them back in. Nothing seemed right. Nothing felt like enough.

At 7a.m. I'm pacing and unable to sit still. Nine years I've waited for a chance to win the coveted Demonic Favour. A chance to shove Ignatius's deal back in his smarmy face.

I arrive at the long drive of Finis Academy campus by 7:30. It's too early, and yet the driveway is crammed with carriages and people carrying bags and trunks.

But it's also swarming with people holding placards, and a perilous number of balled fists.

Jeers litter the air like the cries of newborn kittens.

Screams preach of new worlds, and baritones promise of darkness and unification.

The city's politics weren't always so turgid. I remember my parents: my mother was pro resurrection, my father anti. They seemed to live together in peace just fine. Good-natured debates filled the house, and I'd sit on the floor between them smiling and chattering a concoction of big words like I knew what they meant.

This Ora City is not the same.

Something changed during the years of open opinions, almost as if they seeped into the waterways and infected our bellies. Jagged lines now carve faces, making angry eyes and angrier fists.

It's hard work, but I slalom my way through the carriages and pedestrians, weaving along the endless drive-way. I didn't realise there would be so many of us with invi-tations. Though I suppose half of these are the potential students, and the other half are excited family members wishing their young ones luck.

It must be two miles before I find myself braking and pulling to a stop before the same wrought iron gates where I left Lucy last night.

In the morning light, they seem less imposing and more sinister. Long iron poles stretch up into the low-hanging mist cloaking the Academy. Ivy chokes the sandstone brick. And while the trees outside the campus have shed their leaves for autumn, the evergreen vines inside are bushy and plump, as though the ivy fed on the carcasses.

I take my helmet off. The crowd's screams are shrill, their leers more vicious still. I wince against the roar as pressure builds in my ears. My arms prickle from the rest-less energy.

"Get the fuck off me," a girl bellows.

There's a scuffle, a swarm of bodies pressing in towards the carriages.

"Fucking ashkisser," someone screams.

"It's a university, for demon's sake," the same girl bellows. "Get off me."

I find her voice. She's been grabbed by several protesters. I flick my bike's kickstand down and dive in, barking at the nearest security guard, who leaps into action after me. A man and a woman hold her as she struggles.

I ram my elbow into the man's gut and stomp on his foot. He shrieks, and the woman lets go, flapping her arms at what I assume is her husband.

The girl gains her feet and aims a kick right into his crotch, hard enough even I wince. He drops to the floor.

"Ashkissers," his wife spits at our feet.

"Go fuck yourself," I say and tug the girl away to head towards the gates.

"Hi," she says. She's a Black girl with a set of turquoise braids.

"Midnight." I hold out my hand, and she shakes it. She's shorter than me and wears such an array of styles and brightly coloured clothes that I'm pretty sure she's covered the entire rainbow.

"Lex," she says. "Well, that's not my real name of course, but the kids in my school used to call me Lexicon because I've always been obsessed with language, and the name just stuck."

She's sweet. I like her.

"Pleasure to meet you, Lex. With a name like that, I'm assuming you're here to study Eytomancy?"

She nods, the beads on the ends of her braids jangling

like birdsong. "Absolutely. I'm determined to be fluent in every necromantic language."

"Fluent... is there someone you want to speak to?"

She shucks her rucksack into place, ignoring my question. "So why are you here?"

"To win the favour," I say. The fact Lex changed the subject isn't lost on me.

She cocks an eyebrow at me. "Nothing else? You don't want to be a Doorstop or Detour? Maybe an Echo or Loose End?"

I frown at her. "A what, what and a what now?"

She hustles me towards the gate, so I grab my bike and trot after her while she babbles away.

"You know, you really need to get with the lingo if you want to be the top student."

"Apparently so!"

"I'll help. So, the Echoes are the students who study the memories of the dead. The Doorstops are the Fabric Weavers working with the integrity of the Veil. The Loose Ends deal with the dead who have unfinished business, helping the shades to move on etcetera, etcetera. And then there's the Subtexts, that's me. Though I'll be minoring in Footnotes—also known as Theoretical Death studies."

Gods, my head is already swimming. A wave of warmth rushes up my neck, the confidence I came with draining out of me the more she talks.

We approach the gates. Unlike last night, they willingly open for me. The goyle narrows his grey gaze at me, making me shift position. I hold my bike with one hand and let my fingers skim the cool metal with the other.

There is no hum or vibration this morning. No bite, no blood. Was it all just a dream? A hallucination?

"You okay?" Lex says, staring at my knuckles where I grip the bar tight enough to turn them white.

I didn't even realise she'd stopped to wait for me.

"I... umm, yeah. Let's go."

We're almost through the gates when I hear my name. It lurks in the wind, all whisper and scream.

I try to locate the source. But it's nowhere. And everywhere. It crawls along my skin, slithers in my ears, coats my flesh in echoes.

I scan the long line of carriages behind me, all their windows and doors fastened shut. There's a sea of protesters pressed back by stern security. But no one holds my gaze or waves, no one calls to me.

I glance at the wound on my hand. It's sealed over, but I rub and knead at the itching scab as if it might scratch away the coiling in my gut.

It must have been the crowd.

We break through into campus and a shroud of heavy fog swallows us whole. It sends tingles stretching from my belly to my toes.

Then the mist clears completely.

I falter, spin around only to be greeted by the towering wall of white.

"What the hell?" I whisper.

"So cool," Lex says, bouncing on the balls of her platform trainers.

"There are many *cool* things about the Academy," a tall lady says. She wears narrow glasses, her hair grey, but she bears the yellowest eyes I've ever seen.

"You're a demon," I say, stating the obvious and instantly regretting it. Obviously, she knows she's a demon. But they don't exactly dance in the streets of Ora City. They come to the city to make deals and then return to the underworld or campus or wherever they subsist. Save the few who find they have a taste for our realm.

Lex's mouth twitches like she's trying not to laugh at me.

She sighs. "How astute of you. Park your bike over there and make your way to the cloisters. You'll be greeted and placed into a testing group. I assume you both have your invitations?"

Lex whips hers out, the stark white card sharp against the red whorls and dark parchment of mine.

They both falter at the sight of my letter. It makes my insides shift and plummet. Am I mistaken? Did I not get in? Is this all a desperate delusion I created?

I am a confident woman. But this professor is terrifying. She carries a severity reserved for librarians and mothers of teenagers who *fuuuucked* up. She makes me feel like a child, and I shrink away.

"How odd. It seems like a valid invite, though. Welcome to Finis Academy. I'm Professor Evadne Verrill. Omnia mors aequat."

"Death renders all equal," I breathe, and she nods approvingly.

"I take care of the library."

Of course she does. I daren't interrupt her to say that, though. Lex visibly brightens at the news. Verrill narrows her eyes through her narrower glasses.

"You'll find yourself in my area often, if you know what's good for you."

I'm about to thank her when she steps in front of us, arm out, blocking our view.

She spits out a caustic sentence. All hard edges, clicks and guttural noises.

Lex grabs my hand and squeezes; this must be a necromantic language she's so desperate to learn.

A silvery-white flash erupts from the building behind us. It twists and coils and threads through the air until it loops around Verrill's arms. Screeching ricochets off the building and rends the atmosphere, and I clap my hands to my ears. A charred limb flops onto the cobbles in front of us.

Silence.

Lex is still bouncing on her toes, like this is exciting and not bonkers. Verrill turns to us, flustered, her severe demeanour bent and misshapen. We peer around her stiff form. Hanging at head height is the silvery thread that peeled off the building behind her. Only now it's stitched like a dress hem. As we stare, the thread fades and the strips of air either side undulate like a pregnant belly.

"Wh... What is that...?" Lex asks.

Verrill bristles and kicks the desiccating limb behind her into a bush.

"Off you go," she says, making it clear it wasn't a request. I swallow hard and drag Lex away, though her gaze never leaves the bush.

"I think it was a wraith, or maybe ashspawn," Lex says.

"I thought those things were tucked safely inside the Veil," I say as I park my bike in a bay, lift the keys and hoist my bag onto my shoulder.

"So did I," Lex mutters. "But I guess this is the gateway between realms for a reason."

"Mercedes Midnight," an all too familiar voice says. His caramel-coal tone slices through what was turning out to be a good day.

"Ignatius..." I say.

Lex hovers, reluctant to leave.

"It's okay, I'll catch you up," I say.

She hovers a moment longer and then heads for the cloisters, though she checks over her shoulder twice before disappearing.

"I think it's time we had a talk, don't you?" Ignatius says.

12
MIDNIGHT

Ignatius pulls me aside. "You can't attend the Academy."

I snort at him. "My invitation says otherwise."

His expression darkens; a simmering violence oscillates beneath the surface of his jaw.

"It was you, wasn't it? All nine times?"

His nose flares.

"You bastard."

His hand jumps to my throat. But I have spent too long with this motherfucker not to anticipate his moves. My scythe is buried an inch deep in his side.

"Try it," I choke out against his grip.

He breathes heavy and footsteps rap against the cobbles behind us. He releases me and brushes down my jacket.

"The answer is no."

I smile, a brief twitch of a thing. "I figured you might say that, but once upon a time, you bent the rules of our deal and forced me to become a reaper."

He wavers, realisation washing through his features. Fuck, it's delicious beating a demon.

"Your IOU?" he growls.

I nod. "You gave me an IOU in exchange for being your reaper. I'm calling it in."

I wink at him.

There's a beat of realisation, for both of us. Him realising he just lost, and me recognising that I must be completely unhinged because honestly, the wink is way more than a step over the line.

But not one fuck will be given. I practically skip to the cloisters.

By the time I slide between their slender sandstone pillars, reality has hit, and my stomach is churning. Whether it's anxiety or excitement, I'm not really sure. Probably a little of both if I'm honest with myself.

My fingers caress the weather-worn columns as I wonder how many centuries of knowledge they cradle.

The columns form an arched corridor around the perimeter of the cloisters. In the middle are several ponds housing plump black and silver koi—none of the white, oranges and reds you'd usually see. One lurches left and shoots away, and I realise why it's drained of colour.

"What the fuck?"

"Dead," Lex answers, appearing at my side. "Well, reanimated, so half dead? Hey, is everything okay?"

"Oh, yeah, fine. Don't worry about Ignatius."

"The dean, you mean?"

Right. To Lex he must be an important part of the Academy. To me, he's the cunt that is going to steal my soul.

"I'll explain later," I say and stare at the dead little fish, swimming as if the sun beams and they've not a care in the world.

Reanimated fish, whispers the wind, and I have to

wonder whether the rumours about this place being haunted are true.

The scent of morning rain, petrichor, and decaying parchment drift through the cloisters on the cool morning breeze. It's a light, watery, off scent.

My spine tickles, as though I'm being watched. I scan the cloisters, but see nothing other than students, and gargoyles hanging off doors and stone pillars.

"You need to chill, it's going to be fine," Lex says and pulls my arm over hers.

The further we progress through the cloisters, the more students join us, each one wearing the same unsettled expression.

A sensation wraps around my insides, coiling like snakes. I keep checking my feet, as if I'm one step from something taking my ankles out. Lex is right, I can't spend the next year on edge.

I glance back at the fish. "Bizarre that they're dead and yet moving."

Lex nods. "They're reanimated by the Restarts. It's part of their first term assessments. They have to reanimate small creatures. It's easier to learn with smaller living things before they try human reanimation. Disastrous otherwise. Can you imagine?"

"What's a Restart again?"

She sighs. "Resurrection students. Try and keep up. You'll have to study extra time just to get the base knowledge. Most students come having learned the basics."

"Most students get their invitations earlier than last night."

She frowns. "Yeah, that is odd."

After the first eight rejections, I didn't think it would

happen, so what was the point in studying? I swear I had that ninth rejection, though the invitation it morphed into sits in my back pocket.

A cold prickle nestles between my ribs. Everyone else has probably studied for years and so will be leagues ahead of me.

I'm not giving up. I haven't come this far just to pussy out because I'm not starting term as the top student. I'll do whatever it takes for that Demonic Favour. It's the last resort, the one way I can break my contract and save my soul.

Lex looks me up and down, and hums. "Something tells me you're going to fall in love with being a Detour."

I stare at her blankly.

She sighs again, in a super dramatic way, and I fall totally in friend-love with her.

"Detours are Veilwalkers. Only like the most coveted study programme here. Not everyone gets on, and they're kind of considered the elite. You strike me as one of those lucky kids who will take to it like a reanimated fish in water." She smiles and jerks her head at the pond.

"Kids? I'm probably going to be one of the oldest here. I'm twenty-nine..."

She huffs at me. "Please. You're not the only one who struggled to get in. This was my seventh application. I'm twenty-eight."

A current student in Finis uniform interrupts to hand us maps and papers and then saunters off to hand them to the other shuffling clusters of initiates.

I hold my hand out to Lex. "In that case, I'm formally adopting you as campus tour guide, seeing as you know way more than me, and I am alarmingly clueless."

"Deal." She shakes it.

I yank my hand out of her grip. "Easy there, soldier. Let's not make any of those. I learned that lesson the hard way." I flip my wrist over, showing her my brand.

"Oh, gosh. I'm so sorry,"

I figure if I'm adopting Lex as friend, then I should be upfront about who I am, *what* I am. If she found out later and got all judgemental about it, I'd be gutted.

But before I can explain, a bell chimes out.

Its ding wraps around the cloisters. It buzzes in my bones, clatters my chest.

Rings again.

Again.

A ceaseless beat that grows harder and louder the longer it sings.

Ding.

Ding.

Ding.

Ding.

"Seven rings for seven devils," Lex says.

"And what about the angels?" I whisper.

"There are no angels here," a male voice says. "They abandoned us when Architecti was killed. That's why half the city wants her back."

I knew that, at least. It was the crux of my parents' debates. The benefits and advantages of a city connected to the celestial realm. The balance it brought to magic, versus the law of demonic chaos and the creativity it produces. And then of course, they would meander off into whether or not chaotic magic could be controlled, and if it couldn't, then what? And that was without the debate about what we do now we've lost access to the celestial realm and the political, societal and magical ramifications. There isn't a soul in the city without an opinion on Architecti.

"Can I help you?" Lex interrupts my thoughts.

She's just shirty enough to let this guy know we're a twosome and no one else is welcome, without being overtly rude.

If I didn't love her before, I definitely do now.

"Bastien Malcor," he says and holds out his hand.

Lex merely looks at it like it's an old festering sock. I have to bite the inside of my lip.

He's blond and has the kind of refined white-boy bone structure only a model or jock could pull off. He's handsome, a little effeminate, or maybe just comfortable in his skin. He wears tapered trousers, brogues and a blazer that looks like it should fit right in here, only no markings announce that it's Finis Academy attire.

"Midnight. Nice to meet you, Bastien," I say.

Lex pouts but decides to offer her hand. "Lex."

"As in—" he starts.

"Yes, as in lexicon." She's short with him, but softening.

"So, we have a Subtext student, and let me guess..." He scans up and down my body. "Has to be a Detour."

Gods dammit, I make a commitment to go to the library tonight when everyone is asleep and make a start on catching up.

I'm not letting him think he's got the upper hand though, so I shrug. "What is with everyone assuming I'm here to walk the Veil."

Lex makes an indignant snorting sound. "Oh, please. Detours are all about the vibes. And you, girl, are *all* vibes."

I glare at her, disliking that she's read all of this within about three minutes of meeting me.

"Which makes you..." Lex stares at Bastien, squinting and scanning him the same way he did me. "Hmm, scarred hands, and despite your exterior beauty, you hold grief in your eyes. I'm putting my money on a Restart."

I follow her assessment. The grief lingering in his eyes is stark. Despite the fact he holds himself upright, it's a cold posture masquerading as a barrier. Gods, Lex is good. Her read is exceptional.

Bastien purses his lips and shimmies his shoulders as if shucking off her judgement.

"Bravo," he says, though he looks more put out than impressed.

I laugh. "Not so nice having the tables turned on you, is it?"

He ignores my quip and points at the clusters of students. "I'm assuming you two don't know anyone joining this year, either? There seems to be cohorts of people that have joined together, given the groups walking into the Hall of Unfinished Business."

I shake my head. "Just me."

"Me too," Lex says.

"Then, umm." His eyes drop to the ground, and I realise he doesn't want to be alone. My whole body reacts, a visceral impulse to clutch him tearing through me. I want to know what shape his grief takes and why a scar runs down from his eyelid to his cheek bone. One of his eyes is damaged, his pupil permanently blown and a little murky.

I want to pry the story from him, just as much as I want to learn the truth behind why Lex wants to speak to the dead. A trio, all holding secrets and stories and the burning need to secure entrance to Finis.

"Come on, you can join us, can't he, Lex?"

Lex drags her eyes to mine, a distinct shade of unim-pressed drifting through her gaze, but she sags. She recog-nises the fact he's part of us now whether she likes it or not.

"Yeah, okay. This year is going to be tough, no one should be on their own. Come on."

And together, the three of us walk into the Hall of Unfinished Business. And all I can think is that this is some kind of fucked-up irony, because this is where I intend to finish *all* of my business.

13

MIDNIGHT

The hall is the kind of cavernous reserved for childhood horrors. The same archways that lined the cloister corridors stretch from either side of the room. I crane my head up. The ceiling has a spine-like structure that reaches from one end of the room to the other. Spearing off the sides are support beams that look too much like a ribcage.

"Is that..." I whisper.

"Supposedly," Bastien says.

Lex points at what would be the head end of the spine. "Rumour says it's some giant dead demon. But there's a lot of myth and rumour in this place. No one knows what's real and what's fiction. I think they do it to scare the first-years."

"How about you don't tell me all the horror stories, and I won't have nightmares tonight," Bastien whines.

"Don't be such a pussy," I nudge him, grinning.

At the end of the room, a stage is set above row after row of seating. There's a lectern and stood to the side of it is Ignatius fucking Corvine.

Mother fucker.

"Wow, did he kill your puppy?" Bastien says, looking me up and down.

I tear my gaze away. "No, but..." I pull my sleeve up, showing him the brand.

"Ah," he says.

"Yeah." I yank my sleeve down.

"So that's why you're here? Trying to find a way to break your contract?" he asks.

"Bingo."

Lex touches my arm. "How long do you have?"

Bastien leads us to a row of empty seats.

"A year, just under."

"Shit," Bastien says.

"Yeah, and given I am clearly behind on the basics, I'll be spending my days vag-deep in study."

Bastien and Lex share a glance as they sit.

Lex takes my arm and shoves my sleeve up examining Ignatius's brand. "We could help, you know. Do you have a copy of your contract? I'll bet I can find a loophole. And hey, if Bastien manages to get through this ceremony, maybe he can bring you back after... if... well, you know what I mean."

"If?" Bastien snaps.

"What? I heard some people don't make it." Lex shrugs.

"Encouraging. Real encouraging, both of you," I slouch in my seat.

Lex pouts at me, her expression drooping. She's so forlorn I shove a fake smile on because I can't bear the sight of her looking like that. "I'd love your help. Both of you, if you're sure."

"CANDIDATES OF FINIS ACADEMY," Ignatius booms, cutting our conversation off.

I didn't notice how quickly the room had filled.

"Welcome and congratulations on receiving your invitation to take the Severance Rite. Taking the rite does not guarantee you entry into the campus to study. In order to do that you must complete our sacred ritual. And only the strongest participants complete the rite."

"What happens if we don't succeed?" a voice shouts from near the front.

Ignatius looks less than impressed at the interruption. He scans the audience until he finds the culprit.

His lip curls into a vicious little snarl, one I recognise far too well. It makes the hairs on the back of my neck rise.

"If you're unsuccessful, you don't get in, *candidate...*"

"Yeah, but I heard some students die trying to complete the rite," the young voice shouts again.

Ignatius's expression turns feral. Very little knowledge makes its way out of Finis Academy—it's a vault. And that's what makes gaining entry so sought after. Unless you have family who have studied here and can pass down details, you're on your own. The Academy and its graduates protect the city, and the rest of the mortals go about their business mostly ignorant.

I'm assuming someone in Lex's family studied here for her to be so knowledgeable. The only other way you find anything out is if you're in close proximity to the demons— like being a reaper.

Though this job is not worth the additional knowledge. The only other useful tidbit I've picked up from Ignatius is that a demon's heart crystallises with each contract they create. The more contracts they create, the more possible futures they eliminate for us mortals, and the more magic they harness. Given how dark Ignatius's eyes are, I'd imagine his heart is good and solid about now.

He rounds on the student, even though he's still on

stage, and his looming presence makes the entire front row shrink back in their seats.

He practically growls his response. "Then don't fail."

A mumbling breaks out across the crowd. He didn't deny there was a risk of death.

The mood shifts, every candidate sits taller, more alert. A slow coil of dread settles over the room. Thick and choking. Unwanted awareness of danger settles in the blink of lids and parted lips. Everyone recognises that someone won't walk out of here, but no one is ready to accept it could be them.

"Is it true?" Bastien mutters.

"Yeah. My sister came here about ten years ago. Seven candidates failed to make it through and that was a good year," Lex says.

"Fuck." A pool of cold settles in my fingers and toes. I came here to save my soul. Not end it early. I glance back to check the doors—they're already locked.

Wait. I frown at Lex. "You knew, and you volunteered to go through the rite anyway?"

She sags against her seat, sighing. "Is there anything better than power?"

Both Bastien and I turn to Lex, surprise written across both our expressions.

"That's some dark villain shit for someone wearing such colourful clothes," Bastien says.

"We all want power, Bastien. Even you. It's the reasons why we want it that matter."

"And yours are...?" he asks.

She tuts at him. "I might not be a reaper with a soul to save, but I do have unfinished business. And I can't complete it powerless."

I wonder how many more of us have come to Finis

carrying the same burdens. A strange thing to be bonded by, but the fact we are provides comfort against the churning swirl of my gut.

"Let's make a pact. If we make it through this ceremony, I want the truth. The real reasons you're here," I say.

"If it includes cake and beer, I'm in," Lex says.

Bastien nods in agreement.

Every candidate in here wears tension like soldiers on a battlefield awaiting commands. Necks, backs and shoulders are rigid in seats. Lungs full of a collective breath sticky and coagulated with fear. Fists are clenched, knuckles are white, every brow furrowed in concentration.

Every candidate in here looks like they're going to war.

Bastien leans forward, his voice low under his breath. "I guess you don't come here without a past and a future that you want to rewrite. It's just the nature of death."

He couldn't be more right. In all twenty-nine years of life, I've never wanted anything more than a chance to win the Demonic Favour. It's a need that burns in my bones.

Ignatius claps, demanding attention. "This is an ancient ritual. The severing of a piece of your soul. In the same way that the seven devils and seven angels made the underworld and celestial realms. This tower was built on the bones of our gods. Their magic is stitched into the walls. And it is that same rite you must complete today, if you are to wield that power."

I shift in my seat. I've severed hundreds, maybe thousands of souls. Which means I'm way too aware of how painful this is going to be. And of how dangerous it is to play with soul material.

Ignatius scans the room, and I swear his gaze lands on me. "The stone remembers what the soul forgets. To survive here, part of you must be given freely. Like your future, like your pasts. All possibilities stem from this moment. Most of you will not leave here whole. Many of you will not leave here at all. Omnia mors aequat." A new professor joins him on the stage. "Professor Malifax, let us begin."

14

MIDNIGHT

C andidates are called.

One after another they leave their seats to walk down the main aisle and vanish through a door at the back of the stage. None of them return.

Lex, Bastien and I are fine until the first scream tears through the hall. It's loud and all-encompassing, like the tower sucked the sound into the walls and spat it out again. All three of us hold our ears and lean against each other until it fades. All three of us paler than before.

The longer we wait, the more my gut hardens and my nails cut moons into my palms. I hunger for this challenge and waiting is an exquisite form of torture.

Three hours in, the first candidate dies. We know because the hall blooms in a swarm of entropy moths. The howling screech that rips through the hall wounds something inside me. Was that their last breath for a grieving friend? Lex and Bastien both grab my hands, as if clinging to each other can save the candidate, or maybe it's the vain hope it will save us.

It does neither.

Another hour goes by, and two more candidates die. Each time, their shriek buries itself in my mind. This is so much worse than reaping a soul. Vacant looks and fear I can cope with. But these howls are pure loss. Grief. Anguish and pain as all their possible futures vanish.

With each death comes another swarm of entropy moths. Their fluttering wings growing until the hum is a hiss and rumble that makes the hall vibrate.

This is what I hate the most. I've never liked the moths. Harbingers of souls that need reaping, for me anyway. The more they flutter and fill the hall, the more I fidget, unease coiling like worms inside me.

After the fourth candidate dies, the swarm is so big that the Severance Rite has to pause to clean out the little dust-fuckers.

When they reset, Lex is called.

I squeeze her hand. Bastien stands and hugs her. The way we all cling to each other, you'd think we'd known each other our whole lives. But there's something galvanising about this room and this ritual.

Witnessing death after death.

Soul after soul.

Scream after scream.

This is the kind of nightmare that buries itself deep. It has claws and teeth and the kind of sentience that never dies.

We share matching scars in our hearts now, the kind that no one else understands.

"I don't want to let you go," I whisper to Lex.

She's short, so her hug squeezes my waist. "I'm going to see you both on the other side, aren't I?" she whispers. But none of us know the answer to that, and after what we've witnessed, none of us can lie either. We squeeze her again instead and watch as she makes her way onto the stage and through the door.

Her Severance Rite is short; the next name called much faster than the rest have been. I pray it means she survived and not the alternative.

Half an hour later, Bastien is called.

"If I don't make—"

I shove my hand over his mouth. "You will. You have to."

We hold each other's gaze. One last beat of before held in a single breath, melded with the hope that we get an after. He nods and then he's striding towards the stairs to the stage.

His rite takes longer than Lex's.

Three more candidates pass through the rite, then one dies. Another makes it through their rite only to collapse dead after—so the whispers that follow her limp body in the arms of three professors say.

Professor Malifax clears his throat and straightens his shirt, and I just *know*. I feel it in my bones as if the tower itself is whispering *you're next*.

There's something odd about Malifax. Cold and unfeeling. I shove it away, the excitement and anxiety of today being too much to handle as it is.

I close my eyes, waiting, waiting, waiting.

Nine years I've yearned for this moment. Prayed to the angels that left us, begged the gods who smite us. Pleaded with my parents on the other side to give me this chance.

And now, finally, here it is...

"Mercedes Midnight," he calls.

I stand, acutely aware that there's no one left to hug me. No one to wish me luck or tell me it's going to be okay.

But it will be.

Because I have a score to settle, and a soul to steal back.

The central aisle has to be the longest walkway in history. Every eye left in the room follows me as I make my way towards the stage.

There are whispers. Slurs. "Reaper." "Gravetether." "Ashkisser."

I absorb it all. They think it weakens me, that they can rid the world of another reaper.

But their hate only strengthens me. Makes me burn hotter, fuels the pools of fury that simmer in my gut.

I *will* complete this rite for no other reason than to spite them. Philosophers say spite is a negative, that we should use positivity to motivate us. Well, fuck that. I've never seen a more motivated being than a woman scorned and filled with spite.

I climb the steps, not to my death, but to my future.

Professor Malifax leads me through the door into a dark room with bare walls save for the splats of blood and what looks like chunks of vomit.

The room stinks of charred leather, stale sweat and ammonia that clings thick to the air. The upside is the vomit is covered. The downside is that the stench rubs in my nose like a cold sore.

Professor Malifax passes me a scythe. "This scythe is imbued with Finis Tower's magic. You are to cut through your sternum to the heart of your soul and slice off a sliver."

Cut a piece of my soul? No wonder students didn't make it out. The blade is heavier than mine. Though I can't work out if it's the obsidian stone or the metaphysical weight it bears having killed so many candidates and bled so many souls. It's warm to the touch; I thought it would be cool.

Malifax continues. "Should you complete this success-fully, the blade will transform into a needle and Finis Tower will open for you, bearing its heart so that you can, in turn, stitch your soul with its."

This sounds... *difficult*. I swallow the lump forming in my throat.

"Should you complete the stitching, there is one trial left. You must share a truth with the Tower. Think wisely because the Tower must accept your truth for you to gain entry into Finis."

Malifax closes his hands and lowers his head, mumbling words that sound like nonsense but I'm certain would have Lex squealing with delight.

I sling the blade in my pocket for the stitching and pull out my own. Fuck using a blade every other candidate has.

The ground rumbles, peels of dark ribbons split from the wall. Long, necrotic fingers made of the shadows of gods tiptoe towards me. They undulate in rhythmic patterns, the ribbon-arms must stretch twenty feet from the wall. I want to touch them, bend them around my hands and wield them.

I see the allure now. The awe and wonder that Lex cradled in her gaze.

I close my eyes, bringing my scythe to my sternum. I have torn so many souls from their owners that this should be second nature.

But it's different when it's your own. I guess that's why murder is so much easier than suicide.

Survival instinct wails deep inside me. A protective reflex, making my limbs heavy and my muscles twitch.

I bring the point to my skin. So many times I've done this to others and never felt the sharp sting myself. A light press and the blade slides into my chest.

Hot lacerations surge through me. My veins bulge and pop as my consciousness tries to resist.

The agony is like nothing I've ever experienced. Every nerve sets itself on fire. Heat blisters its way through my chest and buries itself in my limbs, my bones, my veins. It eats its way through every fleshy fibre.

There's a disembodied scream. It's hollow, piercing, shattering. It rattles in my skull, my teeth chattering against the pressure.

It's me. I'm howling so loud I swear the cells in my throat split and tear and leak blood into my gut.

As I slice through my soul, every memory, every moment I've lived surges through me, a tidal wave of visions.

I buckle under the weight of choices.

Of possibilities.

All of them swirling and dancing before me.

I can't do it.

My muscles seize.

My vision spots.

I lean forward and hurl. Blood splatters the floor, making the same pattern so many before me have.

My nose ruptures, hot liquid rushing down and spilling onto my chin.

Ignatius flutters into my mind.

Then Aurelia.

Hatred, thick and oozing, seeps into my mind. It's the fuel I need. Most people are driven by joy and positivity.

Fuck that.

Rage.

Hate.

Obsession.

I will break my contract, no matter what it takes. I grit

my teeth and push up off my knees until I'm standing. I will face my judgement on my feet.

I grab hold of the blade buried in my chest and despite the searing pain, despite my jaw clenching so hard I crack a molar, I tear it from my chest.

A dark smile curls the corner of my mouth as I stare upon the thing Ignatius wants to take from me.

"You can't have this piece, motherfucker," I whisper.

It's a beautiful thin strip. Both regal and divine, it shimmers and floats in the air.

Deep inside me, I am bleeding in a place where I cannot reach. I cannot stem the blood loss, and I cannot heal what I have harvested.

This must be what they meant when they said we wouldn't leave here whole. Such a thin sliver for how gargantuan the chasm is inside me. It gapes like an angry, endless maw I'll never be able to fill.

I'm about to slide my scythe back in my pocket when it shivers in my hand. It trembles harder, quicker, the hilt cracks and the blade extends until it's no longer a scythe but a needle.

Whoa.

I thread my soul through the eye of the needle. It's texture is soft, silken and delicate like a petal. The shadowy arms lunge for me. I grab them and stitch my soul inside the foundations of Finis. This is easier than the tearing. It hurts but it doesn't hurt more than the raging heat in my gut or the aching emptiness that I can't seem to catch hold of. The silvery shimmering thread nestles against the darkness of Finis like a star buried in the night sky.

None of it matters because I will do whatever it takes to win back my soul.

When I'm done, the ribbons of magic coalesce and form a sooty replica of the tower the academy is named after.

"You bleed like you're already dead. I remember you," it says.

The words aren't uttered out loud, but not exactly in my mind either. It's as though I think them, as though they are stitched inside me.

No.

It's not inside me, I'm inside it—inside the campus itself. It's alive? Sentient, I think.

"I'm not dying until I'm good and ready," I say.

"Tell me your truth."

I've thought about this all day. Nothing felt right. I could confess my mistakes, that I'm fallible and fucked up. That the only person I loved threw me away. That my family died for nothing. A stupid debate that resolved nothing and still rages in the city.

The only thing that feels true is what led me here.

I stare deep into the undulating shadow-tower. "Love ruins us all," I say.

I swear it smiles, a feeling that smothers every millimetre of my skin. Seeps into every pore, gelatinous and thick. I shiver; it's not a nice smile. It's dark and viscous like poison.

"That is not true. But it is true, for you, it seems. I'll allow it..."

Relief washes through me until it says, *"If..."*

I replay its words. It will allow it if...

"If, what?"

"If you're willing to take a deal..."

A... what?

Surely this is against protocol? Were the other candidates offered deals? I locate Professor Malifax, but it's as though he's frozen. The only movement comes from the occasional dust mote drifting in the muted beams of stained light.

If this is the only way into Finis, then I'll bite.

"What sort of deal?" I ask, balling my fist.

"Your real truth is that you are here to save your soul... aren't you?"

"I've not hidden that, I assumed you wanted something more meaningful."

"I want the truth. And I want... other things, Mercedes."

That voice. The way it whispers and screams. So familiar, so alien.

"What things do you want?"

"I will save your soul, and in exchange you will reap a single soul for me..."

I laugh. I can't help it, it bubbles up nervous and jittery.

"You're kidding? One soul?"

Is this a joke? I can reap souls all day. Why the hell is it offering me this?

I'm not sure how I can tell, but it shakes its head, a bristly feeling that rushes around me.

"A soul for a soul. Simple."

"Nothing is ever simple. What's the caveat? The clause? The trickery?"

"No clauses, no trickery, no caveats. One soul for yours."

I hear the words, and yet it sounds too good to be true. It almost always is with demons. I swore I'd never make another deal.

But this... This is what I came here for.

Can it really be this simple?

This easy?

Do I get to come out of Finis with my soul and newfound powers? Have the angels finally smiled on me?

I inhale slow and steady, trying to run the possibilities. The problems. But my mind is thick and heady with weariness from the soul severing.

"*Tick tock, Mercedes.*"

I push my brain, plead with it to work. Think of something, anything to reassure me this isn't a giant clusterfuck.

"*I need a decision.*"

My eyes narrow. "Whose soul is it?" There are very few people left that I give a shit about, but I should probably know this at least. I doubt it will change my answer.

It smiles, a feral thing, all teeth and windows and endless gaping holes. I shudder and look away.

"*Ignatius's daughter.*"

My eyes widen. "Ignatius has a daughter?"

"*He does.*"

Oh, my gods, Ignatius has a daughter. And that's who I have to reap to free my soul? The angels really have smiled down on me. This will be the easiest reaping I've ever done. I don't even have to think about the answer. Not only will I free myself, I'll get to witness Ignatius's pain at the loss of his daughter.

"Deal," I say. One brief moment of panic follows when I wonder if his daughter is still just a child. But what problem could Finis have with a child? She could be an ancient woman. I don't even know how old Ignatius is.

A surge of the most intense electric power courses through my body. A pounding headache blooms between my ears. I glance at my fingers, swearing static pops and cracks between my knuckles. A constant flowing pulse pours into me, filling my body from the toes up. The gaping void in my soul replenishes, only for it to drain like a sieve, leaving me both overflowing with power and utterly empty.

Moths materialise.

Faster. Faster.

The room fills with the low hum of thousands of fluttering wings. My heart clenches, that simmering panic of whenever the moths are near. But I chose these moths. I closed off future possibilities by choice. I want this.

Breathe in. Breathe out. I force myself to slow down. Let their velvet wings caress my arms, my cheeks, my neck as they twirl through the air.

When my heart rate slows, I let myself move, staggering right into Professor Malifax. I bend forward and cling to my knees.

"Congratulations, Finis accepted you," he says and helps me stumble towards the door. He frowns at the swarm of unexpected moths but decides not to ask. I guess strange things happen here too often to worry about them.

"Use its power wisely," he says and tugs my top open. His eyes scan my sternum. I want to pull his fingers off. I feel exposed.

His lips curl. "We haven't had many of these today. Congratulations, House Inferos."

I yank my shredded shirt back and slip into the gloom. I can feel the weight of my scythe knocking against my hip—somehow back at my side again.

Despite the darkness, I find my way through a door and out into Finis Academy's campus.

Finally.

Now the real game begins. I spot Lex and Bastien and head over to them when a sickly sweet voice chimes through my focus.

"Midnight?"

My heart nearly rips out of my chest in one giant thud.

My fingers curl at my sides. Those half-moon divots cutting deeper into my palms.

A livid fury boils in my body. I had no idea she was here. The bitch doesn't deserve to be. If screwing my life over wasn't good enough, she had to take my dream too?

"Congratulations," she says as I turn to face my ex.

"Aurelia."

15

LUCY

I spot Midnight the minute she walks through the doors of the Hall of Unfinished Business.

She made it.

Thank the seven devils. Though I think it would be easier for me if she hadn't. But my stomach tightens at the thought. My father might not want me to go near her, but a woman can window-shop from afar.

I lean against the wall, taking the pressure off my knee. I'm fairly certain the bone has healed now, but there's an ache living its best life in my joints.

Midnight's wearing black leathers because she rode here, I assume. They're snug around her ass, her muscular thighs press against the fabric. Her hair is shaved close to her scalp and longer on top. It flops as she pulls her hand through it.

Her shirt, like all the successful candidates is ripped.

I hate that my body reacts to her presence. Perhaps dabbling is worth the risk. Father's only concerned about my magic, and the only way I lose that is if I fall in love, and there's no chance of that. I'm far too busy.

Thalia appears by my side; she nods at Midnight. "I thought you said you didn't have a nice young woman keeping you entertained."

I tut at her. "I don't. She's just a new student."

"Mmmhmm, and one you seem to be admiring."

"Thalia," I scold. "Can you imagine? I'm not risking my tenure for a student. No matter how attractive they may be. What was that professor's name?"

"Jorsin." She nods knowingly.

"That was it."

"Banished to the underworld on top of losing his magic to the mortal. And then she broke it, too. Didn't have control when she used his power, and it shattered his crystalline heart. Just awful."

I kick off the wall, instantly regretting it as my knee buckles and Thalia catches me. Her eyes meet mine, she doesn't say anything. She doesn't have to. She knows what my father is like.

"It's fine," I mumble.

"Is it?" She growls under her breath. "I could rip open the Veil, shove him through. Get Alistair to stitch it up tight enough he can't get back through."

I stifle a laugh. "You're terrible. He's not that bad."

"Lucy..." she says and lets me go once I'm stable. Thalia has always found my father to be difficult. She sees through the charm and allure unlike most female professors.

I clasp her hand. "I did this to myself. The contract..."

She waves me off. "You can't move against him. Blah blah blah. The point is you shouldn't have to. You shouldn't be put in a position where you need to defend yourself and certainly not significantly enough you end up injured."

I cup her cheek. "I appreciate you."

She huffs but leaves me be. In my periphery, I catch

sight of Midnight and my stomach drops. Another student with curly ginger hair and pale, freckled skin gesticulates at her. Midnight's eyes seethe with a coldness that could kill.

Who is she? And why does she make Midnight react that way?

My stomach turns.

It has no right to. Midnight is nothing to me. And even less now I know she's Father's reaper *and* a student. I stand a little taller. I'm about to encourage the professors to sort the students when Midnight notices me.

"Fuck you, Aurelia. Bastien, Lex, excuse me a moment, I'll be back."

She strides over to me, thank the gods, because it's definitely easier resting against the wall. I hobble back but tuck myself under the shade of an archway where we can't be seen by the growing cluster of students.

She raises her finger and points it at me. "Oh," she starts. "You're injured."

"I am." I offer no further information, so she continues.

Her gaze rolls over my body. It falls to my knee, up to my swollen nose, then to my left eye shot through with bloody threads. I take her hand and pull her further into the shadows. I can't have a student ogling me like she wants to devour me in public.

"Stop looking at me like that," I say.

"What happened to you?"

I can't answer that, not to her. Not yet, not now, maybe not ever. "You'll want to get ahead of the class quickly. Study nightly if you can. I'm assuming you're going to study contracts, which means some of your classes will be with me. I'll be sure to treat you like I treat everyone else. There are several texts in the library that will be useful.

Given you're a reaper, you'll be at a disadvantage because no one will want you to succeed."

She steps back. "How did you know...?"

"That you're a reaper?" I sigh. It's probably for the best she doesn't know who my father is.

"You wore a scythe on your hip last night, and I'm a professor of contracts. It doesn't take a genius..."

Her eyes narrow, they scan my body again, lingering on my knee. If I keep blabbering, maybe she'll ignore my injuries, and we can move on.

"Who was that girl you were talking to?" I say, the words slipping out. I bite the inside of my lip, furious that the words snuck out without permission.

She cocks her head up, a slow smirk surfacing. "Sounds like someone's jealous."

She says it so confidently, her ego oozing out of her pores. I am not jealous.

"One orgasm doesn't mean anything."

That makes her raise an eyebrow. But I need to cut it off at the neck. I can't afford this to become anything. I squeeze every ounce of emotion out of my features until my expression is stoic. "I was asking because you seemed angry with her."

She shakes her head as if trying to work out which thing to focus on first. "She's my ex..."

"Oh," I say, not sure what happened or if it's my place to ask. But she offers another nugget.

"She's the reason I'm a reaper."

"I see. So you're not together anymore?"

She snorts. "I'd rather reap my own soul than touch that traitorous cunt." Her expression is like stone and fire. An ancient feminine rage pooling deep in her eyes and simmering in her fists. Whatever that girl did, there's no coming back from it. The knot in my stomach loosens and I try not to think about what that means.

Midnight sighs as she scans my face. "It was your eyes that first attracted me last night. They're beautiful," she says and brings her hand up to push my hair behind my ear. I recoil, too paranoid anyone could be watching.

"You can't do that here, it's not allowed."

"It wasn't until I got here and saw the other demons that I realised they're so beautiful because they're not human."

I can't bring myself to look at her. "No. They're not."

"You're a professor."

I nod.

She huffs out an indignant laugh. "Who'd have thought, the demon professor and the reaper."

I smile softly. "There is no demon professor and reaper. It was one night. A night that can't be repeated."

"Because you're a professor?"

"That, and the fact you're a reaper, and you're mortal and I'm not. The fact you're so young."

She scoffs. "I'm nearly thirty."

I roll my eyes. "And I'm forty."

"That didn't seem to bother you last night..."

My cheeks flame crimson. It makes the corner of her mouth twitch.

She stands straighter, her expression turning serious. "If you think avoiding telling me what happened to you means I'll drop it, you're sorely mistaken. You avoiding the question means it wasn't an accident."

She moves so close to me I have to take a step back. I hit the wall.

"Midnight," I hiss.

"We're both consenting adults, *Lucy*." She exaggerates

my name all sultry and alluring as if that means I can do anything about it.

"It doesn't matter. Not here. I wasn't joking when I said student-professor relations aren't allowed. I'd get the sack. I'd lose my tenure."

"You're prevaricating. Tell me who hurt you…"

She pulls me by the chin to face her, then leans down as if she's going to brush her lips over mine. I place my hands on her chest and push.

Professor Alistair Ironheart steps into view. His eyes slide down to where my hands are outstretched. His laser focus is so acute it makes me flinch.

He swings his gaze between us. "Everything okay, Professor C—?"

"Yes, thank you, Alistair. I know Midnight, outside of the Academy," I say, making sure I accentuate his name. He might think he's being polite, but I don't need anyone sticking their nose into my business.

Besides, as Head of House Inferos, I technically outrank him, and he needs to remember that.

"I see. Well, mind you keep it professional." He gives me a curt nod and disappears.

"I have to go," I say and hobble my way out from under the arch, leaving Midnight in my wake.

Professors congregate around the outside of the Hall of Unfinished Business. It looks like nearly sixty students made it through the Severance Rite. Though that's less than half our cohort of ten years ago.

"Students, if you please, reveal your scars," I say, clapping to signal for silence. I receive a few tentative looks, and then they all brandish the scars over their sternums.

Alistair jostles the students into lines. He wears the Finis Academy uniform like me. It's pressed into sharp lines and against his black skin forms a stark darkness behind his yellow demonic eyes. Long dreadlocks cling to his back. The only part of him that's out of place are a few loose coils that curl around his scalp, needing to be retwisted.

"Why do you need to see the scars?" a male student asks.

"To place you in your Houses," I answer. "Now, come on."

Alistair examines the man's scar and places him to the left. "House Vitalis."

So ensues a rapid sorting and calling out of: Vitalis, Mortis, Inferos.

"What's Vitalis?" the man says.

"House of Life. Your likely area of focused study will be either Theoretical Death studies, Business Dealing, or Memory Magic," Alistair says, tugging at a woman to stand behind him.

Several students are pulled into the House Mortis line. That's for the Eytomancers, Fabric Weavers and Resurrectionists. Contracts is an odd topic because it doesn't fit squarely into any of the seven main magic disciplines. Mostly because it skims across them all. It's the everything and nothing subject.

It takes a while for an Inferos to be called. It's reserved for two types of students: primarily the Veilwalkers, but also those who have the most natural magic potential. The elites. Those most likely to win the coveted demon favour.

Every time Inferos is called, I spend a little longer staring at the initiates. They're my charges now, thanks to Father.

The woman talking to Midnight is pulled into the House Inferos line and a heavy bubble sinks into my gut.

Midnight follows, along with the tall blond guy and short girl with turquoise braids.

Shit.

It would have been more convenient if both Midnight and the woman she's talking to were in another house. That means we'll all be living within the same damn walls.

When the sorting is finished, Alistair takes the House Mortis students, and Professor Helena Stroud takes the House Vitalis cohort. She's our resident head of Theoretical Death Studies. A short, white woman with a scowl for days, I'm convinced her heart is made of steel, and she has a list of strict expectations for her students as high as the Celestial Library.

Which leaves me and the smallest group.

"I guess that means you're the lucky group. Keep up," I say.

"Wait, what about our bags?" The girl with turquoise hair says. She's wearing yellow shorts with brightly coloured flowers, platform trainers and a boyfriend-fit, tie-dye jumper. The combination makes my eyes hurt but my heart warm. I eye her, indicating I want her name.

"Oh, erm, Lex. Nice to meet you." She holds out her hand. I shake it.

"Your bags will be taken to House Inferos. Let's go."

I manage one step before the earth rumbles.

One of the students with Professor Stroud shrieks. It's like gunshot. One student screaming after another.

The ground tremors harder. Several tiles slip and fall from the roof of the Hall of Unfinished Business. I grab Midnight and the two students standing beside her and pull them into the heart of the courtyard as far away from buildings as possible. I glance up at Finis Tower in the heart of the campus. Its soaring peak is visible far above the rest of the buildings. Slate tiles clatter from the roof.

The air fills with sandstone dust as the integrity of the buildings around us fails.

Stroud catches my attention, her eyes flick over my shoulder. I turn and peer in that direction, my eyes widening as I back our huddled group up, fast.

"WHAT THE FUCK IS THAT?" a girl shouts, pointing behind me.

Midnight cranes her head around and stiffens in my grip. The Veil has torn, *again*. A rip at least six feet high in the middle of the courtyard.

This is not good.

The ephemeral fabric flaps in the wind. It resembles shimmering air to the eye, but something is off. Usually, the edges are torn and frayed, flapping like loose curtains. But these are sliced, cut neat and tidy like cake; a detail I file away for later.

Behind the fabric lies the underworld.

Dark, mountainous, barren.

Acrid heat billows from the tear. It's dry, choking and stinks. Fungus fields stretch as far as I can see. And lurking between the slimy black stems are the dark forms of wraiths and ashspawn.

"Shit," Midnight breathes beside me.

It snaps me back to attention.

"Stroud, get the students out of the courtyard," I bark. She nods, flying into action.

"Alistair," I yell, waving him over. He pushes his huddle of students towards Stroud and races across the square towards me.

"Go," I bark at Midnight and her two friends as the air

fills with a pungent scent: sour milk, cigarette breath and fetid meat.

Wraiths.

"Lex," Midnight cries out, pulling her friend out of the way.

But Lex releases a strangled cry, "Bastien!"

The blond man next to her crashes to the ground. His eyes flit from Midnight's to Lex's to mine, and then he's yanked and sliding along the cobbles. Dragged by his ankle towards the Veil. A wraith clings to his leg, but it's weak, necrotic.

Its leathery body is curled, skeletal and wrinkled like dried fruit. Flakes of skin shred with every laboured step it takes. Bastien kicks and lashes out. But even weak wraiths are stronger than mortals. And this one has sunk its claws into his calf.

"Alistair," I shriek.

My heart pounds in my chest. I am not trained in necromantic defence. But my body moves anyway. My hands furl and twist, making shapes I didn't even realise I knew. Dark shadows materialise, peeling off the courtyard buildings. They lurch and jerk through the air as I try to control them. But my practical magic is so much more juvenile and unpractised than my contracts work.

I whisper words of the dead, but my pronunciation is off. The caustic tone needed to coax and control the campus's magic efficiently is missing.

I dig deep, throw my hands towards Bastien and finally, the magic responds. It wraps around his leg, holding him in the mortal realm as Alistair leaps in front to seal the rip. His hands work fast. But my strength wanes faster.

My knee buckles, my nose bursts, blood leaking in

rivers to the ground. The wraith screeches at the smell of it. But it doesn't want to let its prize—Bastien—go.

"Alistair, hurry," I plead.

His hands move faster, the tear resealing inch by inch.

I'm on my knees, sweat pouring down my back.

Midnight pulls a scythe out and lunges towards Bastien.

"No," I cry out, knowing damn well the wraith could attack her. But I'm too weak to do anything other than hold on to the shadows gripping Bastien. The wraith screeches again and drags Bastien closer to the Veil. His foot crosses the threshold.

Midnight hurls herself forward and whips her scythe right across the wraith's neck.

A shrill keening rents the air. A sound that rattles my teeth and makes the hairs on my arms rise.

On the far side of the courtyard, the new students drop to the floor. Bastien lashes out with a vicious kick of his free leg and hits the wraith, booting it clean into the Veil as Alistair flicks his wrists one final time, stitching the Veil shut.

Finally, I release the campus's magic and sag all the way to the ground.

Midnight kneels beside me, her hands ready to pick me up, but Alistair sprints over, his face lined with concern. "Professor Corvine?" he says.

Midnight blinks, once, twice. Her face tightening with realisation.

Static pebbles my vision as Midnight frowns at me.

"Wait. What? Corvine? As in...You're... You're Ignatius Corvine's daughter?"

"Yeah," I say and promptly black out.

16

ARCHITECTI

As dark as the underworld is, the celestial realm is light. Listen, I understand it's a cliché, but I'm not a god. I didn't design our realm, I just live in it.

I was four the first time I realised there was something different about my twin.

Fresh blades of luscious grass tickle the base of my feet as I sit in the middle of the glade. Watery morning light showers my cheeks in warmth, the scent of daisies, spring blooms and dandelion fur fill me with delight as I play.

Other children run and dance and fly through the glade, sing-song laughter drifting on the breeze.

My wing feathers graze the grass, soaking up the warmth as I build a play castle.

I pull beams of light, bending and twirling and shoving them into place, my tongue poking out in concentration. I suck dew from the air into the walls, making the light glisten, and rainbows paint the grass. Taller and taller I build, stitching stardust and debris into the crenellations and windows until a masterpiece stands before me.

I stare at it, my hands on my hips. Something is missing.

"Interitus, come see," I call to my sister.

I pluck another beam of light from the air and squish it up, forcing it to shine like the moon, and place it above the tallest turret.

A little darkness for my sister.

There. Done.

Interitus emerges from the shadows of a silvery tree. Her wings drag behind her, they look sad. The darkened wingtips leave a trail of angel dust as they carve through the grass.

She traipses over slowly. Every step an agony as I bounce on my tippy toes, desperate for her to see. Her eyes never leave my creation.

"It's for us," I say. "To play with." I clap my hands in delight.

Interitus tilts her head to examine the castle but stays silent, so I add, "I thought we could play imagination and make up stories about the people living inside. Look, I added a weapons room and a moon for you. And a painting room for me, and that's a—"

"Prison," Interitus interrupts me.

I blink at her.

Once.

Twice.

A frown forms between my brows. "No. That room is the Great Library."

She shakes her head at me, indignant. "Then it's a prison of words."

She circles the castle, her finger poking at the walls and punching in and out of the crenellations.

It makes me feel funny; I want to tell her to be careful.

She knocks some of the turrets out of line, and I scurry after her, repositioning them.

"Don't you like it?" I ask. My stomach rolls like the dandelion fluff on the wind.

She glowers at the castle.

It's rubbish.

I'm stupid.

I wish I hadn't made it.

It was a silly idea.

Interitus stops suddenly. "I want to see what it sounds like when it breaks."

My eyes widen. It took me four hours to build, I don't want to break it.

I raise my hand to stop her, my wings following. But Interitus is already kicking out, her foot spearing right through the centre of the castle.

The structure implodes. Light sprays my body, glistening particles and rainbow strands clatter to the grass and wink out. The funny thing is, the sound it makes is beautiful.

A tinkling like classic pianos and springtime birdsong. The tinny patter of autumn rain and the crackle of winter fires.

It's a beautiful sound, and yet I feel horrible. Like a piece of me shattered when the castle broke.

It's gone.

Not a single brick or beam is left. I stand there for a long moment, my bottom lip trembling, my toes digging into the grass as I try to understand my sister.

Finally, I turn to her. "Why did you do that?"

Interitus is calm, her eyes and body still compared to the upset vibrating through me.

"I told you. I wanted to know what it sounded like when it broke."

"But..." I whimper.

"Don't you feel it?" she asks.

"Feel?"

She nods enthusiastically. "The *after*. The completeness?"

"It was complete before."

"No," she says. "I *finished* it."

I remain there for a while after she leaves, trying to understand what she meant. Finished, as in ended the castle's life? Finished, as in the castle wasn't complete until it was back in the original forms of its parts?

No matter which way I try and piece her words together, it doesn't make sense. I watch her walking away. Her wing tips no longer drag on the ground, and she stands a little straighter. She doesn't return to the shadows.

Mummy said I was born for creation, and Interitus was born for destruction.

I just didn't think she'd destroy something I made for her.

17

MIDNIGHT

It's late by the time Lex, Bastien and I approach House Inferos. Bastien's leg was dealt with by the medical staff before they'd let us come to our new digs. They bandaged him and gave him some anti-necrotic salve, which seemed to do the trick. He'll be sore for a couple of weeks, but the puncture wounds will heal.

Images of Lucy's unconscious body in Professor Ironheart's arms roll through my mind. Even when I try and focus on the campus buildings and the map, I can't seem to scrub the visions from my mind. I'm not sure if it was the way her head hung limp in the crook of his elbow, or the revelation that she's Ignatius's daughter that's thrown me.

As we traipse towards House Inferos, it's all I can think about: Lucy is the soul I'm meant to reap. This deal with the campus was meant to be the easy way out, the soul I reap without breaking a sweat.

But now I feel...

I don't know, something?

What's worse is that I feel *something* about the fact I feel something.

And honestly, I can't cope with any of that.

The three of us draw to a stop as we gain our first view of House Inferos. It stands, regal and Gothic, all black and stone and glass. Our home for as long as we survive.

Perhaps my last home—another thing I'll try not to think too deeply about.

The main façade is narrow but juts high into the sky with spires piercing the clouds. The mansion extends out on either side and then cuts towards us, making a horse-shoe-shaped building. The outer wings are for the students, no doubt.

Long, pupil-like windows stare down at us—a constant reminder that the campus is always watching. The same campus I made a deal with, and the itch along my spine tells me it's not going to forget.

My parent's images flash in the window. One minute smiling, the next, pale, gaunt and dead. I slam my hand over my face, trying to wipe the image away. When I glance back it's gone. Nothing but glass and the reflection of the ground. Did I imagine it?

Yeah. It's not going to forget.

The mansion is beautiful, though. Autumnal ivy clings to the exterior and crimson and copper leaves bleed down the stone walls. The door stands in a lavish archway with a gargoyle nestled against it, sleeping.

Wind hums and throbs around us, sounding eerily like the campus has a heartbeat.

Midnight, Midnight, Midnight.

That voice.

A whisper.

A scream.

I scan the area, searching for the source. But my name is nothing but a thread on the breeze, like I'm sewn into the fabric of the campus itself. I suppose, we all are after the Severance ceremony.

The sensation of being watched crawls under my skin and settles against my bones. It's no longer just Ignatius I owe something to. It's Finis too.

Lex and Bastien share a look.

"Everything okay?" Lex asks.

I nod, because I can't seem to get a lie out of my mouth, and I'm not sure confessing I made a deal three minutes into being here is the smartest overshare.

She narrows her gaze at me. "If the answer is no, that's okay, too. You don't have to pretend with us."

Her words make my teeth ache, guilt furring my tongue until the words skitter out. "I... No, not really."

Bastien offers me his arm. "Come on, let's get inside and find our rooms. Today was a lot, and I don't know about you, but I'm exhausted."

I slide my hand over his arm, and while his gesture is a comfort, with his limp, I end up supporting him more than he does me.

It reminds me of their offer to support me to break my contract. I've never had help. I've always been on my own. After Aurelia... It's not like I have any family left.

Their offer is lovely, but is it a distraction? People generally are. How much time can I afford to invest in developing friendships when I have to stay focused on winning the Demonic Favour?

I need to study as hard as I can and not get sidetracked by anything else. Not when I'm seemingly starting a mile behind every other student.

"Are you going to tell us what's up?" Lex asks, stepping up to the porch.

"Umm. Yeah," I say, brushing her off.

"She's lying," a weed-like voice says.

The gargoyle is awake and scowling at me. I notice a plaque beneath his feet; it's worn and crumbling but I think it says Vetch.

"Hello to you, too. I'm Midnight."

I tickle under his right ear. It's rounded and plump, a stony earring hanging from it. He has stubby feet and clawed toes nestled under his chin. He purrs like a cat, only grittier. The more I tickle, the more his toes kick against the door like a kangaroo. It's adorable.

"Gerr off," he grumbles.

"Was it that girl outside the severance? The one that got into our House, what was her name?" Bastien says.

Lex smiles the way only an honours student can. "Aurelia."

"She has nothing to do with this," I say, too sharp, too quick for it to be true.

"Liar," Vetch smirks.

I fire a vicious glare at him.

Bastien tugs on his ear. "Quite the character we have as our door goyle."

Vetch narrows his stony eyes to slits. "Vetch will guess your secrets too, boy. Vetch is good at secrets."

"Oh, do go on, this should be fun," Bastien says, leaning against the porch pillar.

Vetch sticks his tongue out, slobbering over his lips, dusty stone drool floating to the ground.

"Boy is gay," Vetch says.

Bastien snorts. "Bisexual, actually. So, no points for you."

Vetch huffs, and both Lex and I glance at him.

"What?" He sticks a hip out in the most camp display

I've ever seen. "Because I look like a jock, I can't find men attractive? Shame on you pair of judgy bitches."

That makes all three of us laugh.

Vetch grinds on his teeth. "Well, boy is holding a secret. Vetch can smell it."

Bastien's throat bobs. "Maybe that secret isn't for you."

He boinks him on the nose and shoves open the door, promptly shutting the goyle up, and together the three of us enter House Inferos.

The warmth of open fires and winter blankets and hot chocolate envelops us as we step through the doorway.

But that fucking voice ceaselessly calls my name.

Midnight. Midnight. Midnight.

I freeze. I swear the letters of my name skitter across the walls, but when I blink, it's gone.

Will it plague me until I reap Lucy? Will I get no respite?

"You okay?" Lex says, touching my arm and making me jump.

"Umm, yeah." I pull a hand through my hair and wipe my palm over my face.

"Convincing," she says.

They stride further into the house, and I rest my fingers against the wall. Maybe I'm losing it, but I don't know any other way to communicate with the campus.

I lower my voice to a whisper. "We made our deal. I told you I'll reap Ignatius's daughter. You don't need to remind me. I'm not even in my room yet, for demon's sake. It's not like I've forgotten."

The wall pulses under my touch. Or maybe it was the vibration from Bastien closing the door.

I need to get a grip. I'm imagining the fucking campus talking to me? I've been here a day, I can't lose it yet.

Our foyer walls are a deep red, the colour of aged blood.

A silvery filigree pattern of lace and spears and abstract moths adorn both the fabricked walls and the tasselled black velvet curtains framing tall windows.

Large lanterns perch in sconces, their flames flickering and sending ember glows and that homely winter warmth around the foyer. A grand staircase sits at the heart of the space, split to allow passage to those dormitory wings.

"Close your eyes," Bastien says. "Can you feel that?"

My eyelids fall shut and I breathe slow and steady, letting my senses stretch and sing. There's a heartbeat here, a thick drumbeat that reverberates around me, inside me. It sounds like sugar and waterfalls. It smells like bonfires and coffee, and it tingles over my skin like a femme's freshly manicured nails.

Fuck. It's addictive. It's power. And now it's home.

"That's our magic," Lex says, then abruptly jumps into a stride across the foyer. "Our rooms."

"How do you know where to go?" I ask.

"I don't know, I just do. Don't you feel it?"

"Actually, yeah," Bastien answers and strides after her. Then I feel the tugging too. I follow after them up onto the first floor and down the corridor to an apartment door.

I'm the last one in. Lex and Bastien have halted in the hallway.

It's not until I shove my way past that my blood runs cold.

"No. Absolutely not," I say.

"I didn't ask for this. I didn't even know you were applying to the Academy," Aurelia answers.

"I don't give a fuck. TAKE A DIFFERENT FLOOR," I shout and shove forward.

Bastien's enormous arms are around me, yanking me back away from her.

"Get off me, Bastien. She's not staying on the same floor as us."

Aurelia rolls her eyes at me, as if I'm the dramatic one.

"I didn't choose this, Midnight. Do you really think I'd have asked to be on your floor? Or even in the same House? I am here to study."

"I don't give a fuck what you're here for. As long as you're doing it as far the fuck away from me as possible."

She shakes her head. "You're not the only one with dreams, you know."

I guffaw. "You gave up your dreams, don't fucking forget that. The only reason you have a dream now is because I sold my soul for you."

Bastien's arms go slack. "What?" he says, releasing me.

"Yeah. She's the fucking reason I'm here."

That hangs in the air, pungent and acrid like the festering rot of a decomposing carcass.

Bastien steps in front of me and points to the floor below. "Go speak to security, Aurelia."

Her shoulders slump but thankfully, she disappears downstairs leaving Bastien, Lex and I alone.

The pair of them stand there, expectant.

"You don't get to make a statement like that without telling us what happened," Lex says.

She opens one of the room doors and pulls Bastien and I inside. Her suitcase is already in there. I'm not sure I'm even surprised. The magic seems to run thick through the walls and halls of the campus.

Lex pushes me onto her bed and nudges Bastien into an armchair, and then she potters out into the communal kitchen, banging cupboards and doors and flicking the kettle on.

She returns with some fruit bowls and three cups of

deep red tea that looks a little too much like blood for my comfort.

"Drink it, it will make you feel better," she says as she hands it to me and I'm unable to hide my grimace.

Bastien behaves like a teenage boy and happily scoffs his fruit and guzzles the tea.

"So?" Lex says.

I sigh and lean back on her bed. "It's a long story. But we were together for a couple of years. Went through a lot of shit together. She was there when my parents died. Anyway. She got sick, and she was the only family I had left. So I sold my soul to heal her."

Bastien leans back in the armchair. "That sounds very benign for how pissed you were."

"Yeah, well, after she was healed, I walked in on... She cheated on me."

Lex winces.

Bastien's forehead creases. "I'm sorry."

I shrug. "It was a long time ago. So long that my time is running out. Finis really is my last chance."

Lex pulls some journals out of her suitcase. "These are my sister's study notes from when she was here. They're ours now. This is going to be a tough year and I don't want to do it alone."

"That's very generous," I say, and she beams at me. "What's your story? I said in the Hall of Unfinished Business if we made it through, I wanted to know what your stories were. What better time than now?"

She sighs.

"Is it to do with your sister?" Bastien asks.

Lex flinches and slumps against the wall. "I made a mistake."

"We've all made mistakes."

"Not like this." Her braids fall in front of her face as she rests her head in her hands.

"I fucked up, made a deal with a lesser demon. My sister was the pride of our family. She'd made it through Finis."

She stalls out, sits up and stares out the window. Bastien and I share a look, but he shakes his head no, so we leave the silence, and wait for her to be ready to tell us.

A moth flutters against the window, trying to reach the light in here.

"The night I was due to have my soul reaped, my sister was with me. She'd come back from some job she was on. I confessed what I'd done, and she was understandably furious."

She turns to us, two streaks glisten down her cheeks.

Bastien gets up, moves to the bed and slides his arm around her, and then uses his other one to tug me in. He squeezes until we're all laughing and collapse on her bed.

My head rests on Lex's stomach. Hers on Bastien's chest.

"When the demon arrived to take me, my sister intervened. The demon took her soul instead of mine. I still don't know why. I don't understand what happened that night."

"And that's why you want to learn the necromantic languages?" I ask.

She nods, her braids rustling against her duvet. "I have to know why. She had such a bright future. And the demon took her so fast, I didn't get a chance to speak to her... to tell her to stop..."

We're silent for a while. Lex's truth lingering cold and palpable in the room.

"My story isn't much better," Bastien finally says,

sitting up. The three of us reposition ourselves and get comfortable.

This time Bastien goes out to make tea. When he returns, it's Lex who pushes him to talk.

"What happened to you?" she says, as he hands her a cuppa and three biscuits.

Bastien sits back in his armchair and picks at his leg bandage. "Anyone know the first rule of resurrection?"

Lex shrugs, unbothered. "Not a class I'll be taking."

"Don't resurrect your family," I say, something I've heard from some reapers who ended up dispatched to deal with wayward family pissed at the loss of their loved one.

"I had an older sister, too. She was a fair bit older than me. She, umm... she died."

Lex's face falls.

"It was natural. She had a dicky heart, she was never going to live a long life, but she was talented too, success-ful. Anyway, it broke my parents when she died. They disengaged. Became depressed."

His words make my ribs ache, filled with longing and regret, and the kind of yearning for something more, some-thing unobtainable you only find buried in the coils of grief.

"I was young and stupid."

"Weren't we all? That might be the one thing we all share," I say.

Lex nods, and Bastien gives us a weak smile.

"I thought magic would be easy to control. Ora City is the gateway, right? How hard can it be?"

"Oh gods, what did you do?" Lex winces.

"Stole a resurrection text and figured I'd give it a go. If I could bring her back, even temporarily for my parents, I reasoned that they'd see she was okay and in a better place."

Lex's mouth hangs open. "You resurrected her?"

Bastien's jaw hardened. "I resurrected her badly. I didn't contain her, and I had no idea you weren't supposed to resurrect your own family. I didn't have a clue what I was doing. She killed our parents. I lost part of my sight." He points to the scar running from above his brow, through his eye and down his cheek.

"So you're here to learn how to resurrect properly," I ask.

He nods, though he can't quite bring himself to look at us. "I never want to make the same mistake again."

Three different pasts. Three mistakes. All of them bringing us to Finis.

I wonder how many students are here because of their past mistakes. Does the campus collect them?

"We're going to rectify them all," Lex says.

And for the first time since being here, I think I believe it. Until I remember what I promised...

What I have to do tonight.

"I'm going to head out for a walk, guys," I say and get up, my scythe pressing against my hip and the whisper of my name in the wind.

18

LUCY

I come to with a coarse and oddly moist scouring pad being dragged under my nose.

"What the fuck?" I groan, swatting it away.

A loud engine hums in my ear and then something fluffy aggressively nudges my head and begins licking my nose again.

I peel open my eyes to find the vibrant orange of feline irises staring down at me. Though, I can also see through them.

"Demon's sake. Get off me," I swat at the cat. It must be one of our campus shade animals. Like the mortals, they couldn't quite let go of their past lives, so they became shades. Most of the time, the Loose End first-years manage to dispatch them on. But a handful of the most stubborn animals gets stuck on campus and end up adopting a student each year.

"My name is Mortem," he meows.

"As in Mortimer?" I say.

He licks his paw, a distinct look of disdain twitching his whiskers.

"As in post-mortem."

I blink at him.

He blinks back.

"Post—" I start.

"Yes," he hisses and swipes his tongue under my nose, licking up the last of my drying blood.

"Get off," I whine and sit up so he falls off my chest. He flops to the bed and begins cleaning his face.

"Delicious," he purrs before curling up and falling asleep.

My nose wrinkles. Gross. I shoo him. But he stares blankly at me.

"Where did the students go?" I ask Alistair, who is sat in a chair beside my bed.

I glance around. I'm in the medical wing.

"Seven bells rang, they were sent to bed."

"I see."

"Are you okay?" he says. "You've only been out about an hour or so."

"I think so," I answer, moving my limbs this way and that. "Magic surge?"

"Yeah, docs think you tapped too much, and it blew your circuits." He taps his scalp.

"Figures." I lie back against the pillow. "Can I leave?"

Alistair nods. "They're not worried, I just thought I'd stay until you woke. Thalia popped in too but was summoned by Arcadius."

"That was nice of her. Honestly, there's nothing I want more than a bath and a glass of wine."

He smiles and gets out of his chair. "I'll see you in the morning for first classes." He rubs my shoulder before leaving.

I get out of bed and make my way to medical reception. The nurse hands me a bottle of painkillers, which I gratefully take, and I leave.

Which is when I remember I'm not going home to my wonderful, quiet bath. I have a new apartment in House Inferos that will no doubt be covered in boxes.

One small silver lining about living in the penthouse of House Inferos is that the view will be fantastic on the days when the mists actually abate.

I head to the staff faculty block and track down the maintenance team to collect my keys and then schlep my weary arse all the way across campus to House Inferos.

Once inside, I trudge up to the penthouse, slide the key into the door, open the apartment and scream.

Familiar orange eyes blink back at me.

"Helloooow," Mortem meows.

"Oh no. Oh, hell no. Come on, shoo. Out."

He sits down.

Fuck my life.

"Out. You. Go..." I try to shoo the cat out of my space, but my hands slip right through his body.

Demon's sake.

"Mortem..." I growl.

"Yes?" he purrs.

I gesture at the door.

He stretches. Bum up, paws down. His back arches, his fluffy tail bristling. Finally, he pads forward towards the door, only to turn around and stroll into the heart of the apartment.

"MORTEM," I squeal, high-pitched and frantic. "I can't... I don't do pets."

"You have moths," he purrs.

"THEY'RE DEAD," I shriek, my hands flapping erratically.

"So am I." He runs around the corner into the bedroom and vanishes.

I make my way inside through the kitchen and into the open-plan living area and freeze. The place is trashed. All my boxes are upturned, my belongings strewn across the floor.

There's the creak of floorboards.

Goosebumps crawl over my skin, I stagger back into the kitchen, yank open a drawer and grab a knife.

Ribbon-like shadows slink along the skirting boards. My heart rate shoots up. My fingers grow cold.

I raise the knife.

Father steps around the corner. "Whoa!" he says.

"Demon's sake. I thought you were a burglar." I chuck the knife in the sink as he opens his arms to hug me.

"What are you doing here?" I ask as I disentangle myself.

"I came to see how the Head of House Inferos was settling into her apartment... And maybe to see if you were okay after the attack. But when I got here, the door was open."

"This wasn't you?"

"Why would I trash your apartment?"

I'm about to say he's done a lot worse but now is not the time to start an argument.

"Then who did?" I ask.

He shakes his head, as if he's as confused as me. It makes a bead of unease grow in my gut. My father is never unsure. His ego makes sure of that.

"Do you think it's the Societas?" I ask.

"It makes the most logical sense. Given what I did to Architecti, they've always had an interest in me. It makes sense they'd come for you next."

The words flow off his tongue so easy. Too easy. But my brain is addled and exhausted, and I can't parse the truth from the lies.

"You'll need heightened security on House Inferos's doors. I'll see to that before morning."

"Okay." I shrug.

"Okay? Lucy, do you have any idea how precious you are to me? I won't let any harm come to you."

He pulls me in tight. Too tight.

"Father, I'm fine."

I wriggle out of his grip, and he cups my cheeks, pressing a kiss to my forehead. "You must be protected."

His words are odd, as if they don't quite fit the mould of his sentence, but I'm exhausted, and a memory trickles back to me: the Veil tear and the neatness of the cut.

"Did you witness the tears that happened before term started?" I ask.

He nods.

"What was the fabric like?"

"Why?" he asks, expression thin.

"Usually tears are frayed, right? Their edges all rough where the fabric bulged and snapped?"

"Correct."

"This wasn't, it was very neat. Too neat, almost like the fabric was sliced. But I've never seen that."

He recoils, his forehead crumpling in concentration. "You think it was cut intentionally?"

"Perhaps? Someone broke into my apartment on the same night there was a Veil attack. So something is going on, and I'd put money on the two events being connected. What I don't understand is why me?"

Father's fists ball. There is something here, something going on, but I see the simmering twitch in his eyelid. He's reached the end of his tether, and I carry the memories of what happens if you keep pushing.

"I have to go. Make sure you lock all the doors and windows. I'll see to it that there's security on the entrances and exits."

I want to protest to ask more, call him out for avoiding the questions but every bone in my body is weary, and if I push him too hard there will be consequences.

"I'll see you in the morning," I say.

He leaves without another word.

The apartment is warm tonight, and I find myself grateful that maintenance started the fire.

Upturned boxes are everywhere. Dresses and jackets spilled over the floor. My academic texts and stationery strewn across the living room.

I tidy what I can before exhaustion eats away at the marrow of my soul and I decide to leave the rest, opting instead to hunt for bathing equipment.

It takes a minute or two, but I find a towel and some soap and head for the shower. My heart sinks when I realise there's no bath. Reluctantly, I switch the shower on. It runs warm so I open the frosted window to stop the steam. I'll just have to be extra careful not to show the world my naked body. I strip and climb in, lathering up my skin.

No wine, no bath... There's only one other comfort I can think of that would make things better.

I slip my hand between my thighs, cleansing my most intimate parts, then brush the thumb over my clit, sending a pulse through my body.

Exhaustion gnaws at every inch of me, but my fingers glide between my folds, picking up the bubbles and using them to massage my apex.

My nipples tighten. I lean back and slide down the tiles. Once sat, I spread my legs.

Midnight's face flickers in my mind. Those crystalline eyes glinting at me. Her expression cocky, assured. A moan slips out. Fuck.

I can't be having thoughts like this, not now she's a student. The last thing I want is to get her expelled. And I definitely do not want to get fired, either. I shove the images of Midnight down deep.

I rub harder, my clit pulsing, my pussy tightening. The smell of vetiver and grapefruit, the scent of Midnight drifts through my senses. What the hell? Images of her sliding her hands down my trousers float through my mind and my body stiffens in response. I'm teetering on the precipice of coming with visions of her littering my thoughts.

A gasp shatters the quiet.

I freeze, my mind shunted back to high alert. I glance out the shower and through the open window, but there's no one there. Though the feeling of being watched doesn't wash away with the soap. It clings to my skin.

I poke my head out the shower, but I'm just being paranoid. I'll take a knife to bed with me tonight, otherwise I'm not sleeping.

I slide down the tiles until I'm sitting again and resume masturbating. One hand skirts low, my fingers gliding between my folds and dipping into my entrance. My other hand finds my clit as I add another finger inside myself. Midnight's name hovers on my lips as I fuck myself into oblivion. Thoughts and images of her swirl around my mind.

My pussy clenches, driving me higher, and I think I whisper her name as I spill over into the best relief I've had all day. The fact it was with my hands in my cunt and Midnight in my mind is something I'll worry about in the morning.

19

MIDNIGHT

I'll slip into Lucy's apartment and reap her soul.

Simple.

The campus will have my back, it wants me to do this, after all. I slip out of our apartment, glaring at Aurelia's bedroom door as I go.

Am I being childish and petty? Yes. Do I give a shit? No. Lucy had to know who I was. She's Ignatius's daughter, for fuck's sake. Gods. She knew that and let me fuck her anyway. She continued to let me flirt with her, for what reason? Some sick joke she and her father have? Use and abuse mortals. Laugh at them while they flounder and pander to the demons.

Fuck her. And fuck him too.

I do need a walk.

I head around the building's perimeter first, marching the energy off. I'm halfway around the mansion when Ignatius storms out the front door.

Interesting.

I reach the rear of the mansion and look up. There's a

window cracked with a light on in the penthouse. She's in there.

Good. That's good. I can just go and take her soul and be done with this whole Finis and Ignatius thing.

By the time I slip back inside the front door, Vetch is snoring loudly, and security guards are stationed in front of him.

Do all campus houses have security? I don't remember seeing any when we passed House Mortis and House Vitalis earlier this evening.

The foyer is empty. I climb the stairs and head to the back of the mansion, using the secondary set of stairs to make my way up to the penthouse.

I press my ear to the door. The hissing rush of a shower drifts through the wooden panel.

I reach for the handle, but the door swings open by itself. I should be thankful. The campus is helping me fulfil my end of the bargain.

But I can't summon the gratitude. Instead, my skin is on edge, the incessant tickle of an insect you can't find.

It's just one soul.

So what if I fucked her. It's not like I care about her. I don't even know her.

My feet carry me inside, slipping into her apartment and through the kitchen into an open living space.

I frown. There are several upturned boxes and items spread across the floor.

It almost looks like someone trashed the place and then did a half-arsed job of tidying.

A ghostly white cat pads across the hallway. I frown. It's way too familiar.

"Hey you," I whisper, and kneel to call it over, hoping it doesn't make any noise.

It nudges my hand just like the cat in the city. I swear it's the same one. It purrs, my hand slips through its body as it drifts in and out of its corporeal state.

It looks up at me and I swear it smirks. Then it sinks its teeth into me.

I have to bite down a scream.

"You little fucking b—"

My hand washes through it as I swat it, but it bounds out of sight before I can catch him.

A moan escapes the bathroom.

And another. And I promptly forget all about the cat.

Sumptuous and deep, it's a moan borne from a body close to orgasm.

My pussy pulses and tightens, excitement leaks into my boxers until I realise she could be in there with someone. Another person could be making her moan and gasp. The bubbling heat I felt outside morphs into something far more dangerous.

Shit.

A burning sensation grows in my chest, my stomach hardening. I push it away, my fingers sliding to my hip and the scythe I always carry.

Violence is always better than emotion. Fuck it, I'll take two souls tonight instead of one. But even as I think it, it feels weak.

I press my back to the bathroom wall and peer inside.

Lucy.

Alone.

My chest cools, my stomach softening. Two things I refuse to acknowledge.

I peek through the gap and thank the archdemon I'm not a man. The sight of Lucy pressed against the shower wall, her legs spread bearing that delicious pink pussy would be enough to give me the kind of raging hard-on that would shove a door open.

Do it, Midnight.

That fucking voice. The whisper and scream that slithers under my skin. Crawls through my mind like a fucking maggot. Wriggling. Relentless. Pushy.

Do it.

Do it.

Do it.

It's an ugly little hiss of a thing.

One little soul.

"Shut up," I bark.

Lucy stops touching herself.

Shit.

I swing away, press my spine into the wall, desperately trying to slow my breathing.

The shower door opens, the sound of her heightened breathing drifting out. Then the door swings shut again. The shower keeps running.

I got away with it.

Thank fuck.

I'm more careful this time as I peer inside the bathroom. Those legs spread, her lips parted where she runs her fingers through her folds.

"Midnight," she says.

I freeze.

Fuck me. Is she masturbating to thoughts of me? Before I can stop myself, my fingers unbuckle my trousers. It's wrong. So fucking wrong, but I don't care, not in this moment. Not if she's fucking herself to thoughts of me.

She eases her hips wider, her glistening cunt spread wide. I can practically taste the sweetness of her come on my tongue. My fingers find my clit and rub. Hard. Furious.

Her lips quiver around a word over and over.

My name.

Oh, gods. She is fucking herself to me, for me. I can't cope. My clit sings, pulses. I'm going to spill over embarrassingly fast.

Lucy slides a finger inside her pussy, and I think my mind enters the celestial realm.

It takes an inconceivable feat of strength not to fling open the door and sink to my knees for her.

She draws her finger in and out and adds a second, stretching that exquisite cunt. Her pink lips swell as she continues fucking herself, her head rolls back, her mouth parts as her breasts rise and fall with her panting. But it's the sight of rosy-pink nipples hardening despite the warm flowing water that has me tipping over into an orgasm.

I jerk against the wall, my legs jelly.

The shower turns off.

I yank my hands out of my boxers and sprint for her apartment door.

I close it behind me just as she exits the bathroom.

What the fuck is wrong with me?

The corridor seems, off. Tension cloys the atmosphere. I didn't do what the campus wanted, and it knows.

For fuck's sake.

Midnight, it hisses.

"I'll get it done. You didn't set a time limit, so arguably I have until the end of term."

A screech follows that sounds like the creak of old floors, the hissing crackle of wood in a fire and the cawing of ravens.

Tricky. Tricky. Don't disappoint me.

But that's the thing. I should have done it. I should have reaped her tonight, and instead I watched her fuck herself over me. And now instead of contemplating how to reap her, all I can think about is how much I want to make her come again. How much I want to know every dirty dream and thought in her head.

And that is not good news.

20

LUCY

Before classes start, I make my way down to the demonic contracts library. Mortem follows, weaving in and out of my legs. I swear he's trying to trip me up. The little shit strolls into the library, hops up on one of the tables, gives me the evil eye and then falls asleep.

The contracts library is located in Finis Tower's basement and houses copies of every contract every demon has ever created.

Except one.

Mine.

The librarian insists I'm wrong and that I've just not searched properly.

I have. I asked Father the location of the contract once. I was eleven. It resulted in him taking his belt to my arse. It was a long time before I asked again. He caught me searching in the archives for it, and when I questioned him, he refused to engage in conversation, stating that, "it's in the library where it should be." And that's the same response I've gotten every time since, too.

I browse the aisles for an hour every few days, my fingers running along fraying and tattered parchments. Each demon's mark is slightly different, their contractual wording nuanced in the necromantic verbiage and grammar. It's fascinating the ways in which demons can tie a mortal into knots.

"No joy today?" Mrs. Atasap, the contracts librarian asks.

"No joy today, or any other day," I sigh.

"My eyes are forever open and hunting for you, dear," she says and bids me goodbye as I leave the library and ascend Finis Tower's staircase.

I make my way back across campus and into the Negotiations Lecture Hall.

I always take the first class of every new intake. Why? Because contracts are the basis for all demon magic. The more contracts we create, the more future possibilities we steal, the more magic we harness.

My class is already sat when I walk in.

We are in a borrowed classroom. There's steep, tiered seating facing a mass of chalkboards along one wall. The sides of the hall are all shelved with relics and items from the dead. Meaningful trinkets, old bones and other things the shades needed to help them move on.

My gaze lands on Midnight first, she's sat in the back row with Bastien and Lex, the two students in her apartment in House Inferos.

Midnight is wearing black leather trousers, her scythe harness strapped to her thigh and a vest top showing off her toned shoulders and arms, the cut of her biceps visible even though she's nowhere near a gym.

I swallow and refocus on my notes. I need to get rid of this ridiculous obsession with her. I'm a middle-aged woman with a professional tenure at the greatest academy in the realm, and I do not need my attention misplaced on a student who is likely to get me fired.

"Students of Finis Academy. Welcome and congratulations on passing the Severance Rite. This year is going to be the hardest of your life. Graduates of Finis are well respected for one reason and one reason alone... can anyone tell me what that is?"

It's the same opening speech I always give. Something to put the fear into them. Set their competitive natures alight.

I'm met with silence followed by uncomfortable coughing and the rustling fabric of bottoms shifting in seats.

A woman raises her hand near the front row.

"Yes?"

She gives the man sat next to her a hesitant glance and then says, "Because we're qualified?"

Oh, dear demons below. I stare at the woman, astonished. Is she joking? If this is the standard we're letting in, we don't stand a chance against the Societas.

"While accurate, that is, on this occasion, incorrect," I say.

The woman shrinks in her seat.

"The reason is this: Our pass mark is simple... survive the year."

A peal of nervous laughter ripples through the room. But my face remains expressionless.

A man in the front row raises his hand. "Could you elaborate, Professor?"

"Certainly. You will, of course, receive points throughout the year, and there will be an overall top student. But in order to receive your qualifications, you merely need to survive. That, in itself, will be a challenge."

The man glances at the student to his right, his Adam's apple bobbing visibly. I don't class myself a sadist at all. I'm far more masochistic, enjoying the release that pain gives me. However, there are a few moments when my morals slip, and I rather enjoy tormenting the new students. This is one of them.

"The good news for you is that there are many ways to gain points. The bad news is that there are many more ways to die."

"Like what?" A brunette man sat a few rows back asks. His friends all jeer and clap. I guarantee they're wannabe Veilwalkers; the ego is dripping off them.

"I'm glad you asked." I inhale and then proceed to rattle off a lengthy list at top speed. "Wraith attacks, ashspawn attacks, sigil and or rune backlash, death by haunting, suicide, in-class duelling, incorrect Veilwalking, fabric fuck-ups, death by fear, accidentally cutting your soul, losing your soul, breaching the Veil while inadequately prepared, pissing the Tower off, and I suppose getting hit by falling bricks, given our current tremors. Those are off the top of my head, shall I continue?"

The entire hall is silent.

"I didn't think so. Now, today is the introduction to contracts. Can anyone tell me why we start here?"

"Theft is the basis for all demonic magic," Midnight shouts from the back.

A couple of the students hiss out an "Ooouch" and a couple of others shout "Burn."

"Would you mind putting your hand up in class. What's your name?"

Even from the front of the lecture hall I can see the smirk she gives me.

"I think you managed to pronounce my name just fine last night, don't you?"

I freeze. The students reach a frenzy, squealing at her banter and cheering for her. My cheeks flush red as I try to work out what the hell she's talking about? How dare she talk to me like this in front of the entire cohort. I clench my jaw. Her eyes glitter up in the stands. I swear to the archdemon I will—

"Midnight," she moans her own name in the exact tone that slipped out when I was in the shower last night.

Oh. My. Gods. Heat blooms everywhere from my cheeks to my pussy.

The noise I heard in the shower. I poked my head out the door but heard nothing. I assumed I was on my own and it was just new apartment noises. Was she... she wouldn't?

How dare she humiliate me in front of the entire class.

I grit my teeth. "Well, Midnight. You can stay behind after class and write me an extra essay on the ethics of appropriate class behaviour."

"Oh, I'll happily stay behind for extra class," she says, and there's a rumbling of 'whaaaayy' cheered around the room.

I ignore it and turn to the chalkboard, my neck as scarlet as my cheeks.

My hand shakes as I write *contracts vs covenants*.

"Does anyone know the difference between contracts and covenants?" I ask.

Bastien flings his hand up.

"Bastien?"

"Covenants are the angelic version of a contract."

"Good, at least someone in House Inferos is academically inclined."

Midnight's smirk grows deeper, as if she knows she got to me.

The rest of the class goes smoothly. I take them through the basic anatomy of a contract and the most regularly found clauses.

When the class files out, Midnight stays sat in her seat.

The last student files out, and I lock the lecture hall door.

"What the hell is wrong with you?"

She stands up and slowly makes her way down the tiered seating as if she has all the time in the world.

"You're the one jerking off over a student."

I gasp, check the door is actually locked.

"Did you break into my apartment last night?" I hiss.

She's in front of me now, stepping closer and closer until I hit the wall. She leans in, trapping me in place with one hand against the wall and leaning into my other ear. Her breath is hot, the scent of vetiver and grapefruit rich and heady.

"The real question is, did you masturbate over Daddy last night?"

"Midnight," I gasp.

But I'm no longer thinking straight. My mind has short circuited. My breath hitches.

"You... you can't talk to me like that. You can't behave like that in class, either. It's not okay. We could both lose everything. They fired a professor here a couple of years ago for fraternising with a student."

She pulls back, her expression shifting from molten lust to a deeper heat, a fury etched into her bones.

"How long?" she tugs her hand through her hair.

"How long what?"

"How. Long. Have. You. Known. Who. I. Was?" She spits every word.

Oh.

She shakes her head and steps away. The space between us suddenly vast, and cold.

"Wait," I say, and surge forward, though every rational cell screams at me to let her be angry. To use the situation to put much-needed distance between us.

"How fucking long, Lucy? Why wouldn't you have told me?"

"Because I didn't know. At least not at the graveyard."

"Then when?" she snaps.

This time, it's me getting closer. She rests her arse against the shelving filled with trinkets and bones. She's furious, her nostrils flaring, and yet I still find myself stepping closer.

She's seething. Heat simmers beneath her skin, but it's pliable, changing. It seems to swing between rage and, and... lust?

I tell her the truth. "The morning of the Severance Rite."

She shakes her head at me. "I hate everything you are."

An urge swells up, my fingers twitching, my feet driving me forward. Midnight's energy frissons with lethal vigour. But I ignore it and lean close, pressing my forehead to hers.

"You don't. You hate my father."

"No," she says, and suddenly I'm spinning. My back slams against the bookcase. She grabs my throat with one hand and slides her scythe under my chin with the other.

"One swipe and it's all over," she says, but I'm no longer sure if she's talking about my life or hers.

My heart hammers so loud I feel the beat in my tongue. I swallow against her fingers.

"Please don't do this to hurt him. I just want to be free. Like you."

"What?" she says, the hardness in her gaze faltering.

She releases her grip on my throat, her thumb rubbing gentle circles where I assume she's left marks on me.

My tongue slides over my lips. Is it wrong that I like the idea of her marking me?

"What do you mean you want to be free?" Midnight asks.

I glance at the door, making sure it's still locked. Gods forbid someone came in. Telling Midnight this is a risk. If anyone found out what Ignatius did, binding someone underage into a contract, his reputation would be defiled. And that is the one thing he won't tolerate. Even Thalia guesses at the truth.

But I am tired of carrying this burden on my own. So I decide to do the unthinkable.

"You aren't the only one Ignatius has locked in a contract," I whisper.

She folds her arms, her expression thinning. "Say more."

"When I was a child, he saved my life by forcing me into a contract. So you're not the only one who wants freedom."

Her head hangs low. "Trapped, just like me." But her words are quiet, spoken to herself rather than me. "That motherfucker."

"Let me help you," I say, an idea forming.

"You can't help me. I have less than a year until he reaps me. Finis and the Demonic Favour is my last chance at salvation."

"Exactly. Hear me out. Let me train you. You won't win without additional training. The students with families that have come here for generations start with an advantage."

"Why would you do that? What's in it for you?"

"Well, it's not for free. I can't break my contract by myself because it forbids me from making a move against Ignatius."

"And how exactly do I do that?"

"Does it matter? If I help you win that favour and you break your own, does the cost really make a difference? What are you willing to do to save your soul, Midnight? How far would you go?"

My words are potent. She stares into the distance, her vision unfocused. She snaps to attention and holds out her hand.

"Fine. You got yourself a deal."

"Oh no, Midnight. That's not how I seal my deals..."

21
MIDNIGHT

Ten Years Ago

It takes me a week to figure out how to summon a demon safely. I mean obviously anyone can do it, but demons are notorious for trickery, and I don't want to get fucked over any worse than I already am.

And I don't just want some low-level, entry-type demon, either.

I need one with power. One that can actually save Aurelia's life. Otherwise, the sacrifice I'm going to make will be for naught.

I heard that the more you want a demon, the more powerful that demon is likely to be—the text I found said they were drawn to emotions. Given the level of desperation I have to save Aurelia, I'm not taking any chances with safety because I'm likely to summon an archdemon.

I'm all set up on consecrated ground—a local church cemetery. There were so few texts available, but the one I did find said consecrated ground and salt can help control demons. But I don't have anyone to confirm that, so this is all guess work.

Salt first.

I draw a reasonably sized circle.

Place the herbs, crystals and the mirror down to ward off anything else from jumping across the Veil.

I drag the blade across my palm and fling the drops of blood into the circle. Then open my mouth, ready to recite the words I've memorised. But I'm cut off.

"It's all bullshit," a voice rumbles behind me.

I shriek and spin around, brandishing the knife at the intruder.

"Who the fuck is there?" I bark.

My heart is in my throat, blood rushing to my ears. I checked the graveyard on the way in, I was definitely on my own. This site doesn't even have security.

A shadowy figure leans against a tree. He's tall. His hair and eyes as dark as death.

"Who are you?" I say again, this time my voice trembles.

"I," he kicks off the tree and steps into the moonlight, "am who you summoned."

I hesitate, glancing back to the salt circle, wondering if I have magic powers because I didn't even recite the words.

He must read my thoughts because he rolls his eyes.

"Like I said, all bullshit."

"Then, how did you come to be here?"

He folds his arms, staring down at me. An impressive feat given I'm tall for a woman. "Because you summoned me. Keep up, I'm a busy devil. What is it you seek?"

This is really happening. I'm going to be able to save Aurelia.

"My girlfriend. She's sick..."

"So take her to the doctor," he drawls, his voice deep

and rumbling in a way that would make even straight men reconsider their sexuality.

"Terminally sick. I want you to save her."

He narrows his eyes at me. "It costs a soul to save a soul."

"I know." I researched enough to know the price. But I also know you can negotiate.

"Give me fifty years with her."

He throws his head back and laughs, a great booming sound that billows around the cemetery.

"I'll give you two."

I read that deals like this go one of two ways. Either you successfully charm them enough they are open to negotiating, or they get bored and leave. I figured to grab his attention I'd have to go big. I'm never going to have a full life, not with an ask this big, but I could get some time with her.

"Forty," I bark back.

That wipes the smile off his face, he turns to leave. Okay, shit, I was too bold.

"Twenty-five," I offer.

"Five," he counters.

"Ten. Final offer." It's a brash move from me, but I'm desperate and he knows that, or he wouldn't have come. And devils do like their deals.

He spins to face me, his face as glimmering and dark as a starry sky.

The longer I stare upon him the colder my body grows. It's the first time I'm truly afraid. My heart races so fast my chest hurts. I can't breathe.

He leans down into my face, brandishing a crooked smile at me.

"Ten years, one soul for another. And no comebacks."

He holds his hand out.

"That easy?" I breathe, my words barely audible.

"That easy, *Midnight*."

"I didn't tell you my name."

"You already gave me your soul..."

I glance down, our hands clasped. The word *deal* a whisper and an echo in the air.

Entropy moths materialise, fluttering around me, their wings brushing my hair and cheeks and arms. They're soft, sweet, oddly beautiful despite their awful meaning.

I always thought I was fated for more. But is there any greater life than one lived in service of another. And I love Aurelia enough to sacrifice everything for her.

I thought it would be a momentous occasion. Thought we'd sign in blood. That there would be a thunderclap or a rift in reality.

But I sold my soul with nothing but the dead and the stars to witness.

He turns my wrist to display his mark.

"You're mine now, Midnight. Ten years." He glances at his watch as it ticks past twelve.

"Oh, and happy birthday."

Then he's gone, and I'm left standing in the graveyard hoping and praying that I made the right decision. That Aurelia and I can make the most of the next ten years.

I thought I'd be elated, that I'd run home singing and screaming and full of hope for the next decade.

But my fingers have turned cold. My stomach has dropped, and there is an immeasurable weight pressing on my chest that I can't seem to get rid of.

When I walk through the door, Aurelia bounces off the sofa.

"It's a miracle. I'm healed!" she says, running to embrace me.

"I know," I say, my voice monotone.

She halts mid-step.

"What...? What do you mean 'you know?'"

I open my mouth to tell her, but no words come out. Only a breathy scream.

"What the fuck did you do?" Aurelia says, her expression darkening.

"I told you... I wouldn't let you die."

I pull my sleeve up and display Ignatius's mark.

"No," she says, stepping back as if I'm diseased. She shakes her head, pulling her hands over her face. "Not like this."

"You're going to be okay, that's what matters."

"How long?" she barks.

"Does it matter?"

"Of course, it fucking matters. What the hell is wrong with you? Does life mean so little to you?"

"No, Aurelia, it's that you mean everything to me."

"SO YOU'D GIVE UP A LIFE TOGETHER?"

"You were going to die. Now we get ten years."

She goes still. "Ten years?" Her eyes fill, tears spilling down her cheeks.

I reach out to clasp her wrist and pull her to me. But she snatches it away.

"Don't touch me. Who are you? Who does that? Who sells their soul like that?"

She leaves me alone in the hallway with nothing but the clock on the wall and the tick, tick, ticking.

It's louder than before.

Just me and the clock.

And an ever-increasing weight on my chest.

22

LUCY

Midnight's eyes glimmer, the blue flaring hot like fire. I smile and slide into her personal space all over again. But this time she welcomes it. All the fury melting into something far more molten.

"What are you doing?" she asks.

She tries to back up but she's already against the shelving. She knocks several books, a couple of jars and some bone shards off in her vain attempt to escape.

I rise on my tiptoes and bring my lips millimetres from hers.

"Sealing the deal, Midnight, what else?"

"Sealing it how?"

"It won't hurt a bit... it's just a kiss."

"This isn't a fucking fairytale," she says. But her words are as weak as her resolve, all of which are fading as fast as the marks she left on my neck.

I plunge my lips onto hers. She goes rigid beneath my touch.

Her lips tingle against mine—magic. I've always

thought deal creation a strange sensation. Like whispered promises and warm sandy beaches. Like the smell of crackling winter fires and creamy hot chocolate.

Moths materialise around us. Futures, dreams and possibilities dissolve as she commits to another deal and seals her fate. A surge of power runs through my body. It's intense and electric. Golden energy courses through my body and settles between my legs, in my chest and fingers and mind. So rarely do I make a deal, but gods is the power exquisite.

Something snaps inside me. My hands are everywhere. They skulk up the back of Midnight's head, my fingers bristling against the neatly shaved hairs. She must sense my need, magic electrifying every nerve in my body—a desperation seeping into my bones. She deepens the kiss. Until finally, I break off.

Our lips are pink and swollen. Midnight's expression is needy.

"Sorry, I... got carried away," I say.

Midnight glances at the empty lecture hall. "There's no one here."

"I apologise. That was inappropriate. If anyone found us..."

But my body, thrumming with newly formed magic, doesn't give a flying fuck that we're in a lecture hall. Or that despite the fact the hall is locked, anyone could unlock it, or the next class could arrive. All my body seems to want is an orgasm.

"Inappropriate, and yet you want more anyway," she says, a smile lingering in her tone.

"No. That's..."

"So you don't want me to fuck you against this bookshelf?"

"Oh, fuck, I—" I have to squeeze my thighs shut and shake my head. But I am well aware my eyes will be betraying me.

Midnight's lashes flutter at me as she bites her lip.

Fuck, I will regret this.

She lunges for me, and I lose the ability to be rational. My mouth sinks onto hers. She rips my jacket open, her hand slides up my waist, caressing my breasts. Nipping down the side of my neck.

I moan against her.

"More. Need more." I need everything. Magic flows in every cell and crook of my body. I'm alive in ways I haven't been for so long. And that is a problem. If I made contracts regularly, I wouldn't be behaving like a jacked-up teen.

But I don't. And so here we are.

Midnight hoists my top up and yanks down my bra cup, exposing a breast and I lose the last shreds of control I've been clinging onto.

My nipple tightens before she can sink her tongue and teeth over the peaked nub.

"Oh, fuck," I moan as my mind drifts on the ebbing waves of magic and lust. I want her tongue, her teeth, her fingers. I need to be fucked. And I need to be fucked *hard*.

She pulls me off the bookshelf and spins me to face it.

"Hands. Now," she growls, pushing them flat against the shelf.

From behind, she unbuckles my trousers and slides them to my ankles.

"What if we're seen?" I squeal with the one logical brain cell I still have.

"Then they'll get a good show, won't they? Now, be a good girl and spread your legs. Daddy's fucking famished."

I am so screwed. I obediently spread my legs as wide as

my trousers will allow. There are no rational brain cells left. They've migrated to my pussy. I'm soaking, needy and eager.

She lowers herself to her knees, her hands find my cheeks and spread me. She stretches my pussy with such obscene force that my lips part and a rush of air slips between my thighs.

"Fuck, your pussy is divine."

My hands grip the first thing they find, my knuckle bones straining the skin on my hands.

"Please, fuck me," I beg.

She tilts my hips, exposing my pussy further and I moan at how filthy the image of me must be. Legs splayed, pussy and arse on show.

"Stop teasing me and fuck me," I say.

A growled hum billows from her chest as her hand lands on my cheek. I shunt forward, knocking several jars off the bookshelf.

Her fingers smooth over the stinging prints until her teeth sink into the flesh, and I groan against the searing pain.

Her tongue spears my pussy, jutting into my entrance and making me cry out as waves of pleasure ripple outward. She licks me from clit to hole and back again, mopping up every drop of excitement.

"Fuck," I moan.

She licks faster, her tongue doing things that make my body shiver and tremble against the tides of pleasure washing through me.

I moan her name, scream for more as I lose myself in the sensations of her touch and the rhythm of magic flowing through me.

Black ribbons rip from the wall and coil around my

hands as more and more magic builds the closer she pushes me to orgasm.

She pushes two fingers inside me, her tongue finding my ring of muscle, and I swear stars splinter across my vision.

I'm so out of it, I nearly slip off the edge of the bookcase. My hands grip harder, and—wait. I'm not holding the bookcase, it's a bone. Thick too, but the end is rounded smooth, worn from erosion. The other end is balled—a joint. Possibly a humerus or maybe a femur?

No.

I can't.

It's sick.

It's completely shameless.

And yet...

I slide the bone between my thighs and gasp.

"I need... I need you inside me."

"Fuck," Midnight says, her words dripping with intensity as she takes the bone from me. She stands and leans into my ear, warm breath trickling down my neck.

"You really are a depraved little slut, aren't you?"

My body melts, her words make my breathing quicken, my mind turn molten. She lifts me by my hips, spins me to face her and lowers herself to her knees.

"Is there any image more divine than a woman on her knees for you?"

She raises an eyebrow at me. "There's one..."

"Oh?" I say.

"Mmm. A woman on her knees crawling to you."

She sinks onto my pussy, sucking my swollen clit between her teeth. I nearly explode in her mouth. She brings the smooth end of the bone to my cunt and pushes.

My legs tremble as waves of electric pleasure radiate over me.

"Yes, more."

She laps at me harder, ravishing my clit with attention. The bone thrusts in and out, she angles it better, making it rub against my G-spot.

"Oh fuck, oh fuck," I say as my pussy clenches around the bone.

I grind my cunt into her mouth, taking everything she gives me. I want more. Need it. I want everything. My mind drifts in another realm, saturated by magic and pleasure and waves of building orgasm.

Her tongue softens, flicking quicker and gentler than before. The perfect contrast to the hard bone pumping inside me.

My fingers find her hair, squeezing the roots at the scalp. *Harder. Faster. More.*

She drives the bone in and out, faster, harder, her tongue matching pace. Until I'm grinding so hard against her face, I swear she'll be as marked as my neck was earlier.

She thrusts the bone in again and again, tipping me further and further over the precipice until I white out. My head lolls back, my mouth opens in a silent scream as she obliterates my world, and I come the hardest I ever have. Black ribbons billow around the lecture hall, darkness descending over us. When I finally come down to earth and the magic dissipates, she slides the bone out and runs her tongue up and down every side.

"You did not…" I mumble, still orgasm-addled.

"Did you or did you not just come?"

I nod.

"Then I earned it." She licks up the final drops of my come and then places the bone back on the shelf.

I will never be able to look at it or this bookshelf the same way.

She frowns and glances at my neck.

"What?"

"I must be seeing things."

"You going to elaborate?" I ask as I hoik my trousers up.

"It's just, in the graveyard I thought I saw something on your neck, but it vanished, and the same thing happened just now. I saw something but it's already gone."

"What was it?"

"I have no idea, I've never seen a symbol like it."

23
MIDNIGHT

Two Hundred and Forty-Three Days To Go

Classes are relentless.

Bastien, Lex and I sink into a routine. We eat breakfast together. Some of our classes cross, but most do not. We meet in the refectory for lunches, and most often dinner in the apartment with our books spread out on the communal table. Each of us brings class problems to the others. We share knowledge generously, and all of us benefit from it.

Aurelia keeps to herself. I think she's found a group of friends, annoyingly Darwin, one of my old reaper pals, is in that group.

"I heard a conspiracy today. Architecti wasn't the bad guy—her sister was," Bastien says, shovelling chicken into his mouth.

"Nope, I heard it was the elder angel, and she was in love with him and took the fall. Proper age-gap romance style," Lex adds, pinching the chicken Bastien just picked up and gobbling it before he has a chance to protest.

I pull the demonic runes dictionary towards me and continue flicking through it.

"Why do you keep reading those when you don't take any Eytomancy classes?" Lex says.

"I find them interesting," I say. Which is a total lie. I want to find the symbol that appeared twice on Lucy's neck. I've spent weeks hunting and failed to find anything useful. I've managed to sketch a couple of lines for Lucy, and she's convinced it's something to do with her contract. Given our deal and my promise to help her, I'll continue searching and reading.

I catch Lex glancing at my wrist and the brand, so I pull my sleeve down.

"Sorry," she says, sheepish.

"How long?" Bastien asks.

"Two hundred and forty-three days."

Bastien raises an eyebrow. "Not that you're counting."

I give him a sad smile. "The only certainty I have is the relentlessness of the ticking clock. Anyway, Architecti—for or against resurrection?" I say, changing the subject.

"Ooh, a debate, love them. For," Lex says.

Bastien's mouth drops. "You're kidding?"

Lex shrugs. "It's not like I'm a Societas member or anything extreme. I just think if she was resurrected, maybe the angels would return."

"Yeah, and all-out war, I imagine," Bastien says between mouthfuls of eggs. How he can eat a full-blown protein pile this early in the morning, I don't know.

"Maybe. Or maybe things would go back to the way they were, when we had access to all kinds of magic. Covenants benefit mortals much more than contracts, and we don't have those anymore," I add.

Lex claps and points at me. "See? Midnight's got it."

"I don't know, none of the demons have tried to over-throw mortals or restructure our government," Bastien says and gets up to make coffee.

"They don't have to." I close my textbook and pack my bag for the day.

"How so?" Bastien asks.

"They steal our future, what else do they need?"

That makes Bastien falter, a flicker of comprehension sliding into his features. "I never thought about it like that."

"No. And the demons don't want you to either. That's the problem with authority, and why healthy debate matters. It opens your mind," Lex says, packing her books.

Bastien hands out three coffees in to-go cups, and we head out for class.

"Classes are stepping up today," Professor Alistair Ironheart announces. Another professor stands at the front of the room with him, one I've seen hanging out with Lucy.

"Good morning, I am Professor Thalia Morrow," she says.

She's older than Ironheart, her hair is streaked with grey, though gracefully so. Her eyes are as mismatched as her hair, one blue and one golden. She has an ethereal quality to her as she glides across the room, though equally, she has an edge that screams *do not fuck with me*.

She continues. "Due to the acceleration in studies, we are doubling up. As Veil students, you should be spending this term studying the theory of both Veilwalking and Fabric Weaving."

"We don't want to weave fabric, though," the same

arrogant student who shouted out the morning of initiation says. He's been obnoxious like this all term.

"What's your name, boy?" Thalia asks.

"Hadrian Umbriel."

She examines his face, her voice turning cold. "If you have no skills in Fabric Weaving, how do you expect to cut yourself a hole out of the underworld should you get in trouble?"

"Don't plan on getting into trouble," he scoffs.

Thalia's eyes fill with enough malice that even her sunny gold irises turn icy.

"Well, Hadrian, seeing as you have so much confidence, you get to go first." She turns to the class. "I want the Fabric Weaving students on the left, and the Veilwalkers on the right. Pair up."

We all move fast. Thankfully, Aurelia partners with someone else. Hadrian is situated next to me, but I get left with a blonde girl who is honestly so wispy and frail-looking, I'm amazed she had the strength to make it through the Severance Rite, let alone the last term of gruelling lectures.

Alistair claps for silence. We oblige and Thalia continues.

"Doorstop students, you're going straight into cutting. I want you to make a six-inch incision in the Veil fabric. Professors and Teaching Assistants, I need one with each pairing. The Doorstops will cut, and Detours, I want you to slide your hand into the Veil and back out again."

The blonde girl I'm partnered with raises her hand.

"Yes?" Thalia says.

"How do we cut?" she asks.

Thalia grins, not sweetly. Her teeth are a little sharper than I expected. "You've not done cutting yet?"

Alistair pouts. "Arcadius insisted on a defence focus for the first term. Given the number of tears over the last few weeks, I am now inclined to agree with him."

"Fine. You cut like this." Thalia closes her eyes, raises her hands and dark ribbons peel off from the walls.

"Call the magic to you, eyes closed, hearts open. When you feel a tingle in your fingers, grab hold and tug. It will come. Fabric students, you're predisposed to sensing the Veil. Hold your hands up and glide them through the air until you feel a hitch. A broken stitch, like when your heart skips a beat. That is where you cut."

She demonstrates, her hands moving through the air. The Doorstops all gasp when her fingers halt suddenly.

I frown.

The blonde girl touches my arm and says, "We can see the fabric. And it's Silvana. We partnered once last term for ashspawn defence, but you were exhausted that day, so I figured you wouldn't remember."

I shake her hand and whisper my name. "Apologies. I'm Midnight."

Thalia brings an index finger and middle finger together, then does the same with her other hand. The undersides touch, and she makes a sharp sweeping motion.

There's a series of oohs and gasps. I fidget on the spot, uncomfortable at not being able to see what they can.

"Think we've got a runt here," Hadrian says, pointing at me.

"Go fuck yourself," I snarl.

"Umbriel," Thalia snaps, her top lip curls, and I swear she'll seal his hand in the other side if he doesn't watch it. "All yours..." she snarls and gestures at the tear.

He swallows, looking less confident and holds his hand out.

Thalia cocks her eyebrow at him. "I thought you could see the cut?" She smirks, and Hadrian blushes. His friends laugh at him, and I'm instantly less pissy.

She sighs and moves his hand to the right position. "Feel the frayed edge?" she asks.

His brow furrows in concentration, a line of sweat appearing. "THERE!" he says, and his hand vanishes.

"Whoa," I breathe, along with half the other students in here.

He goes grey, yanks his hand out and promptly spews at Thalia's feet. She makes the reverse swiping shape with her hand, and I assume the cut seals back up.

She glances down, her nose wrinkling. "I forgot how pathetic first-years were. Clean that up, Umbriel. Right, everyone else, begin."

I take back everything I said about Silvana. She might be small, but she's a beast with the fabric. She slices first—as a Doorstop it's a lot easier for her. I, however, am not so good. She guides my hands to the frayed fabric, but it takes me three attempts and an extra ribbon of magic from the classroom walls before I can slide my hand through.

I don't puke, but I do get a nosebleed.

Despite the blood pissing down my face, all I can taste is sour milk, stale cigarettes and a hint of old meat. No wonder Hadrian puked. I have to rapidly swallow down both blood and bile to stop myself doing the same.

This could all be over. The campus. That fucking incessant voice. It hasn't left me. Not since I made the deal. It's in the windows and walls. It follows me to class and into my dreams. It whispers in the wind and poisons my thoughts.

It wants Lucy.

And I don't want to give her to it.

"You okay?" Silvana says.

"Yeah. Sorry. Just clearing my head."

The class moves on. By lunch, all of us are sweating and exhausted. Most of us are covered in bruises. One student lost a nail—an ashspawn bit it and yanked it out of the nail bed.

Thalia strides up to Aurelia. "Well done, I was extremely impressed with you. Keep this up, and that favour will be yours, without a doubt."

Aurelia beams.

I seethe.

With less than eight months left, I need to double down and increase the number of extra training sessions I'm doing, or I can kiss my soul goodbye.

24

LUCY

We're in the library tonight. Midnight is practicing Veil stitching and cutting.

The library isn't the best location, but I have a ton of contracts to mark, and I needed some resources from the vaults. So here we are.

"No," I say and slide in behind her.

She huffs in my ear as I move my arms over hers, repositioning her hands into the correct position for a more effective long stitch.

"There," I say, lacing my fingers through hers. My lips are close to her neck, my breath trickling down into her collar.

"It's intensely difficult to focus when you are this close to me."

"I'm pretty sure I could be further away and directing you, but where's the fun in that?"

"What a deviant professor you are."

She spins suddenly and plunges her lips on mine. We shouldn't, it's dangerous and risky, even at this time of night, but she smells like hot skin and citrus, and I drink in every ounce of her lips.

Her tongue slides into mine, her hands between my legs as she caresses my crotch.

I moan into her kiss.

Thud.

I freeze. Midnight leaps off me, shoving me behind her as she puts her arm out to guard me.

"Oh gods, Professor Malifax, I didn't see you there," I say, pushing past Midnight to greet the Severance Rite professor in the vain hope he didn't see me with my tongue down Midnight's throat.

"Mmm, that much is evident. Pretty hard to see anything when you're tonguing a student."

Oh. Shit. He very much saw then. Midnight swallows audibly. This time, I push her behind me.

"It's not what you think," I say.

He laughs, it's sinister and cold and I know he's not buying our bullshit.

"I think you have some explaining to do, don't you?"

He lunges for me. What the fuck?

His fingers grip my arm so hard it hurts. "You're coming with me."

"Get off her. What the fuck is wrong with you? Stop manhandling her," Midnight says.

He draws a blade on Midnight, halting her as he points it right over her heart.

"One more move."

"What the fuck is going on?" I say, trying to pry his fingers off me.

When it doesn't work, I twist and drive my knee into his balls. "I said, get off me."

He drops the blade and groans as he buckles forward gripping his crotch.

"Who the hell are you?" I snap.

But he's already recovered. He lurches for his blade and swings up. I duck out of the way and scream.

"You're coming with me."

"The fuck I am," I bark and back up.

He charges at me with the blade, and I scream and run. Midnight sprints after us, smashing an emergency alarm on the library wall as she darts out the door on our heels. I run hard and fast. But the glint of the blade is always in my periphery, and he gains on me.

"KEEP GOING," Midnight bellows after me as the library sirens scream through the night.

I break out into the courtyard moat area and run hard for the drawbridge. But it's shut.

Who the fuck shut it? In forty years, I've never known the drawbridge to be closed.

How the hell am I getting out of here?

He careens into me, and I go flying, almost falling into the moat. I roll and save myself as Midnight lands a blow to the back of his head, making the blade sail out of his hands.

I throw myself at it, grasp the hilt and yank it out of his reach milliseconds before he gets to it.

"You're fucked now," Midnight says, pulling her bone-like scythe out of her hip holster. The pair of us circle him.

"You better start talking," I snap.

"The Societas will not stop hunting you. You will be taken, and she will be resurrected."

Thalia comes surging out of the Great Library. "What the hell is going on?"

Malifax freezes, his skin grows clammy.

"I may not have secured you, but the Societas will resurrect her. Omnia mors aequat."

The threat is punctuated with a crack, and then yellow foam fills his mouth, his eyes roll back and he drops to the ground like a stone.

"What the fuck?" I say.

Thalia jogs over, takes one look at Malifax and shouts, "Medic!"

Verrill's head pokes out of the library door and ducks straight back in.

But I can't get over Malifax. He was all out for attack and then he just stopped. It was like something terrified him.

"Are you okay?" Thalia says and wraps her arms around me.

"I think so," I say.

"Go, get back to House Inferos. Midnight, will you escort her?"

"Of course, Professor," she says and gestures for me to follow her.

Father runs into the courtyard as Midnight guides me out. He slows to a walk and then halts to stare at us with narrowed eyes as we pass by.

My throat thickens. What is he thinking? What does he know? Midnight keeps her distance and her hands to herself. Neither of us says anything. But Father follows us at a distance.

As Midnight reaches for Inferos's door handle, her fingers trembling, my father's cold eyes are still on us.

It doesn't open. She growls at it, shaking the handle and slams her fist against the wood.

"Gently," I say. And twist the handle.

She pouts at me, as if opening a door isn't the easiest thing in the world.

"I swear the campus hates me," she says.

"Of course it doesn't."

I glance at Father as we enter House Inferos.

Midnight's mouth thins as I close the door behind us.

"This isn't great," I say.

"No. The Societas had a mole, and they're after you..."

25

LUCY

Midnight closes the door and patrols around the penthouse, checking the windows and the front door about fourteen times before she's satisfied.

She double takes at what I assume is my apartment's moth room. Her face scrunches and tips this way and that. Her mouth forms around the words *what the fuck.*

"I swear they weren't here when—"

"When you broke into my apartment to watch me masturbate?" I say, folding my arms and leaning a hip against my kitchen counter. Probably not the most appropriate time to joke, but I need to lighten the mood after what happened tonight.

Her jaw hangs loose. "I... umm. It was just a little light stalking..."

"They're my..." I start, but Mortem strolls into view and distracts me.

"They're her pets," he says.

"You call those 'pets?'" Midnight answers.

"I mean, no... *I* don't."

Mortem meows. "They're pets, like me."

He's solid enough that I lean down and give him scratches under his chin. "Actually, I believe you foisted yourself on me."

He bites my hand and then rubs his head into my shins, asking for more scratches. "I'm the best part of your day and you know it."

Midnight throws the moth room several surreptitious glances. "But they're..." Her face scrunches so tight I don't know how she can see out her eyelids.

"Dead?" I ask, the hint of a laughter twitch tickling my lips.

"Yeah," she says almost whiny. "Why would you want dead moths?"

"Well, they're reanimated so they're not, like, dead-dead."

She glares at me.

"Okay, they're dead. But at least they won't break my heart by dying."

"That is... a bizarre thought process. Whoa," she says as one of them flies at her head and she attempts to swat it out the way.

"Careful. They're extremely delicate. Stay still, I bet it will—"

It does.

It lands on her forehead.

She goes rigid and this time I do laugh. She looks extremely, *intensely* uncomfortable.

"I would like you to get it off me," she says very calmly but with absolute authority.

I do not, in fact, get it off her.

I burst out laughing.

"Now. Please," she says, more insistent and an octave or

two too high. But I'm gone. The more she protests, the more I buckle.

"It's just a moth," I say through breathy hysteria.

"I have a strong aversion to them, given what the ashkissing entropy moths do to me."

"These aren't entropy moths. They're just normal ones."

It moves, dancing across her brow. She flinches and makes a high-pitched sound.

I can't.

I collapse to my knees, holding my belly.

"This. Is. Not. Fucking. Funny," she growls.

Which, of course, makes me howl so hard tears leak out my eyes.

I can barely see when another moth, my most delicate of all—its wings frayed like the skeleton of an autumn leaf, flutters out the door.

"Oh, fuck no," she says and starts to stagger away. But Mortem drops to the floor, his butt wiggling. Then he flies at an unimaginable speed down the apartment and leaps up to catch it.

"Mortem," I bellow, but he ignores me, chasing the moth, hissing and swiping at it. The moth and the cat skitter in and out of rooms until I'm convinced the moth is winding Mortem up as much as Mortem is trying to catch it.

The moth on Midnight's forehead finally flutters away, and she visibly sags. There's even a hint of sweat on her skin.

"I can't believe a big, strong reaper like you, who just chased after and beat the crap out of a Societas member, is scared of a little moth."

She strides down the corridor towards me. "One, I am

not scared. I just don't like them, there's a difference. And two, they're hideous little creatures."

I raise an eyebrow. "The uneducated see horror where the educated see beauty."

She slides to a halt in front of me. "So educate me, Professor." Her words dip, that sultry tone I've heard her use too many times. We said we wouldn't sleep with each other anymore. That we'd keep things professional while she was at the academy, especially if I was going to be training her.

It's been... excruciating.

Every time she strides into a room, my pussy clenches. Every time she beams when she successfully executes another form of magic, every time she looks at me with those piercing blue eyes, another piece of my self-control chips away.

She is temptation incarnate, and I have to be honest, I am struggling to keep my hands off her. Especially when she indulges me with these flights of intellectual fancy.

"Well, did you know that many of the moth species don't eat when they become adults and leave their pupa?"

She squints at me. "What? How do they survive?"

"That's the point. They don't. Much of their life is as eggs, larva, pupa and then the ones that don't eat only live for five to twelve days as adult moths."

"Then why not feed and live longer?"

"Because the energetic cost of building and carrying that digestive system is expensive. Plus, they'd have to spend a good portion of the little time they have as moths eating. Food is expensive. So when they're in the pupa, they sacrifice digestion, they don't even have mouths. The result is less time as moths. But they can focus on their sole purpose: mating and laying eggs."

"Not a bad life, getting off for your entire adulthood."

"Midnight," I scold.

"What?" She shrugs. "Okay, fine, that is quite interesting. But I don't think that's what we should be talking about. How did Malifax keep his association quiet for so long?"

The moth that landed on her head flutters in my direction. I hold my hand out. Its faded wings are so worn I can see through them. He won't last much longer, they eventually crumble to dust unless you constantly reanimate them. He's a delicate boy as he drifts down and lands on my finger. I bring it close, tilting it this way and that.

"They fascinate me," I say and wave my hand, encouraging him to fly back to the room where his food is.

Midnight strides towards me, cupping my chin and turning my face to hers. "This is important. Put the moths aside. Why is the Societas interested in you?"

"Who knows. Father thinks it's to get at him. He was the one who disposed of Architecti, after all. Maybe the Societas were after the old Head of House Inferos."

She shakes her head. "You've been the Head for a couple of months now. Malifax knew that along with the fact Dregan was gone. Try again," she says, folding her arms.

"Then maybe he was after my father," I say, trying not to get huffy.

"Then why wouldn't he go straight for him? Malifax knows the campus, he would have been well aware of where your father was and where he could find him. No. I think this is to do with you."

I purse my lips. I'd already come to the same conclusion. I just didn't want to admit it, because saying it out loud makes it real. Just like I've already concluded it must be something to do with the runes on my neck. There's nothing else unique about me.

"You know, don't you?" she says, narrowing her gaze at me.

"No. I suspect though…"

She paces the apartment. "Why you? What could they want with you?"

Her brain whirs loud as she strides up and down, up and down. I wait, knowing she'll come to the same conclusion I did. Her body moves bold and confident as she thinks. It makes the question I have to ask her easier.

She halts suddenly. "The runes?"

I nod.

"Then we have to make them appear again…" she says, her features brightening, knowing we can take action in this mystery.

"Yes… But… I've been thinking about that, and the fact we've only seen them twice."

"That's right, we saw them—Oh," she stops mid-sentence, her eyes widening as once again, she comes to the same conclusion I did.

"Oh dear, Professor," she growls.

My skin heats. I've been avoiding this conversation, knowing the risks we'd have to take. And the fact I am barely clinging to my self-control around her as it is.

"That is a real shame… isn't it…" Her expression glimmers.

I shake my head, trying and failing to suppress the smile.

"You're incorrigible."

"Says the woman needing an orgasm." She saunters over, nudges my thighs apart, sliding hers between mine and pressing up against my pussy.

My breath hitches.

"I think, Professor, that you want... correction. I think you *need* me to spread your legs. Bend you over that sofa and finish what I started in the library."

I whimper because that's exactly what I want and need. Her fingers come to my belt, which she unbuckles, followed by my trousers.

She slides to her knees and pulls my shoes, socks, trousers and underwear off.

And I don't stop her.

Because it's not just the runes I want, it's her.

She starts on my top and bra until I'm fully naked while she's still fully clothed.

There is something about the dominance of that. The fact I'm utterly bare, vulnerable, desperate.

And she is wholly in control.

She pushes between my legs, spreading my naked pussy with the force of her hips. A cold rush of air caresses my cunt as she lifts me by the thighs and places me on the kitchen counter.

She keeps her eyes on me but grips my knees and shoves them further apart.

Her eyes never leave mine, but they want to. I know it by the way she bites her bottom lip that she's clinging to my gaze instead of raking them down my body.

"Midnight, we shouldn't."

She grins.

"Midnight..." I whine.

"Oh, I heard you. But there's a difference between shouldn't and can't. And..." she kneels between my legs. My pussy is spread so far open, my lips are parted. I squirm at being so on display—the vulgarity of it. But fuck, her eyes are hungry, obsessed. Lust pools in her gaze as she takes in every inch of me. It shifts the tension clinging to my insides. Dropping it into a warm coil in my belly. I like making her look like she's starved.

I push my hips out a little further. Her nostrils flare and she turns away, leaning her face into my thigh.

"Tell me no," she says against my flesh.

"No," I hum, unable to keep the brattish giggle from my voice.

"Lucy," Midnight hisses my name like a curse. "What's your safe word?"

"Do I need one?"

"Maybe not tonight, but you will at some point."

I sigh. "Tonight... listen... this... we've been here. It's too risky. Yes, I want the runes... hell... I want you. But we can't do this. So it's a one-time thing. If we were to get caught... you saw what almost happened tonight. You'd get kicked out. I'd lose my job."

"That all sounds great. But we're locked in your apartment, and I want your safe word."

I keep my mouth shut. But the word bubbles on my tongue, desperate for me to let it out.

"Now, Lucy." It's a demand. Fuck, it makes me melt, makes my pussy glisten inches from her mouth. I want this. I fucking need it. My clit is still swollen and aching to be touched.

"Satan," I whisper, cursing my traitorous mouth.

Her brow cinches in question.

"He was a demon from a distant realm. He, well, the realm itself could be a myth for all I know. But he was a fallen angel, like Architecti. It just... it was the first thing that came to mind."

"Fine. Satan it is."

She leans into my pussy, a moan slipping from her lips. "Wait," I say.

She lurches back. "Such a cunt tease."

"I'm just kidding. I wanted to see you flinch."

She sighs, "You little brat."

She hoists me up by my arse and flings me over her shoulder, landing a healthy slap on my cheek. I squeal as she carries me like that and throws me on the sofa.

"Turn around and hold onto the top of the sofa," Midnight says.

"Wh-What?" I stumble over my words, a flutter of something adrenaline-like twisting through my belly.

"Do it." Midnight's eyes darken, and my body moves of its own accord. I place my hands on the back of the sofa, my knees making depressions in the cushions.

Midnight stalks back to my pile of clothes and the... oh my gods. She picks up my belt and wraps it around her fist.

"What are you doing?" I ask. I go to move my hands, but her eyes snap to my grip.

"Did I tell you to move?" Her voice deepens, becoming all chesty and authoritative. My pussy clenches knowing what's coming, fearing and craving it in equal measure. My nipples rub against the sofa fabric and stiffen in antic-ipation.

"Bend over," she demands.

"Pardon?"

"Don't make me ask you again. This can go one of two ways..."

I bend over.

"Further," she says, flexing the leather belt. The crackle and creak of leather sends a shiver through my body and a line of goosebumps up my arm. And yet, between my thighs, it's pure pulsing heat.

"See, I think you've been harbouring a secret from me... haven't you?"

Have I? I don't know what it is, but I love her tone and the tension cording her neck, so I play along.

"Mmmhmm," I say and flutter my lashes at her.

"See, I think you've been hiding the fact you're a dirty little sub from Daddy."

Oh, my gods. My knuckles whiten on the sofa, my heart rate skyrockets.

"Midnight," I say, breathy. I haven't had a dom in so long, and she is everything I could want in one. More so.

Her hand comes down on my arse. The sting pulses over my cheek, radiating in waves of hot tingles.

The whimpered sound that slips from my lips stops her in her tracks; her gaze turns molten. Desire and lust mingle in the heat between us.

"I've never had a daddy," I manage.

She rounds the sofa and tips my chin up. "Oh, baby girl. I'm about to rock your world. Remember, you are in control. You can stop me. Just say your safe word. Okay?"

I nod.

"Say it for me now," she says.

"Satan."

"Louder." She lets go of my chin.

"Satan," I cry out.

I don't feel her move, but the leather creaks once more and then it comes crashing down on my ass. I shunt forward, toppling into the back of the sofa and losing my footing.

I gasp and let go to clutch my ass. But Midnight barks at me.

"Hands on the sofa."

I do as I'm told, the blistering sting burning my skin.

But she rubs her palm over it, and it melts, dissolving into something warmer and deeper.

"Slide your fingers to your entrance and touch yourself."

I crane my head to look at her. "You want me to touch myself in front of you?"

"I watched you masturbate in the shower, now is not the time to be shy."

My neck flares hot, but I do as I'm told and slide my fingers to my core. Predictably, I'm soaked.

Gods.

"Now your clit. I want you to bring yourself to the edge."

I hesitate, but when I realise she's deadly serious, I slowly rub at my clit. It swells instantly at my touch.

The belt comes down on my other cheek. I gasp but it quickly dissolves into a moan as my fingers drag bolts of pleasure from my clit, and she eases the sting with her palm.

Fuck me, the intensity sends my mind somewhere else. Somewhere that only touch and sensation and the throbbing between my legs matters.

We repeat the cycle over and over. The stark difference of my soft fingers to the sharp sting of the belt is too much. My body is on fire, my nipples harden to painful points. Midnight's eyes drag the heat everywhere she stares.

She's still fully clothed, and I don't know whether I'm desperate for her to be naked or about to come over that fact.

"Stop," she barks.

"But I'm so close," I whine.

"Exactly."

What the hell? I want to throw something at her. I

genuinely consider lobbing a sofa cushion at her or using my safe word. But I'm not in physical pain. I'm safe. In control. I *could* say my safe word just to take myself to climax, but then this would be over. And I don't *hate* the orgasmic torture.

Her eyes narrow, her lip curls and it's the kind of expression that sends my stomach fluttering. Not with arousal, but this time with anxiety.

"Given the events of this evening, there's something we need to address. I asked you a question the day I came here. And you didn't answer it."

Oh, fuck. I shake my head. I can't go there. I just can't.

"Lucy..."

The belt comes down on my arse.

"Midnight," I plead.

"Do you need to say your safe word?"

"I..." I genuinely consider it.

"Tell me who hurt you and this stops. I need to know if they're connected with the break-in tonight."

I hang my head between my arms. The belt swings down across both my cheeks. I scream as the sting instantly welts the skin.

"Touch your clit," she demands.

"Oh, oh fuck," I moan as pleasure flows in rhythmic waves between my legs. Excitement coats my fingers as I push inside my entrance and pull them up to my clit, rubbing harder and faster than before.

The belt comes down again. My whole body is alive, screaming, singing. Goosebumps pimple my skin, and my pussy begs for release. Pulses of familiar electricity build up, every flick pushing me closer to the edge.

"I'm so close," I gasp.

"Stop," Midnight demands.

"Midnight," I scream, as my fingers fall away from my swollen pussy.

"Who hurt you? You're going to tell me, or we can keep doing this all night. We need to get to the bottom of this."

"You don't have to protect me, I'm not your responsibility."

"You don't get to decide what I do and don't protect. Now. Are you going to tell me who hurt you or do you want the belt?"

I whimper, my legs already shaking. But I turn my back to her and give her my arse.

Her teeth grind against each other, the leather crackles in her hand as she wraps the buckle in her palm and shortens the leather. I take a deep breath just as the band lashes down on me.

I scream, my skin heating, a line of sweat trickling down my spine. I can't do it. I wobble. My safe word perches on the edge of my tongue.

Midnight must be able to read my body as she draws near. The heat from her flows over me. Her hand hovers above my backside, scarcely a millimetre above my flesh and yet close enough that the heat of her palm soaks into my skin. She sinks against me and moves in circles, rubbing and smoothing the aching skin.

"Tell me, Lucy. Or give me your safe word."

Tears sting my lids. It's all too much. I don't want to tell her. If I tell her, I open the door to the shit in my life. It's not for her to deal with. Even Thalia doesn't really know.

If I keep it to myself, then it doesn't have to be true. I don't have to face what he's like. I can keep pretending that our relationship is fine. I won't lose him.

"Fingers. Clit. Take yourself right to the edge."

A cold rush of air washes over my back when she moves

away. My hand returns to my pussy, I'm dripping. Tears are rolling down my cheeks as I move over my clit, two fingers dipping in and out of my entrance, gathering up excitement and using it to ease the friction on my clit.

I jerk as my clit pulses hard. There's no way I'm holding out again, my whole body is taut.

"Lucy," Midnight growls my name.

"I'm going to..." I moan, my fingers moving faster.

The belt follows, so hard I break. A sob rips from my chest. My pussy tips, the rippling blister of the belt shoving me over the edge into an orgasm. Two words slip from my lips as I sag against the sofa.

"My father."

The belt clatters to the apartment floor, the metal buckle tinging against laminate flooring.

The ringing of release.

Of a confession forty years in the making.

The sound of a weight I didn't know I'd been carrying finally lifting.

26
MIDNIGHT

Lucy sags against her sofa, her body completely spent. But there, glistening on her neck, is the hint of the symbol we were hoping for.

I reach out and hesitate. Her skin shimmers.

"Wow," I breathe.

The symbol is there, but I can't quite make it out. It's too faint.

She rolls over, lying flat on the sofa. "What's wrong?"

"It's there, it's just so light it's hard to make it out. Look in the mirror."

She attempts to get up and stumbles, and I realise this is not what I'm supposed to be doing. I should be caring for her while she's in this state.

"Come here," I lift her into my arms and carry her to her bedroom where there's a full-length mirror.

"See," I say.

She frowns.

"Demon's sake, Lucy, it's right there."

Her face crumples. "There's nothing there."

I huff and place her down on the bed. "Get under the covers, I'll be back."

I fetch her some water and some scraps of paper, then I ferret around until I find a pencil. I return to Lucy and pull her chin around. "Fuck, it's gone," I groan.

"How inconvenient," she says, but her eyelashes flutter at me.

I set to sketching what I could see of the rune. I'm finishing the last bit when she snatches the drawing from me.

"Shit," she says and scrambles out of bed, jumping to the mirror and pulling at the skin. "Why can't I see it?" She claws at her neck.

I get off the bed and tug her hands away from her throat. "I told you, it's gone. I can't see it now either."

"You have to do it again."

I frown. "Do what again?"

"Whatever you did to make it appear. I need to see it."

The first two times, I made her come. This time, she made herself come with my help. I wonder if that's why it was fainter and didn't last as long.

"You sure about that? What I did was fuck you... all the way to an orgasm. This time you made yourself come... And you insisted it was a one-time thing."

"Oh, I see," she says.

I wink at her, knowing it will wind her up. "Hmm, so I couldn't possibly make you come again."

"That is bad news." She drops to her knees and crawls along the floor. Her breasts are round and full and swaying with her body as she crawls on her knees. It makes my mouth water.

"Gods dammit, Lucy... we need to talk. Not fuck."

"But, Daddy... I need another orgasm... please," she says as she halts at my boots.

I stare down at her naked flesh. She sucks in her bottom lip; my pussy aches with need. I've already lost.

But when she lowers herself to my boot and places a kiss on the toe, I snap. My boxers are soaking and my pussy is desperate for touch. I raise my foot, tucking it gently under her chin and push her onto her back.

Keeping my heel on her chest, I strip. Top first, sports bra, then I unbuckle my belt. I release the pressure on her sternum to remove my boots and trousers. Then I lay my body over hers, shift back until my cunt mounts her face and lower mine to her pussy.

She's swollen and sticky, her scent intoxicating, and I am gagging to taste her.

My tongue slips between her folds, and I lap up every exquisite drop of wetness. She tastes fucking divine, and I moan as I lick down her slit.

Her tongue finds my clit before her lips close over it and she sucks. I close my eyes and rock over her mouth, letting the sensation of her lapping wash waves of pleasure through my core.

She bucks underneath me, sensitive from her first orgasm, but I don't care, I want to drag another one from her.

I twist my arm over her thigh and slide a finger into her pussy. She's warm and so wet for me that I glide in and out, my tongue flicking at her apex.

She moans against my pussy, desperately hanging on to her orgasm as she builds me higher and higher.

But the closer she gets, the more she moans and the quicker I climb. Her pussy clamps around my finger, her hips tilt as she trembles and comes in my mouth.

Her sweet release sends me over the edge, my body stiffening as I fall apart on her face. I lay there, motionless, unable to move from the sensory overload until I remember why she wanted this.

I climb off and help her up and there, brandished on her neck, is the symbol, clearer and bolder than I've seen it before.

I guide her to the mirror but her face falls.

"You can't see it?" I ask.

She shakes her head, tears spilling down her cheeks. I scoop her up and carry her to the bed, resting myself against the headboard, sliding her between my thighs. I finish drawing the symbol and then hand her the paper.

"Thank you," she says.

I lean in, pressing my lips to hers. She freezes and then relaxes, moving her mouth against mine, slow and hungry.

I deepen the kiss, my hands caressing her head, gliding through her dark hair. The world shrinks to me and her, and the soft mattress beneath us. And it's the first time I think I may be in trouble.

I love the way her body feels under my fingers. The deep spicy smell of her perfume. It's addictive and moreish and I want to bite and lick my way over her skin until I'm sated.

She lays in my arms a while, both of us coming back to earth and I remember that awful confession.

"We need to talk," I say.

She goes rigid in my arms. But we have to discuss it.

"Your father..." I say and leave it hanging in the air. When she doesn't offer any information, I probe again. "What do you mean he is the one who hurt you?"

"It's complicated."

She tries to wriggle out of my grasp, but I pull her closer

against me, enveloping her with my arms and tugging a blanket around us.

"Uncomplicate it, Lucy."

She resists, fidgeting against me until she realises I'm not letting her go. She huffs and settles against my chest.

Her hair tickles my chin, but I drink in the scent of crackling fire, autumn flowers and warm summer wind. I have to suppress the urge to inhale her deeply. To bottle her scent and keep it forever.

For the first time, I find myself wishing I could keep *her* forever.

"I told you, I'm trapped in a contract. He made it when I was born. I don't know the full story, only that there was a contract which saved my life and that the contract has consequences."

I run my fingers up and down her arms. "Explain the consequences."

She turns her face into my chest and huffs. "Mostly that I can't move against him. I can't fight back. If I attack him, or even sometimes just threaten him, the results aren't good for me."

"Your eye and knee at the Severance Rite?" I ask.

She nods. "I get nosebleeds, my bones break. Bloodshot eyes. I've thrown up blood when things get really bad. I imagine that if I kept going, I'd end up dead."

"What kind of sick, fucked-up contract is that?"

"One that means he always wins. It's why I need your help."

"He needs to win against his child?"

"I think it's more that he needs to win full stop. He's manipulative and sometimes aggressive, but there are good parts to him. He's never actually hit me. My injuries are self-induced when I try to fight back. Besides, he saved the city, didn't he…"

"Why does that sound like a question?"

She presses her lips shut, as if sealing in a secret.

"I'm failing to see anything good about that man," I say.

She sighs, twining her fingers into mine. "When I was little, every full moon, he'd take me down into the basement, and we'd watch the Veil and make up stories about the shades that would drift in and out. He used to make me draw my nightmares out when I was scared, and then we'd burn them together in the cloisters."

"And what about now? He hasn't stopped being your father just because you're an adult."

She releases my hand and tiptoes her fingers over my skin. "Things are harder now. I fight back more. But…"

"But that means you get injured more?" I ask.

She nods.

"I see."

"You going to tell me why you want that Demonic Favour?"

I shift, untangling us. It was easier making her talk than having to admit what happened to me.

"There's not a lot to tell, really. I thought she was the love of my life. She got sick. I sold my soul to save her."

She gets out of bed and roots in a couple of still unemptied boxes until she finds a set of pyjamas.

"Then why aren't you with her now?" she asks, sitting back on the bed and picking up the drawing of her symbol.

"She broke us," I say. But Lucy's frowning at the image, turning it this way and that.

"What is it?" I ask.

She shakes her head, staring at it. "It just can't be."

"Can't be what?"

"They're contract runes."

I frown at her. "Why do you have contract runes on your body?"

"I wouldn't. Not unless…"

"They're your own contract runes?"

Her head snaps up. "I think this is how we break my contract."

27

ARCHITECTI

It's our thirteenth birthday. A special celebration in any angel's life. When we're born, a moth egg is placed against our mouths, and our first breath gives life to it. The breath reshapes its genetic structure and bonds the egg to our soul, forming the source of our magic.

While we're babies, our parents nurture the eggs, but as soon as we're walking, we're taught to care for and nurture these eggs. It was a challenging task for Interitus.

It's in her nature to break things, not care for them. This, it seems, was the one exception she made. Probably because she understood that if it died, so would her magic.

The eggs turn to little larvae by the time we're five and spend the next few years growing and developing until our twelfth birthday—the last day we spend with them as they cocoon themselves in a pupa, sealing them, and our magic away for an entire year.

Penance, the elder angels call it. The year when we discover what it's like to be mortal—of a sort, anyway. When we understand what it's like to be powerless.

Interitus did not like it.

Not one bit.

She changed. The visceral anger she carried beneath her skin mutated. Grew like a tumour, thick and fibrous until she became nasty.

Bitter.

Feral.

I found the first dead rabbit three weeks into our powerless year.

It didn't get better.

I don't want to make out like Interitus is all bad. She isn't. The morning of our Emergence Ceremony, she trotted into my bedroom with a replica pupa. She handed it to me, a smile wide on her lips.

"It's for you," she says.

I take it from her, and I'm amazed at the delicacy of the stone. It's been carved and chipped out of some kind of crystal.

"I didn't think you liked art."

She shrugs. "I got to break pieces of the stone off to make the shapes. That felt satisfying, so I kept going. And I figured it looked more like your pupa than mine. I tried obsidian for mine but it didn't work out as well, so I threw it against a wall."

I clutch the carving to my chest, understanding how, for once, she created something through destruction.

"Do you see, sister?" she says.

"See what?"

Her wings ruffle, the tips have grown darker this year. The ends are almost black as night now.

"That even though you were born to destroy, you are still powerful beyond measure? You can still create."

Her eyes narrow at me. "Not all power comes from creation, *Architecti*." She spits my name.

I've annoyed her.

I should have been more careful with how I spoke, the words I used.

My eyes sting with tears. I wanted to be nice, to make her feel good.

"I'm sorry, I didn't mean it to come out like that. I think what you've made is wonderful, and I adore it."

But I can tell it's too late. She's shut down, the coldness of her eyes hardening as she retreats out of the room.

My heart sinks, a coiling low in my belly that tells me she will punish me for my mistake.

Dozens of angels congregate in the great hall to witness the emergence of our moths. Our pupae sit on a plinth in the middle of the room. We stand a few feet away. It's been a year since I held my power. Since I felt the thrum and light of magical energy. My fingertips ache to hold the swelling rise of power again.

The pupae look flimsy, as they should. At last, the silk has worn thin enough our moths can emerge. My stomach won't stop somersaulting with excitement.

Murmurs ripple around the room, poorly disguised whispers that compare our pupae, that note the differences. I hate that they only use kind words to describe mine and ugly words to describe hers.

I stand next to her and slip my hand into hers. "Don't listen to them," I whisper.

But she grips my hand, squeezing harder and harder until my knuckles grind against each other, and I have to bite down a yelp and yank my hand away.

"That's how it feels," she says.

"How what feels?" I cradle my bruised fingers.

"Them. Their words. It grinds me down. Wears me thin. They don't want me here. It doesn't matter what lies you try and whisper into existence. I know it's true."

I'm about to answer, but the high elder angel steps in front of our pupae.

"Welcome, angels, to another magnificent Emergence. This rite is significant in every angel's life. For a year we are stripped bare, cut off from our divine right to celestial magic."

The angels clap, only it's a fluttering of wings rather than slap of hands. It's a light ruffling sort of sound that feels like bubbles and sunshine.

"The pupa does not falter, it does not yield to will nor pride. It shapes only what was always there—hidden, waiting, growing."

My skin heats with excitement and my wings bristle up and down when I can't contain my energy.

There's a soft crackle, like the breaking of an egg. The elder stops speaking and turns to the pupa, a smile of delight breaking across his expression.

"So it begins."

Our pupae move, their surfaces undulating and pulsing as the moths try to wriggle their way out.

Mine glows from within, a sun-like orb forming at the peak. As the light blooms so too does the heat in my belly. Magic thrums as my moth emerges.

Interitus's pupa cracks and crinkles, like the crunch of feet on gravel. Pieces of the cocoon flake and flutter to the floor. Her fists ball and flex by her sides. She's as keen to get her magic as I am.

Both our moth casings split. Wings protrude. We turn to each other. Both holding distinct expressions.

Mine bold and rounded with joy. Hers narrowed and darkened with chaos.

My moth pokes its head out, wriggling and pushing until finally she frees herself, and the crowd gasps as her body unfurls.

She is glorious.

Infinite.

Radiant.

I'm hit with wave after wave of magic flowing into me. The more her wings uncurl, the more the magic flows until I buckle under the weight of it. It fills my body until it's all that I can see and breathe and feel.

It tingles through to my toes and right to the tips of my wing feathers.

Finally, my moth flutters off the plinth and flaps her way across the room to me.

Her wings are magnificent. They shimmer like woven constellations. Her body is delicate like spider thread glistening with dew. When she reaches me, the elder kneels at my feet and proclaims:

"The Crowned Moth. The bearer of infinite threads. For one hundred millennia, we have not seen such a powerful moth. She has returned to us."

She perches on my shoulder and the rest of the angels kneel before me. I don't understand what's happening.

Interitus's moth snaps her pupa in two. The shell clattering to the plinth. All eyes fall to the dark little creature.

Its wings are not made of starlight like my moth's are. They're serrated and sharp like shards of obsidian. It does not flutter to Interitus, it stalks and skitters and hunts its way across the room until it lands proud on her equally proud shoulder.

The elder angel's eyes widen. But it is another angel that whispers its name.

"The Severed Moth, bearer of finality's end." The speaker's voice is strained. I can't find her in the crowd, but it doesn't matter because a cacophony erupts.

"What does this mean?" one angel shouts.

"Are we doomed?" another screams.

"Enough," the elder knelt below me says. "We must consult with the celestial table."

Interitus strides out of the hall, a path forming either side of her as the angels move away.

"Wait," I say to the elder.

He pauses, rounding on me.

"What aren't you saying?" I ask.

His eyes draw down, a softness that makes my gums itch.

"Angels aren't meant to be twins," he says.

"Why not."

His lips draw thin and he presses them together as if he's trying to hold the truth in.

"Tell me."

"Our magic is powerful. But it is supposed to be contained inside one vessel. Not split between twins."

"Why not?"

"Because it doesn't always split evenly."

I frown, scratch my temple. "You mean like fallen angels?"

He nods. "Sometimes one angel goes bad."

He leaves me standing there with my moth fluttering above my head. As the hall clears, a thread coalesces in my chest. It bears the markers of the same broken little shard I kept from that castle I built as a child. Frayed and sharp-edged. Tainted. Ominous.

I don't understand. He didn't say Interitus was bad. Did he? I feel like that's what he meant. That Interitus is bad. But she isn't. She's my sister. And I love her.

This isn't right.

This feels all wrong.

This is going to end badly.

Very, very badly.

28

LUCY

One Hundred And Fifty-Two Days To Go

The high of discovering the rune is celestial dampens as nothing else surfaces and the weeks blur into months. The academic year drains faster than I'd like to admit. Not least because Midnight's clock has become my own.

My deal with her to help me break my contract won't supersede hers with my father—his came first. So no matter what, if he reaps her, we're both screwed.

There haven't been any more Societas breaches on campus since Malifax ended himself. And the Veil tears have slowed too, though not ceased. Father concluded Malifax had been causing a good portion of them, at least the ones where they appeared to have been cut rather than bulged and frayed naturally.

Father added more security guards to protect the students—and me—but the way they loiter both around campus and House Inferos has further added to the tension on site. It seems to leak from the walls like sweat.

Students hurry and skitter across campus rather than meandering and indulging in academic chat.

It has also made studying with Midnight difficult. Security doesn't give a toss why you're out late. They want you indoors in safety, and they're happy to tell Chancellor Arcadius about anyone who disagrees.

"Good afternoon, Professor Corvine," Thalia's chirpy voice says as I stroll towards House Inferos.

Aurelia is with her. My eyes narrow as I study the pair, they're awfully friendly. Midnight won't like that, and I can't say I'm a fan. Aurelia seems to sense she isn't wanted and makes her excuses and heads inside House Inferos.

I give Thalia a hug. "For how dire things are on campus, that is a very perky attitude."

"Oh, I don't know. I feel like things are going my way at the moment. Got a few projects in the works I'm rather excited about."

"Well, I'm glad someone is." I smile and glance at House Inferos wondering if her mood is anything to do with Aurelia.

"You seem less perky," she says.

I weigh up telling her. She's my closest friend here, a mentor and someone who propelled my academic career. But things are odd at the moment. While there haven't been any further break-ins, it does call into question who you can trust.

"Where do you sit with the Societas?" I ask, amazed that the words slip out.

She bristles, her eyebrows shooting up.

"Is that really what you're asking?" she says, pulling me into a section of tree cover between House Inferos and the Restricted Records building.

"I'm aware that we shouldn't really discuss it, given the

campus has taken the stance of no on the resurrection. But intellectually, I wondered where you sit."

She pinches her mouth and then nods. "I am ambivalent, truth be told. I think very few things that are black and white. The resurrection included."

It's a non-answer, but I suppose I didn't expect anything else. As staff, we're not really allowed to have public opinions. I guess I expected her to be honest with me.

"Have a lovely afternoon," I say and give her a weak smile.

"Fine. Wait," she says.

I halt.

"I'm sixty-forty."

"Against?"

She doesn't answer. I turn to face her. "Sixty-forty *for*?" I raise an eyebrow at her as she nods, a hint of pink crawling up her throat.

"I suspect that it may unlock new magics for us. I certainly feel like it would for me. I think our hierarchy, both demonically and within the institution, is far too male. Is Architecti a chaos agent? Yes, but she's also female. Call me a misandrist if you will, but I rather think a female leader might do some good for once."

This was more like the answer I was looking for. I dig in my bag and pull out the ragged paper Midnight drew the symbol from my neck on. It's frayed and crinkled where I've kept it on my person, shoved in pockets and bags ever since. I hand it to her.

"What's this?" she says, turning it this way and that.

"A contract rune."

"Well, I gathered that, but it doesn't look like any I've read before."

"No, nor me. I was headed to the Restricted Records building as there are some texts I want to compare it to. So far, I've been unable to match the linguistic shapes to any necro language we're aware of, let alone translate it."

"Where did you get it?"

I take a deep breath. Once I tell her this, there's no going back. "It was on my body."

Her eyes widen; she scans the symbol again. "Your contract..." she whispers. "My gods, Lucy. Tell me you've translated it."

I shake my head. "It's incomplete. I thought I'd be able to translate it with what I had, but it seems I've failed."

"Then make it appear again. Isn't this everything you've ever wanted?"

"It is. But getting the symbols to appear is complicated."

And by complicated, I mean lethal to my tenure and Midnight's Demonic Favour if we were caught.

In the evenings, I help Midnight consolidate the classes she took in the day. I've been trying to moderate how hard we work, but she keeps pushing until she has a nosebleed or passes out.

The level of determination is admirable, if a little extreme. But the real issue is that every time we train, it's excruciating for both of us. I have to position her body, help shape her hands. We're constantly in each other's personal space, our lips and mouths millimetres from each other. Her scent, vetiver and grapefruit, is intoxicating. It worms into my nose and makes my body ache to touch her. Each night, I have to fling myself away, only to suffer by watching her curl shadowy fingers of magic around her toned arms. That's without her thighs bulging in her jeans. I'm not sure if it's from all the work she does on her motorbike or the combat training she does for the reaping job, but what I do know is that I've worn a callus lump inside my cheek from biting it.

Thalia glances from me to the rune and then her expression glimmers. "By complicated you mean... it appeared after you—"

"Yes. Thank you, we don't need to go into the details."

She chuckles. "You're such a prude sometimes. I've heard of people eliciting other emotions to get the runes to appear, but quite often, a jolly good fucking does the trick nicely."

"Demon's sake, Thalia. Do you have to be so crass?"

She shrugs, laughter making her lips twitch. "It's only sex."

"*Anywaaay*, it's only ever happened with one partner and it's not really... well, that's complicated too."

"Is it, though? Don't you want answers?"

"I really do." I want to break the hold Ignatius has on me more than anything.

She squeezes my arm, encouraging me to go for it. But I push her off.

"They're mortal..."

That makes her stand tall. "Okay, that is more complicated."

"Exactly."

The sun dips low in the sky, though its attempts at showering the campus in warmth are limp at best. Winter is almost upon us. The buildings, usually covered in lush, green, creeping ivy are scant. While the ivy remains, it's sparser than in high summer. This deep into autumn, the campus buildings are covered in gnarled twigs and branches amongst the dark green leaves.

Thalia scratches at her scalp and draws my attention

back to her. "Is there any chance of you falling in love with them?"

I shake my head. "It's very unlikely. They are... younger than me. Our lives aren't exactly on the same path."

But something about the way the words come out seems... wrong? I'm not lying. At least, I don't think I am.

"If that's truly the case, and you're not in danger of falling for them, then your magic is safe. Invite Complicated over for dinner and ask them very nicely to get on their knees for you."

I give her a gentle slap on the arm, and she chuckles. "You're incorrigible."

"I like to think of it as chaotically cheeky. But I'll go with incorrigible."

"Thank you," I say.

She winks. "Sometimes a little chaos is worth the results. Just stay safe and be discreet."

As she walks off, I have to wonder whether she knows exactly who Complicated is.

29
MIDNIGHT

One Hundred Days To Go

I'm sat at the kitchen table in our House Inferos apartment when Lex strolls in. Her turquoise braids are now a deep purple, and she wears an orange jumper, tie-dye trousers and yellow platform trainers. She sticks her head over my shoulder looking at the scribbles I drew of Lucy's runes.

"Whatcha doing?" she asks, bouncing on her toes and biting into something that looks way too healthy to be edible.

"Trying to figure out what the hell this means," I say.

She scoffs, "You're not going to be able to read that."

"Oh?" I say and pluck her apple out of her hand.

"Well, it doesn't look like a demonic or necro language. So it's not something we study here."

Her face scrunches as she examines it, as if the fact she can't read it is deeply offensive.

"Evening, folks," Bastien says, dramatically shoving open the apartment door. Aurelia is in the corridor. I narrow my eyes at her as she strolls past. But Bastien slams the door shut cutting her off and strides into the kitchen to put bread in the toaster. I'm still livid she's in the same house as me, but grateful she found a room downstairs. Bastien has at least attempted to be civil to her, no doubt they were having a 'civil' conversation outside. Lex refused, claiming she was dead to her.

If only.

We haven't spoken more than five words to each other all year, and I don't plan to share another five. Especially since she's topping me in most classes and likes to smirk at me every time any exam results are released.

Lex interrupts my stream of Aurelia hate by plucking the paper from my hand and proceeding to pace up and down the kitchen.

Bastien's toast pops. I duck around his arms and pilfer a slice before he can take it.

"Do you mind?" he says, swatting at me.

"Not in the slightest." I butter it, add jam and take a giant bite when Lex stops suddenly, as if she were freeze-framed.

"What's wrong?" I ask.

She reanimates and sprints from the kitchen. I glance at Bastien and then we both head after her.

We find her in her room, pulling out boxes, and emptying stuff from her wardrobe.

"You going to explain?" I ask.

But she doesn't respond until she waves a very tatty-looking book at us.

"What is that?" Bastien says, his nose wrinkled at the sorry state of it.

She goes *off* at full speed as the pair of us try to keep up.

"I knew the shape of the rune, but it doesn't follow

any of the grammatical rules of any demonic or necro language. So, I was thinking in the kitchen, was it a forgotten language? Was it cypher encoded? But I knew there was something I was missing because it *was* familiar but wrong. Which got me thinking maybe it was a dialect or something we haven't been taught yet. But obviously it wasn't because I'm months ahead of our reading schedule, I would have known..." She takes an enormous dramatic breath and stares at us blankly, letting silence descend.

"Demon's sake Lex, stop being a vaj tease. What were you missing?" I ask.

She laughs. "That's the thing. I wasn't missing anything. I said it didn't look like demonic or necro language *because* it isn't."

"Then what language, pray tell, is it?" Bastien says.

"That's the weirdest part... It's celestial. Only nobody has seen or written in the celestial language in decades..."

If that's true, then why the hell does Lucy have angelic runes on her body?

"I have to go," I say, plucking the sketch out of her hands and leaving the apartment.

I stroll across campus, sticking to the shadows. While it's not against the rules to be out of doors after lights out, it is still frowned upon. Especially with the amount of security patrolling campus. But it's the campus itself that I'm more concerned about.

I've been dreaming of that voice. The whisper that's becoming more of a snarl.

A threat.

A warning.

I've still not reaped Lucy. It wants what it's owed. But we never agreed to a timeframe, so it can be as angry as it wants with me. I am not obliged to reap her on a set dead-line. No matter how much pressure it applies.

And it *is* applying pressure.

I scan the area ahead of me, it's deathly still and quiet. Security must be patrolling the northern end of campus, and yet a gnawing sensation trickles down my spine.

"Leave me alone," I breathe into the night.

Finis doesn't respond, but my skin prickles like I'm being watched. As if the buildings have eyes and ears and claws. I've noticed more and more doors stay locked to me, or they swing shut harder than necessary, slapping my behind as I walk through. My belongings go missing and then reappear. The worst of it though, are the memories it pulls from the sliver of soul it has. It projects Aurelia breaking my heart into mirrors and windows. It shows my parents' death over and over.

Some days I wonder whether Finis is haunting me or whether it's me and I'm losing the plot. Maybe I've pushed too hard, trained too long and the magic is cracking my mind. Or maybe it's that ever-fucking present ticking clock, the draining of time that's sending my body into a freefall of fight or flight, burning up my adrenal glands and screwing my mind for shits and giggles.

A ribbon of dark sinuous magic is following me—a perpetual reminder that I am indebted, and the campus hasn't forgotten. I shrug my jacket tighter around my shoulders, desperate to get out of the open and into a building.

I reach for the door handle but my hand slips through nothing.

"Finis," I growl.

The door creaks open, I step forward only to smack my head against the wood as it slams shut. I take a breath, call my magic ready to force shadowy threads into the lock, but the door swings all the way open.

As I step inside the clock tower, both my magic and the sinuous stalker dissipate. The creaking hinges echo out a huffy laughter that follows me all the way upstairs.

"Fucking campus."

I haven't told Lucy about the deal I made with Finis, and I don't intend to. If I can win the Demonic Favour and hold the campus off long enough, it will void our deal and Lucy stays safe. So why tell her when I am going to do everything I can to protect her? But the fact she bears a celestial rune? That I can tell her.

I knock on the loft door at 11 p.m. Lucy opens it, and I wave my latest exam results at her. "I came third. The training is working."

"Jolly good, because I brought you a load of homework."

My face falls as she thrusts an enormous pile of books into my hands.

"I've marked up the key sections, but if you can read them all then even better," she says.

"In all the free time I have, you mean? Between classes and reaping, and additional training and trying to maintain a friendship with my roommates, keeping my barely used bike running and helping research your contract rune?"

"Right, exactly. Between all those things." She smiles.

The clocktower loft is a large room, with the clock mechanism's cogs and dials and wires taking up much of a wall, though there are several windows level with it looking down on campus. Despite how large the clock is, the room is silent, too silent. I wonder if the building has swallowed time like it's swallowed the ticking of the hands.

"This is the only view of campus better than my penthouse," she says.

I approach the window and slide in next to her. The campus is stunning, even under darkness. Tonight is one of those rare evenings where the fog cloud has evaporated; the crisp bite of winter chewing up what heat is left and spitting out dotted skies and silvery moons instead of puffs of mist and dew.

As we stare out at our walled universe, our bodies press against each other. Her arms radiate heat, and gods, is it enticing. I ache to touch her. To slide my hand around her waist and pull her in. We both agreed that no matter how much we wanted it, being with each other was too dangerous for us both. But it makes every day agony. My body yearns for her in ways I can't explain. She's recoded my DNA, mangled my brain until I see her in every pull of magic, every cut of the Veil and every line in every book. She's all I think about and it's exhausting.

"Magnificent, isn't she?" Lucy says, craning her neck to see Finis. Even this high up, it's hard to see the top of the Tower.

"A feat of architectural genius."

She smiles softly at me and before I can stop myself, my fingers find their way across her neck, brushing rouge streaks of hair away from her skin.

The exhaustion takes hold of me, and I am weak, so I let my lips glide over her cheekbones, one then the other.

She keeps her hands to herself, trying to resist. But we are rarely alone, and it is inevitable that her body melts under my touch.

She whimpers softly.

I press a kiss to her neck. "I know we agreed not to. But

we're safe up here, and this is killing me, Lucy. Night after night. So close to you, and yet…"

She presses her palm to my jaw, brushing her lips over mine. "You have no idea how much I want to…"

She doesn't finish the sentence, and it slices another piece off my heart. I've never wanted a woman the way I ache for her.

"I have a gift for you," I say, hunting in my pockets for the sketch of her celestial rune.

"After." She claps her hands. "Training first. You had necromantic defence today, didn't you?"

"Yes, those teachers from Sangui City are savage. I thought the professors here were tough."

She grins like a sadist enjoying my academic pain and pulls out a piece of white chalk. I take it, kneel and draw a circle in the centre of the room, reciting what I know as I go.

"Professor Malrec said to draw a necro-protection circle. Then we cut a one-inch hole in the Veil and use a shade-summoning spell."

"Did you get to the memory orb attacks?" she asks.

"Sort of. I wasn't very good. Hadrian and his commies were disruptive, and they all took to it so easily that they overshadowed everyone else. But the rest of my grades this week made up for today's defence class."

She strides over to the pile of books, pulls one of the middle ones out and lays it on the floor in front of me.

"I am not an expert in memory magic. But once upon a time, I took a course as I wanted to examine the influence of certain memories on the effectiveness of contract clauses."

"I'm listening," I say, crossing my legs inside the chalk circle.

Mortem materialises in the middle of the room, plods

over and plonks himself down a foot away from the circle and passes out again.

"Useful cat," I mumble.

He raises his head, opens one eye to glare at me and falls asleep again. I push my sleeves up and call the campus's magic to me. I am getting better at controlling it; it's the one thing Finis doesn't fight me over. Despite the hauntings and perpetual reminders of our deal, I have a piece of the campus inside me just as much as it has a sliver of my soul inside it.

When I close my eyes and summon them, the shadowy ribbons fly directly to me. I wrap them around my hands and feel for a notch in the Veil.

"What memories were you taught to use from the shades?" she asks.

"Negative ones, since that's usually why they're stuck here."

"Standard memory magic 101. But, after my course, I experimented. Your mileage may vary, but I found the happy memories were far more potent. Try it and see."

"Happy memories as a weapon?" I ask, trying not to sound too indignant.

"Isn't happiness the greatest weapon of all?"

Her words take me by surprise. I falter and lose the Veil notch as I process what she's saying. How many people use happiness as a weapon? A threat? It's certainly used to push people to work harder.

If you study more, pass this exam, you'll achieve what you want. If you get this job, you'll be able to buy that house.

That's happiness, right?

I mean, I'm hellbent on breaking my contract because

that's going to make me happy. But have I weaponised my own happiness against myself?

I find another notch and slice a small hole in the Veil. Bending my hands around the campus's magic, I contort my fingers into the right shape and then whisper words Lex has made me repeat over and over to summon the shade.

A thin wisp appears like a waft of smoke, then it pools and blooms. I step out of the circle, allowing it to fill the space. It's strange looking through a face. Lucy stands the other side of the circle.

"Good, Midnight. Very good. Draw out the shade's memories, but where they told you to hunt for the sharp edges, I want you to look for the ruffles. Let the magic ease into the shade, don't be aggressive with it."

I follow her instruction, trying not to focus on the fact she's in her element as she teaches. The fact that her skin glows as she guides me and witnesses my development. I try not to notice the way she smiles when I command the ribbons of magic or the way her entire body beams as I make a perfect incision in the Veil.

The shade is fully formed now, she hovers before me, translucent. A curvaceous woman with a pleasant smile.

I extend the shadowy ribbons of campus magic towards her and she flinches as they drift through her ethereal form.

I close my eyes, let my body feel for the memories. One hits me immediately. It's much easier than hunting for the fractured edges. People suppress bad things, that's why it's so much harder to find those memories once they're dead. It's why those memories fragment. I like to think of it as our body's self-defence mechanism.

But this woman has hundreds of happy memories. I grab hold of three, lassoing the ribbons and coaxing them out.

"Does it remove them from her mind?" I ask Lucy.

She shakes her head. "No. The campus magic makes a replica before extraction. Now bring them out carefully. Keep your hands steady because you can do damage if you go too quickly."

I do as she says, and then spin my hands, swirling and looping them until the memory compresses into a bright white orb.

"Wow," I say, surprised that it is so much easier this way.

"I told you. Happy memories are always underestimated. Seal the orb so it becomes stable." I do. The shade smiles at me and drifts back towards the hole in the Veil. Her form dissolves back to smoke and drifts through the opening, which I stitch closed when she's gone.

I compress my hands over the orb the way a child would squish colourful dough. I push until sweat forms on my brow and my arms tremble from exertion. For once, my nose doesn't rupture. But I am spent by the time the orb takes on a glassy, solid feeling.

"Done," I pronounce and display it to her.

She beams at me and then her eyes glint. "Again."

Ah, fuck.

Lucy makes me repeat the process a dozen more times, until I am so fast that she actually loses count. What is both surprising and delightful is that I didn't get a nosebleed this evening.

"I'm getting stronger," I say. "Now for your gift..."

I pull out my copy of her rune. It's as crumpled as hers is. She frowns.

"I know what it is... I was in my apartment studying and Lex took the drawing from me. I didn't tell her anything, but she took it and compared it to some old book of hers and told me what it is..."

Her mouth falls open. "You're lying."

I shake my head. "All this time we've been looking in the wrong places... Looking for demonic languages."

Her eyes widen, and she takes the paper. "It's not demonic?"

"No. It's celestial. That's why you couldn't find it."

She looks up at me, her face growing pale. "Why the hell do I have celestial runes on my body?"

"*That* is the real question," I say.

She lights up the way the sun does every dawn, her features beaming with delight. "We have to celebrate," she says.

And then she leaps into my arms and plunges her mouth onto mine.

30
MIDNIGHT

I pry Lucy from me, untangling her arms and cupping her face. My heart hammers in my throat. My fingers pulse with the same need as my cunt.

I am done.

Done waiting.

Done hiding. Fuck the rules and the campus, I need her.

"You're going to meet me by the front gates, do you understand?" It's not a question and there is no compromise.

"I…"

"Lucy," I growl.

"Yes, Daddy."

Fuck me. My jaw clicks as I bite down and internalise a stream of obscene things I plan to do to her.

"Go. Now," I say. "We need to celebrate."

She sneaks out the front gate, I take one of the other exits, riding my bike around to the front and finding her hidden a few hundred metres up the campus driveway in the trailing branches of an evergreen tree.

I hand her a helmet. She peers at it, her face crumpling, but I give her the same expression I did in the clock tower.

"This is not up for discussion."

An hour later, I'm pulling my bike into the carriage parking lot of the new DnD club in town.

"These clubs are special," I say as I tuck our helmets onto a rack in the parking lot. "Everything that happens in here stays inside the club. We have a free pass. It's imbued with magic from the Whisper Club in Sangui City but modelled on the New Imperium sex clubs. In other words, we get to have fun in here without the worry of being caught, and even if we are, no one can say anything."

Her eyes burn at the news. Her tongue glides over her bottom lip, and I revel in the knowledge that tonight is going to be exceptional.

We enter the club, greeted by a door that, for want of a better explanation, feels you up like a dirty old man as you pass through it. The club smells a little like iron and a little of mint and lavender. Odd. But that's what happens when city magics are mixed.

It's dark, the walls covered in black-and-maroon velvet, with Chesterfield buttons in a uniform pattern on the bottom half of the walls.

The entryway opens into the main area of the club, where there's a bar and a dance floor. Tables are dotted around the space with dancers spiralling up and down poles entertaining or engaging guests. But what catches Lucy's attention are the windows running the perimeter of the room. As she peeks into each of them, examining the different types of kinks and sex play on offer, the skin of her neck and face heats.

She stops suddenly and turns to me. "I... want this... us.

But not here..." She points to her chest, hovering over her crystalline demon's heart.

I grit my teeth. "No emotions?"

She nods, not quite able to look at me. "If I fall for you... I lose everything. It's not just about my tenure. When a demon falls for a mortal, our magic transfers to them, and we're left totally vulnerable."

I knew this but hearing it doesn't hurt any less.

"I get it," I say, and this time, I can't bring myself to look at her. Because deep down I think it might already be too late.

But I won't tarnish our celebration tonight with my pathetic heart.

"I'm sorry," she whispers, but I choose to ignore it and drag her past more windows. We pass another room with a naked man in it. He has another guy on his knees. The naked one slaps his cock against the one kneeling and then spits in his mouth before ramming his dick in.

Lucy's nose wrinkles.

"Was it the penis or the spitting?" I ask.

"The spitting. I don't mind plastic cocks, actually quite like them," she says, looking queasy.

I laugh. "So spitting is a hard line. Good to know, we all have them."

"What's yours?" she asks.

"While I'll give anal, I won't receive."

"Noted. So... umm... are we going to talk about what we do want...?"

This makes me smile. "It my job to provide. I seem to remember you enjoy being spanked."

"You also called me a whore," she whispers.

I smile, knowing exactly which room to take her to. I grab her hand and pull her down the corridor and into a red-themed room. She needs to have control, and she wants to be free because she's trapped in real life. This is how I help her.

She steps inside and gasps. The room is full of toys and devices, some even I haven't seen before.

"Take your clothes off," I demand.

She obeys, sucking in her bottom lip and chewing on it. But it's the way her eyes flare, all fire and flames, that makes my heart squeeze. She is the memory I want to die with.

If Ignatius reaps me in a couple of months' time, then I hope her smile is the last thing I see. But I can't think like that, not when she's been clear—no emotions. So I take a moment to shut them down. If all I can have from her is transactional, sex but no love, a deal agreed in souls, training for help, then so be it. I'll take whatever she's willing to give me, because I'd rather take a piece of her with me than die never having held her heart in my hands.

"You are in control," I say.

She nods.

"Tell me your safe word."

"Satan."

"Good, Lucy. That's very good," I say. Though I think the words are meant more for me; praise for myself for shutting down every ache, every yearn and every desire for more from her.

She's fully naked and breathtaking. I brush her hair back from her face, lean close to her neck and whisper.

"What do you fear?"

She freezes, takes a long moment of thought, and then she whispers, "Ignatius."

My blood boils, hot and frothing. My moment of reticence gone. Screw dying at his hand. I live for the day I get to reap *him*.

"Fuck Ignatius, I'm your daddy now."

Her lips part.

"Say it," I demand.

"You're my daddy," she pants, and something seems to crack in her. Her eyes go molten in a way I've never seen. She needs this.

"Are you going to be a good little slut for Daddy?"

She nods.

"Get on your knees, baby girl."

She drops like a stone to the floor. I unzip my trousers slowly. Her eyes light up. She's been craving this. It's been weeks since we touched each other. I pull my boxers down and step out of them. I glance at the nearby shelf, finding the toy I want.

But first.

"Open your mouth," I say. She looks hesitant. Of course, this is how that man was in the other room.

"Do you trust me?" I ask.

"Yes."

"Why?"

"Because I'm in control?"

"Yes, you are, baby girl. Now, open your mouth or bend over."

She opens her mouth, and I step forward and sink my cunt onto it. Her eyes close, and she moans as her hands grip my legs, squeezing as her tongue immediately begins licking and lapping between my folds.

My legs start to shake. But it's worth it to see her on her knees for me. I reach forward and loop her long hair around my fist. I hold her in place and start to rock my hips, grinding against her tongue and mouth. With every flick, my clit pulses. She's a fucking fiend with that tongue, ravishing me with long strokes then light soft ones. I'm panting, grinding my hips down onto her mouth.

Until I yank her away from my pussy by her hair. She pouts at me.

"Oh, you like the taste of my pussy?"

She nods and licks her lips. Gods, the sight of her savouring my excitement fucks me right up. My nipples tighten inside my sports bra, my pussy clenches.

"Such a beautiful whore. Look at that filth on your lips."

I use my thumb to wipe away a glistening smear of my excitement from her chin, and her eyes blow wide.

I slide my thumb over her tongue, deeper, deeper until she gags. "Fuck, you're pretty when you gag. Now, I'm likely to squirt, and if I do, you are going to be a good girl and swallow it. Do you understand?"

She nods.

"Use your words, Lucy."

"Yes, Daddy."

Fuck. Me. I'll confess, I've always been into daddy kink, but I've never had anyone use it to ruin me the way it ruins them.

"Get on the bed," I say, my tone flat, disinterested.

When she stays put and grins at me, I pull her along by her hair.

"If you brat on me, there will be consequences."

She makes a panicked breathy mewling sound until it dissolves into a panted moan.

My cunt proceeds to soak itself and make my thighs sticky.

"Gods, you keep making filthy sounds like that, and I'm going to come before I can suffocate that pretty little face of yours."

I let her hair go long enough to push her onto her back. I pull the rest of my clothes off and then climb up and straddle her waist. How the roles have reversed. At night, on campus, she is the teacher and I am her student.

In here, tonight, she is my girl, and I am her daddy.

"I'm not letting you come up for air until I come. So if you can't breathe, you tap my leg, I'll lift up. Understand?"

"Yes, Daddy."

I have to shut my eyes and take a second. Every time she purrs those words it flips a switch in my brain. As if those two words have corrupted every synapse I have.

"Oh, baby girl, I am going to fucking ruin that mouth of yours."

I kneel over her head and lower my pussy to her waiting mouth. Her eyes roll shut as she lets out a sigh of pleasure.

Gods.

Her tongue slips between my folds, mopping up all the excitement she made with those filthy little sounds of hers.

She uses her whole mouth, her lips and tongue glide over my cunt. Long strokes sweep over me, her tongue dipping in and out of my entrance.

"Fuck," I moan.

I lean back, reaching an arm around to finger her core. She's drenched.

My restraint snaps.

I rock my hips, grinding over her mouth.

"Touch yourself," I say as I sit up and grip her hair, pushing her deeper into the bed as I ride her face.

She pulls her knees up so she can reach herself and rubs two fingers over her clit. I can't decide whether fucking her face or watching her finger herself is more pleasurable.

"Fuck, Lucy," I say as my nipples pinch.

She reaches her free hand and squeezes one of them. I

moan and grind down harder on her. Her hands find my arse and squeeze, working my hips, making me rock faster, faster, faster.

Her tongue laps and licks, circling and slipping through my folds and inside me. My clit draws tighter and harder until I lift up.

"Open," I say as I tip over the edge into a haze of pleasure.

My head rolls back, my eyes shut, the liquid starts slow. But I'm hungry for more. I move my hand over my clit, rubbing fast and hard as the release flows through my clit a thousand miles an hour. Electric pleasure shoots from my core to my toes and a rush of liquid gushes over her face and fills her mouth.

She stares up at me, her mouth open and full of my come.

I smile and push her chin shut.

"Swallow it," I demand.

Her throat bobs and I think I die, right there. She takes my fucking soul and rips it right from my body. Ignatius is fucked because his princess is now mine, and she already owns my soul.

I climb off her and lie next to her on the bed.

"That was amazing," she says and slips her fingers through mine. She holds me like I'm hers, like I belong to her.

Somewhere deep in my mind an alarm goes off. A reminder that she doesn't want any emotions. That I can't get attached.

This is never going to be serious.

Once my contract is broken, once she's free of Ignatius, there will be no reason for us to spend any time together.

But when her thumb caresses the back of my hand, her

fingers slot against mine and it feels as though they've always been there.

As though they always will be. And I struggle to understand why we can't be together.

I made a promise, though. I told her no feelings. So I'm keeping it that way. I pull my hand out of hers and head to the shelves where I find a strap-on and harness.

"Spread," I say.

"Yes, Daddy." She grins.

I wanted to ruin her, but I think she's already destroyed me. Her legs are spread wide enough to part her lips and show me her glistening entrance.

"You really are the perfect little slut, aren't you? All wet and ready to take Daddy..."

She smiles. I take her fingers and bring them to her pussy, sliding them down her centre, making sure they're good and wet before crawling up her body to place them against her lips.

"Be a good girl and open up for me."

Her mouth opens, and I push her fingers over her tongue. It gives me a deliciously dark idea. I don't usually like taking a cock, but I'm going to make an exception for this.

I slide it between my legs to my entrance and push. It hurts, so I take a second to breathe and force myself to relax.

"What are you doing?" she says, sitting up, a cinch forming between her brows.

I pump the cock in and out until it glides like silk and it's wet enough for what I want.

I climb into the harness, attaching the dildo, and pull Lucy to the edge of the bed.

"You said you didn't mind cock..." I say.

"I don't."

"Good. Then get on your knees. This one is going to taste delicious. Tap my thigh if it gets too much."

She kneels and places one hand against my leg, then opens her mouth and waits.

"I think you are the most beautiful creature I've ever seen, sat there waiting for me to give you my cock."

I slide the blue plastic shaft between her lips. She's tentative at first, but her confidence builds as she twirls her tongue around the cock. She bounces up and down, her eyes rolling shut as she laps up my juices.

I grab her hair and loop it around my fist, pulling her down on the cock. She makes a choking sound.

"My leg if it's too much," I say

But she responds by sinking lower onto the dildo. Her eyes stream as she gags, soaking the strap with saliva.

I pull her off, lift her under her arms and drop her onto the bed so she's on her front bent over, her arse facing me.

I kick her knees wider so I have a view of her glistening slit. I slide into the gap and draw my tongue from her clit all the way up to her arsehole.

She squeals as I touch her ring of muscle, and it makes my whole body heat with a carnal need.

I moan into her folds as I lap at her pussy. She tastes sweet and heady and a little sharp. It's heavenly, and I ravish every millimetre of flesh I find. Licking and sucking and nibbling until she's panting.

Her fingers bunch the bed sheets as she balls them in her fists.

"I'm going to come," she moans.

I lick harder, faster. Her body writhes under me. I pull my hand back and slap her arse. As I bring my fingers to her entrance, she's so wet I can slide two straight into her pussy.

"Oh gods," she pants, her back arching.

I pull my fingers out, bring the cock to her entrance and then I slam in all the way to the hilt.

"Midnight," she cries my name, pleading as I drive her to the edge of pleasure and then switch up.

I bring my hand down on her arse hard enough to leave a print. It's perfect, her white cheek and my red handprint. I wish it would stay there forever.

Marked.

Mine.

I drive my hips forward, over and over, slapping her arse harder and harder. I slap because I want her. Because she doesn't want me. And because even if she did, this is all going to be over in a matter of weeks anyway.

Her face is pushed into the covers, a fucking mess of my come, her saliva and tear-streaked cheeks. My pussy throbs at the sight of her.

The first hint of that rune appears on her neck.

"Harder," she begs. "Fuck me harder."

I slam my cock in, lean down and slide my hand to her clit. It only takes two strokes of my fingers before she's screaming obscenities and falling slack on the bed.

"So fucking beautiful," I breathe. But it's the silent words that come after that terrify me.

So fucking mine.

"Can you see them?" she mumbles, when her breathing comes back to normal.

"Yeah," I say, the moment passing, tucked away like a happy little memory orb. But I don't think about that.

I don't think about the way her hand felt in mine, or how desperately I want to spend my life watching her light up as she teaches, or all the ways I want to make her body fall apart with pleasure.

Instead, I hop off the bed and examine her neck, taking her to the mirror.

"Well?" I ask.

"I still can't see it."

"That's interesting," I say. "Because there's the faintest hint of a second…"

31

LUCY

It's so late it's early by the time Midnight and I sneak back into House Inferos. Tonight was... incredible. Which is why it was also awful. I have to stay strong, keep my emotions locked away, I can't risk falling for Midnight, not if it means losing my power.

But the way she worships my body, empowers me by giving me control. It's rewiring my brain. Changing my chemistry and I don't know how much longer I can hold out.

In the face of my goal and how much closer we are to finding out what Ignatius did, how can I give up because she's dangerous to my heart?

I can't contemplate the fact it's her I dream about, her I wish I drank my morning coffee with and her I wish I fell asleep next to.

She is dangerous, this whole fucking thing is. But what if it leads to my freedom?

Vetch raises his stony judgemental eyebrow at us as the door creaks open.

"I think we need to talk," Lex says, her hand on her hip, foot tapping as the foyer lights flick on.

Bastien winces behind her, raising his hands in defence.

"Where have you been?" Lex says. "I told you about the rune and you vanished. It's been hours. And why are you investigating celes—"

Midnight lunges and plonks her hand over Lex's mouth.

"My apartment," I say, resigned to the fact we've been caught, but I'd rather it was Midnight's friends than Ignatius.

We schlep up the stairs and I close us inside, putting the kettle on. We sit around the dining room table, sipping tea and picking at biscuits.

"Is this anything to do with Malifax the other day?" Bastien says.

Midnight hesitates. "We're not sure. Probably is the best answer. They're convinced Lu— sorry, Professor Corvine has something to do with the resurrection."

"Lucy?" Bastien says, a smug expression sliding into his features.

Lex's gaze flits between me and Midnight, settling on me. "The celestial runes were for you?" she asks.

"It's..." Oh gods, I can't tell them. It puts my job on the line, it puts Midnight's place at Finis in jeopardy. If they were to tell someone, it would destroy everything.

Bastien leans forward. "Look, you might as well tell us, we've worked it out anyway." He slides his middle and index fingers over each other in a scissoring motion.

Vile.

Why are men like this?

Midnight slaps him upside the head.

"Can we focus?" Lex yawns.

I glance at Midnight. "Should we trust them?"

She nods at me. "They have my back."

"They need to have mine too," I say to her.

"I trust them."

"Okay." I nod.

Midnight explains everything. The additional training in exchange for helping me break my contract. She tells them about my contract and the fact that when I orgasm, she can read the runes on my body. That garners several raised eyebrows but no further judgement, so she tells them about Malifax and how the Societas are convinced I am linked to Architecti's resurrection.

Lex wipes a hand over her mouth and her lips move as if she's whispering at a rapid rate of knots.

"What is it, Lex?" I ask.

"Ignatius trapped Architecti, and in a way he also trapped you. And now your body is covered in celestial contract runes, and Architecti is..."

"Celestial," Midnight finishes for me.

I sit bolt upright. "Shit..."

"What?" Lex says.

"I've never seen my contract. I've always hunted for it in the demonic library because Ignatius is a demon."

Bastien grins. "But the contract runes on your body aren't demonic."

"No, they're not," I breathe.

"So your contract was never going to be in the demonic library?" Midnight says.

"I don't think so."

All three of them grin.

"Then I guess we're taking a trip upstairs," Bastien says.

"Except the Celestial Library has been shut off for years. Even my sister's cohort didn't have access to it," Lex says.

"Looks like we're going to be breaking and entering," Midnight replies, a devious glint forming in her eye.

"We can't. There's no direct access to it from the campus. The floor was magically sealed off when the angels left, and they added a ton of security," I tell them.

"What kind of security?" Bastien asks.

"The dangerous kind," I answer.

"Sounds like my kind of evening," Midnight says.

"I'm serious. Encoded runes seal the doors, and there's also the minor point of the angels themselves. If one of them were to find you, they'd erase your memories and probably wipe your entire personality from your brain to protect their knowledge. And that's without the fact we have wraiths controlled by some ancient magic guarding the doors."

"That is a lot," Lex says.

"Yeah," I agree and slump against the sofa.

"Let's not give up. You said no direct access to it *from campus*. But that sounds like there might be direct access to it from somewhere else," Bastien says.

I shrug. "In theory, there should be access to it from every realm."

"Including the Veil?" Midnight says, sitting up.

"Theoretically, but there's no way we can do that. None of us are trained enough, and even if we had someone like Alistair weaving for us, we'd be sitting ducks in the underworld. Even if we only stepped through it and cut our way straight into the Celestial Library."

We fall silent.

Lex busies herself in my kitchen, opening cupboards and pulling packets this way and that until she finds more tea. I almost ask what she's doing rifling through everything, but I find it endearing that she decided to make herself at home.

As if summoned by the thought of food, Mortem strolls into the kitchen and rubs himself over my calves. I scratch at his ears and under his chin. He plonks himself at my feet and falls asleep.

Midnight is staring into space, her eyes locked onto something none of us can see. Bastien's brow is furrowed deep in concentration.

Lex flips the kettle on and gets fresh cups out for us all.

"So the dangerous part is the underworld?" Midnight says.

I nod.

"What if we skip it entirely? We could cut a hole in the Veil to the underworld and immediately cut another deeper hole right back to the celestial world. Maybe stitch the frayed edges together."

"Like a wormhole," Lex says, pouring tea for everyone. She hasn't even asked how we like it. I'm surprised when she puts a cup down in front of me and it has the hint of honey in it. Just how I like it.

"That's impressive," I say as she passes out the rest of the mugs.

"It's my party trick." She smiles.

"This sounds more than possible," Bastien says.

I shrug. "It is in theory. Theory being the operative word."

Midnight rubs her hands together as if itching to get going. "Plus, it would bypass the wraiths as we'd cut straight through the Veil into the library."

"And we wouldn't have to deal with the rune locks on the doors," Lex replies.

"Or that," I answer, already seeing where this is going.

"So, *in theory*, the hardest part is cutting the Veil twice in quick succession?" Midnight asks.

"And stepping through it without getting caught or attacked by a wraith," I confirm.

All three of them give each other the side-eye. Oh gods, I can't be responsible for putting three students in danger.

"No. No way. We can't."

But I've already lost this battle.

"*We* can't," Midnight says, and her eyes fall to Mortem. As if summoned by the sheer weight of a gaze on him, his ear twitches and he lifts his head off his paws.

The scowl on his furry face is impressive.

"I do hope you're not referring to me," he meows.

"A wraith won't attack you," Midnight says.

"Are you out of your hairless minds? I'm not walking through the Veil. I'm a shade for a reason."

"But you could also open the door for us," Bastien says.

He slow-blinks at Bastien, only it looks less like a sign of affection and more like a sign of dismay at the sheer idiocy coming out of our mouths.

He yawns, licks his paw beans and then pads over to sit in front of Midnight and Bastien. "Do I look like I have opposable thumbs?"

"Well, you have enough attitude to open a thousand locked doors. I think you'll find a way," Midnight says and leans down to tickle him under his chin.

I'm about to warn her that's a bad idea, he bites. But Mortem leans in, letting her stroke him and head butting her. His form becomes more and more dense, his colours changing from translucent to fresh snowfall white.

Then he sinks his teeth into her hand, and Midnight shrieks.

"You little bastard," she yells and goes to bonk him on

the nose, but he shifts back to noncorporeal. Her hand falls right through his face, and she head butts the table.

Bastien busts out laughing, and Lex nearly chokes on her gulp of tea.

I swear Mortem outright chuckles, though it sounds more like a hacked purr.

He dashes away down the corridor with Midnight chasing after him, leaving the three of us cackling.

32

LUCY

Three weeks later, after countless evenings of training and practice, an inordinate amount of tuna bribes for Mortem and several evenings of completing extra defence classes and perfecting their Veil cuts back to our realm, we're ready.

It's ten to twelve, the night is cool and thankfully misty, providing ample cover for us. Though that just makes me worry more.

It's too easy.

Mortem pads across the Great Library roof towards us, his belly swings left and right.

"Have you put weight on?"

"I was hardly going to say no to the tuna, was I?" He radiates contempt. I tut at him.

"You're cute with a bit more fluff, but if you don't fit through the very precise Veil cuts we've practiced, I'm going to resurrect you just to murder you myself," I say.

"Everyone got their kit?" Lex asks.

Bastien holds up two necroflares. Something that will ward off wraiths if it comes to it—and if they're aimed well, blow them up, sending them right back through the Veil.

"Timer," I say, holding up the stopwatch I pilfered from Thalia's desk earlier.

Lex waves a celestial dictionary of runes she found. It's nearly eighty years old and half the pages are missing, but it's better than nothing.

"We have two minutes for the shift change of the wraiths, on the strike of twelve."

"Yeah, easy," Bastien drawls. "All we have to do in two minutes is reverse abseil up several hundred feet of tower, cut a hole through the Veil, *twice*, throw a cat through, open a door and hope we're all inside before the new wraiths return." His skin is a sickly white colour.

"I resent the phrase 'throw a cat,'" Mortem hisses.

"This is going to be fun," Midnight says, bouncing on her feet.

"I think you and I have two very different concepts of fun," Mortem says. "I'll see you up there." He vanishes.

"Call your magic," I say, and all four of us open our hands and draw ribbons of campus magic towards us.

They carve the night up, eight jet black threads of billowing smoke slicing through the mist. My gut drops, chills settle over me.

I don't like this.

We're too open, if anyone were to look up. And it doesn't matter if the students are meant to be asleep. Someone is always out of bed after lights out. I shouldn't be asking them to risk their places here for me, but what choice do I have?

"Ready?" I ask, glancing at my watch. All three of them nod at me.

"In three. Two. One. Go." I whisper the last word and

hit the timer. All four of us throw our ribbons up to the turrets, looping them around and tugging them tight. We've practiced this so many times, our hands bare the calluses of tired necromancers.

"Locked in," Lex says.

"Me too," Bastien follows.

"Locked and ready," Midnight says.

Together the four of us lean over the edge of the library roof with nothing more than hope in our hearts.

Bastien bares his teeth. "Hate heights."

The shadowy ribbons lock around our bodies and jerk us off the edge, drawing us all the way up to the top of the tower. I try not to look down, but as the wind rushes in my ears and we're pulled hundreds of feet into the air, I falter.

I instantly regret my life choices. My vision swims so hard I have to hold a hand over my mouth so I don't puke.

I check my stopwatch. Twenty seconds have passed as we finally climb over the parapet ledge and drop onto the exterior balcony outside the Celestial Library.

"Go, go, go," I say. "Make the cuts."

Midnight and Bastien are the most effective at cutting, so they take the lead. Bastien twists his fingers and makes a sweeping motion as Mortem materialises at his feet.

A sheen of sweat appears on his brow as he stitches the frayed edges with campus magic, giving them enough stability for us to hang the second cut off the first.

Midnight shuffles into place.

"Forty-five seconds down," I say.

Midnight's features crumple in concentration as she examines Bastien's cuts and swipes her hands this way and that.

"Close your eyes, picture the library, feel for the difference in vibration. It's a different kind of notch compared to the Veil. It will feel lighter, fluffier, like blowing bubbles in the night sky."

"Got it," she says, and slashes her fingers apart.

The three of us gawp at the hole. A tunnel sliced right through the fabric of not just our realm but the celestial one. No one has seen inside the Celestial Library for four decades.

"Go," Lex barks. We don't have time. She picks up Mortem, tickles him under his chin and says, "Don't fuck this up or I'm feeding you to a wraith."

He hisses at her, but she's already pushing him through the tunnel.

He, inevitably, gets stuck.

"Demon's sake, Mortem," Midnight growls and shoves his furry arse hard. He yowls, though much of the sound is lost between worlds. I'm pretty sure he calls Midnight some expletive that really shouldn't be coming from a cat.

"You could always poke him in the arse," Bastien says.

There's a moment of reflective pause. Mortem goes deathly still. Bastien brings his finger towards Mortem's puckered butt. "Last chance, Mortem," he says.

The cat explodes forward.

In all the months of living with Mortem, I have genuinely never seen his legs move that fast. Suffice to say he plops out the other side of the Veil in a plume of fur clumps and hissing. The glare he gives Bastien is vicious enough to slice the lips off his smirk.

"Go," Lex wafts a hand at him. If a cat could pout, that is the expression he gives us. He turns his back on us and trots off, a few remaining fur clumps fluttering off his back.

"Shit, look out," Lex says as a sinewy black finger nudges at the Veil edge.

"Seal the cuts," I shout.

Bastien and Midnight launch into action as the wraith's arm tugs at the stitching.

"Midnight," Lex urges.

The stopwatch shrieks at me.

"Fuck, thirty seconds left. Come on, Mortem," I breathe. My foot taps as Midnight and Bastien battle to close the haemorrhaging Veil. The wraith's finger bursts through, slicing a one-inch cut.

Midnight's nose erupts, blood pissing down her face.

"Shit," Lex grabs Midnight and hauls her out of the way as the wraith's hand bursts through the stitching.

"Use the flare," I bark at Bastien.

"Pocket," Bastien says, jumping in to pick up the threads Midnight dropped.

I yank the flare out and snap it, shoving it into the gap around the wraith's hand. Light flashes, and an explosion makes the fabric bulge, shoving all four of us back against the parapet.

Lex slips.

Bastien and I grab her as she teeters on the edge.

"MORTEM," Midnight bellows as my stopwatch chimes.

"We're fucked now," Bastien says, hauling Lex back away from the edge. Three wraiths materialise, their dark sinewy bodies creeping across the parapet, mouths hung low, teeth yellowed and far too sharp. The magic that binds them to the tower is looped around them in the form of golden collars and leashes and masks. But they do nothing to slow them down in the face of an attack.

The library door clicks and swings open. The four of us sprint across the balcony. The wraiths scream; a shrill sound like the shattering of glass and grinding gears.

I make it through, followed by Bastien and Midnight.

But Lex halts in the door. Her eyes go wide; she blinks once. Twice.

And glances down at her shoulder, where a wraith finger has punctured right through.

Midnight grabs her, yanking her inside, pulling her off the wraith's finger. I slam the door shut. Blood billows down her shoulder.

"This is not good," Lex says as she slides down the door. "Go. I'll just wait here, okay?"

"We're not leaving you," Midnight answers.

"You will or we did this for nothing. You're going to have to come back for me, anyway. The wraiths know we're here, and we can't go out the same way we came in, which means cutting new holes in the Veil. I just need a minute."

Her dark skin turns grey.

Mortem hops onto her torso and licks at the wound. And to my surprise, it stems the flow of blood.

"Delicious," he says, "Just the dessert I need after cleaning my arse."

Lex's skin goes from grey to green, and I swear Mortem smirks as he resumes licking.

"Go, before I commit cat-icide," Lex says.

33
MIDNIGHT

The Celestial Library is so bright inside it feels like a spring morning. Bastien, Lucy and I reluctantly leave Lex to rest with Mortem keeping an eye on her and using his odd ghost spittle to lessen the bleeding. We spread out, searching down aisles and racks of parchment and scrolls.

It smells a little musty and a layer of dust covers everything. Such a waste. There's so much knowledge in here, I can't bear the thought of it going unused, unexplored, unknown. My fingers trail the spines of several texts. They burn with the need to steal, to pilfer the knowledge buried within the pages and words trapped in this shining vault.

I have spent my life believing that fate is predetermined, that no matter what I do, I fucked up when I signed a contract. But walking these aisles, the number of Architect moths still fluttering inside here, despite four decades of entrapment, gives me hope. Hope that maybe there is a way out. If this library holds a way out of the prison Lucy's father created for her, maybe there's a way out of the one I created for myself.

Gods.

Hope is such an insidious emotion. I want to quash it. To shove it somewhere where it can't threaten me. But this library is filled with possibility. What if a method for breaking my contract lies in here?

I lose Bastien and Lucy for a while, only to stumble upon them back in the central aisle.

"Any luck?" I ask.

They both shake their heads.

"This place is enormous," I say. "We need to be more strategic before Lex bleeds out."

Bastien touches Lucy's arm. "Would your runes help…?"

I frown at him. "You can't be serious?" I bury my head in my hands, heat rising up my neck.

"What can't he be serious about?" Lucy says.

He shrugs. "This place is massive, and we're running out of time. I'd put money on your runes calling to their source, or maybe helping like a map. I don't know, but it's worth a shot if it saves Lex…"

"In here? It's the Celestial Library…" Lucy dances from foot to foot, but I'm out of ideas too, and Bastien has a point.

"Do you have a better idea?" he asks.

Neither of us come up with anything.

He smirks and flicks his tongue like a snake. "Be quick. No pressure, Midnight, but now would be a good time to work your magic. I'll check on Lex."

He vanishes and the pair of us face each other awkwardly.

"Listen. We don't—" Lucy starts, but I place my finger over her lips, shutting her up.

"You need to stop."

"Buthhh," she mumbles against my finger and then

sags when she realises she won't be able to get her words out.

I brush a lock of hair behind her ear. "When are you going to realise that I love every moment of being with you?"

I stiffen, realising I shouldn't have used the L word, not in any context.

"What I meant to say—"

This time, she cuts me off, pulling my hand away from her mouth.

She holds my gaze, our eyes lingering on each other, hungry, exchanging so many unspoken words. Things that our bodies have come to accept but our minds cannot. Things that we wish we could whisper but admitting them would mean... I can't even think about what it would mean.

How is it we've ended up here? How is it that our promise to make it all about the contracts has become a lie to protect our hearts? To protect her power.

I can't have her. There are too many obstacles in our path.

I'm meant to reap her. She is forbidden from loving a mortal. I *am* mortal and she isn't. I'll die, she won't. Her father hates me and loves her. We were never meant to be.

But that doesn't stop me sliding my hand behind her head and pulling her mouth to mine. When I kiss her, it's not with the urgency I should feel. It's not with the cocky lust I felt in the graveyard.

And it's not with the heavy weight of knowledge that one day soon, this will end.

My lips move as if nothing else exists.

As if the angels have stopped time just for us, and I can finally believe we control our own fates.

As if this single kiss will save us both.

She tastes like heaven. Like a thousand different caresses under a thousand different skies. Like dreams and hopes and all the wishes I've ever had. But what terrifies me most is that she tastes like every forever I've ever ached for.

She must feel it too because she steps us back, down an aisle, our hands ravishing each other. This isn't fucking anymore. This isn't a quickie. It's not sex for the sake of contracts and runes.

This is something else, something more.

We practically trip and fall out the other side of an aisle into an open space. We break apart long enough to find a fountain at its centre, dark and glistening like a waterfall of stars. Architect moths flutter in and out of the flowing liquid, their wings making new sprays and flows as they drift around the fountain.

In a corner is what I assume to be a reading area, filled with pillows, blankets and seating. I tug Lucy towards it, and we collapse on top of them. A puff of dust billows up and makes both of us laugh and cough.

She slides her hand into mine. "What happens when this is all over?" she asks.

I shake my head. "Every answer to that question has a consequence, Lucy. How can I tell you the truth when I don't even know if I'll be here after?"

She brings her thumb to my lower lip, pulling it down. "Then lie to me with your body, your mouth, your tongue. Lie well enough I believe we'll be okay."

So that's what I do.

I slide down her inch by inch, adorning her exposed skin with kisses and pecks and nibbles. My teeth graze her, inciting a mesmerising display of goosebumps. She arches her back as I tug her trousers down, exposing her neat pussy to the air.

I part her legs, gazing upon her glistening flesh. My chest aches at the sight of her, my mouth watering at what I know will be an exquisite feast.

I lower my mouth to her clit and suck it fully into my mouth. She is divine tonight, a little sweet with an edge of something deeper. I lick and slide my tongue over her clit. Each flick a prayer and a plea to the angels still listening.

Let me have a little longer with her.

Please?

I lap at her pussy, drawing my tongue up and down in long lavish strokes, trying and failing to memorise the taste of her, the feeling of her hard little bud against my tongue, the shape of her folds and the heat in her core. I never want to forget. No matter whether I save my soul or end up in the underworld, she is the memory I want to take with me.

I place a finger at her entrance and slowly tease my way in. Her back lifts off the pillows. She's soaking in a way she's never been before, hungrily accepting me inside.

"Two fingers," she pleads.

I oblige, adding a second and curling them into the shape I know drives her wild. I drag my hand in and out, drawing every ounce of pleasure I can from her.

She pants and moans and begs me for more.

I lap at her clit. The more sounds she makes, the more wetness clings to my boxers.

She does this to me.

My clit pulses between my legs in time with her panting, and I swear that I could come from the sound of her melting under my touch.

I glance up at her neck and see her runes are already visible. They glow so bright I almost stop fucking her. I gasp against her clit; my fingers bear down, and she cries out.

"Midnight," she cries out as her pussy clenches around my fingers and her body falls over the edge.

But I'm left staring at her throat, wondering why the runes appeared before she came.

"I felt them," she whispers.

I help her pull on her trousers.

"They appeared early, didn't they?" she says.

I nod. "Probably just because we're in here, right? The whole celestial meets celestial thing."

"Yeah, potentially," she says but neither of us are looking at each other.

And I'd bet good money on the fact she doesn't believe that any more than I do. Something has changed. Shifted between us in a way that can't be taken back.

We always thought the runes appeared because I was making her come. But what if it was never that? What if it was always because of how I made her feel?

That is not something either of us can address.

She clutches her chest.

"What's wrong?" I ask as she stumbles her way through the library. She moves with purpose as if she's leading me now.

"Yeah. No. I... my heart... it's. Doesn't matter." She takes a deep breath, her shoulders tilt away from me, her back rigid, distant. She charges forward and doesn't wait for me.

Something is wrong.

We pass through three aisles before she slows her pace. And then she halts suddenly, rifling through a rack of parchment.

Her fingers still.

"It's here."

She brushes the contract. There's an almighty crack.

The ground shudders.

"A Veil tear? Shit. I thought we'd be okay in here. We need to get out. Now," I scream.

Lucy grabs the contract, and we run back to Bastien and Lex.

"You're going to have to make the cuts by yourself, Midnight," Bastien says.

Lex glances up at me from the ground, but she's barely conscious and Bastien is covered in her blood where he's applying pressure to her wound. He's right. If he releases the pressure on her, she'll bleed out.

"I'm sorry," Lex mumbles, her eyes rolling open and closed.

"You stay with us, Lex, or I swear to the archdemon... Mortem?" I say.

He materialises, chewing on a translucent tail. I scrunch my face up as the ground judders again, the violent shaking making Bastien slip and have to readjust his position on Lex.

"Is that a— You know what, never mind, I need you to get the door open for us," I say.

He does that thing with his mouth that looks like pouting.

"Or would you like to die in here," I growl.

"Already dead," he purrs.

"And yet you could still be fed to a wraith," Bastien jabs at him.

He sighs. "Fine."

It's ugly. The fizzing in my chest doesn't help my focus, nor the fact that we're celestial-side, so calling the campus's magic in a realm I've not worked in is significantly harder.

I manage to call one ribbon of magic from the walls, but I need two—I can't do this at half tilt. A headache sears through my temples as I refocus, concentrate on the campus, and coax more from the walls.

The ground trembles harder.

"Come on, Midnight, faster," Lucy breathes.

She and Bastien have Lex standing and secured under her arms. I draw my fingers in slicing motions so familiar muscle memory moves them now.

But it's messy, and the Veil parts more than I intended.

The scent of stale coffee and boiled flesh envelopes me.

"Wraith!" Bastien screams as a skeletal arm punches through the gap I've made in the Veil.

I throw my fist up, scythe in hand, and sever the limb. The wraith screeches so shrill and piercing I slam my hands over my ears.

"Hurry," Lucy says, pulling my hands back down.

I refocus and reach out to draw as much magic as I can from the building, sucking in every ounce. It swells and builds inside me until I feel like I'm going to burst or throw up or maybe a bit of both.

Dizzy, I make the second cut, but it too is haphazard and I don't quite manage to sever all the threads, so I have to cut again.

It's too much.

My nose bursts, a searing stab cuts through my mind. The kind of pounding headache that makes my vision cloud red. Not good.

I can barely see through one eye as I grab Bastien's arm and help shove the three of them through.

Mortem materialises in the room as I reverse the magic and seal us back on campus. But it's not clean, the fabric is frayed and the stitching uneven, which, given I only have one working eye, was the best I could do. And the wraith must sense the weakness. The air around the piss-poor stitching bulges in rhythmic thumps as the wraith attempts to shove his way through.

My vision smatters with grey dots, but I manage to stay conscious.

Lex, however, does not.

"Move," Bastien says, and the three of us lift her and run all the way to the medical wing.

34
MIDNIGHT

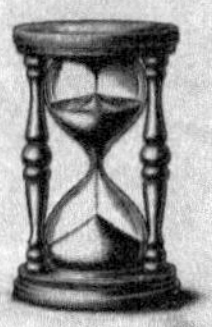

Nine And A Half Years Ago

The door to our bedroom swings open.

Aurelia is sprawled on the bed, her legs open.

A woman lies between them, her fingers buried in Aurelia's pussy, her tongue licking down her slit. A moan rips from Aurelia's lips.

"More, oh yes. Harder."

They haven't seen me.

I can't move. Like a fucking fool, I stand there watching my soulmate destroy every piece of my heart.

I blink once.

The life I thought I'd have dissolves: dinners, family meals, carriage rides at sunset. The ring I was going to buy her.

My stomach hardens.

I blink again.

Aurelia cries out, her back arching off the bed.

A cosy cottage with open fires, marshmallows toasted

in the middle of the day because we're too excited to wait for nightfall. Toes curling through sand and feet padding through long grass.

My fingers go numb, lead drops into my heart.

I blink once more.

Aurelia's pussy grinds into this woman's face, her eyes squeeze shut as she comes.

Soft kisses under moonlight. Warm coffee in the mornings. A lifetime of bringing her banana-on-toast the way she likes it. A face wrinkled by memories.

Strange thing, letting go.

Grief.

Rage.

And spontaneous loss.

A coldness settles in my limbs. Then a sharp clarity as I'm freed from the burden of love. Of a life dependent on another. Of the obsessive need to serve her.

Her whims, needs and desires.

It's freedom.

I cling to it, knowing freedom will bring me joy. I cling to it even as my cooling heart betrays me. And fuck, I cling to it despite reality leaking down my cheeks in giant rivulets.

It is only now, when her body settles on the bed and both of them are panting, that their energy dips low enough to feel the frothing presence of my rage.

Aurelia's eyes open.

One beat.

She stares at this other woman, lust thick and heavy in her eyes.

Two beats.

She tenses. A growing awareness that something is

wrong. The woman draws her tongue in one long final lick over Aurelia's cunt.

Three beats.

Aurelia tenses, her eyes slowly drawing across the room to meet mine.

She screams. Shuffles back away from the woman, desperately trying to cover her swollen pussy.

Like that matters.

Like hiding her nakedness can erase what's seared into my mind.

She covers her mouth.

I laugh.

Fold my arms.

Wait.

As if she can say something that will fix this. I don't want it fixed.

Not now.

Not ever.

She opens her mouth, the faintest hiss of a word.

"Don't," I bark.

She's crying now. And I'm laughing harder. I must look like a psychopath. Hysterical, mouth open like the maw of a lion, all teeth and fury. Head kicked back, leaning against the doorway.

The woman is scrambling now, pulling clothes on and scurrying away. Like her leaving will make it better.

But I'm in the doorway.

She approaches. There's no other way out. She has to go past me. I must hold murder in my eyes because she trembles as she nears me.

"E... excuse me," she stammers.

I lock onto her eyes and stand immobile. I will not move.

She makes herself tiny, pressing her spine flat against the doorframe as she tries to squeeze by without touching me.

She keeps her head turned away, focused on her goal: the exit.

"Boo," I growl and jerk forward.

She screams and lunges, tripping and careening towards the floor. Her hands are full of her clothes. She doesn't put them out to save herself and smacks her head on a stone tile.

She's motionless for a moment, and then scrambles up, her head bleeding.

We're the same now, she and I.

Blood leaks down her cheeks the way tears run down mine.

She meets my gaze for one long second, her expression crumpled, smeared with my girlfriend's come.

My fingers slip to my hip as if I carry a blade. She doesn't know I don't.

Her eyes follow.

She steps back.

I could do it. Take her life. Ruin mine.

She's not worth it.

Neither of them are.

She doesn't wait any longer, she turns and runs, slamming the door and vanishing.

Slowly, I turn to Aurelia. Now the woman is out of sight, the heat of my anger is extinguishing.

But I need it. Holding onto it will keep me strong. Every other emotion is a waste. Why feel sad when this is clearly already over? Why feel grief when I already sold my soul?

I close my eyes, trying to sink into the furnace deep in

my chest, but it's betraying me. Locking itself away. Abandoning me when I need it most. I grab at it. Trying to hold the threads of pain, but they're slippery, like oversoaked rose stems.

"Midnight," Aurelia says. Her words are soft. How odd that my name on her tongue used to fill me with stars and moondust. She made me feel like I was immortal, like every time she whispered my name it etched another year into my soul.

My eyes flash and she recoils. There is no point having a conversation. This is over.

"You broke us," I say.

She laughs. It's so sudden, so unexpected, that this time I'm the one recoiling.

"And you have a saviour complex." She sits up on the bed, her legs still bare and dares to brandish her rage at me like she's entitled to it.

"Do you have any idea how suffocating your love is?"

"I saved your fucking life, Aurelia. I gave up my soul for you."

"Oh, please. You were on a mission to self-destruct. I told you over and over not to try and save me. But you didn't listen. And then you're all up in my face every second of every day, never giving me a chance to breathe or live."

"YOU WERE GOING TO DIE." I'm screaming now, and I'm not sure if it's at me or her. I don't understand what is happening or how we've gotten to this place.

"AND YOU STOPPED ME LIVING ANYWAY."

"You ungrateful cunt." My fists ball. A deep need to break something fills my gut, my lungs, it's all I can breathe, all I can see. But she won't let up. She won't stop screaming.

"And you're an obsessive, controlling freak."

"Get out. Get out and never come back."

She gets up from the bed and begins packing her shit, and I slide down the wall.

I stay there, staring at nothing. Listening to the sounds of my future disintegrating. Each item she packs is another splinter, another fracture in the life I thought I was going to have.

All of it shoved into two suitcases and a rucksack.

She pauses by the front door. I don't look at her. I don't look at anything much.

She must wait for at least three minutes. Whether she's contemplating saying something, apologising, hurling more abuse, maybe telling me she still loves me, it doesn't matter.

In the end, she says nothing, just walks out.

The door clicks shut. It's the loudest thud. The heaviest crack in my heart.

I sink to the hardwood floor. Cold seeps into my bones as I cry, alone.

Silent.

No one mops my tears or hears my screams.

I stay there until day turns to night. Until the moon rises and the stars wrap a cloak around me, stitching me back together like a patchwork quilt. Nothing quite fits anymore. Nothing quite works. But when morning comes, there are no tears left.

There is no love left in my heart.

There is only the knowledge that I have nine years and six months left to break my contract. I will not let my soul be reaped for her. Aurelia does not get to live while I die.

It twists and gnarls into a thirst. The kind of primal

hunger that only the obsessed and the deranged can understand.

I must have vengeance.

I must have redemption.

By the time I haul myself off the floor, I am raw thirst. I am pure revenge.

And it flows deep, deep, deep in my veins.

35

LUCY

Lex survives her brush with the wraith and spends thirty-six hours in the medical ward before losing her shit about missing lectures and discharges herself. She had a transfusion for the blood loss. The wraith punctured through her chest, somehow missing every vital organ. She was incredibly lucky, all things considered.

Father, thankfully, accepted the lie that it was because of a Veil tear and that we'd been close by to intervene.

I pull my contract out of the drawer, the contract I have coveted for forty long years, only to shove it away and slam my fist on the desk.

What a fool. Hope surged through me the night we found it. I thought this was it, that I'd be able to read it, dissect it and find a loophole.

Except it's written in a celestial language. I can't fucking read it any better than I can see the runes on my neck.

Useless.

But I didn't want to tell them. Not when Lex risked her

life for me. Was injured *because* of me, and for what? A fucking useless document.

Wasted.

And I have never felt more pathetically mortal than I do now, wallowing in my bitterness and failure.

It's one of many reasons I've avoided Midnight. It's been three long days. I know she's hurt because on the second night she left a letter under my door with five words scrawled in her messy script.

What did I do wrong?

My chest caves in reading it, the script blurring as I trace her scrawl. She didn't do anything. That's the problem. She's always been respectful and supportive. I'm the one failing to keep my boundaries. I was clear we could never be more. But my brain and body are refusing to listen. Perhaps Father and the Corvines were right all these years. Mortals are dangerous and they don't realise why.

It is the ultimate reason why we can't be together.

She's too young, too human, too 'student'.

No matter what I want, the truth remains the same, that if I utter those words to her, my power will siphon and bury itself in her soul.

When we were in the Celestial Library, I swear my crystalline heart cracked. I thought I was too late to stop it. That it was going to shatter and leave me there, helpless, in an abandoned, banished library. But I buried the feelings, and that is why I've had to avoid her, even though it feels like I'm tearing out chunks of myself in order to stay away.

But tonight, there's a celebration ball. The students had their practice exams, in preparation for the finals next month. The results will be posted shortly. I'm just hoping the training we've been doing has paid off for Midnight. I'm certain it will. She's improved beyond all measure. Has she improved enough, though? We'll have to see because the other students are ruthless.

I rest against one of Finis Tower's circular turret windows and peer down at the moat. Maintenance have laid glass over it, making a dance floor between the Great Library and Finis Tower. It's enormous. They've hung twinkling fairy lights from the tower's turrets all the way down to the library roof. It resembles a starlit sky, even from up here. A band plays on the porch of one of the towers, and all five years of students congregate and mingle around the base. Alcohol flows freely this evening; one of the rare occasions the staff and faculty turn a blind eye. Booze and magic aren't the best mixture.

We're guaranteed to have at least five students in the medical wing by morning, no one will turn up on time to class tomorrow and I'm betting there will be at least one Veil tear.

Midnight walks through the library arch and onto the circular dance floor.

I grip the window frame; it creaks under the pressure. She must sense me, for her eyes track the area and then scan up.

The moment she sees me, the corner of her lip twitches.

She bids Bastien and Lex goodbye and heads straight into Finis Tower.

I consider leaving. Finding another room, hiding away from her, but what's the point? I should confess. I wore this dress for her.

I shouldn't have, not when it just opens up the pathway for more.

We can never be more.

We are purely transactional. I keep telling myself this.

And yet...

Before she reaches me, I inhale vetiver and grapefruit, a scent that makes my body hot and my nipples tight.

And yet...

When she walks through the turret doorway, my heart betrays me. A hitch and a beat that thuds like another crack of crystal.

I swear my stomach dances like callow moths.

And yet...

Even though the light haloes her, making it hard to see more than her silhouette, I can tell it's her.

The way her body moves through time and space has carved a path through my mind. I smile because I have memorised the way she stalks the campus halls. She doesn't stroll like the privileged elite who don't fear failing. And before turning to face her, I know her fists will ball instead of her sharing the fact she's pissed at me, hurt by me.

I keep all of this tucked away because I shouldn't know any of it. Because I shouldn't lov—

My heart splinters, and I lean forward against the glass and push the feelings away, down, down, down into a vault where I can never reach them.

The searing heat in my chest eases, my breathing returning to normal.

"Professor Corvine," she says, and I almost melt on the spot as I face her.

Her mouth parts, her fists clench and relax at her sides and a small smile kisses the corner of my mouth.

Her attention lingers on my dress, trailing from hem to collar.

It's black, mostly, with a slit cut all the way to my upper thigh. A set of deep red rubies decorate one breast and climb into a peak on my décolletage. The dress cinches at the waist and trails behind me. It's extravagant, elegant and deeply sexy. Not something I often feel in my forties, nor when I was in my thirties, come to think of it.

When did I stop dressing up to feel good? When did I stop going out and living life? When did work become my main focus instead of living?

Tonight is for living. And, apparently, for taking extreme risks.

I find myself gawping at her. She's wearing an all-black suit, boots and a black shirt that's only buttoned halfway. I am uncomfortably certain that she's not wearing a bra. The bulge of her ample breasts teases the line of buttons. A long string necklace plunges into the gap between them.

I swallow, hard.

Her hair is freshly shaved on the sides, the impeccable neatness of a barber's blade evident from the sharp lines sculpting her face. The rest of her hair is gelled into a wet look and slicked up and back. But it's her bright blue eyes that undo me. That make me want to strip the skin from my bones and hand her my soul on a platter.

"You're beautiful," I say without meaning to. My fingertips brush my traitorous lips, surprised at their confession.

"Have you looked in the mirror?"

This. It's these comments that ruin me, blast through all my barriers and fuck me up. How am I supposed to keep her at arm's length?

The music kicks up a notch outside, the volume growing sufficiently loud enough that we can hear the thudding base beat through the turret windows and the melody lilting on top.

"I, umm," Midnight starts, and pulls a hand through her hair. "Are you still pissed at me?"

I tear my gaze away from her. "I was never upset with you. I was trying to protect this..."

I point at my heart, and her jaw flexes, one curt nod.

"Figured. I can leave."

She turns.

"No," I shriek. Too fast, too desperate. I have to get a grip.

"No?" Her brow furrows.

"I'm sorry I ignored you. That was wrong of me. I just got up in my emotions, and I'm struggling to keep control of them. We have to ignore each other out there. But if you're not mad, I'd like to have at least one dance with you in here?" I ask.

Every cell in my body pleads with her to say no, to push me away and tell me we can't. But I'm the one holding back. I always have been.

"Or has fate decided I'm not to be so lucky this evening?" I say.

"I'd take your hand and dance with you till the coals of hell burned my heels and crumbled my bones to ash."

Yeah, I am fucked.

Her eyes glimmer. "I thought you didn't believe in fate," she says.

"I don't, but if it's on my side, I'm not going to say no."

Midnight holds out her hand and bows. I step forward and then continue pushing her all the way to the door and lock it behind us.

She walks me into the middle of the room and slides her hand around my waist and then leads me in slow circles around the room. I lower my head to her shoulder and just breathe.

"There have been so few quiet moments this year," I say into her shoulder.

Midnight kisses my forehead. "Tell me what you're thinking."

"I'm imagining all the things that can never be," I whisper.

Her hand strokes my back, and I wonder if she's thinking the same. There are barely thirty days left and still so much to do.

"The demon and the reaper, hey?" She huffs against the top of my head.

"Something like that."

"I want you to tell me all of the futures," she says.

I sigh as she spins me around and we slide to another section of the turret room.

"I'm thinking about all the campus walks in misty mornings that we can never have."

Her movements speed up, I'm not sure if I've pissed her off, until she says, "Or the lazy mornings in bed, where I bring you coffee and those god-awful eggy circles you like."

"You mean a pancake?"

"Yeah, fucking awful things."

I laugh against her shoulder and then stop suddenly, my voice cracking. "I'm thinking about how we'll never grow old together, wrinkled hands that won't carve calluses in each other's palms."

Midnight spins me out, and I go twirling across the room. "I thought you said our fate is our own? This is the most fatalistic I've ever heard you."

"I'm just tired."

She tugs me and I spin in so fast my back ends up against her chest. She leans in and kisses down my neck. I moan and lean in as she kisses down my throat.

"You don't have to do this, Midnight. You don't need to fuck me this evening."

She tuts at me, one of her hands skimming up the slit in my dress, dragging the fabric with it until her fingertips graze so close to my folds. I'm not wearing underwear, but she hasn't realised yet.

"Need? Fuck, Lucy, don't you get what you've become to me?"

I shake my head, trembling beneath her grasp. I don't want to hear this, I can't. I am barely hanging on to my self-control as it is.

She sighs against my scalp, placing a kiss on top of my head. "You can't love me, I understand that. But it's too fucking late for me. You have stitched yourself into my soul. You are in my marrow, in every breath I breathe and every thought I have. You are more than need and desire. I will crave you long after my soul has been taken. I will yearn for you in this world, and the underworld and any other that drags me from you. And until then, I will fight to find a way to keep you, because you are mine. No matter what fate says, you will *always* be mine."

"Your words are poison," I whisper, tears falling down my cheeks.

I have no resilience left.

"Sometimes the truth feels like poison," she whispers and then spins me around and hoists me into her arms. She powers us forward until my spine hits the turret window.

"Midnight, the crowds, wh—"

But she cuts me off with her mouth plunging over mine. Her lips are plump and needy. Her tongue pushes its way into my mouth and caresses mine. She tastes of mint and cider. My body responds to her the way it would a drug.

Instantly pliable.

Instantly aroused.

If I were wearing underwear, they'd be clinging to me. But instead, my thighs stick to each other. And the thought of her discovering my bareness only makes me wetter.

What am I doing? Why am I risking everything?

Her hands are everywhere, tugging and pulling and caressing. One of my breasts falls out of my dress, and she moans at the sight.

"Perfect," she breathes, her tongue licking a hot circle over my nipple before she sucks it into her mouth. Her eyes fall shut. She sucks almost to the point of pain, and it makes me whimper.

"Fuck," she pants.

"We shouldn't," I say, but my words are pathetic and whispered in between moans. I tug her shirt out of her trousers, my hands skirting up the hard lines of her abs and to her own erect nipples. I tweak them and the feral expression she gives me elicits such a delicious bolt of pleasure between my thighs I have to squeeze them shut.

"Then you shouldn't have come dressed like that..."

I suck my bottom lip in.

"You dressed like that for Daddy, didn't you?" she asks.

"Yes," I whisper, and I think I might die if she doesn't touch me.

"Oh, baby girl. I am going to ruin that pussy tonight. I'm wearing something just for you too..."

She tugs my hand away from her breast and down, down, down until I find a hard bulge. I jolt.

"You're packing?" I ask.

She grins.

"Wait, I was ignoring you. Were you planning on picking up a woman tonight?"

"Only one," she says and slides her palm against my

thigh and up, up, up the slit in my dress. Everywhere her skin caresses mine, my body comes alive. She leaves static in her wake. Static and hope and promises she can't keep.

Her fingers find my core and she goes rigid.

"You're naked."

This time I grin.

"Were *you* planning on picking up women tonight?" she practically growls at me, her fingers growing stiff against my centre. The possessiveness pooling in her grip... She owns me tonight; there's no question of that. I give up resisting. She can take me.

"Only one."

She leans in to kiss me. "Good answer." Her mouth finds mine as her fingers glide against my pussy, slipping through my folds and teasing my clit. She rubs just hard enough, her fingers dipping down to use my excitement to ease the friction. It feels illicit.

I want illicit. Dirty. I want her to use me and treat me like a fuck toy. I want her to fuck me and ruin me and cut my heart out and steal it for her own.

My head lolls back and clunks against the window, the impact shoving reality in. "Wait, shit. We need to move away from the glass."

"No," she says, "you need to be discreet."

She resumes her movement, rubbing faster against my clit, winding my body tighter and higher. But I can't bear it, I need more.

"Please," I whisper.

The need to have her inside me, the need to feel her mouth on my clit, it's overwhelming. My hips move on their own, greedy and desperate, forcing her fingers to slip an inch inside me.

She pulls away, tutting.

"If you want something, you need to use your words."

I am well aware of what I want tonight. It's why I dressed the way I did.

"Get on your knees, Daddy, you look like you're starving."

Midnight pulls her fingers from my cunt and smears them over her lips. Her tongue skitters over the glisten.

"Mmm, delicious. Open," she demands, and I die.

There and then.

I open my mouth, and she slides her finger over my tongue.

"Divine, isn't it?" she says as she lowers herself to her knees, one leg at a time, her eyes never leaving mine.

My heart races about ten thousand beats per second. I swear it shatters as I gaze upon Midnight.

How is it she can hold every ounce of power in this moment and yet I'm the one telling her to get on the floor?

"Fuck," I say, taking in the sight of her beneath me.

"Tell me, what you need," she says. The hooded look in her eyes makes me dizzy with want.

I slide my hand to her chin and tilt her up to face me.

"I want you to eat," I say and slide my thighs apart, grip her hair and force her onto my pussy.

She moans against my cunt as her tongue flicks my clit. She makes filthy moaning sounds as though she's drinking the finest wine.

She moves closer, brings her fingers to my entrance and pushes inside me.

"Gods," I say and make a racket as I lean against the window again.

My hips roll forward and grind against her sinful mouth. One hand holds her to my cunt while the other presses against the window frame as we find a rhythm. The harder I grind against her, the quicker she moves. Her tongue ravishing me, her fingers pounding inside me.

"Fuck. Yes. More, Midnight. I need more."

She curls them inside me, hitting my G-spot. My pussy clenches down on her fingers as the rhythmic motions of her tongue, hard then soft then hard, have me screaming out her name. I come apart on her, cracking the window frame with my grip.

She sucks my clit between her teeth, forcing aftershocks to ripple through my thighs. Finally, she ceases the relentless assault, only to stand up and undo the zip on her trousers.

"Wh—but I just—" I say, realising I was never actually in control.

Her fingers lace through mine, bringing my hand up to my throat, tracing where I assume the outline of the contract rune sits.

She grips my throat, pulls me away from the window, and spins me. My chest crashes against the window frame, my breast still exposed.

"Midnight," I gasp. "What if someone sees?"

"I thought we made our own fate? That we can control our destiny. So control it, baby girl," she says, nipping my throat as she kisses and licks and bites.

She slides her hands to my hips and over my arse, drawing my dress skirt up, exposing my thighs.

"You should check if the door is locked," I say, my exhale making a fan of steam over the window.

But she ignores me, bringing the head of the dildo to my entrance and dipping in and out, testing, soaking the head with my excitement.

"Gods, Midnight, we can't."

"Like I couldn't eat that pretty little pussy of yours just now, you mean?"

"Yeah," I whimper. "Like that." I love the filth that comes out of her mouth. None of my partners have ever been so vocal or spoken to me like that. How is it words can have such power? Why is it the filthier she is, the more my body gives itself to her?

She weaves spells with that tongue. Her hand slides against mine, flattening against the windowpane. With her other, she guides the strap inside me.

Slow and steady she grinds until she's sheathed to the hilt. She releases my fingers, her hand coming to my throat and squeezing just a touch. Enough for my pussy to clench against the cock inside me.

She pulls her hips back, yanking me off the window and slams into me, crashing us against the glass. She squeezes my throat as she drives the strap home, and I swear I sees stars.

"Oh, my gods," I choke out.

She is relentless. Pulling the strap out and driving it home, over and over. Pumping in and out of me until my thighs tremble and my pussy pulses with such a vicious ecstasy, I swear I'm going to pass out.

The glass shivers, I'm certain we're going to either crack it or dislodge the pane entirely.

Her hand tweaks my nipple, pulling and tugging at my breast as her teeth sink into the muscly flesh of my neck. My knees threaten to give out as she slams into me.

Heat pools between my legs. But it's not enough.

"I... I need more," I pant.

She leaves my nipple and lowers her hand between my legs. Her fingers glide over my sensitive clit.

"Oh, fuck," I whimper. My body tightens with her

movement. I close my eyes, sinking into the thuds against the glass, the way she cocoons me, makes me feel safe. The way I wish for a thousand nights like this.

For her arms to always find mine.

She drives in and out, in and out. My hips tilt to let the strap press against my G-spot.

"Do you like it when I fuck you like this?" Midnight whispers against my ear lobe, her breath trickling down my flesh and setting my skin on fire.

"Yes, I need it harder. Rougher. Fuck me like you mean it, Midnight. Fuck me like this is the last time."

A rumbling sound rips from her chest as she grabs my throat and hauls me back, dragging us haphazardly towards a table. The strap slips out, but she bends me over the table, pinning my arms above my head with one hand and yanking my dress up with the other. She kicks my feet out and pushes the cock to my centre.

She thrusts in with one hard sweep.

"Oh, fuck," I cry out, and wriggle against her. She holds me down firmly, and my pussy pulses at the restraint. Yes, this is what I want. To be manhandled, owned. Fucked like she's lost control. Like I am consuming her every waking thought.

"Do you need your safe word?" she whispers.

"NO," I practically scream at her. "Gods, no. Harder. I want more."

Her hand draws back and slaps against my arse.

I gasp, but it quickly becomes a moan as the strap continues to pound into me.

If anyone were to walk in, to see me, pinned to the table, ball gown hoisted up, being fucked like a dog. Gods. It's humiliating. So why is it that thought nearly sends me toppling into an orgasm?

Midnight slaps my cheek again, blistering heat radiating from her palm.

"You like it, don't you?" she growls as she drives into me.

"Yes," I whimper.

"I knew you could take it. Daddy's perfect little slut."

Fuck me. My mind is molten. I'm gone. I shift into some other universe.

"Say it again," I beg.

Midnight pulls her hips back and slams into me. Harder. Harder. We shunt the table across the room until we're thrusting against the wall making the most godsawful racket. And some part of me realises we're too loud, too noisy, but I'm too whacked out on bliss to give a shit.

Her hand finds my clit and rubs in time with her pumping, bringing me so close. My whole body is electric, as if every nerve and every cell have been struck by lightning.

With every pull of the strap out of my pussy and every slam back in, I feel the ridges glide against my walls. The heat of her body against mine, the press of her breasts into my back.

"If I tell you, are you going to come for me?" Midnight says.

"Yes," I pant, and I will because I can't take any more. My cheek slips against the table, wet? Tears? Tears for the fact this is the best sex of my life, and I know I can't have it again.

"Mmm," Midnight says as her hands grasp my ass and spread my cheeks.

I wriggle trying to hide my other hole. But instead, cold wetness dribbles onto it.

"What are you doing?" I shriek.

"Using you as I see fit, Lucy. Because you're Daddy's perfect little whore."

My world tilts as she rubs a finger around the entrance I never thought I'd want touched.

She slides the strap slower now, letting my body come down away from the orgasm I was so close to.

"Safe word?" she asks.

"No," I say.

She slides her finger to my tight ring and my back arches off the table, the sensation alien as she pushes her way in. But she continues her thrusting in and out of my pussy, keeping the pleasure coiling low between my legs.

"Just relax," she says, and I try but I'm barely in control of my body.

I'm so full.

Too full. I shouldn't be this full, but she's gentle, gentle enough my body responds.

She pulls her finger out and slowly pushes back in.

"Oh. Oh, fuck," I say, and my eyes roll shut.

She moves them in time, her finger and the strap, then she adds another finger, and I can't...

The image of me bent over the table, being used like a fuck toy. What if someone walked in? Saw Midnight with a strap-on in my cunt and her fingers in my arse. It's too much.

It's filthy.

It's degrading.

She's debasing me and it's making me come.

She drives the strap and her fingers in over and over until I swear I'm lost in some corner of my mind.

I spill over, black out, my body and mind separated as I drift into endless pleasure. Every cell fires and stars drift across my vision as a soul-crushing orgasm rips through my body.

I'm vaguely aware of my name being called. Repetitive, insistent.

Midnight hauls me off the table, her face serious.

"What?" I say, pissed that she's pulling me out of my post-orgasm haze all too quickly.

"The second contract rune... It's clear as day."

36
MIDNIGHT

Thirty Days Left

I hand Lucy a hastily drawn scribble of the rune. She takes it and slips it into the boob cup of her dress.

"Thank you. But..."

"But?" I say, the air souring.

"We have to stop this," Lucy says, adjusting her dress.

"You don't want to," I answer, inspecting the turret window for cracks. There are none, surprisingly. I think we got away with it.

"What I want is irrelevant. I... I told you at the start this could never be anything more... and what we're doing..."

"It is more?" I say.

She turns away from me.

"So what? You're breaking up with me after letting me fuck you?"

She kneads her temple. "Do you have to be so crass?"

"Do you have to be so cowardly?"

"Cowardly? Fuck you, Midnight. You have no concept at

all of what will happen to me if I so much as utter words of confirmation."

She's right. To love her, all I have to do is fall; to love me, she has to sacrifice everything.

I'm just the idiot that fell first.

I need to get out of here. I need to leave and get my head in check and stop myself from falling any harder or faster. She was clear it could never be more. I chose not to listen.

I turn and walk out, leaving her in the turret alone and find my way back to Lex and Bastien.

Finis must recognise my growing reluctance. It is always with me. It follows me now, stalking me through the reflections in the windows, as I make my way downstairs.

Those flickering images, sometimes me, sometimes my parents, sometimes horrible lies and warped nightmares. An image of Lucy, dead and rotting floats like a gnarled watercolour in the window. I shudder as my name is chanted like a whisper on the breeze. Finis is impatient, and for the first time, I am afraid of what will happen.

I find Lex and Bastien, both already animated.

"It's a bit cruel for them to post the results during the ball," Lex whines. She's recovered now, but she has a nasty scar over her shoulder blade. I left Lucy in the turret to clean herself up and adjust her dress so she didn't look like she'd been fucked within an inch of her life.

"Says the girl at the top of their class," Bastien scoffs.

I note that Aurelia is third in Lex's primary subject.

Second in Bastien's.

My teeth grind against each other. I'm not top three in anything I've checked so far. But what did I expect? Despite all my extra study, I spent the first half of the year at the bottom of the group. It's thanks to Lucy I've crawled my way to the mid-ranks and higher. I frantically scan the papers hanging on the outside of Finis Tower searching for my name.

It seems I have made progress, for I'm in the top ten percent of every class I check. But that's not enough progress to chase off the gnawing knowledge that I made a deal that will see me choose: Lucy's soul or mine? And the longer I spend with Lucy, the more I struggle with the concept of reaping her.

I find the most important results, the Veilwalker scores, and torture myself by scanning from the bottom up.

My name isn't there. What the hell?

I reach the middle of the class, and my name still hasn't appeared. I scan back down to make sure I didn't miss it.

Hope.

A dangerous creature, I swear it was designed by demons as a form of torture. One sent to lure you in, taunt you with possibility, with futures never meant for you.

I keep searching. Lex's hand slides into one of mine. Bastien's on the other side.

"Oh, my gods," Lex whispers.

I reach the top ten students, and I still haven't seen my name.

A swell of something warm and bubbly nestles in my chest like birthday cake and hugs from friends. My eyes sting, everything blurs.

Top five. Still my name hasn't appeared.

4th: Silvana Danswick

Surely... not. Can I really have a chance of winning the favour next month? We're thirty days out. But what if I've scored close enough...

3rd: Mercedes Midnight.

The bubbles pop. The cake turns sour, and the hugs vanish, leaving me cold.

"I knew it was too much to ask," I say, dropping Lex and Bastien's hands and turn my back on the scroll just as Hadrian shoves past me and sees his name next to first place.

The worst bit wasn't Hadrian. It was...

"Listen, she's not even going to be in your final exam. Not when it counts," Bastien says.

"Oh, please. It all counts. And top student isn't just top of their own subject. It's top of everything. And Aurelia is in the top three of every fucking subject she's taken," I bark.

I'm going to have to study harder, longer. More hours in the library. I'll drink more coffee, cut sleep. I don't care what I have to do to get to the top of the student rankings. An absurd thought occurs to me that at this point, if I hadn't already sold my soul and was trying to get it back, I'd consider selling my soul to win.

Gods. What the hell is wrong with me that I value my soul so little? Or perhaps it's that I valued someone else so much that I'd have done anything for them and *that* cost me everything.

Caring. Love.

Maybe Lucy is right, we should quit while we're ahead.

Aurelia strides past me, her hand locked in her new girlfriend's. She doesn't even look at me. The pair of them are dressed beautifully, but that's about as much of a compliment as I can muster for the bitch who stole everything from me.

She can't win that favour. She just can't.

The music behind us at the ball kicks up a beat as Aurelia gasps and claps her hands together behind me. It sets my teeth on edge. Lex and Bastien must notice because they sling their arms over my shoulders and drag me away.

"She's not worth it," Bastien says, handing me a glass of some sort of booze, which I down in one. He blinks, takes the glass and exchanges it for another, which I also down.

"Okaaay, maybe we won't have any more of those just yet," he says.

We stroll around the tower, doing a full loop, examining the bars and food stalls. Bastien eats enough for all of Ora City, and Lex picks at the odd thing, preferring to steal bites of Bastien's food than actually order her own.

I'm too pissed off to eat.

A couple of students stroll past me, and I double take. Must be the booze. But I don't recognise them, and they're wearing uniform, tonight of all nights.

"What's wrong?" Lex asks.

"You ever seen those two before?"

"No?" she says. "Maybe they started term late."

"Is that a thing here?" Bastien asks.

Lex shrugs. "My sister had a late starter."

But something feels off, like an ant trapped under your shirt. I can't get rid of the sensation. We make our way to the front of the tower, and Lucy is standing there with several professors, Alistair and Thalia—the two professors I see her with most often, among them.

Ignatius is behind her. He catches my eye and narrows his gaze at me. He indicates for me to come to him, so I break off from Lex and Bastien and head over.

The two students I don't recognise linger near the drinks table Lucy is at. Professor Stroud joins Alistair and Thalia in conversation.

Lucy appears elegant and put back together save for a couple of rubies missing from her chest; they must have flicked off while we were fucking. My eyes glance up to the window, a smirk tickling the corner of my mouth. Aside from the missing rubies, you'd never know I fucked her.

"What do you want, Ignatius?" I ask, moving us away from the group of professors into a nook near a bar.

"Is that really a way to talk to the demon holding your soul in his hands? Hmm?"

"I have a party to attend unless you have something you need me to do?"

"There are three souls I need you to reap tomorrow."

"Fine, send the details in the moths as usual."

"Eager to get rid of me tonight, aren't you? You wouldn't be hiding anything from me, would you?"

"Like I could," I say.

Lies. I'm hiding too much from him.

He leans close. "I see the way you look at my daughter. She is not for you."

"Why? Because I'm a lowly reaper? Or because I'm a mortal?"

His lip curls. "Both..."

But that's not it, is it? There's something he's hiding from me or maybe from her. "There's more, isn't there?"

"If she falls in love with a mortal, her powers will be lost. I can't... I won't allow that to happen."

There's something in his expression. Something I'm missing. I may not be close to Ignatius, but I've known him for a decade, I'm used to his ego, his charm, I can tell when he's lying. And while it might not be an outright lie, there *is* something.

"No...That's not it. Why don't you want me near her?"

"You don't know what you're talking about, Midnight. You're naive to think you can barrel up to me with this ego and accusations. You're mortal, that alone means you're not good enough for her."

"And yet, you haven't denied it. Maybe it's not me you want her to avoid. But it is something about me, or is it a relationship you don't want her having? Is the threat a human? Perhaps it's all tied to her contract…"

His expression darkens. I've hit a nerve. Good.

"I'm going to figure it out, Ignatius. And when I do, I'm going to make sure she knows how to break free from you."

He snarls. Lurches towards me, grabbing my shirt.

Thalia bursts out laughing, distracting both of us. I slip his outstretched hand, spinning out of his grasp as Thalia flings her arms out, laughing so hard she knocks several glasses over.

"The best bit…" I say, and only demons know what possesses me to keep pushing him. "I've got nothing to lose by pissing you off. You might reap my soul, but you can't for another thirty days."

He flashes so dark I swear he swallows Finis Tower whole. Thalia is still laughing when Mortem appears out of nowhere.

"Hey, Mortem," I say and kneel to pet him, but he darts away and heads straight for Lucy, who's reaching for a drink.

Mortem hisses and leaps at her, disappearing through her dress and I assume sinking his claws into her ankle because she lets the glass go and hops around, screaming.

Mortem appears under the drinks table. What the fuck has gotten into him? Why is everyone so weird tonight?

Lucy pats down her leg, realising there are no marks, and then reaches for her glass. But it's gone.

"Helena, I think you took my drink," she says.

"I'll grab you another one, sorry, I thought it was fresh," Helena says.

"Well, it was, but never mind, you keep it."

"Thanks, I'm gasping," she says and gulps down half the glass.

She swallows but her face turns a funny colour. She steps back.

"Oh," Helena says. "Oh, dear."

Her face contorts, she buckles over and throws up like a waterfall. The liquid comes first. Then what I assume was her dinner and then blood.

So much blood.

A scream rips through the courtyard.

Lucy staggers back.

Ignatius surges forward. Thalia and Alistair both reach for Helena.

"GET A MEDIC," Thalia screams.

I clock the two students who I didn't recognise escaping out the library archway.

"Lucy," I bellow.

Chaos erupts as Helena drops to the floor, her mouth foams as she seizes. Space is made for her, but that's the last thing I see as I drag Lucy away. Ignatius catches me with Lucy's hand threaded through mine, and my stomach churns. He might not be able to touch me for a month, but he can make my death painful.

Bastien and Lex spot me and charge after us.

"Get her back to House Inferos," I bark at Bastien.

"Like fuck, that was my glass," Lucy says.

"Exactly. That's the second attack on you, and I want to know why."

"*You* want to? It's me they keep coming after. You're not going after them without me," Lucy says.

"Wow. At least you don't argue like a married couple," Lex says.

"I would like to point out, they are, in fact, getting away," Bastien points a lazy finger in the direction of the cloisters.

"Fucksake," I growl and yank my scythe out. "I swear to gods, Lucy, you get injured, and I'll reap your soul for you."

"So dramatic, and just over a professor…" Lex says, her expression implying the fact she's fully aware that Lucy is anything but *just* a professor to me.

Something I'll have to deal with later.

The four of us chase after the students but they're way ahead.

Lucy calls the campus's magic, and dark ribbons peel off each building as we pass. She whispers words into the threads of one. "Tell Obidiah to keep them on campus."

The ribbon twirls and then vanishes.

We manage to catch up to the supposed students as their hands claw and pull at the gates.

"Stop there, motherfuckers." I say and run my scythe along the iron railing, sending sparks flying.

Reap her. Reap her. Reap her.

That voice, all whispers and shouts, slithers into my mind. It forces pressure through my brain. I buckle under the weight of it, clutching my temples as a searing pain makes my vision white out.

Not now, motherfucker. I force the campus out of my head and wipe the sweat away from my brow.

"Don't hurt us," the man says. He's wearing Finis uniform, something most students are not doing tonight, which is one reason they stood out. But now I'm close, I can see the Societas emblem emblazoned in ink on the underside of his wrist.

"We were told to do it," the woman with him says.

But what concerns me is that both of their eyes keep skittering to Lucy. Bastien scruffs the man.

"You better start talking," I say and slide the scythe under his neck.

"Please," the woman begs.

"Talk. Before I lose my patience," I snap.

"I'd tell her something useful—I've seen her pissed off," Lex adds.

"The Societas sent us," she says.

"Something I don't already know," I say and slide my scythe to the man's wrist, forcing it to flip over to display his tattoo.

Motherfucker.

"Talk," I demand.

He stays silent. So, I slip the scythe to his pinkie and flick my wrist, severing the digit from his hand. He shrieks, dropping to his knees as blood streams from the open wound.

"Stop! I'll tell you," the woman says. "There's a theory within the Society."

"Speak faster," Bastien says, gripping him tighter as I slide the scythe under his index finger.

"Th—they think that Lucy is the key to resurrecting Architecti," the woman stumbles over her words as she tries to get their story out fast enough.

"Why? What the hell has it got to do with Lucy?" Lex interrupts.

"We're not high ranking enough to know," the man pants, looking rather grey.

My eyes fall to Lucy. She's pale, her eyes skittish as she takes it all in. But the woman glances from Lucy to the man.

I move the scythe to her throat. She wasn't expecting it,

she expected me to keep the violence to the man. What she failed to comprehend is that I'd burn Finis to the ground if it meant Lucy stayed safe. The woman stumbles against the gates.

"P—Please," she begs.

I snarl. "You should know, I love it when a woman begs." I bring the blade up to the crease in her neck. "And I am really good with a scythe, so talk before I get bored and do something you regret."

"Okay, okay, okay. I don't know exactly. But I heard the elders talking about something Ignatius did to her. That's all I know, I swear."

"That's too bad," I say and push the scythe through her throat and sever her soul.

"Midnight," Lex gasps.

"NO," the man screams, but I'm already shoving Bastien out the way and plunging the blade through the man's spine.

They drop to the floor, soulless. Dead. I'm breathing hard. Lucy is white as a sheet.

"Lucy," I say, reaching out to her.

But she turns and runs.

37
ARCHITECTI

I t is an easy mistake to think that angels are good or incapable of evil. Just as it is an egregious error to assume that demonkind is evil or incapable of good. The gods made us in their image, and yet, we have free will.

The most heinous error of all is to assume that the gods are infallible.

We are as they are. And it is our free will that means we can *sin*, just as demons can *save*.

Today, Interitus and I are eighteen.

Today, we will gaze upon the Mirror of Fate and witness a vision of our futures.

This ceremony is far less regal than the others. We are to enter the Room of Fates, locate the Mirror inside and see what it shows us. It sounds so simple, and yet it is the hardest rite of all.

What if we do not like the future it shows us?

What if our fate terrifies us?

Worse, what if it thrills us?

Interitus stands beside me, our hands entwined on the door handle.

"Are you ready?" she says to me.

"No. Are you?" I ask.

She smiles, a dark little thing made of shadows and blades.

"I don't care what the mirror says. I already know my fate."

"How can that be so?" I ask.

"Because I've decided it. No matter what the gods throw at me, I shall carve it from their bones if I must."

"Interitus," I scold. "You can't talk like that. What if they materialise? What if they hear?"

"I think you're missing the point, dear sister."

I frown at her, our hands twisting the knob.

"I. Don't. Care," she whispers.

For eighteen years, I have tried with all my celestial being to love my sister, and I do. It has always been us, together, with our parents gone much of the time doing what celestials must do. This is the way with angels—we are a community, raising children together.

When I felt alone, she was there.

When I felt afraid, or sad, or jealous, she was there.

But the thing I didn't like to admit, is that sometimes she was the reason I was afraid.

We step in to the Room of Fates and stand before the mirror just as millions of angels have before us. This mirror has always existed.

And it will stand long after we are gone.

Interitus, in an unusual bout of politeness, lets me step in front of the mirror first.

The Crowned Moth flutters from my shoulder, dancing around the mirror's gilded frame. The surface ripples and shifts, flickering with an infinite number of futures, made bigger by the fact my moth dances with the mirror. Its starry wings flirt with the blanket of stars shimmering beneath the mirror's surface.

A tower appears, I stand atop it, my hands twining with the stars, weaving possibility and futures. Tears fall down my cheeks.

I don't understand.

My hands weave a tapestry of souls and civilisations, love and art and the most beautiful memories. But the longer I stare at myself, the more I realise I am not crying in sorrow. It is because I am burdened. Burdened by the weight of choice, of carrying so much free will. For every thread I weave and cut, there are an infinite number of others. It's too much. My power lies not just in creation, but in the responsibility of that creation.

This is not the future I thought I had.

The mirage trembles.

Interitus has stepped into the mirror's view.

I swear the tower I am standing on flickers, one moment I stand on it, the next I am trapped in it. But as soon as the vision appears, it's gone.

Interitus laughs. "Such nonsense. Look." She pushes me out of the way, and my fate dissolves. In its place, a ruined garden. Dead plants, a derelict castle. The stars I so carefully weaved fall from the sky like hail.

Interitus appears in the mirage, her wings are fully blackened. She smiles next to me, her teeth sharper than they were, I swear.

Every step she takes another path crumbles and dies. And she smiles harder.

It makes cold slip down my spine and into my wing tips.

"You have the gall to stand there and judge me," she spits.

I huff at her. "You're a destroyer."

She snaps her head towards me. "And you're naive. I am not destroying anything. I am not causing the end of things. Merely acknowledging them."

"Not if you're choosing to end them for the mortals."

She snarls. "And you're doing the same by providing a predestined future. You're creating the illusion of free will but you're no better than me, sister."

"You're deluded, I don't choose for them, I give them possibilities to choose from."

"AND THEY CHOOSE THEIR ENDING." She shakes, but I realise too late it's not fear or frustration.

It's fury. I gasp as I scan along her outstretched arm.

"Interitus, what have you done?"

She tilts her head at her hand, which is buried deep inside the mirror. She grips the mirage between her clenched fingers.

"Be careful, you could—"

Her smile cuts me off. It's vicious, and toothy, and full of venom.

"I am so tired of your self-righteousness. I don't want to be at war with you," she says and slowly pulls her hand out of the mirror.

"And yet you fight with everyone."

I realise my mistake a heartbeat too late. The rage starts in her eyebrow, one sharp arch that filters into her eyes. They grow cold and hard and dead.

It makes me swallow.

"I'm sorry, Interitus. I didn't mean it. Just... Just be careful. The mirror."

Her neck cords.

"Interitus, please, it's older than our bloodline. Don't do this because I said the wrong thing. I'm sorry."

I call the Crowned Moth to me, desperate to weave any future that isn't the one unfolding before me. But I'm too late.

My moth isn't fast enough.

I reach for her starry wings, but my magic is panicking. She's producing too many futures and none of them are in my control. She sinks under the weight, as possibility spawns thousands of Architect moths from her wings.

Interitus, with her hand still buried inside the mirror, clenches our fate in her fist.

The sound is hideous. A creaking like nails clawing at a chalkboard prison. Like metal shrieking against metal. Like the howling of a mother losing her baby.

I clasp my hands to my ears.

The mirror wobbles, its surface bulging and flexing.

"Please don't destroy it." I get on my knees and beg.

"I will not have my future determined. Not by you or the elders or the fucking gods."

She rips her hand from the mirror, and it bursts. A million, trillion futures erupt. Stars and fate and futures scatter around the room in light and dust and screams.

The mirror bleeds life onto the floor. I scramble up, desperate to stand it up. Desperate to grab my moth and weave a future where the mirror heals and fixes itself. But my moth is exhausted. My panic overwhelmed it.

I scoop up the pieces and furiously try to put them back into the frame. But it's too late. The Mirror of Fate is broken and I can't fix it.

"What have you done?" I whisper.

"You did this," Interitus says.

"No," I shake my head. And it's the first time I've openly disagreed with her. "You did this. You went too far this time."

She smiles. I've always loved it when someone bestows a smile upon me, but hers, I've grown to hate.

She picks up a piece of the mirror and hands it to me.

"And what do you see now, sister?" she asks.

I can't answer, because as my eyes draw down upon the mirror, I am sickened. But more than anything, I'm terrified by the singular looping future I see before me.

38

LUCY

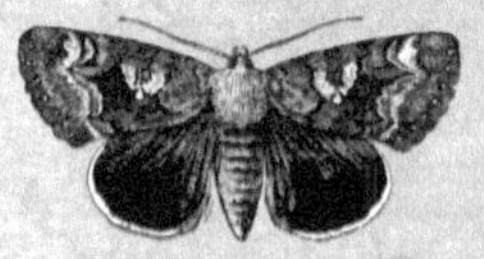

Helena's cremation is a simple affair. We bury her in the campus cemetery two days after the incident. Her celebration, like all funerals in Ora, begins in Church Vitalis remembering her life and ends in Church Mortis where we remember her death.

The professors are muted, the energy on campus dimmed compared to the loss of Malifax. He was a traitor, Helena was beloved.

And it's my fault. She died in my place. She died because of me.

Because the Societas are convinced I can somehow resurrect Architecti. But they're wrong. They're so fucking wrong, but only Father and I can prove it.

It doesn't matter how much he tries to convince me otherwise, it's my fault she's dead.

I take a couple of days off teaching to get some headspace, to think, to torture myself with the contract. It vexes me. I have tried every contact I have to see if there are any codexes or former professors who could translate angelic runes. But there are none. The ones that can still read it—

and they are few and far between—are reluctant to engage with anything celestial for fear of the Societas. Those I dared to show snippets of the contract to said while they could read some celestial runes, this was beyond their skillset.

Dead end after dead end.

No books or texts exist. They were all either burnt or vanished with the angels. Lex leant me her dictionary, but it's so rudimentary, and these runes are complex. It's as though every ounce of angelic language was sucked from our realm when Father disposed of Architecti.

I put my head in my hands, the frustration gnawing into my bones.

One of my moths flutters across my living room, its wings are so threadbare I really need to reanimate it again or I'll lose him. But it's such a gruelling process for their little bodies I'm always reluctant to put them through it.

He seems tired as I let him flutter around my cheek. I imagine he's kissing me hello.

"Sweet thing," I say and carry him back to the moth room just as there's a soft knock at my penthouse door.

It will be Midnight and her friends. Reluctantly, I pad to the door. I wondered how long it would take them to visit. Bastien and Lex barrel in, their arms full of texts and papers.

Midnight follows, her arms equally full though she doesn't look at me.

My body strangles me in a cocktail of sensations: my heart sinking while my stomach flutters like one of my young moths. Strange how we can hold conflicting things inside of ourselves. My fingers twitch, desperate to reach out to her, to hold her and touch her.

"Studying hard, are we?" I ask.

"Finals are killing everyone, don't even think I'm going to make it to the exam," Lex moans.

"And I thought Bastien was the dramatic one. We're still a couple of weeks out," I say, smiling.

"Rude," Bastien huffs.

I am about to highlight that he's making my point for me, but I figure it'll be lost on him.

Lex chucks her stuff on the table and opens the cupboards. "Bastien, can you make that thing again? It was delicious."

"You mean the chicken salad?" he deadpans.

"Don't be like that, you know it had a fancy sauce." She shuts the cupboard and hustles him into the kitchen while Midnight and I stand opposite each other, neither of us quite sure of what to do.

Her eyes flit to my neck, lingering there longer than normal.

"Is it on display?" I ask.

She nods.

I lower my eyes to the floor. Even her proximity is bringing out the runes now. I don't want to consider what this means, what the consequences of this are.

"I'm sorry I reaped them. I didn't mean to scare you," she says.

"Is that what you thought?" I ask.

She nods, her eyes welling up.

"Gods, Midnight, no. Thank you for doing it, you saved me. They wanted me dead."

"Then..."

"It's my fault she's dead. It just shook me, is all. I needed some time out. From..." But I stop myself because saying it would hurt her, and I don't want to do that either.

"From me," she finishes.

"I…" I start.

She holds her hands up. "No. It's fine. I get it. I knew from the outset you weren't able to commit, to have feelings for me. You were straight with me, and the fact that I developed feelings for you, is on me."

She takes a seat at the table and opens her books.

"Midnight…"

But Lex and Bastien return holding food and drinks for everyone.

"I just can't get this contract essay right," Lex whines while shovelling chicken and salad in her mouth. "All the clauses are clunky, and I think I'm missing obvious contractual issues."

"Give it here," I say, holding my hand out for the parchment.

I scan it, and it's actually exceptional. "I only see one issue. You've missed an obvious loophole here. Not going to tell you what it is, but this is where it should go." I point at a sub clause in her document, and she nods.

"Thanks, Prof."

I smile at her, all the while painfully aware of how quiet Midnight is. It makes my insides squirm recognising that I'm the one responsible for the haunted look in her eyes.

"Speaking of contracts," Bastien says, raising his eyebrow at me. "How has it gone?"

I shrug. "Not well." I get up from the table and pull the contract from the drawer. "I can't read it. And anyone I've tried to contact was a dead end."

Lex rubs her hands together as she nestles next to me and examines it.

"The fact it's in celestial runes…" Lex pauses.

Midnight rakes her hand through her hair and looks at me. "I guess it's to be expected, given your neck."

"And yet, Ignatius wrote the contract, so arguably it should be in demonic scripture," Lex continues.

"It's proving quite the mystery," I say.

"What do we do? How does it get read?" Midnight asks.

"It doesn't. I don't know anyone at Finis who can read angelic runes. In fact, I'm not sure I know anyone in Ora City who can. Not alive, anyway."

Bastien shifts in his seat. A light sheen breaks out over his brow.

I narrow my eyes at him. "Spit it out."

He rubs his forehead, licking and chewing at his bottom lip.

"Bastien?" Lex snaps.

He raises his hands in defence. "I know someone who can, or they could, at least."

"Define *could*," Midnight says, leaning on her chair legs to swing in her seat.

"She's dead," he groans.

"Says the resurrectionist," Lex scoffs.

He gives her a shitty stare. "What's the first rule of resurrection?"

"Who cares? I dropped it the first week we were here. I'm not in your classes, remember?"

But I know where this is going and why he's so uncomfortable. "Don't resurrect family," I say.

He points at me. "One point to the prof."

"It's your sister?" Midnight asks.

He nods. "Who is rapidly turning from a shade into a wraith. So... not exactly who we'd want to ask for help."

I slouch back in my seat, trawling through anyone I've met or colleagues of colleagues I might know that could help, but I come up empty.

"I'm out," Midnight says. "I don't know anyone."

"Me too," Lex says. "Had my sister known anyone, she'd have told me because she knows what a language nut I am."

Bastien pleads with me silently, his forehead lined. I search my memory for anything or anyone else I can think of.

"It's fine," I say. "I'm not putting this burden on you. You've all done too much for me already."

"Fuck that," Lex says. "Midnight's our gal, and if you're her gal, then that makes you our gal by default."

Midnight nods, Bastien too.

"Professor or not, you're one of us," Bastien says.

"Thank you, that's kind. But truly, this is my problem, not yours."

Midnight sighs. "I'm sorry, Bastien. Looks like you're our only option."

"I agree. Fuck," he says and puts his head in his hands.

39
MIDNIGHT

Twenty-One Days To Go

Bastien is white as a sheet. He paces basement floor minus six as Lex, Lucy and I try to locate a safe room for him.

This floor is mostly row upon row of cages and safe rooms, except for the giant practice room at the heart of this level.

We stride down the gloomy corridors, checking room after room.

Lucy and I continue sharing surreptitious glances; we're going to have to talk properly. Things are different between us, and we're avoiding talking about it. But we're running out of time. I have less than three weeks until the final exam and three weeks exactly until my birthday. If we don't talk soon, there may not be any more time.

I shouldn't think like that. I should assume I'll win the favour, and Lucy will be free of Ignatius.

Whether it's the incessant tinnitus-like whispering the

campus is doing in my ear, or the slick sensation of being watched always present on my spine, I am losing faith.

A melancholy has settled in my bones; an inevitability that things will end. Has fate finally caught up to me? Maybe it's just the ever-present weight a reaper carries.

"Any luck?" Lucy says, jolting me out of my thoughts.

Lex shakes her head as we walk down the next corridor.

I sidle up to Lucy and lean in to whisper, "We need to talk."

She snaps her attention to me. "Now?"

"I get that it's not convenient, but when else are we going to talk? There's only three weeks until the final exams and my birthday. We don't have a lot of time."

Her lips press into a flat line, but she nods. "Okay, talk."

"Wow, so open." It's childish, but I'm hurt.

"What do you want me to say?" she whisper-hisses at me.

"Oh, I dunno, how about how you actually feel?"

She fires me a look that bears the weight of a thousand emotions. She ages a decade in one fleeting glance.

"How I feel is irrelevant."

"Is it?"

"Yes, if I want to live. Don't you get that?"

I grit my teeth. I'm pissed at her tone. Pissed that she has feelings. More pissed that she's not admitting to them and royally fucking pissed that if she does admit to them, she'll render herself powerless.

I must be seething because Lucy stops dead.

"For fuck's sake, Midnight. What do you want me to do? Confess and what? Lose my power? For what? A relationship that's going nowhere?"

"Wow, just wow."

She looks at the floor, kneads her forehead. "I didn't

mean that. I— Gods. I'm sorry, that was really shitty of me. But... we can't talk about this."

She staggers, her hands clutching at her chest.

"What's wrong?" I say under my breath, the first hint of panic seeping into my ribs.

"This is... This is why I've been avoiding you, why I can't tell you how I feel." Her voice is softer now. When she steadies herself and moves her hand away from her chest, a wispy ribbon of red protrudes from her skin.

"Oh my gods. It happens that fast?" I say, all the rage seeping out of me and leaving me with a cold coil in my gut.

"All it takes is one slip, one truth told to you in an offhand comment, and I lose everything."

"I guess, I always thought... So... this really isn't going anywhere?" I exhale, my throat thick, a hard lump making it tricky to swallow.

She doesn't respond to that. What would be the point?

"What happened to believing in free will? In our ability to change our future? I thought I was the pessimist?"

She doesn't respond to that either, and it makes my blood boil in my veins, my stomach swirl with hot thoughts and a crippling pain that shoots between my ribs.

The red smoky magic slides back into her chest and seals itself inside her crystalline heart. I bite the inside of my cheek until I taste copper, the searing heat and spike of pain calming me and grounding me. It's the only thing that stops me from clawing my chest open, ripping my heart out from between my ribs and stamping all over it.

What hurts the most is understanding what she's thinking: why bother giving your heart to someone when you know they'll be dead in a few weeks?

My eyes sting.

I move away from her. I don't want to be near her. All of

this was for nothing. Because one way or another, we're not meant to be together. Be it because I'll leave her powerless or because her father will come for my soul.

That thought makes me angrier than it has any right to.

Bastien rounds the corner, giving me something else to focus on. "We need the safest of safe rooms, ones where the exterior walls have had their Veil fabric reinforced. Plus, a room with wards on the walls, so that whatever we resurrect can't go any further than the room we're in," he says.

If we were just resurrecting a basic shade or reanimating animals, it wouldn't matter so much. But bringing a desiccating shade back to Finis is dangerous as fuck, especially when it's a family member.

"And just to be absolutely clear, you're all sure there's no one else we could find?" Bastien asks.

"I mean, sure, there's a girl I know from a different city who knows literally everyone, but she got married recently so I suspect she's busy," I say.

He pouts at me and continues pacing up and down and around us in circles until I grab him by the wrist and hold his hand, forcing him to stay by my side.

"You're doing my head in," I mumble.

"Sorry," he says.

I rub the back of his hand trying to give him some reassurance.

"It's going to be okay, bud."

He tilts his head at me and mouths, "Is it?"

Probably not, this is wildly dangerous, but thankfully I don't have to answer him because Lucy stops dead at the end of the corridor and says, "This is the one."

Mortem materialises, chewing on a translucent tail. It's honestly beyond me how that floof ball keeps finding mice tails. He's never managed to catch a moth let alone a rodent, at least not to my knowledge. Makes me wonder where he's getting them.

Lucy seals us in the room, just to make doubly sure that Bastien's sister can't escape, and then calls her magic. It zips away from the walls in thick, shadowy wisps. She places them around the door frame almost like Sellotape, ensuring there are no gaps. When she's done, she turns to us.

"No one in, no one out. That means you too, Mortem. I know you can materialise, but I don't want any out routes for Calyx."

"Meow." Mortem dips his head. He's been far better behaved since the library, and quieter too. I don't know if it scared him into behaving. But I miss the grumpy bastard and all his quarrelling.

He sits at my feet while we wait for everyone to get ready.

"Lex, you're on salt and demonic runes. Bastien, we need your blood on the mirrors," Lucy says, jostling everyone into position.

Lex makes the circle large enough that trapped-in-the-middle Calyx won't be able to reach us, but also small enough that we have room to step back and her not touch us if she lashes out.

Bastien steps into the middle of the circle and places the mirror in the centre.

"Wait," Lucy says, holding her hand out as Bastien has the serrated edge of the blade millimetres from his skin. "You don't have to do this."

Bastien rolls his eyes. "When are you going to let your friends look after you?"

Lucy's lips part. Her eyes go glassy. Then she lowers her head and nods, stepping back.

Bastien slices his hand and lets it drip onto the glass. He takes a vial out of his pocket and opens the lid.

He mumbles words under his breath, sprinkling Calyx's ashes onto the mirror. Then he hops out of the circle, his skin looking as grey as his features are grave.

I open my arms and wrap them around him. Lex jumps in on the other side and Lucy, to my surprise, throws hers around him, too.

"We believe in you," I mumble into his shoulder.

We step away to give him space. He takes three long, deep breaths and calls his magic.

Dozens of gnarly dark ribbons peel off the walls and wrap around his fists and arms, making him look like a swollen thundercloud.

He throws the first thread of magic towards the circle, using his hands to coax them into spinning.

Another goes, then another. Until the salt circle is no longer visible. The black shadows spin and swirl around so fast, they become a seething mass. It's a fucking tornado in my mind. A tornado of magic and chaos. I edge back, both impressed with Bastien's magic and mildly concerned we're all about to die.

Bastien buckles to his knees.

"Keep going, Bastien," I shout. I want to go to him, to slide my hand in his and give him my energy, but it's impossible and it wouldn't work anyway. I've mastered resurrecting the rodents and small mammals needed to get a good grade, but it isn't my speciality like it is his. He's on his own.

He bares his teeth, his brow glistens with beads of sweat, but the ribbons of magic keep spinning faster and faster.

Resurrecting family isn't just forbidden, it's also difficult. Our bodies and minds fight doing it subconsciously because we know it's wrong.

Bastien lurches forward and throws up, the pile of liquid far too bloody.

I glance at Lex, her face wrinkling. Bastien holds his hand up.

"Stay back," he says. "I've got this."

His nose erupts, blood pours over the floor, straight onto the salt circle.

"Oh fuck, he absolutely does not 'got this'." I lunge for Bastien and yank him back.

"SALT," Lucy bellows at Lex, who is already opening the canister and hurling salt onto the floor to complete the circle.

The dark ribbons of magic surge and spiral into a funnel, swirling so fast it creates wind inside the room.

This was such a bad idea.

I drag Bastien away, but he passes out cold becoming a dead weight. Sweating and puffing, I manage to get us to the edge of the room—the safest distance I can.

"I'm sorry about this," I whisper to him and then slap him hard across the face.

He jerks up, gasping for air. "Did I do it? Is she back?"

We glance behind us, and as the black sinuous ribbons dissipate, there, standing in their shadowy remnants, is the most hideous creature I've ever seen.

"Yeah, I think you did it."

40

LUCY

Midnight won't look at me. Her skin is mottled and taut, she cracks her neck, and I am grateful she's this way and not the opposite. If she withdrew and became forlorn, I'd fear I'd done irreparable damage.

She drags an unconscious Bastien away from the salt circle and proceeds to slap him across the face.

I wince, but he comes around as the seething mass of magic and shadows coalesces and then evaporates.

The thing that stands before us is grotesque. Neither shade nor wraith, it is a gross violation of both species.

Patches of what was Calyx are ghostly like Mortem, shimmery white and translucent. But there are large areas of wilted skin. Necrotic and gangrenous, withering into flaking black pustules and blisters. One of her shoulders looks dislocated and where her mouth once was is a gaping maw with hundreds of teeth.

I glance at Bastien. He kneels before her weeping, not at her appearance, but at her eyes. They remain as they were when she was mortal. Round and blue and this evening, full of sorrow for her brother.

"I need your help," Bastien says.

She nods slowly. "Always," she says, her voice soft and dreamy, almost ethereal.

Then her body jerks and spasms, she hurls herself against the circle boundary, screeching. Some of the salt sprays out from the impact. Lex twitches, the jar open in her grip, ready to reinforce if necessary. Bastien shuffles back and throws his arm out. A loop of magic peels off the wall and encircles his fist, which he flings at his sister.

"Calyx, please stay with me, don't let the wraith take over."

He loops more and more sinewy ribbons of magic around her arms and feet. One slips around her neck like a collar and finally binds her in position. His expression is strained, years of regret etching grooves into his skin.

"Why should I help you?" she spits. This time her voice is gravelly and cold, every word rasped like she swallowed glass and sandpaper.

It makes me shiver.

He reaches towards me, his fingers wriggling. I hand him the parchment, and he shows her.

"I need to know what it says," Bastien pleads, his bottom lip wobbles as he takes in the sight of his very dead sibling.

She laughs. It's a shrill curdle that eats at your bones. "After what you did? You made me hurt them, Bastien. Our own flesh and blood."

She twitches and a translucent projection appears before her. It's wispy and sepia and plays in staccato movements.

Bastien sobs, one guttural cry from deep within his chest.

Oh gods. She's replaying a memory. This isn't the first time he's resurrected her, I recall. She slaughters everyone but him. He stands among the broken bodies and bloody pools, wide-eyed and trembling as he forces her back through the Veil. Then he's all alone.

The ribbon of magic holding her collar bursts. Bastien is frozen in a looping cycle of memories. He's choking. We're going to have to intervene.

I call magic from the walls and bind her again. But she's strong, far stronger than my magic can sustain. I'm no resurrectionist, I don't know all the proper spells to keep her trapped.

"Bastien, get a fucking grip," Midnight says through bared teeth.

But he's stuck in the past, and screaming at him isn't going to help. Not this time.

I slide my hand over his shoulder, thinking perhaps he needs coaxing out, a gentler form of encouragement. "You're not alone anymore. We're here for you, Bastien."

He blinks, shaking his head as if ridding himself of her hold. He touches my hand and squeezes and then focuses on what's left of his sister.

"I am sorry I called you back then, it was a mistake. Will you forgive me?"

She throws herself forward, smashing against the circle and tumbling back. As she crashes to the ground, it seems to snap her back to more shade than wraith.

She hauls herself up. "I forgive you, but the wraith... it's stronger than me."

Bastien scoots forward, his hand outstretched.

I grip his shoulder, pulling back. "That's close enough."

"What can you tell us about these runes?"

Her head twists left and right so far it makes me queasy.

"Let me out, and I will," she rasps.

"I can't do that," Bastien says.

She screams, bends double and then jerks back, bursting the bindings I made and sending me hurtling. I smack my head against the wall and slide to the floor, my vision spotty.

Midnight darts across the room, kneeling to check me, but I'm fine. Just bruised. Her expression softens, the anger fading, though it still simmers beneath her skin.

I reject her outstretched hand, not out of spite, but because I am okay, I can help myself. But her eyes darken, her teeth clench and she marches away.

"I didn't—" I start, but what's the point?

Maybe it's better to let her be angry with me.

Calyx throws herself against the salt circle, over and over until a piece of her forehead cracks and necrotic ghost skin flies around the room. It splatters against the wall, making a vile squelching sound and turning my stomach.

"I love you," Bastien says. "And I'm so sorry."

Calyx stills. Her bright expression going cold as she collapses to her knees. Her maw hangs open; a piercing sound erupts from the void. The walls rattle and rumble, and I thank the archdemon I found an empty room with reinforced Veil structures.

Giant necrotic tears fall from her cheeks. "I can't. It won't let me," she says, her voice finally returning to a soft lilt.

"Okay," Bastien nods. "Okay, go and rest in peace."

Her expression contorts and twists and morphs. Her shoulder cracks, her spine snapping forward and back as she fights for control.

"It's coded," she says breathless. "You... You need a codex to unlock the words."

He sits up, so do Lex and Midnight. Finally, we're getting somewhere.

"Where can I find a codex?" he breathes.

Her body jerks left and right like she's being shot. She must be fighting the wraith inside her. Her face contorts and reforms. Serene one moment, gnarled the next.

"Not somewhere..." She screams then, her voice descending into the grating rasp once more.

"Maybe you should let her go, Bastien," Midnight says.

"Midnight's right, time to send her back." Lex fists a load of salt and reinforces the circle as best she can from a distance, chucking the salt at the thinner places.

"No," he pleads. "We're so close. What do you mean 'not somewhere?'" He asks, inching nearer and nearer the salt circle.

Lex glances at me and then to Midnight. He's losing his ability to let go. We need to act.

"Someone," she shrieks, every trace of softness gone.

"Bastien," I plead. "Now."

"I can't," he sobs.

His knees are dangerously close to the edge of the circle. All three of us use our bodies to push him back away from his sister.

"Please," he whines. "She's all I have left."

"You have us," Midnight says and kisses him on the forehead, finally understanding that he needs comfort and not encouragement.

The wail he lets out reaches straight into my heart. This is why we don't bring relatives back. It's too hard to say goodbye all over again.

"I love you," he says, over and over. "I'm sorry."

"S... S... Someone," she manages.

"The codex is a person?" I blurt.

She nods.

Bastien and Calyx hold each other's gaze for a moment longer. Calyx is bent forward, her shoulders heavy, exhausted. Bastien draws his hands together and splits them. The magic holding her here severs and she dissolves, her hand outstretched, seeking one more touch.

He kneels, blood pouring from his nose, his hand still outstretched. It's no longer pain in his expression but agony. It's so acute I'm not sure if he will ever recover, and it's my fault. They did this for me, and all I'm doing is causing them pain. Bastien slouches, Midnight pulls him to the ground. He curls up into the foetal position. Midnight spoons him from behind, Lex snuggles into his chest, and they let him cry.

People never die when we want. But perhaps that is the only way it should be? If we knew when our end would come, like Midnight, would we eat ourselves up contemplating how to live meaningfully? Or would we bury our head and deny the truth.

We're all messed up, whether we fight fate or face it.

41

MIDNIGHT

**Nine Years, Five Months,
and Twenty-Nine Days To Go**

The first thing I do when I haul myself off the bedroom floor is shower, drink a toxic amount of coffee and then march myself back to the cemetery I summoned Ignatius in.

Fuck Aurelia.

I intend to break my contract and spend the rest of my life wishing her a sickening amount of bad karma.

I draw the same salt circle as last time. Even though it didn't contain him, I feel safer making it.

I place the mirror in the circle. Slit my palm and drop several droplets of blood on the mirror.

Nothing happens.

Weird.

Is it because I don't want the demon the way I did the last time? The desperation to save Aurelia was acute, now I'm just pissed.

My fingers find the brand on my wrist and rub as I continue to summon Ignatius.

A tingle scratches my fingertips.

The cemetery tilts. Dark clouds billow and throb in the sky, shadows crawl across the graveyard like the skitter of spiders.

They swirl around me, faster and faster as if I'm caught in a tornado.

My body is yanked backwards, my arms fling out to support me, but I never hit the ground.

I fall down.

Down.

Down.

When I do hit the ground, it is not in the cemetery.

I am in an office, blinking up at a ceiling. There are walls lined with shelves of books and jars and specimens and interesting tools and trinkets. My eyes land on a shelf of blades, my fingers twitching to hold them, use them.

I stand up to find a large mahogany desk, behind it a wall of achievements and the occasional framed piece of artwork from a child.

Candles flicker in sconces.

The door flings open, making me flinch. Ignatius strides in and glowers at me.

"I'm busy. Speak fast," he says.

"I want my soul back."

That stops him mid-stride. I stare at him.

He stares back. When I continue the staring, he makes an odd guffaw sound. "Wait, you're serious?"

"Deadly."

This time, he laughs. A full-bodied, head thrown back howl made of malice and cruelty.

"And what? You think I'd just give it to you?"

"Aren't all deals negotiable?"

"Before they're signed, sure."

"You broke your end of the deal," I hiss.

That makes his eyes narrow into venomous slits. He strides to his desk chair and sits.

"This should be good. Please, Mercedes, explain how I have cheated you."

"Aurelia..."

"Did she die?"

"No."

A nasty sneer curls his lip and makes spite dance in his features. "Then I fulfilled my end of the bargain. I gave you what you asked for."

I stand tall, my body tense and rigid. My fists clenching and unclenching.

"I didn't ask to be cheated on."

His face twitches as if he's trying not to smirk. He leans forward on the desk, clasping his hands.

"Let me get this right... you thought, because your girlfriend—"

"Ex."

There's that twitch again, and it makes me want to pick up one of the blades from his shelves and cut it from his smug face.

"You thought because your *ex* cheated on you that it would negate our blood contract?" He raises an eyebrow.

"I thought it was worth a shot."

"Nothing breaks a contract, Mercedes."

"My name is Midnight. And that isn't true, is it?"

He leans back in his chair. "Oh?"

"There are several recorded cases of contract breaks. Renegotiated, angelic blessings from the Crowned Moth and..."

"And?" he says, raising an eyebrow, clearly knowing exactly what the last method of contract breaking is.

"And the death of the demon."

He laughs, wipes his nose. "And you thought you could what? Summon me in that salt circle and stab an angel blade in my back?"

I shrug. "Anything's worth a shot when you've nothing left to lose."

He tilts his head at me, examining me. My arm sears hot, the brand flaring bright red. I'm dragged across the room until he lunges for my wrist and pulls me halfway across his desk.

"For wasting my time, I'm going to make you my personal reaper."

"No," I snarl through gritted teeth and try to wrench my hand away. I will not let him control even more of my life and what little time I have left.

The brand on my arm grows so hot it makes my eyes water. I bite the inside of my cheek against the rapidly blistering skin. My brand morphs and changes. The stench of burnt flesh fills the air, and I gag.

I wriggle harder, desperate to stop this, to change my fate. But I should have learned this by now. We mere mortals do not control our fate. We are nothing in a world of angels and demons.

Several entropy moths materialise and flutter around my head, sealing my fate.

That cunt.

Finally, he releases my hand, and I recoil, stumbling back and cupping my still sizzling wrist.

"You will spend the next nine years reaping souls for me, Mercedes, and then you'll have the pleasure of reaping your own soul."

With every ounce of poison I can muster, I say, "And if I refuse?"

"Feisty, aren't we. I already have control of your soul... but I tell you what. I like your sass, and I'm in a good mood today. I'll give you one IOU during the nine years to be used however you like. No questions asked."

"A favour?"

"Cute, but no. It's just an IOU. I suggest you use it wisely."

That was a mistake. I will find a way to use the favour against him. If he thinks I'm going to bend over and accept the loss of my soul, he's wrong. I don't care what he makes me do, I will never give up.

I smile, big, bold and toothy. "I'll use it now. Break my contract and let me out of it."

His expression turns cold. "Sass wears thin. Nine years, as many souls as I desire, and a single IOU in exchange. Now, choose your scythe and get the hell out of my office."

He jerks his head in the direction of the shelves of blades. He flicks his hand, and three dark ribbons of shadowy magic materialise, projecting out from the wall and coalescing in the corner.

"The shadows will take you home."

I reluctantly head to the shelves, always keeping the shadows in my periphery. My fingers skim across the rows of blades, trailing over the hilts. The ribs, grooves and gilded handles are all as stunning as the intricate detailing on their curved blades.

But none of them call to me. I don't just want a blade. I want a weapon I can use on a demon.

I dismiss a dozen in rapid succession. Too heavy, too small, too dirty, too old.

My eyes catch on a bone on the shelf above; it's locked

in a glass case, lain on a silky bed. But I swear it shimmers, almost as if it's made of stars.

My fingers fumble over the latch and push the lid up. I need to choose a scythe, not a bone, but I feel like it's calling to me anyway.

I hover just above the bone. It's a finger, but the bone doesn't look like any I've seen before, it shines like the deepest night sky.

I stroke the bone, and it trembles. When I pull away, there, laid on the silk fabric, is a scythe. The hilt is still curved and ridged, the bulbous knuckle forming the tip. But protruding out is a silvery-white blade made of bone.

This is the one.

I can't explain why, but it calls to me. I need it.

I swipe it, slot it in my pocket. It sits heavy against my thigh, unnaturally warm as if it hungers for the souls I'll reap. Or maybe it remembers the soul of the titan who once wielded it. It's special, that much I recognise. I lower the glass case and glance at Ignatius. He doesn't bother to look at me, his head buried deep in scrolls.

When I look back at the silk bed, another bone has appeared. I squint down only to realise it's not really there. A ghost of a bone, but you could only tell if you knew to look closer.

I step into the shadows, the oddest sensation settling in my gut. Warmth that spreads to my chest, setting my heart to racing.

Even as I disappear into darkness and Ignatius fades, I feel like I've won. Like I took something of his, and he doesn't even know it yet.

42

LUCY

Someone knocks softly at my apartment door, and I know before I even get out of my chair who it is.

It's been ten days since we resurrected Calyx.

Ten days and no Midnight. She hasn't come to my classes. We haven't studied at night. She must be worried about the finals. She came to Finis to win the Demonic Favour, and she won't if she doesn't study relentlessly.

If she's not concerned about it, I certainly am. I've tried her apartment every day, left messages with Lex and Bastien and shoved letters under her door.

Nothing.

It also means I am no closer to deciphering my contract, and she knows that.

I don't want her to put the favour at risk because she's pissed at me, or worse, use me as an excuse to self-sabotage.

Which is why I pull the door open and I'm instantly cross. Her shoulders are drawn in and tight while furrowed lines darken her blue eyes into swirling pools of rage.

She's more than mad at me.

How dare she. What exactly does she expect from me? To give up everything? Make myself completely at her whims and in need of her protection?

"Hi," I say, and have to force myself not to sound shitty. To at least give her a chance to explain why she's here.

She won't look at me when she speaks. "Could we please continue our study? Finals are imminent, and I would like to continue with our deal, should you see fit to want that."

"Is that meant to be an apology?"

This makes her head snap up, her expression thinning. "And what exactly am I supposed to be apologising for?"

I huff. "Oh, I don't know, maybe the fact you know I can't read that contract without you. So you punished me by withholding the one thing I need."

She shoves past me into my apartment. "Well, don't worry, I put my favour in jeopardy, too. So I guess we're both fucked now."

"Mature, real fucking mature. A bit like your demands, your expectations. You want more from me than I can give. And when I didn't give it you, you went dark. Walked away like a child instead of talking this through."

"What the hell have I demanded from you? Other than meeting your half of our deal?"

I close the door and stride into the living room area after her. She's pacing. Wearing lines into my carpet where her boots grind into the floor.

"You don't have to use words to make demands, Midnight," I say.

She stops still. "You fucking hypocrite."

"I beg your pardon."

She sniffs, wipes her forehead and glares at me. "And

you don't have to use words to tell me you have feelings for me."

I baulk. How are we here again?

"This was supposed to be a deal. I help you win the favour, and you help me break my contract. You agreed to that."

She flings her hands up. "Neither of us knew that fucking you brought the runes out. Things change, Lucy. That's part of being human."

"I'm no—"

"Don't you fucking dare pull that shit with me. You feel, therefore, you have human experience."

I shake my head. "Your feelings won't leave you power-less, vulnerable."

She scoffs at me. "How can you know so little about mortals? Don't you get it? Don't you understand what happens to us when we fall in love?"

I fall silent, her words sinking in. Finally, after what feels like an aeon, I speak.

"You're in love with me?" My eyes sting hot and watery.

"You think you're so different." She's snarling. Furious with me because she loves me. She resumes pacing and ranting. "Humans don't have crystalline hearts, no, and our power doesn't rest inside them, but fuck, it might as well."

"What do you mean?" I say and step closer. Her bright blue eyes are all flames and passion.

She shakes her head at me. "You set yourselves apart like you're so fucking different. But when a mortal truly falls in love, they may as well rip out their beating heart and hand it to their loved one. That's the power another holds over us. Love is making yourself wholly vulnerable. It's giving yourself to another. There's no one more capable of hurting you than the one you're in love with. It's why

Aurelia broke me... and it's why having you in my life remade me."

Her words cut me so deep, my crystalline heart shivers. How is it she can penetrate my defences without me noticing? I stiffen as my chest squeezes; I swear hairline fractures form on the surface of my heart.

She is danger.

She is my ending.

My undoing.

And I can't seem to walk away. My feet lead me towards my demise. My heart trembles but my body holds firm in the face of the passion oozing from her every pore, every clenching and unclenching of her fists.

She makes me feel wanted, and yet there's an ache in the back of my throat that reminds me we're doomed.

This is where she seems so young, so innocent. She can't see that love isn't enough. No matter how much we might yearn for each other, we won't make it through this.

"Tell me you see it?" she says, fury coiling in her expression. "Answer me, dammit."

She's shouting. I know better, though. And I want to save her from this pain, but I am as fallible as she is. I'm inches from her now. Heat swirls between us, barbed and serrated it hooks beneath my ribs and draws me closer, closer.

"Say something..." She's pleading now, and I know what she needs.

Words aren't going to help because I can't tell her what she wants. Not without sacrificing myself. I've come too far, I'm too close to being free of my father to lose it all now.

But I can give her my body.

My fingers find my shirt buttons and slowly undo them. I take the shirt off and drop it in front of her. My trousers follow. Until I'm stood in my underwear. I unclasp my bra, my nipples already erect by the time it falls to the floor.

She swallows as she holds my gaze, her eyes never dropping from mine, even though her breathing increases.

Maybe it's wrong, toxic even. But I don't know what else I can give her. What I can do is surrender my body to her. I just have to keep hold of my heart. But is it enough?

I slip my hands against my hips and drag my underwear down my thighs and step out of them.

I am utterly naked. She is still fully clothed, unmoving. A fact that makes excitement pool between my legs. Wondering what she will do with me, how she might punish me even though I'm giving myself as fully as I can to her.

I lower myself into the Nadu position. Sat on my calves, my hands open, palms rest on my thighs. My head lowered.

"Use me," I whisper. "Take your frustration out on me. Hurt me, Midnight. Hurt me the way I'm hurting you."

She inhales a sharp breath. "Fuck." The rigidity in her face loosens a fraction. I'm winning, getting through to her, easing the pain in the only way I'm capable of.

Shucking her jacket off, she throws it on the armchair. She cracks her neck, darkness swims in her eyes and it makes gooseflesh spill down my spine.

Tonight will be rough, exactly the way I like it.

Midnight moves to the dining room table and swipes everything off it in one movement with her arm.

"Who's your Daddy, Lucy?" She's furious and it makes my entire body electric. My skin breaks out in a cool sweat, my nipples form hard buds. One touch and I'll melt.

"You are," I breathe.

She nods, satisfied.

"Get on the table."

I stand up and make my way to the edge and hop up.

"Open," she says in a rumble coming from her chest. "Wider, Lucy." She says my name sing-song, as if she's exhausted by me and I'm an inconvenience. I see the game she's playing, the role she's taking on.

"Don't fuck about with me tonight," she says, her tone low and heady.

I suck my bottom lip in and push my knees as wide as I can, putting my pussy on display for her. Her lips twitch as she rakes her hand through her hair. I'm getting to her.

"Who do you belong to?" she says.

"You, Daddy," I say, and I swear my pussy must be glistening by now.

"That's right. Now tell Daddy where your toys are."

My grin deepens, knowing that even though I shouldn't use sex as a distraction, this *is* what we both need tonight.

"Top drawer," I cock my head towards the bedroom.

"Don't move. That pussy is mine. I want it on display for me when I return."

She takes a few minutes, but when she strides back in, she's topless, her breasts round and firm. I am desperate to put my mouth around them and suck one of her pink nipples between my teeth. The thought makes my mouth water with the aching need to taste her.

I drop my gaze lower. She still wears her leather trousers, but now a strap-on is secured in place with a vibe ring for my clit. In her hand, she carries a flogger, a paddle, and knot of rope.

She steps between my legs and places the toys on the table then grips my chin hard, forcing me to look at her. Her posture and movements still hold that simmering heat, the cloying mix of lust and the burn of anger beneath it. It drives me wild, like I hope tonight is going to be.

"Safe word," she says.

"Satan."

"You are mine, Lucy, do you understand?"

I hesitate too long.

Her hand rears back and slaps my pussy. I squeal and shunt backwards up the table. She holds my chin tighter, making the sting instantly morph into something silky. The moan that spills from my lips is raw. It affects her. Midnight's lips part, her eyes flash.

Her fingers clasp my jaw hard enough I'm certain they're going to leave bruises. It's wrong; I should tell her to ease up.

But I like it.

I *want* the marks. I want more of them. Want her to mark my body hard enough that even when this is over and we part ways, I'll always carry a piece of her.

Which is why I am very careful what I say next, knowing the reaction it will elicit.

"My *body* is yours, Daddy."

Her nostrils flare, frustration written in her expression. She slaps my pussy again, and I half scream, half moan as sharp tingles spread from my clit deep into my core.

She flips me over so my chest is pressed to the table, my arse in the air for her. Then she loops the rope around one wrist, chucks it over the table and ties my other wrist. She throws the rope under the table and picks it up, the other side knotting me in place, keeping me pinned to the table.

"Whores give their bodies. Is that what you are?" she snarls over my back.

She doesn't stop to ask me to move, just kicks my ankles out, displaying both my holes and my soaking pussy. My toes struggle to touch the floor. I'm barely able to keep myself in place. It makes my heart race, my breath short and a bolt of pleasure rush between my thighs.

The flogger comes down hard on my cheeks. It's the lightest sting but still makes me tremble.

I crane my head as she swishes her wrist this way and that, making sounds only someone practiced with one can. The kind of whistle and crack of leather that's both threatening and sexy simultaneously. I squeal in anticipation.

Whip. Whip.

She cracks the flogger on each side. I moan, my legs wriggling on the table. I can't see behind me and not knowing what's coming makes my heart rate spike. A warm, wet tongue swipes from my clit all the way to my arse.

"Oh gods," I cry out.

A clatter startles me. Through the crack in the table, I spot the flogger, and I brace instantly. The paddle comes down on my now-sensitive cheeks.

Once. Twice. Three times.

I scream as the sting burns viciously hot. My hard nipples rub against the table. There are too many sensations.

Her tongue assaults my clit with lavish licks and laps, the sensitive bundle of nerves already engorged.

She's relentless.

Pissed.

She sucks my clit between her teeth, applying enough pressure it makes me arch my back and sends a bolt of adrenaline coursing through me. She's taking me right to the edge. Pushing me, testing how much of myself I've really given to her.

I turn molten as she eases the pressure and resumes licking. My body floods with every hormone and emotion simultaneously. Her tongue carves me in two as she explores every millimetre of sensitive skin.

Worshipping it.

Praising it.

Making it hers.

She sucks and nips and licks and bites until my legs tremble so hard I have to grip the edge of the table to hold on.

A cool breeze flows between my legs as she backs off, then the head of the dildo meets my entrance and hovers. Teasing, tempting.

"What do you need?" she says.

So many things. To be free from Ignatius. Free to love her. But I can't have either of those things, so I choose the alternative.

"To not feel," I pant. "Make it all go away."

Because having pieces of me ache for Midnight and not being able to give them to her hurts worse than having my soul reaped.

She thrusts deep, spearing my pussy and shoving me against the table.

"Fuck," I cry out.

She pulls the dildo out and drives forward again, until she's hilt deep, the vibration from the ring pressing against my clit.

"Oh gods," I whimper.

She leans over me, her nipples caressing my back.

"You think I'm going to stop?" She breathes against my back, dropping kisses over my skin. "And I don't mean fucking you."

Oh gods, she means loving me. Making me fall for her. I try to wriggle, but the restraints have me locked in place. The first hint of panic coils in my gut as I try to move.

She thrusts in and out, and the loops of adrenaline morph into something else.

"Do you?" she whispers and then sinks her teeth into the fleshy bit of my shoulder. I cry out, the blister of teeth radiates as her hand smooths the skin.

I lie there moaning and turning to mush as she pumps in and out of me.

"You're mine. Tonight, tomorrow and every day you can conceive of. I am not letting you go, Lucy. No matter how long it takes, I will *come* for you."

The pressure lightens on my back as she stands up, dragging me to the edge of the table to relentlessly fuck me.

Over and over she drives into me, the vibrations bouncing on my clit. On. Off. On. Off.

I can't speak, I can't move. Pinned in place taking everything she gives me.

"Do you understand yet?" she says.

But when I don't answer, she brings the paddle down on my arse.

I rear up, barely rising two inches before the restraints pull me back down.

Paddle.

Paddle.

Paddle.

My cheeks are raw and burning, her hands caress the sting away. The pounding slows to a rhythmic thrust.

"Mine," she says.

Thrust, thrust.

"Mine."

In. out.

"Harder," I whisper.

She kicks up her hips. Pumping into me so hard we shift the table forwards.

"Harder," I beg. I want it to hurt; an orgasm wrapped in the delicious burn of pain, everything heightened, everything more.

But two wet drips plop on my back, and I realise this hasn't broken me.

It's broken her.

And that makes me crack. My eyes glaze, my own little pools of salty wetness forming under my cheeks.

"Harder," I sob.

"Mine." She thrusts and slaps and thrusts.

My body winds tighter and tighter. Cool drips raining on my back.

I'm yours, I think.

"Mine," she whimpers.

A raw throb settles between my ribs. For her, for me, and for everything we can't have. For everything I want laid before me and I'm unable to take.

"Say it," she pleads.

And this is all I can give her.

"I'm yours," I breathe as she picks up speed and rams into me over and over. Driving my body right to the brink.

"Come for me, baby girl," she says and spanks me again, driving the cock deep and pressing the vibrating ring against my clit in a relentless flow of pleasure.

I spill over, moaning her name and cursing my soul.

43

MIDNIGHT

Eleven Days To Go

I untie Lucy as fast as I can and carry her to the sofa. I give her a blanket.

"Get the contract. It's on my bedside table."

I rush to get it and as I bring it back, the same symbol on her shoulder forms on the page.

"Whoa, you really are a codex," I say and lay it on the coffee table in front of us.

The rune dissipates from her skin, appearing on the paper and then reforms itself into words.

Severance Clause:

This contract is binding for eternity unless Architecti is released.

I read the sentence over and over wondering why it jars. And then I understand.

"Why does it say 'released'?" I ask, my tone a little colder than it should be.

Lucy doesn't answer. She blinks at the contract, mumbling the wording over and over. I get up and pad to the kitchen to get us some water and put my shirt back on. I settle next to her, tugging her under my arm. Aftercare is important no matter what is going on.

"Do you understand what this means?" I ask and place a kiss on top of her head. I recognise that perhaps I shouldn't be providing such intimate care. She was clear— we're in a contract, nothing more. No matter what I want. No matter what I think she wants. Why am I torturing myself by being this close?

Lucy's puts her head in her hands. "There's something I have to tell you."

I stay quiet, giving her the space to open up.

"This is... it's the one piece of information I've held precious since I discovered it. Telling you... it requires quite the level of trust because it's my only leverage against my father. And you are *his* reaper."

"You don't trust me?" I say, trying not to sound hurt.

"That's not... I didn't mean it like that. I've just spent so long fighting my father on my own, I don't know how to do this with someone else. I asked you for help, and I recognise I've been resisting accepting it."

"What did I say earlier? You're mine. I am not letting you go no matter how hard you resist. You can trust me because you are the only thing I want in this life. Even if that life only lasts another eleven days."

She swallows, her eyes dropping away from mine. It stings.

"I didn't think it would be relevant."

"That what wasn't relevant?"

"Architecti... she's... she isn't dead."

"What are you talking about? Of course she's dead."

"No, Midnight, she isn't. Or not exactly, anyway. I don't know what she is now."

"You're not making any sense," I say.

She takes a deep breath, trying to focus her thoughts. "My father tricked her and imprisoned her. She's in some kind of purgatory, I guess. I don't know how he did it, only that she isn't actually dead. So, the Societas are wrong. They don't need to kill me to resurrect her, because she never really died. She's just trapped."

"Fuck me," I breathe, running a hand through my hair. "He tricked the entire city. We all thought we were safe."

"That's the thing, everyone is safe while she's trapped. What did it matter where Architecti was? She was gone and that was the point. It's why I never told anyone."

"And you have the gall to call me naive. You took the side of a man who lied to millions of people. Made them think he was their fucking saviour when really—"

I stop dead and glance at the contract, the words in dark ink on the parchment. Heat flashes in my cheeks. "Oh gods, he used you."

"What?" she says.

I point at the contract, my head swimming. "Don't you see? He used you. He trapped Architecti. This contract is between him and her and inked on your body. And the Societas are convinced you're the key to resurrecting her. This contract is the key, I don't know how, but I think the Societas are right. They're just wrong about resurrection."

Her eyes widen as she turns back to the parchment.

"He fucking used me..." she whispers.

A knock at the door startles us both.

"You expecting company?" I ask.

She shakes her head, wraps the blanket around her like a towel and cracks the front door open.

Lucy gasps and stumbles back. "Father…"

Oh, fuck.

Ignatius's eyes fall straight to the runes on her body, then scan the apartment, the debris of sex and kink. His skin deepens to a rouge that reminds me of lava. He snaps to face me.

I've never feared him. Not once. But tonight, I get close. He stalks across the living room, scruffs me by the neck and hauls me off the sofa.

"What did I tell you about Lucy?"

I grab at his wrist. His grip is too tight, I can't breathe, let alone speak.

"Put her down," Lucy's voice cuts through the tension.

Ignatius flinches.

"Now," she says, and I spot a glint of steel jabbing his side.

His grip loosens. She stabs the knife in.

"Release her properly."

He opens his hand and I stagger back.

"Can I trust you two long enough for me to gather clothes?" Lucy says.

"Don't look at *me*," I say.

Ignatius gives her a curt nod, and she dashes from the room. Neither of us move.

She returns with impressive speed.

"What do you want?" she barks at him.

"Why do you have celestial runes on your body?" Ignatius asks.

"You are well aware of why, perhaps *you* should tell *me*," she says.

Ignatius rubs a hand over his face and notices the

contract on the coffee table. "How the hell do you have that?"

"I'm not answering any questions until you start talking," Lucy says.

I'm in a dangerous position now. I should leave. Thanks to Lucy, I have leverage on Ignatius, but I don't want to jeopardise her if he finds out.

"Why are you here?"

"I came to protect you," he says, suddenly looking old.

"You cause her more pain than protection," I blurt and instantly regret it as he lunges for me.

Lucy steps between us, holding the knife under his chin. "Don't touch her."

He backs off, raising his hands. "Fine. There was a break-in. The Societas. I think we're in imminent danger."

"Where?" I ask.

"My office. They stole a bone."

"A break-in is awful, but why do you care so much about a bone? Just source a new one," Lucy says.

"I can't."

"Why?" I ask.

"Because it isn't just any bone. It's angelic. It's Architecti's finger, and it's one of the only weapons in existence that can kill a demon."

I frown. "I thought demons were immortal..." But there's more, something niggling at the edges of my mind.

"We are to mortals. But angels have the power to kill us. You have to be protected," Ignatius says and stalks to the windows, checking the latches.

"Why? Because if I die, Architecti is released?" Lucy says.

He stills.

A thick pause hangs in the air.

"I'm sorry," he says, and Lucy's lips part, a gasp escaping.

I'm not sure if it's the truth that's hitting her or the fact Ignatius actually apologised.

And that's when it hits me. I used Architecti's scythe in the Severance Rite.

"Oh my gods, she's here... isn't she?" I whisper.

Ignatius glowers at me. I brace myself, expecting a fight. "Yes," he says.

One word and everything falls into place.

Midnight, Midnight, Midnight.

That voice, that whisper and scream. It was never the campus.

"Who is where?" Lucy says, her eyes switching between us.

Ignatius sags. "Architecti. I trapped her here."

Which means I never made a deal with the campus. I made it with Architecti. A fallen angel. One who wants Lucy's soul.

Oh gods, what did I do? What will she do if I don't reap Lucy?

"I take it you've unlocked your contract?" Ignatius says.

Lucy nods.

Ignatius moves towards Lucy. "Which means... have you told her? Are you in love?"

Lucy shakes her head, her eyes glassy as she covers her mouth with her hand.

"What does it matter?"

"It matters because regardless of what you think, you are my daughter, and I do love you, and I don't want... You have to be protected at all costs."

"We've unlocked part of it..."

Ignatius continues checking the windows, the doors,

bathroom, any entrance and exit while the pair of us stand still, feeling helpless. My fingers slide to my scythe.

"Wait," I say.

Ignatius stops what he's doing.

"Where was the bone? What did it look like?"

"It was a finger bone. It was in a glass box."

I unclasp the leather holster and pull out the scythe I've carried for a decade.

"Like this?" I say and as I present it, it shifts and morphs back into a bone.

His eyes widen. "It was you..."

He hurls himself at me, but Lucy charges him and they careen into the kitchen counter.

"You will not fucking touch her," she screams.

"I didn't steal it today. I've had it the whole time. I took it the day you made me a reaper. I don't know what magic it has, but a ghost of a bone reformed in the glass case the second I removed it. You'd annoyed me, and I liked having one up on you."

He sags against the floor and Lucy clambers up.

"And no one else knows you took it?"

"No."

"Then that is something. I guess I'll be collecting that from you in a few days."

And there it is, the godsawful truth that lingers between us. Lucy's eyes flash.

"You will not reap her," she snarls.

"Lucy, sweetie, she made a contract. It's binding."

"Like mine, you mean?"

"Exactly."

"Then I guess I'll unmake mine."

He smiles softly at her, cups her chin the way a proud

father does. "That tells me you still haven't unlocked the final rune."

"You're not taking her from me," Lucy says, and it's the first time I've truly seen her fight for me. A hint of red smoke forms between the buttons of her pyjamas. I tense, expecting him to see it. He doesn't.

Instead, he says something that turns my blood cold.

"You won't. Not when you find out what you have to do to break it."

44

MIDNIGHT

Forty-Eight Hours To Go

The last week was exhausting. If the weight of my ticking clock weren't enough, I now carry Ignatius's secret too. The lie the entire city believes...it's all unravelling.

Ignatius has been skittish all week. Every time I see him around campus, he glares. A threat, a warning, or perhaps an omen of what he plans to do if we spill his secret. He hates the fact I've been helping Lucy unlock her contract, but his tight shoulders and pallid skin tell me it's less rage and more fear.

What is he afraid of?

We still haven't unlocked the final rune, despite best efforts. But I know the truth lays in it. And I can't think about any of it because today is the day I win the favour. I have to.

I've spent a year obsessively studying. Lucy fulfilled her promise of helping—we spent every second of the last week practicing and training. It's on me now. My biggest competition is Hadrian, and to my surprise and disdain, Aurelia. There's no fucking way I'm letting Aurelia beat me.

Not today.

Not again.

Today is a two-part exam. While they've been testing us on all our subject areas, our final marks for the top student are allocated based on our performance in our two best subjects. Mine being weaving and walking.

My friends and I make our way to Finis. We all clutch each other knowing this could be the last day we're together.

Bastien pulls me into a hug so tight I have to tap out.

"Gods, Bastien, don't suffocate a bitch before her exam," I mumble into his chest.

"Sorry, I'm proud of us, that's all. Thank you for the support this year, it's been..."

"Yeah," Lex says, pulling us both in again. "It has. And two days from now, when it's all over and Midnight is still with us, we're going to get shitfaced. Got it?"

The three of us smile, but mine never meets my eyes and I'm not sure either of them believes the words.

We part ways and each descends the stairs to our levels. Even though my primary subject is Veilwalking, my assessment is on level minus five.

I step down, down, down, but the stairs seem to meander and drift and the fifth floor never appears. The hair on the back of my neck prickles. Today isn't the day to fuck about, Finis.

My heart rate escalates. I move faster. I swear I already passed floor three. But there it is again.

And then again.

I stop. Rub a hand over my face and force my heart to slow. I will not let the campus get under my skin today. I hold a hand against the brick and silently tell Finis I will not be fucked with today.

Then I move again. Whether it's my veiled threat or the fact a breeze wafts over me that feels like a smug huff and tastes like satisfaction, or the fact I'm now unnerved, floor five finally appears.

When I locate the central hall, a ton of Doorstops are already waiting. They fidget in their seats, rub their knuckles anxiously and throw skittish looks across the room. I've shown enough proficiency in Veilwalking that they're primarily assessing my weaving today, with walking threaded in for easy bonus points.

I scan the observation deck; Lucy catches my eye and gives me a wink. She's sat with a pile of parchment, marking exams, I imagine.

The professors have thought about today and put out a ton of refreshments, though they mostly go untouched. Too many pallid complexions and furrowed brows. At least I'm not the only one feeling sick.

We're taken in one at a time to be assessed while the rest of us just wait.

The ticking clock on the wall grinds on my nerves. I have enough reminders of what tomorrow will bring without an incessant ticking.

Midnight.

That voice, no, Architecti, calls. I ignore it. In forty-eight hours I'll be dead if I don't win this, so what does it matter if she doesn't get Lucy?

Professor Alistair Ironheart walks out of the assessment room and calls my name.

"Mercedes Midnight?"

"Here," I say and traipse my way over, but I leave my

stomach where I was sat. Bile licks at my throat as I slip into the testing room and close the door behind me.

The archdemon Chancellor Arcadius sits at a long table with Alistair and a couple of the teaching assistants and a professor I recognise but can't remember their name, T something, I think.

"Don't be perturbed by the audience, they're mostly assessing me for my conduct and organisation of the exam. Professor Taplin is making sure you don't cheat. But that's it," Alistair breathes in my ear.

"Okay," I say.

"There are three assessments," Alistair begins. "I will make rapid cuts of the Veil, and you are to stitch them as effectively, neatly and as rapidly as you can. For the second assessment, you'll need to cut a hole large enough for the Chancellor himself to step through, seal him in and then unseal and release him. And last, the most dangerous test. We will strip you of your campus magic. You will need to draw on your own stores and emotions to weave a thread of magic strong enough to cut the Veil. You will enter, seal yourself in and then cut your way out, closing the Veil behind you. All without Finis magic."

I try to process everything he says. I didn't realise we were having to step inside the Veil without anyone to protect us. We've not done that before. Thank fuck I took additional defence lessons. And for the first time in a decade, I'm quietly pleased I'm a reaper. Knowing my scythe is strapped to my hip gives me a little—but not much—relief.

I've already forgotten the first assessment, but thankfully Alistair takes me through it again before moving me inside a salt circle and placing himself on the other side.

"Ready?" he asks.

I close my eyes and take a deep breath.

"Good luck, Midnight. Omnia mors aequat."

I call the campus magic to me, opening my hands and connecting to that piece of my soul that's buried inside the Tower somewhere. Buried, I realise, with Architecti.

Dark ribbons fire off the walls in quick succession until my hands are smothered in pulsing magic.

"Ready."

Alistair smiles, perhaps a little too widely. But this is our favourite game, and I am the best in class. He winks and then he fires magic out in a lightning-fast explosion.

His hands move left and right, up, down, behind me, in front. He's fucking quick.

The air fills with Veil rips, little glimmers of the other side floating wherever his magic cuts.

But I am just as good as him. And I fling magic at the tears in rapid succession. My fingers move so fast I surprise myself. My mind switches off, my body moving on autopilot.

Sweat trickles down my neck, but I remain focused, predicting Alistair's movements and coming in milliseconds after him to stitch where he's cut.

His eyes widen as I speed up, stitching every cut he made until I'm right behind him. I grin as he grows tired, and I continue to match him stitch for cut.

Finally, he staggers back, sweat running down his temples, breathing hard.

"I'm out," he says. "Bravo, Midnight. That was excellent."

My lips twitch, I try not to appear too smug, especially with Chancellor Arcadius and the other professors taking notes behind their desks.

Alistair passes me a bottle of water as he glugs from another then wipes his brow and resets the room.

"Chancellor Arcadius, if you please," Alistair says.

Arcadius pushes his chair back, the feet scraping along the floor, and makes his way to the circle. His nose turns up when he crosses the threshold. I mean, fair. I don't know any demon who's a fan of salt. It's usually pretty harmless to them once they're a devil like Arcadius and Ignatius, but I guess old habits die hard.

"Midnight," he says and inclines his head at me.

"Ready?" Alistair says.

I nod.

"Begin."

Honestly, this test feels easier than the first. While it's a large cut, the practice I've done means that cutting the Veil is as easy as using my scythe. I feel for a notch and swipe my hands up; the only difficulty is making a cut larger than my arm span.

I close my eyes and push the magic out, my muscles burn as the slice reaches the height of Arcadius's head. I dig deep and fling the magic the rest of the way, and the cut rips with a foot of space above his head.

I baulk when a wraith slips into view. But Arcadius flings his hand out and the wraith is thrown back, rolling and tumbling at least fifty feet away from the tear.

He steps through and glares at me. "I prefer it this side, so make sure you get me back."

"Yes, sir."

I bring my hands together, stitching and threading the Veil and sealing him inside.

Alistair steps in to check my stitching. When the scar vanishes, he says, "Seal complete. Begin cutting."

This time, I decide to show off a little, I draw more

magic than necessary from the walls until my arms are coated in throbbing black ribbons all the way up to my shoulders, and then I fling the lot at the sealed cut.

It slices in one very neat, very complete cut all the way to the same height as before.

Alistair lets out a whistle as the Chancellor steps back into the room.

"Impressive," he whispers.

I restitch the cut and the assessment finishes, my confidence sky high.

They allow me a few minutes of breathing space before the final assessment. Lex had told me about this one—her sister had to do it as well. She said the best emotions to use were the negative ones. Grief was particularly effective.

I hated hearing that. Of course, it would be fucking grief. Grief is what drove me to Finis in the first place.

What better memory to use than the grief of what happened to me?

"Midnight, when you're ready," Alistair says and guides me to the centre of the circle.

He squeezes my shoulder and whispers, "You're killing it, keep going."

He draws a sequence of patterns over my chest and the scar that sits on my sternum. There's a white light, a searing heat and then an emptiness like nothing I've ever felt. It's awful. I hadn't realised how deep the campus has crawled into my mind and body.

"Begin," Alistair says.

I draw the memory of Aurelia into sharp focus. Her open legs. That woman. The cold press of tiles against my cheek as I laid there all night. The seething hatred. I play the memory over and over until my lids sting with unshed tears and a furnace burns in my chest.

Magic pools around my fists. Slow at first and then faster and thicker, billowing the same way the campus's magic does.

My magic smells different, as it should, since the source isn't Finis. It's darker, bitter, it smells stale and sharp, like mildew exposed to winter. Is that what grief smells like?

I take one last glance at the room and then I sweep my hands open in a severing motion and cut a hole in the Veil large enough for me to step through.

I throw Alistair one last glance. He nods at me, and it's comforting. Then I step into the Veil.

My breath is stolen as soon as I'm inside, the arid air is hot and billowy like the first waft of an open oven.

It sits heavy in my chest, smoky and clogged with decay.

I stitch the Veil shut, waiting for the scar to disappear. As the last stitch fades, my vision whites.

Midnight, at last. a voice says, both a whisper and a shout.

Architecti.

I can't see anything. Everything is white and blinding, the Veil has vanished and been replaced with a white room.

"You have to let me go, I'll die inside the Veil."

You owe me a soul.

"There was no timeframe."

You've had a year.

"Is it really you...?" I say trying to scan my mind for anything I can think of to escape.

Yes.

All this time, I didn't want to face the truth of it, but the more we uncovered about Lucy's runes, the more the nagging grew in my gut.

"A real angel?" And for a moment I forget myself, forget that she is fallen, a murderer, and I fall to my knees.

Yes.

I swear a feather brushes my cheek, gentle, tender. But she's a killer?

"I can't kill Lucy. I won't bring you back to wreak havoc on our world."

Your city has been deceived. I am not your enemy. They walk among you, disguised. You have to help me. It is your destiny.

My destiny is to be reaped by Ignatius.

Do you really believe that?

I smile. "If you're asking me if I want another fate. Of course."

"What if the only other way is to reap Lucy?"

"Then I choose her."

"Fate repeats. We'll see. I think there is another destiny meant for you. I can't hold you here any longer. I have to show you who I am..."

There's a heavy pressing sensation on my chest, and then my vision fills with colour and stood before me are two young angels and an enormous, looming bridge made of glass and smoke.

45

ARCHITECTI

Interitus has been erratic for days. Pacing, having outbursts, arguing with our peers, even shouting at some of the elders. She has grown restless in a way that I am struggling to appease.

The archelder asks me to take her for a walk to establish what is wrong. I didn't want to, but he pleaded, and I complied because that is what I always do.

We've walked for miles, to the edge of our celestial realm. I thought we were walking randomly, but Interitus edges ahead, picking up the pace until a sheen of sweat appears on my brow. I realise too late where she is leading me.

"Must we walk to the bridge?"

She snaps her head around to face me. "Must you act so scared? It's just a bridge, sister."

"Yes," I hiss. "That is a direct path to the underworld. It's dangerous. We should head home."

I tug on her wing tip, but she snatches it out of my hand, a feather pulling loose. It's a black one, more of her tips are black these days. It crawls up the white of her wings, spreading like a virus.

"Sorry," I say, clutching the feather to my chest.

Her eyes narrow at me, her mouth flexing as if she's chewing on something. She says nothing, simply turns on her heel and marches in the direction of the bridge. She knows she has me.

I turn to see our home, the city of fates. It seems so distant now, so tiny. The glass spires and skyscrapers slicing fluffy clouds and reflecting the light into rainbows.

My mouth sours, and I'm not sure why.

She is planning something, I'm sure of it. The way my stomach roils tells me it is nothing good. Nothing that will end well.

I could leave.

I could abandon her and make my way back to the city. Sense tells me that is the right choice, but my mind can never forget the images from the mirror.

The chaos.

The destruction.

Millions and millions of endings over and over.

I can't leave her because I understand what the mirror was telling me. It is my destiny, my responsibility to stop her.

Every step we take closer to the bridge, my chest grows heavier. The type of heavy that your subconscious says is a warning, but your consciousness tells you to ignore.

Interitus opens her arms wide as she steps onto the bridge.

"Fate is just another word for dictator," she says as I catch up to her.

The bridge is enormous, stretching further than my eyes can make out. The entire thing is made of a glass that was once crystal clear, but the ash from the underworld rising to meet it has stained it smoky. I hang back; this is the most dangerous place in our city. Our wings don't work here. It's the one place that if we fall, we cannot save ourselves.

"Interitus please, fate is about as far from dictatorship as you can get. Now, come on, let's head home. I'm tired."

She smirks. "And I'm exhausted." She edges further and further onto the bridge.

I roll my eyes, having to shout my sentences at her. "From what? We have wonderful lives, we're free and fulfilling our roles. What more do you want?"

"More, Architecti. I need more."

"How can you want more, when we have everything?"

A sneer curls her upper lip. "Your eyes are closed. Our system is broken. Fate *is* another word for dictator. It determines who we must become. What we do with our lives. What we do with theirs..." She points down towards the mortal realm and the underworld.

I shake my head no. "We create possibility."

"Yes, we. Not them. We are not gods, yet we are behaving so," Interitus says.

"You're wrong. Our souls are capable of creating infinite possibility."

She sighs, her eyes softening. "That's not true. We can only do that at the expense of our soul. To truly give them free will, we must die."

"Their lives are short. The number of possibilities we provide feels infinite to them. It feels like free will."

Interitus scoffs. "And yet, it isn't. Don't you see? This where the problem lies, sister. *We* are creating their options. We are still controlling."

"Interitus, what is going on? You have never cared

about the mortals." I make my way onto the bridge, every step like dragging anchors, my stomach heavy, legs jellied. I can't look down or I'll throw up.

"You're right. I don't care about the mortals. But free will is just an illusion, even for us angels. And that I do care about. Look at the Mirror... our fates have already been determined, and I do not approve of mine."

I turn away from her. "The Mirror is no more. You saw to that."

"Yes, and much freer we all are for it. No one should control our destiny but ourselves. So, I got rid of our method of seeing it. But that was just the start."

She lurches right suddenly, stepping onto a ledge that juts out the side.

"INTERITUS," I shriek.

Blood rushes to my ears. My eyes bulge. I wave my hands at her, encouraging her to come back, but she ignores me and keeps stepping out, out, out, onto the ledge.

It dangles perilously over an infinite drop.

I can't control my tone anymore, I'm shrieking, desperate. "You speak of the gods with such malice, and yet, you are no god either. Now come back from there before you slip."

"A wise word from my sister at last. But... I think not. Why don't *you* join me?"

She intentionally jerks this way and that.

Dancing her feet up and down.

My heart is in my mouth, beating a million thuds a second. If she falls, there's no way home.

But then I remember the Mirror. Dying by jumping off the bridge is not her fate. Neither of our fates. If nothing else, this should provide a comfort. But I can't seem to swallow down the bitter panic.

I tell myself over and over that if I step onto the ledge, I'll be able to pull her back to safety. I will do it successfully because other fates await us.

One foot onto the ledge, my chest tingling and heavy. My breath short.

Angels are meant to fly, and this place clips our wings. It's wrong. Unnatural. I throw my arms and wings out for balance. They might not work if I fall, but while I'm on the ledge, they work perfectly to keep me balanced.

"What makes you think you're strong enough to decide your fate?" I ask.

Interitus rounds on me, all teeth and growl, one long finger pointed at me. "What makes you think you're weak enough you can't?"

I stall. Thrown by the question.

That was my mistake.

My arms lower for a split second as I consider whether I'm weak. I have never seen myself as so.

Is she right?

Am I weak by choosing to believe in our system? Our culture is thousands, tens of thousands, millions of years old, it has run smoothly for all of time. Who are we to determine whether it is right or just? Was it weak to say yes to the elder? Should I have stood my ground?

Interitus slides right to the lip of the ledge and stands on tippy toes. "You think too small, sister. Your dreams are too tiny. What do you even do?"

"I create."

She nods, slow, steady. "From what do you create?"

"The mess of humanity."

"Yessss," she hisses. "Now you see. Without chaos you cannot create such beauty. But where does chaos come from?"

My lips part, one last breath drawn, my eyes wide with horror.

"From destruction," I whisper, my words barely audible as the gravity of realisation dawns on me.

She led me here.

This was never a walk for me to calm her down and bring her back to the elders.

She was leading me here to an inevitable conclusion. I laugh, the last of my naivety abandoning me with my final realisation. She really did choose her own fate.

I close my eyes knowing what's coming.

The Crowned Moth curls inside my shirt collar, trembling against my skin.

Interitus's hands shove hard.

The warmth of her fingers seeping away as I tip back. Into nothingness.

My wings automatically spread out, but they're useless, unable to flap against the pressure of a fall to the underworld.

The sun streams, warming my cheeks, a sharp set of thoughts accompanying me as my consciousness slows.

How could my own flesh and blood push me? Make me a fallen angel? Perhaps it is selfish, but there is a fleeting moment in this long, long fall where I think: at last, I am free of her. No longer do I have to bear the responsibility of protecting the world from her.

A shadow passes over me.

My blood freezes.

I blink my eyes open.

The shadow grows larger and larger. Wings spread. A face full of teeth and a glint in her eye more vicious than I've ever seen.

She may have pushed me.

But she chose to jump.

Oh my gods, she jumped.

As my eyes roll shut, an infinite number of futures, possibilities, and fates drifts through my mind.

All of them ending in chaos and destruction.

My last thought is but a whisper, a hope, a final prayer.

Interitus, what have you done?

46
MIDNIGHT

Thirty-Six Hours To Go

I come to standing in the courtyard of Finis Tower.

"You okay?" Lex says.

"Yeah, you were away with the Fae for a hot second," Bastien adds.

"What?" I say and try to shake off the vision. I don't even know how I got here. Did I finish the exam?

"The results are going to be here any minute," Lex says, bouncing on the balls of her feet.

The courtyard is crammed. Every student waits with bated breath.

Lex, Bastien and I stand hand in hand as Alistair and Thalia pin the results up.

We rush to the wall with everyone else. All of us fighting to reach the grading lists. Whoops of joy and celebration echo around the tower and slowly the crowd thins enough we can push to the front.

This time, I don't torture myself.

Bastien and Lex hold my hands so tight my fingers go

numb. Lex is top of her class and fifth overall in the cohort. Bastien is second in his resurrection class and seventh overall.

All of us inhale in synch and hold a collective breath as we come to the Veil results.

My heart rate slows as I stare at the list of names. A hollow ringing trills in my ears.

I blink.

It has to be wrong.

I blink again.

Lex makes a strangled sound next to me.

Bastien rips the paper from the tower wall and scrunches it up. They're shouting. Noise fills the courtyard. But I can't hear anything. I continue blinking at the space where my name was.

Next to a number two. Beneath Aurelia Ravena.

She won.

She fucking took everything from me, and now she's taken this.

I lost.

My chest is hollow, fluttering. Heart rate erratic. Everything is numb and loud and so, so silent.

I take a step. And then another. I need to keep moving.

Run.

Yeah, I should run.

I still have my scythe, I could fight him. I won't give up.

A year of fucking training, working every night, every break, every spare second and all for Aurelia to snatch it from me.

Fucking Aurelia.

I really thought I stood a chance. My fingers curl around my scythe, furious that this is the choice I'm left with: my soul, or the woman I love.

How is that a choice?

Fuck the Demonic Favour. Fuck Ignatius. Fuck Aurelia. Fuck Architecti.

Architecti. Oh gods, there is a far greater danger in our midst, and no one realises. I'm not even sure Ignatius knows.

"Where's Lucy?" I say to Lex and Bastien.

They shrug at me.

"Are you okay?" one of them asks. But I'm already making my way inside and down to the observation room. She said she was going to watch the exams.

I scan the observation deck. Lucy was definitely here earlier.

I check the whole of the fifth floor. Every practice and exam room, the reading areas and the other observation deck in case she moved.

She's vanished.

I return to the first observation area and notice a stray notebook. Probably just a student's. But my feet take me to it anyway.

It's leather, stained and worn, that soft velvet only well-loved leather can produce. There's a fountain pen knocked on the floor, ink splats haloing the nib. The lid missing.

My eyes narrow, I open the front page to see an inscription:

If lost, please return to the contracts office and Professor Corvine.

My fingers go cold, my chest heavy. Why would she leave her notebook?

I head back to the courtyard, but she's not there either. My stomach turns. I can't imagine her leaving before she saw the results. My throat goes dry. Ignatius said there was a break-in, what if the Societas got in again today, knowing we would be distracted with the exams.

A group of professors stride past.

"Hey, Professor Morrow, have you seen Professor Corvine?" I say, trying to suppress the quake in my voice. Her brow cinches, one neat little line. Thalia seems off, but I can't place why.

"No? She was watching your Veilwalker exams last I saw her."

"You didn't see her leave?"

"No, sorry, perhaps she's gone to help with organising the celebrations later."

There's a rumble around us. The earth trembles and it's far louder and more aggressive than usual. My arms fill with goosebumps.

My gut coils in on itself, my tongue sours. Something is wrong.

She didn't just leave. My contract with Ignatius will have to wait.

"I... I need to go."

She didn't say goodbye. She abandoned her notebook. Something isn't right. Lucy wouldn't vanish without saying goodbye. Not on exam day, not after everything she's done to help me.

Bastien appears outside the Great Library entrance.

"Hey? Where did you go, what's happened?"

"Lucy is missing."

"Missing how? Where have you checked? She probably went back to Inferos." He shrugs.

I grab him by the arms, forcing him to look at me. "I'm telling you, she's missing."

"Okay, okay, I'll help you look."

"I'm going to check her apartment. You check the lecture halls and her office."

We part outside the Great Library, and he sets off to the southern area of campus while I head north towards the three Houses.

I bump into Lex en route and she helps, heading towards the theatre, pubs and shops, agreeing to meet us at the cloisters.

When I reach the penthouse in House Inferos, my blood turns to ice.

Her door is open. My fingers tremble as I push it open to see the apartment trashed. Her belongings are strewn across the floor. Kitchen draws upturned. Cupboards thrown open.

The frail skeleton moth lays dead on the carpet, one wing torn clean off and discarded a foot away from the rest.

"Oh," I say and my eyes sting. It's so stupid, it wasn't even alive, and I hated them. But it's this dead moth that unleashes the flood gates.

I pick him up and carry him to the moth room and rest him against the foliage.

"Mortem," I shout.

He materialises instantly. He trembles, his fur stuck out at all angles, his eyes wide as he mewls at me. He pads across the floor and jumps into my arms.

He's never done that, never sought affection.

It makes bile claw at the back of my throat. I stroke him until he ceases trembling.

"What did you see, buddy? What happened?"

He makes a dry hacking sound. Oh gods, eww, a hairball at this time?

I put him down as he makes strange arching shapes

with his body and wretches until a vile, squelching lump plops on the floor.

He looks up at me with sad eyes and toes the lump.

"You have got to be kidding me," I say. My nose wrinkles as I reach down to prod the gloopy fur. There's something hard inside it.

"Eww," I groan as I poke the middle of the furball and pull out the lump.

"What the hell?" I say as I scrape the goop off to reveal a hard metal pin. The logo of the Societas.

"The Societas have her?" I say, my head snapping to look at the miserable not-quite-dead cat.

"Meow," he nods.

I bolt out the door. I can't do this on my own. I have no idea where they would have taken her. All I know is that if I don't get to her fast, they'll kill her.

I run until my thighs burn and sweat flings off me like rain. I run straight to my death sentence and into Ignatius's office.

I shove the door open so hard it bounces off the wall.

Ignatius stands, his eyes hot and dark.

"What do you think—"

"Lucy is missing," I cut him off. It's only then that I see the horns protruding from the man sat in front of Ignatius's desk.

Chancellor Arcadius. Oh shit, oh shit, oh fuck.

"I—I mean Professor Corvine, she's... gone. I went to take my paper to her apartment as I was late and needed the mark. And her door was open. Her apartment was trashed. Her cat... he said the Societas took her."

That statement causes the chancellor to round on me.

"This is the truth?" He towers above me; he must be over seven feet tall.

"Every word of it, sir."

The chancellor glances at Ignatius. "Fix this. And don't fuck it up."

"Yes, Chancellor," Ignatius says.

The chancellor strides out of the office, slamming the door shut.

"Architecti isn't the angel we need to worry about," I spit.

"You're not making any sense."

I shake my head. "It was never her. She isn't a fallen angel."

"What the hell are you talking about?"

"Her sister pushed her. You trapped the wrong angel."

I have never seen a devil pale the way Ignatius does in this moment.

"You're wrong," he snarls.

"You trapped the wrong fucking angel, and you used Lucy to do it. And now she's in jeopardy because an entire fucking society wants Architecti back."

He pulls a hand over his face. "You don't understand. I had to do it."

"Do what, Ignatius? You're not saying anything helpful and every second we stay here, Lucy is in danger."

"If the Societas have her, I know where they'll have taken her..."

"Just like that?" I say, suspicion narrowing my eyes.

"It's not necromantic physics, Midnight. They want to resurrect Architecti, where do you think they'll be?"

It takes a second. But then I scold myself for not thinking of it earlier and going straight there. "The basement. As close to the Veil as they can get safely."

He swallows, his skin turning grey. "We have to get her back or..."

"What did you do?" I say, stepping away from him.

"There's a reason the Societas can't release Architecti."

"Speak faster, Ignatius…" And I know I'm playing with fire. If I spoke to him at any other time like this, he'd probably reap my soul there and then. But tonight is different. Tonight is happening because he fucked up and I am here to help.

"Architecti is an angel. She's celestial. You can't just use any old magic to bind them. It's like trying to trap a wraith with a shoelace."

"What did you use?" A chill settles in my core.

Ignatius has never seemed old, always youthful in that way only immortals can pull off.

But right now, he seems as ancient as the gods themselves.

"Ignatius… what did you use?"

He blinks, startled by my question. He swallows hard and finally looks at me.

"The Veil. I used the fabric of the Veil. If they release her, they bring down the Veil, too."

47

LUCY

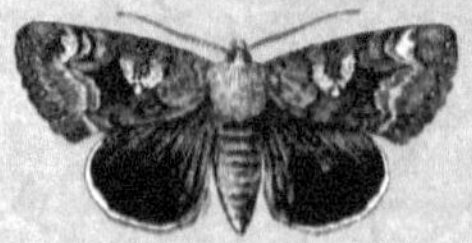

I peel my eyes open. My head pounds, a hammering throb that's close to a hangover. I must have been drugged. How someone managed to abduct me in the middle of exam day, I don't know, but then I suppose everyone was too busy with the exams to notice one missing professor.

There's not much light, though there must be sconces filled with flaming lanterns somewhere because a dim glow illuminates my surroundings.

I'm in some kind of cell. The walls are stone, cool to touch and have a slight silken glaze to them.

Outside the cell seems to be a corridor. I squint, straining to see in the flickering lantern light. I make out the end of the corridor and my blood freezes.

It's the gateway to the Veil.

An enormous stone archway replaces the corridor's end wall. The stone is a mix of pale, shimmering marble, and dark onyx. The curved stone appears ornate, with finely carved threads twined together like rope—one dark thread, one pale—a representation of the fabric itself. The oldest goyle on campus, Gardon, sits at the peak of the arch.

He must sense me because he turns to glance at me and scowls.

Beneath him, in the archway, hangs a shimmering curtain. The most direct way into and out of the Veil. Though only the most trained necromancers go in and out here. Up on the surface, whenever you cut a hole in the Veil it's like opening a thin capillary. This portal is a floodgate; you're essentially slicing the Veil's jugular.

Why the hell am I down here?

"You're awake," a familiar voice says.

"Thalia? Oh my gods, Thalia, help me. Get me out of here."

She emerges from the darkness but something about her is different. Her mismatched eyes glower at me through the darkness. She holds a snarl on her features I've never seen before. Her shoulders are tight but wide-set, radiating power and confidence typically reserved for devils.

"Thalia?" I say, quieter this time.

She bares her teeth in a hideous smile, and they seem far, far sharper than before.

My stomach drops out. I back away from the iron bars.

"What's going on?" I ask.

She stalks towards me, a key in her hand. It clinks in the metal lock and sets my teeth on edge.

"Out," she says, her voice flat.

I hesitate; Thalia has always been so loving and affectionate towards me. I don't understand what is happening.

"Move," she barks and yanks me by the arm out of the cell. Her grip is a vice. I tug my arm, but her fingers dig harder, pinching my skin where she drags me. More and more people emerge from the darkness to line the corridor.

All of them bearing pins above their left breast pockets. A symbol that makes my heart stop.

The Societas Mortis Architecti.

They all bow their heads as we pass; it's reverent, respectful. But I don't understand. My mind is trying to compute what's happening.

"What are you doing with them?" I whisper. But as the words fall from my mouth, a rift carves through my heart.

She is not with *them*. They are with *her*.

"All this time?" I whisper. "It was always you?" A trickle of cold flows down my back. I tug my arm again.

Her nails slice into my skin where she refuses to let go.

"Always me," she says.

"But why?"

She laughs, harsh and grating as we approach Gardon's arch and the Veil.

"You really have no idea who I am?" She shakes her head at me as if dismayed. As if I'm the fool for not knowing.

"Who? What do you mean?" I breathe as she stops us by the undulating expanse of the Veil. She extends a finger to the shimmering surface and draws it down from top to bottom, as if tasting the icing on a cake.

A waft of acrid air fills the corridor; it's sticky and smoky and makes me cough.

"The real question, Lucy, is who are *you*."

And then she shoves me hard. I stumble back and fall between the folds of the Veil.

I'm back on my feet, screaming and lurching forward, but she's already sealed the Veil shut, the scar healed over without a trace.

I'm trapped.

Fuck, I'm trapped. My heart rate climbs to a thousand

beats a second as I frantically search my mind for the magic to cut myself out. But I'm inside the Veil with no access to the campus's magic. I call upon my own magic. Reach for a memory, an emotion. Anything. But my heart is beating too fast. My mind whirring a stampede. I can't reach it, it won't come.

Oh gods. Oh gods. Oh gods.

I scan the area where I'm standing. It's as barren and desolate as it is hot. Mountainous peaks of dark, craggy rocks and flat ground with barely a living thing in sight. Any plants I see are scorched and brittle, their stems and branches bone-white with skeletal leaves having scarcely more colour.

I'm going to die here.

And that's when I realise that is the point. If Thalia is part of the Societas, then she wants me dead. Did she trap me here to somehow resurrect Architecti?

Sweat beads on my brow and spills down my temples. Then something moves in my periphery.

Fuck.

I attempt to call my magic. Even though every cell in my body is screaming at me not to, I close my eyes and reach for it. But there's nothing there. I can't feel Finis.

Despite the heat, the hair on my arms rises: danger.

I open my eyes.

A group of wraiths stalks towards me. Shit. My body turns icy.

Is this how I die? Demons are immortal if we stay healthy and safe, but just like vampires, there are ways to kill us.

They advance on me, step by step, their sinewy, leathery bodies skulking and sinister. Their mouths drop open, ringing my sentence out in shrieks and gnashing teeth. I stagger back, desperately searching for a weapon, a rock, anything I can use to defend myself.

There's nothing.

I am alone.

This is where it ends. The Societas has won.

Ten feet.

Five.

Three.

One long skeleton arm sweeps out towards me.

I shut my eyes, resigned.

But the impact never comes.

I open them, confused. Gossamer wings made of starlight and sky fill my vision, surrounding me, separating me from the wraiths.

They twist and twirl and reform the Veil until I am standing somewhere not quite there, and not quite anywhere.

An in-between.

The wings shiver and shrink and flutter before me until they belong to the most beautiful moth I've ever seen. I try and capture it, but my vision clears, and a translucent form of Finis Tower surrounds me, as if I am inside the ghost of it. I walk forward, attempting to return to campus, but I stumble into an invisible wall.

Like a window.

Wait. Not a window.

A prison.

Oh, gods. "Architecti?" I whisper. My heart climbs into my throat, my entire body trembles as I realise I've found my way into the prison my father created to trap an angel.

"Hello, Lucy."

"Please don't hurt me," I plead. "I'm not my father." The

starlit moth flutters to Architecti and sits atop her shoulder, nestling into her neck as she steps into view.

She's the most beautiful creature I've ever seen. White wings hover at her back and stretch high above her. Her bronze skin is smooth and ageless, her eyes are bright and smiling. So strange that such a beautiful entity can be so awful.

"You misunderstand. I am not here to hurt you. I am here to explain."

"Wh—what?" I say, unable to stop my face scrunching.

"I could not let Interitus kill you."

Interitus? She continues talking.

"There is one more rune you must unlock."

"How do you know about the runes?"

She glances at the floor, her tone soft as she says, "A contract as powerful as ours needed a sturdier vessel. Parchment can be torn, broken, destroyed. The clauses overwritten as simply as spilled ink."

My head swims as I parse out what she's saying. I don't... No. It's not true, it can't be.

"Who am I?" I breathe.

"Not who, what."

"Wh-what am I?"

"You are everything. A promise. A beloved. You are our words and our meaning. Once upon a time, a demon made a deal with an angel... You are the product of that. The binding of a celestial's power to a demon's. You, my blessed child, are the manifestation of my attempt to save us all."

"I don't... I don't understand."

She nods, her wings ruffling as she speaks. "That's okay, there is still one more rune."

"Why don't you tell me what it says?"

She smiles softly. "Do you care for her?"

"Midnight?"

She nods.

"With all my heart. But if I tell her, if I give myself to her, I'll lose my power, my security, my identity."

"My sister is going to bring about the end of days. She is determined to eradicate fate. You are the key to stopping that. Ignatius thought he was clever putting me inside this prison. But I knew what he was doing. I agreed to the entrapment because it was the only way to render my sister powerless."

The beautiful moth flutters off her shoulder as Architecti opens her hand and a second moth, one with dark serrated wings appears. They flutter in tandem, spiralling and twisting as they dance around each other.

The ground rumbles, the tower shakes, the translucent skeleton of Finis trembling all around us.

"There isn't time for me to explain. You must go. This isn't how you die. You have another destiny..."

"I don't believe in fate. We make our own futures."

Her eyes soften as she gazes at me. "Does it give you comfort to believe that?"

"I know it to be true."

"For some, that may be so. But you and I... we serve a greater purpose. Our destinies were sealed long ago."

"Then what is it? My fate?"

She cups my chin with her palm, tipping my head up to her.

"My child, you already know. The question is, what is Midnight's?"

She presses a kiss to my forehead. It's like being kissed by every ocean and every wind and every fire in the world. Architect moths materialise, colour blooming everywhere.

Wings flutter and kiss my cheeks, my arms, and I am filled with hope and sorrow and wonder and disdain.

Midnight fills my mind, her smile, her piercing blue eyes and slicked back hair. Over and over, she appears.

A million futures, a million possibilities, a million dreams scatter across my vision.

Tears flow down my cheeks as my mind and body are overwhelmed with all her futures. I buckle under the weight of her glorious life. She *can* change her fate. Hope surges through me, my heart ready to explode.

She can beat my father.

One way or another, she will find a way.

Until I realise there is one thing all of her possibilities share.

My heart plummets.

A single horrifying truth settles like lead in my bones.

Inevitable.

As if this truth were stitched into the very fabric of my being. I always knew. Deep down, this is why I held myself back. Why I never gave myself to her.

Inevitable.

It was always inevitable.

I want to claw the visions from my soul, scour my fate from time with wire bristles and bleach and poison.

But the more I scream, the more I fight, the heavier the realisation settles.

While she is in every future I see...

I am in none.

48

LUCY

Midnight lays me in bed. The soft comfort of silk pillows and the faint scent of perfume are the last things I remember. Time must pass because even as I sleep, my dreams cross from night to day to night, the sun skimming my cheeks and warming my body.

There is something foreign in the air. A slow coagulation. The thickening of a pool of blood destined to be nothing more than a distant stain and fading memory of violence.

It all feels inevitable.

My stomach coils, the weight of dread pressing thick and fibrous on my ribs.

The Societas nearly killed me. I might be safe for now, but it doesn't feel over.

Not yet.

There is something missing, some piece of information that will make it all make sense.

When I wake, Midnight carries me into the bathroom and lowers me into a bath. She soaps my body, cleanses my hair and razes the hair from my legs. She dries me, dresses me in nothing but a silk gown.

And she does it all in silence, as if savouring every second, every touch, every moment we have left.

Because that's what these are, our last moments. I don't know how I know that, but it's a truth that lingers between the threads of my soul.

"Just stop it, okay?" Midnight snaps as she follows me back to the bedroom.

"Stop what, Midnight?" I say, my voice as tired as my bones.

"You're acting like you died."

"We all die."

"Well, you're not dead yet, so stop acting like it. Just don't. I can't stand another—"

She cuts herself off, turning away from me as she stalks into the kitchen.

"Another what?" I say, striding after her.

"Just forget it. Go back to bed, you need to rest."

But I don't want to rest, not yet. I need to know what happened and everything is blurry.

"Where's Thalia?" I ask.

Midnight halts. "Missing. Ignatius has hushed it all up, of course. Said she's on leave. How can he be a hero helping me to save you only to turn round and lie to everyone moments later?"

"The lies have always come easy to him."

"I'm so over all of this," she says. "I can't..."

I grab her wrist and pull her to me. She glances down. I've never taken control like this, I am always the submissive. I like my place. There is nothing I love more than her in control. But not tonight. Tonight, I am exhausted, and I need answers.

I want to control something, take something back. I release her.

"You can't what?" I say, my voice hard.

Midnight's nostrils flare, her fists clenching by her sides the way they do when she's cross. "I can't cope with another Aurelia."

She sags. I let her hand go, and she continues, as if a dam broke.

"I get that our fate is predetermined. But she just gave up. Wouldn't fight. Once she knew it was terminal, she just stopped. Laid in bed all day and refused to try, she wouldn't look at magical solutions. She wouldn't do anything. I just wanted her to fight. If she couldn't do it for herself, then do it for me. Keep pushing because she wanted another day, another week, another month with me. But she didn't. She accepted her fate and gave up, and it broke me."

My heart aches for her but... "I'm not Aurelia."

"I know," she nods. "I'm sorry. I knew as soon as I made the comparison it was wrong. You're nothing like her."

I'm not. And yet, part of me wonders if I have given up. I have always fought. Spent my life fighting my father. Injury after injury, and yet tonight, things are different. Am I resigned to my fate? Whatever that may be.

Tonight, I need something different. Need control. Power.

"Get on the floor," I say, that professor tone lacing my words.

Midnight hesitates. This is not how we work. Something defiant flashes through her gaze. But she nods.

"I don't sub, but for you, I will gladly get on my knees."

"Such a good boy," I purr, testing the water. Her shoulders heave a deep sigh.

Interesting.

"My safe word is moth," she says, and I laugh.

"You're kidding?"

"I hate them, I'm hardly going to say that word in the bedroom."

"Okay, well, I don't think you need a safe word, I just need to be in control for once. I can't explain it."

I rest my backside against the kitchen counter and loosen the robe ties, baring my pussy to her.

She licks her lips, hungry.

I grab her by her hair and draw her to me. She winces against the tug, but her eyes quickly turn molten.

I spread my legs open for her and pull her to my cunt.

Such a simple pleasure, a woman on her knees for you, licking and sucking your clit. My robe slides open, displaying one nipple that hardens in the cool air.

I watch as her tongue dips in and out between my folds and she moans in pleasure at my taste.

But I'm not ready to come. I want to have my way with her first. I yank her off my pussy and slide out from her grasp.

"Undress," I say. "Leave a trail of clothes on your way to the bedroom. I want you naked on the bed, waiting for me."

She does exactly as I ask, dropping an item of clothing every few feet until I hear the flop of her body onto the bed.

I take my time making my way through the apartment after her. Savouring the fact she's having to wait, to do as I bid. It's heady, this power over another, I see why she likes it. Anticipation grows the longer I hold out, the longer I resist my own urges.

But as I step inside the bedroom, my newfound willpower cracks. I slide between her legs and run my tongue down her slit. She's warm and wet and tastes fucking divine. I moan against her pussy as I drag my tongue up and down.

She bucks her hips, grinding against my mouth. I curl a hand around her thigh, holding her in a bruising grip, and bring my free hand to her pussy. My fingers tease her entrance.

"More," she says.

I slide my finger inside her cunt, thrusting slow and steady until she's wet enough I can slide another in.

She gasps. "Oh fuck, Lucy. Faster."

I curl my fingers, loving the way her pussy clenches around me. I drive my hand in and out, until she's writhing against my mouth. My tongue ravishes her clit quicker and quicker until her back arches off the bed. Her hands fist the duvet, and she spills over into an orgasm.

But I'm not done. One isn't enough. I climb on top of her, flipping around and laying my belly flat on hers. I shuffle back until my pussy rests against her mouth.

She grips my thighs and pulls me down onto her face, dragging her tongue over my clit.

I lay my head on her pelvis and lower myself to her apex. I suck her into my mouth. She cries out as I flick my tongue hard against her swollen, sensitive bud.

I'm still aroused from the kitchen, so it doesn't take much for me to climb to the same place she's in.

It's too much. She's too much. The taste of her pussy in my mouth as she ravishes mine makes something split inside me. I scream her name as pulses of hot static swirl between my legs. Our rising climaxes, building and building.

I rock against her as she lays there and takes every flick and lap of my tongue. I angle myself to slide a finger back inside her and she jolts, whimpering against my pussy.

She pushes my legs open and slides a finger into me. We move together, hips bucking, tongues ravishing clits, and moans filling the bedroom until we both tip over the edge and I am blinded by an orgasm that reaches every cell in my body. It sends a pulsing electricity from my scalp to my toes.

And I drift somewhere else.

Runes fill my vision.

Celestial.

Contractual.

Demonic.

They swirl and twist and reform until deep in my mind a singular rune forms.

One that twists and morphs, crumbling into a single sentence.

One that tells me how to break my contract.

One that shatters everything.

49
LUCY

Two Hours To Go

"Will you come with me?" I ask.

"I'll go with you anywhere," Midnight whispers. "We have until twelve tonight. Ignatius will come for me on time, I've no doubt."

I give her a soft smile. I was never going to let that happen.

"Let's walk," I say.

Midnight's brow cinches. She wants to ask what the runes showed me. What I know. But I'm not ready to tell her. Not when there's so many other things I want to say.

I was so determined to believe we controlled our fate, that we could change our future. But this all feels inevitable. Like we joked, maybe meeting in a graveyard was an omen after all. Perhaps this was always where we were heading to. Are some loves destined to fail, while some are destined to soar?

I smile to myself, wondering if I was wrong all these

years. Was Midnight right? Was this always going to happen because our fate is sealed?

Maybe we never stood a chance.

My chest hurts. Every breath aches like a cancer in my marrow. The words I know I have to say build and build in my throat until I swear they're going to suffocate me.

"Okay, I'll get dressed," she says and climbs out of bed.

She knows. She has to. Or perhaps it's subconscious.

I wonder if she'll enjoy the fact she was right, that we were always destined to end up here: the demon and the reaper.

I hope she'll forgive me for what I have to make her do.

We slip out into the night, hand in hand, no longer hiding. What's the point? None of the academy rules matter anymore. Nothing other than what we do tonight matters.

We walk through the maze and enter the Garden of Death.

"Tell me what our life would be like," I say.

Her fingers stiffen where she holds me, and she draws in an audible breath, but whether it's a defence mechanism or denial, she doesn't question my tense.

"I'll tell you what it will be like," she says, stroking the back of my hand with her thumb. "We'll have a modest house, but an enormous library, filled with books and texts and contracts."

"I like the sound of that," I say and close my eyes trying to imagine it. Nothing appears. My mind is blank because it won't lie to me. Not tonight.

"We'll always eat dinner together and every evening, I'll massage your feet because you'll have spent all day standing and lecturing."

"Mmm, you would make the perfect wife," I say.

"I'll spend my days fixing bikes, and I'll build my own

garage and business on our land. People will come from all different realms to bring me their bikes."

"I'd run you a bath every day," I add.

"We'd summer in Lantis, finding some secluded beach to read on."

My chest burns, as if each memory we'll never make nestles between my ribs and swells.

We draw to a stop at the centre of the garden. There's a fountain that runs all day and night; it's dark, the liquid reflecting the night sky. It glistens with stars and dreams, and I think this is a nice image to end with.

The ground rumbles, another Veil tear somewhere on campus, a seemingly constant occurrence these days.

"Midnight... I—"

"Don't," she says. "If you say it, you'll lose your power."

I give her a sad smile. She doesn't even realise my power is already gone.

I lean in and kiss her, surrounded by the scent of night blossoms, her grapefruit and vetiver perfume filling the air. My lips move over hers.

So soft, so slow.

She tastes like moonlight and memories. I savour every drop, trying to burn the feel of her onto my soul. I want to take her with me and never forget any part of her.

My lips are wet. I ease away to see streaks carving her cheeks.

"Please don't do it," she says.

"Do what?"

"Whatever it is that made you kiss me like that. It felt like goodbye."

My mouth thins with the desperate need to hold in the words I'd rather keep secret. I glance at my watch. It's five to midnight.

"We've run out of time," I say.

This is the truth I have to share.

That to be free, I have to lose everything that means anything to me. But worse, this will make me the villain in her eyes. And yet, I'm setting her free. I just have to break both our hearts to do it.

This is right. She'll understand eventually.

"I'll fight him. I won't go down without trying. I got you back from the Societas, remember. Maybe he'll negotiate..."

I cup her cheek, and she stills.

"I need you to do something for me," I say.

She shakes her head, a soft no before I've even told her. Funny how the heart already knows what the mind refuses to accept.

"Please," Midnight says, her voice cracking. She gasps as several entropy moths materialise.

It's already done. The moths are here, there's no going back.

A shift happens inside me, my crystalline heart cracking as my power siphons out, slow and steady. Red smoke twists in the air around us. I thought it would hurt. I thought I'd shatter and burn and every bone in my body would crumble.

But this is none of those things.

I just feel free.

She has freed me.

One final crimson ribbon bursts from my chest and spirals around us. A lightness comes over me as if I have shed a thousand burdens.

"No, no, I won't accept it," Midnight says, waving her hands, swatting the magic away. I grab her wrists and pull her against me.

"You don't love me. SAY IT, TAKE IT BACK," she screams.

"But I do, Midnight. I've always loved you."

Ribbons of magic swirl faster, spinning around us. I expected some godsawful stench, like stale coffee and broiling flesh. But instead, it smells like spring mornings, the crisp heat of summer's first warmth and evergreen sap.

The ground rumbles, harder this time. Several slate tiles fall from the roof of Finis Tower. I know what is coming tonight. I just hope the Academy survives it.

"I don't want your magic," she says. And this is where I realise it doesn't matter how much I try and explain who I am, or what I am to her, she won't accept it. She'll fight no matter what.

"It will save you," I whisper.

The last ribbons hover around her head, finding any and every way inside her body even though she swats at them and tries to push them away.

"I'm already doomed, Lucy. You don't have to do this to yourself. Not for me. You can't save me."

I can't bring myself to look at her when I say this, because for all the sacrifice she's going to have to make, this is selfish. I will make her do this no matter what. It's the only way I can truly be free.

"But you can save me," I whisper.

She trembles against me, but it doesn't seem to matter how close I hold her. Nothing can make this better.

"Do you remember you promised you'd help me break my contract?"

"Y-yes," she whispers. Her sob breaks me in two. My chest aches so much I swear my heart will stop beating before I can do this.

"I need you to fulfil that promise for me."

"I can't," she says.

"You have to. Take out your scythe, Midnight." My voice is cool and calm, so steady where hers is shattering.

"No, I won't." The tears run freely now.

"Don't make me force you," I say and release her from my grip.

She shakes her head at me. "You can't. I have your magic, you said that yourself. You can't make me"

"You made a deal. It's binding no matter who holds the magic. Take. Out. Your. Scythe."

She shrieks as the weight of my words forces her to her knees. This is the last time I'll feel the surge of power coursing through my body; the last time I'll wield demon magic for my own cause.

A sheen of sweat covers her brow as she fights herself, fights the weight of contractual magic controlling her limbs.

I see the moment she shifts from devastation to anger. This is what I needed—her furious—it's the only way she'll survive this. Her face contorts, deep lines carving canyons through her features. She grips the blade in her hand.

"How could you do this to me?" she says.

"There is no other way."

"So you make me responsible for bringing back a fallen angel? For the massacre of millions of innocent Ora City residents? All for what? To free you from your father?"

"Will it make it easier if I'm the villain?"

"You were never supposed to be *my* villain, I was..."

"You were what, Midnight?"

She laughs, it's dry and humourless. "I was supposed to reap you. And I never told you, this whole fucking time. I made a deal with the Tower in my Severance Rite. It would break my contract if I reaped a single soul. It wasn't until after that I discovered that soul was yours. But I couldn't do it because I fell in love with you."

The ground rumbles as if hearing her confession. I smile. "Don't you see? You were always meant to do this. You're the one that believes in fate. So fulfil your destiny, Midnight. Take my soul, free yourself from Ignatius. No more contract..."

"Fuck y—" she starts but I place my lips on hers, one more kiss. One more goodbye.

"LUCY, NO," Father screams behind me. But the ground quakes. The Veil rips, and the screeching of freshly freed wraiths fills the air.

I wrap my fingers around Midnight's and pull the scythe up to my neck.

"One little cut, and it's all over."

"Lucy," she begs. The way she whimpers my name slices through the air. It's hollow, so much pain held in four little letters.

A tear rolls down my cheek as I draw the scythe tighter to my throat. But I can't do it myself, she has to reap me.

"Midnight..."

She holds my gaze, her eyes watery, brow furrowed all the way down to her soul. Her bottom lip quivering.

"I was going to let Ignatius take my soul to save you, I wasn't going to do what the Tower asked. Fucking ironic that I'm here, again."

"Don't you get it yet? It was never the Tower, it was always her, Architecti. She is the one you made a deal with. This was always going to happen. We were always meant to end up here. Do you want me to say you were right? That we can't fight our destiny? That everything I fought for was for nothing?"

She shakes her head, tears rolling over her lids. "I don't believe that anymore."

I laugh; it's bitter. "Well, I do."

"I won't reap you."

"You don't have a choice. There's no time for me to explain who I am, *what* I am."

"I don't care what you are, I need you, here with me."

"That's not how it's meant to be."

"LUCY," Father screams again behind me, but it's swallowed by the campus siren, by the screams of students, the campus coming alive with lights and professors.

"It's time," I say. There are so many things I wish I'd said, so many things I should have told her. Perhaps that is my lesson and my punishment.

I'll never get to tell her that I love the way she frowns when she's concentrating. Or that it makes me smile when I watch her polish and care for her bike. Or that I appreciated how hard she tried to like my moths.

Or that, no matter how much she professes to hate Mortem, I know that they secretly love each other.

"No," she growls. "Fuck you."

I hoped it wouldn't come to this, that she would have the strength and understanding to take my soul and free herself.

"If you love me, you'll let me go."

"And if you loved me, you wouldn't give up."

I take a deep breath, my last, and I savour the fresh night breeze the way it coils in my throat and fills my lungs.

My watch strikes the top of the hour.

"Happy birthday, Midnight. May it be the first of many more."

I close my eyes and use the bargain one last time.

She screams as the weight of the deal bears down on

her hand, forcing her to slice through my soul, to cut me from my body and set me free.

Bright pain explodes in my chest. It sears white and hot and burns from the inside out.

And then there is only freedom.

Darkness plummets over my vision as my body disintegrates, and the last thing I see is the devastation written on Midnight's face.

50
MIDNIGHT

Time's Up

I never thought death could be beautiful until I hold Lucy in my arms as she dies.

Her expression is serene, her eyes closed and peaceful as particle by particle she dissolves. I grip her, pleading, holding tighter, forcing her to stay. I use every ounce of my strength to fight to keep her. But the more I cling, the faster she fades until she's nothing but a swirling mass of sparkling dust and runes.

And then she's gone.

My hands clasp at nothing but air, and I'm screaming and screaming and screaming.

Ignatius fights his way past wraiths and students and shredded sections of the Veil to reach me.

"What the hell did you do?" he bellows.

"She made me," I say, my face streaked with tears and sweat and heartbreak.

The ground ruptures, accompanied by a thunderous crack as if the earth itself shrieks. It floods the campus in a tsunami of noise. I lurch forward into Ignatius, the pair of us thrown to the ground.

Finis Tower screeches as a jagged fissure carves its way through the building from top to bottom.

Ignatius pales. We scramble to our feet.

Professors and students alike scream.

Finis Tower shudders and tilts. A terrible creaking rents the air.

Like a giant yawning maw, the fissure ruptures into an enormous hole at the heart of the tower. The entire campus freezes and stares up at the tower, transfixed.

Our symbol of power, protection and prosperity is under siege.

Dozens and dozens of mouths hang open, eyes watering as they gaze upon the destruction of Finis.

Brick by brick, our tower, our power and our home collapses in on itself.

The air fills with dust and bricks and shattered slate. And when it's over, in the silence and smoke, students and professors fall to their knees. Others grab each other and cry.

Only two remain standing: Ignatius and me.

The largest Veil tear I've ever seen carves the space where Finis Tower used to stand and haloed in the cut is a figure.

Ignatius sucks in a breath, his eyes bulging as he finally reanimates and backs away, step by step among the rubble and people.

"Run," he breathes.

But as the figure solidifies, she looks so familiar.

"Thalia?" I say.

But it's not the professor—she appears, marching down from the churches. She carries a darkness in her eyes that makes me shiver. But what makes me stagger back are the most enormous white wings tipped in black looming behind her.

What the fuck?

"At last," the woman cloaked in Finis's ashes says.

I don't understand why she looks exactly like Thalia. She steps down from the crumbled tower, her eyes laser-focused on the professor.

How the hell do they know each other?

"Midnight, it's time to run. *Now,*" Ignatius growls.

I do. The last thing I see is Thalia drawing long, serrated blades from behind her and sliding a foot back. She readies herself in a stance that has only one meaning: war.

Then she smiles, all teeth and snarl. "Hello, Architecti."

WANT TO FIND OUT WHAT HAPPENS NEXT...?

PREORDER INTERITUS NOW

**THE STORY CONCLUDES IN INTERITUS -
BOOK TWO OF THE DEALS OF DARK DESIRE DUET**

The campus lies in ruins. The Veil is shattered. And the angel who fell millennia ago has risen once more.

As Midnight grapples with the devastating choice she was forced to make, dark truths about the past collide with an even darker future. With Architecti's sister now walking among them, the delicate balance between realms threatens to collapse entirely. Some bonds are forged in creation, others in destruction—but the most dangerous are those born from both.

The Crowned Moth and the Severed Moth. Two sisters. Two powers. One inevitable ending.

INTERITUS RELEASES IN 2026.
Preorder your signed copy exclusively at:
www.rubyroe.co.uk/products/interitus
and receive character artwork, a bookmark and sticker with every physical preorder.

ABOUT RUBY ROE

Ruby Roe is the author of lesbian fantasy romance. She loves a bit of magic with her smut, but she'll read anything as long as the characters get down and dirty. When Ruby isn't writing romance, she can usually be found beasting herself at the gym, snuggling with her two pussy...cats, or spanking all her money on her next travel adventure. She lives in England with her wife, son, and two devious cats.

instagram.com/sachablackauthor
tiktok.com/@rubyroeauthor